"They say, in fact," the prince went on, "that a princess who married the King of Khotan smuggled silkworms in her headdress to her new home so she would be certain of silk garments there. Raising silk is indeed a woman's art. And how not? They love it well, and it loves them. At one time it was forbedden to all but the First Empress, but the Son of Heaven was moved by the pleas of his ladies, and the poverty of the weavers and dyers to rescind his edict. And ever since, our court has blossomed," the prince said, with another smile at Alexandra.

She look aside. Anyone else would have thought it was modesty. Alexandra had to be considering what had just struck him: They would accept this man's companionship and protection, would accept the friendship he seemed to offer. And then they would betray him.

SILK ROADS AND SHADOWS

SUSAN SHWARTZ

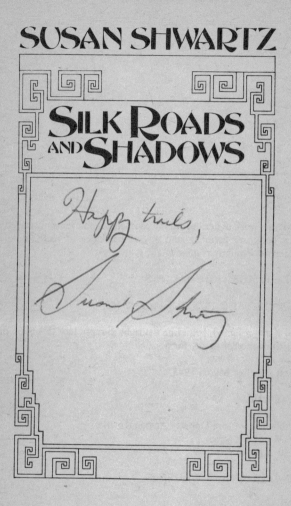

SILK ROADS AND SHADOWS

Happy trails,

Susan Shwartz

TOR

A TOM DOHERTY ASSOCIATES BOOK

SILK ROADS AND SHADOWS

COPYRIGHT © 1988 by Susan Shwartz

First printing: March 1988

A TOR Book

Published by Tom Doherty Associates, Inc.
49 West 24th Street
New York, NY 10010

Cover art by Nancy Wiesenfeld

ISBN: 0-812-55411-6
Can. No.: 0-812-55412-4

Printed in the United States of America

0 9 8 7 6 5 4 3 2 1

DEDICATION

For Marion Zimmer Bradley,
who said this was a novel
and told me to write it.

ACKNOWLEDGMENTS

I want to express my thanks to Dr. Marsha Wagner, Vice President for instruction at the China Institute in New York City, as well as to Sandra Miesel for articles on T'ang tombs and the Simposh (now, after a forced conversion to Islam, called Nuristanis), and to Andre Norton. With characteristic generosity, she shared a twenty-year collection of books on China, and gave me the Bowman, Spearman, and Officer.

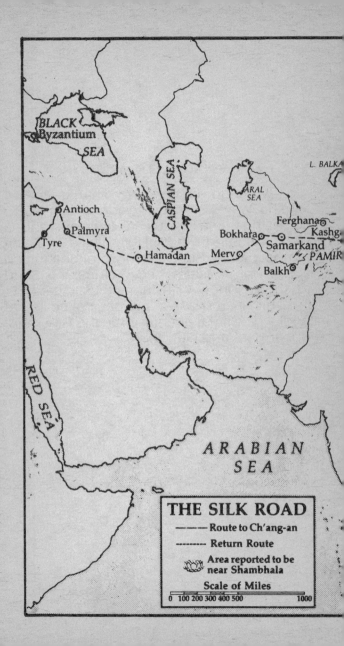

EN SHAN
Hami
Turpan
Kucha
Aksu
TAKLA MAKAN
Miran
Khotan
TIBET
Dunhuang
Huang Ho
(Yellow R.)
THE GREAT WALL
YELLOW
SEA
Lanchou
Wu River
Ch'ang-an
(Xing)
CH'IN
(CHINA)
IND
NDIA)
INDIAN
OCEAN

NOTE

The Chinese curse, "May you live in interesting times," definitely applies to the mid-ninth century, when *Silk Roads and Shadows* takes place. In Byzantium, this period saw the overthrow of the Amorian dynasty with the assassination of Michael III, "the Drunkard," and possibly one of the worst emperors (842–867) in the Empire's history, by his erstwhile-favorite, Basil, subsequently the founder of the Macedonian dynasty.

In T'ang dynasty China, already shaken by the attempts at revolution a century earlier, a Taoist emperor did indeed launch a purge of foreign religions (including Buddhism) that made England's dissolution of the monasteries centuries later look like an afternoon's peaceful leafletting. Western readers who like to think of Taoism as a benign cult that stresses unity with nature may be warned that nature also involves earthquakes and typhoons—and offers an emperor no reason why he should avoid these particular manifestations either.

Such actions changed China irrevocably. Before 842, the mania in China for things Western can only be compared to our present-day fascination for things Chinese. After 842, China turned increasingly xenophobic. Ultimately the country withdrew behind its walls from world trade.

Readers interested in the legend of Shambhala (from which James Hilton probably drew his classic *Lost Horizon*) might enjoy Edwin Bernbaum's *The Way to Shambhala* (Anchor Press), which combines travel and Buddhist teachings, providing a toehold onto the Diamond Path for anyone brave enough to walk it. Those wanting a more detailed treatment of esoteric Buddhism in Central Asia might look at the UCLA Arts Council catalogue, *The Silk Route and the Diamond Path*, an extraordinary blend of art, theology, and some formidable maps. The region and trade within it, centuries before Marco Polo, are covered by L. Boulnois' *The Silk Roads* (George Allen and Unwen). And anyone who even glances into Edward Schafer's *The Golden Peaches of Samarkand* runs the risk of turning into a Sinologue. This extraordinary book describes the art, music, food, trade, and history of T'ang-dynasty China in a way that will fascinate new readers and old China hands alike.

I should probably apologize for endangering the fabulous Byzantine silk industry, which did indeed start in Justinian's reign when Nestorian monks smuggled silk out of Central Asia. In several spots I've juggled with chronology in order to install the Varangian Guard in its palace barracks somewhat earlier than actually occurred, to rehabilitate the weak Amorian dynasty in Byzantium, and—since turnabout is fair play—to eliminate the much stronger Macedonian dynasty.

I have also wreaked havoc with the People's Republic of China's excavation of the First Emperor's tomb outside Ch'ang-an (present-day Xian), which has already turned up some 7500 lifesize terra-cotta statues. But possibly my worst offense has been to wish a turbulent princess like Alexandra on an Empire already noted for its strong women.

Though I've played these games with history quite deliberately (and, very likely, come up with a few errors I don't know about yet), let me justify them by saying that writers of historical fantasy are like people who stack dominoes in intricate patterns. Occasionally we give things a little nudge to make sure they will fall the way we want them to.

Prologue

The Emperor of the Romans was drunk again. His new favorite, Basil, told Prince Bryennius that it was a fever. He would be unable to watch the prince play polo. Another fever. Bryennius nodded agreement and regret, despising himself as he did whenever he agreed with Basil. But it was best not to cross Basil the Patrician; people who did that had a way of disappearing from Byzantium. Then it was more than bad manners to mention their names, in or out of court; it was bad sense. The Church frowned on suicides.

Bryennius recalled summers of blue and green and gold when he and his Imperial cousins had been close. He sighed, then turned back to his own rooms in the palace. At least no one had seen the upstart Basil dismiss him, a prince. And he had hidden his loneliness well. He flung himself down with a cup of wine near the scandalously secular mosaic he had commissioned, too discouraged to admire it, or follow his earlier intentions of going to the stables.

He missed his cousins. There had been four children in the palace then: himself; Princess Alexandra and her elder, more placid sister, Princess Theophano; and Michael, of course, the tall, lordly elder boy who won the games (except when he chose not to), and always had a kind word and sometimes a gift for the younger children. He usually let Bryennius try his horses, too.

Then Bryennius had lost them all: Michael to the throne, and Michael's two sisters to holiness. Alexandra had been thirteen, Theophano fifteen, when they had left the palace for the convent over which their aunt Theodora, a holy woman and noted scholar, presided. As spare princesses, they had had few choices. They could be married off to patricians powerful enough to deserve them but not strong enough to threaten the new Emperor. Or they might marry foreigners. But Alexandra had declared that Frankish princes smelled bad, Armenian ones worse, no proper match for a *porphyrogenita*, a princess born in the Imperial porphyry birthing chamber. So that left one option. They could marry God, as had their aunt, and the widow Danielis, who had aided Theodora in building up the island convent's library.

From the few letters Bryennius had from her while they were growing up, he rather thought Alexandra liked her convent. She had burrowed into its library for tranquil years; her letters were full of references to history—and mild scoldings to a cousin who, she had learned, was turning out frivolous. That was not his fault, he had retorted. No one could refuse a prince military training, but they had refused him a career in the armies. Perhaps, he thought, Michael's advisors feared his becoming a successful general. Thank Mary, Mother of God, he was too old to survive being made into a eunuch.

Then Theophano returned to the palace. Where she had once been plump and placid, now she was thin, easily frightened. He had seen her only once.

"I wanted out," Theophano had wept the one time he had managed to speak privately to her. "Even if it meant marrying a barbarian, I had to leave. But my poor sister is trapped there. She doesn't even know it's a trap, either."

"What kind of trap?" Bryennius asked. Useless he might be—devoted to polo, fine horses, and seductions—but he loved his Cousin Alexandra.

"The books," Theophano whispered. "Books and scrolls and strange languages. They—Aunt Theodora and Lady Danielis—wanted me to read them, and I was never clever, Bry', you know that. And then . . ." She broke off, her eyes bulging with fright.

The Patrician Basil had entered the room, moving quietly, as he always did, the better to hear them. He bowed to the prince and princess, then disposed of them, as he always had.

"I think that Princess Theophano is easily tired. She should devote her energy to preparing for her marriage to the King of Sicily. Don't you agree, Highness?"

Bryennius had not seen Theophano again until her marriage, when she wept again, but this time with relief.

He sighed. That line of thought was unproductive. It made him boil with anger at Basil, too; and that was dangerous. Far more pleasant—and far safer—to consider which of three women to lay siege to for the evening, and which of three horses to purchase. Glumly, he decided on a target and to buy all three horses. As he turned to call for paper and ink, a hiss from the garden onto which his rooms opened brought him around, chased dagger in hand.

So even as an idler, Basil found him too much of a risk to keep alive. Heart pounding, Bryennius edged around to the doorway. Perhaps it would be just one assassin; he thought he could kill one man in a moderately fair fight.

Someone entered the door, Bryennius pounced, and a woman wailed her outrage and fear. It was Alexandra's nurse, Demetria, whom Alexandra had most reluctantly left behind in honorable retirement when she had entered the convent. Panting and frightened, the woman bowed to him—the boy she had spanked for stealing sweets.

"Your pardon, old mother," he said. He turned his chair about to spare her the sight of the mosaic, eased her into it, and handed her his wine cup, which she drained before extracting a sealed note from the heavy folds of her black robes.

"Cousin Bryennius," ran Alexandra's rapid, elegant writing, "I have found the cause of the Basileus' 'fevers' —which his heir is destined to catch, too. For their souls' sake, and mine, help me escape this hellhole!"

So Alexandra had discovered the trap that terrified Theophano and had asked his help? Finally, he would have something worthwhile to do! Urgent questions drew the facts he needed from the old woman. Yes, her son captained the ship that brought supplies to the convent. Yes, men were occasionally permitted on the island. No, Demetria had no idea why Alexandra might be unhappy or afraid, seeing as she was holy and safe in God's keeping, bless her soul . . . and the old woman was weeping again.

Delighted at his own competence, Bryennius bought a crewman's rough garments and bribed a mercenary to lift grapples from the war supplies. Disguised, he sneaked on board Demetria's son's ship. It tacked across the harbor to the convent. Then Bryennius was hugging the walls, creeping from shadow to shadow, his heart hammering at the sacrilege Alexandra had demanded of him.

Someone tapped his shoulder, and he all but screamed until he whirled and saw Alexandra. A man, almost as short as she, was with her. Bryennius started to snatch her up for a quick hug of welcome, but "no time!" gasped his cousin. She kilted up her skirts like a wild girl, and they ran for the ship.

As they scrambled on board, Alexandra was frantic, crying to the captain to cast off as they loved the Emperor and their City.

"For God's sake, cousin, what's wrong?" Bryennius cried. "And who's this with you?" Alexandra was as thin and intense as ever, but the little man huddling near her had a decidedly Persian cast of feature.

In the convent up above the dock, lights started to appear. Suddenly a shriek of rage rang out, and Alexandra sank to the deck.

"They know we're missing! Captain, if you let them take you, they won't just have you executed; they'll kill you themselves and drain your soul."

The captain signed himself in terror. All Byzantium feared necromancy. To have a princess flee a convent because of it was blasphemy worse than Bryennius had dreamed possible. Quickly they cast off.

Alexandra's odd companion came up to Bryennius, standing so close to him that the prince recoiled. "Prince, are you armed?" he asked, his accent surprisingly pure for an Easterner. He had the manner of a priest and—to Bryennius' surprise when he asked—the name of the Basileus' favorite. Probably a heretic as well as unluckily named . . .

"Are you armed?" he repeated the question insistently.

Bryennius nodded.

"Then I beg you, if we are captured, kill me."

"We're not going to be captured!" Bryennius spat.

"But we're not moving," Alexandra gasped. "Captain, what's wrong?" Her voice was shrill, as if she expected trouble.

"The tide, Highness. There's no tide!" The man's voice, hoarse from years of shouting orders, trembled with fear.

"Then let's row!" Bryennius cried.

Even the heretic strained on the oars. Just as Bryennius thought his heart would burst, the undertow struck. When they fought the swift, savage current, it surged into a maelstrom.

"Get down, cousin!" Bryennius screamed at Alexandra, who almost lurched over the side of the boat. She

drew a tiny phial from her drab garments, fumbled it
open, and threw it over the side. The waters whirled
once more, then subsided.

Alexandra sank down, gasping. "Oh, your face, cousin. That was holy water, not sorcery."

Bryennius flexed his hands, blistered and raw from the
oars. "Now," he said firmly, "Alexandra, cousin or no
cousin, you owe me an explanation right now! What in
the name of hell . . ."

"The name of hell . . . that's it, Bry'," Alexandra
gasped. "The Crown Prince, my little nephew Michael
—he's going to be very sick. No one in the court knows
it yet, but he's going to be sick. Yes, there go the bells and
semantrons. They've started to pray for him now. He has
the fever my brother has, and its name . . . oh, God, its
name"—she laughed hysterically—"is Basil. Or Aunt
Theodora and her friend Danielis. They plan to seize
power."

Bryennius darted a glance at the monk.

"No, not that Basil. He's as much a victim . . ." In the
reddish glow of Byzantium's night lights, Alexandra's
eyes were wild, the whites as huge as those of a horse that
smells fire in its stable. "It's all of a piece, Bryennius.
You were the one who told me that the silk trade was
waning. The vestments in the church started to fray, and
there was no silk to replace them. Aunt Theodora didn't
seem to mind, either. That made me curious."

Alexandra, Bryennius knew, always had been too
curious for her own good. "You know, Byzantium used
to have to buy its silk from Ch'in. The gold we paid—no
wonder all Ch'in's people have golden skins!

"But when we learned that worms made their silk,
they refused to sell them to us. Then in the reign of
Justinian the Lawgiver, Nestorians like Father Basil here
smuggled silkworms out of Ch'in in their staffs at the
risk of their lives. Since then—at least up until now
—Byzantium has produced silk of its own."

Bryennius nodded. Every Byzantine took pride in the

City's silk. It was the Emperor's own care. The silk was even woven in the palace's closely guarded factories by women more skilled than a thousand Arachnes. Only the secret of making Greek fire was more strictly kept. Both proclaimed Empire to the barbarians: strength, beauty, truth, and power; the embodiment of splendor on earth, anticipating the greater glories to come. If the silk trade failed, then Byzantium too was failing.

"How has this to do with magic?" Alexandra asked.

"I was about to ask," Bryennius said wryly. His hands stung and he felt like all the strength had drained out of him.

His cousin shivered. "It's all of a piece," she said. "Byzantium faltering, my brother himself . . . Bryennius, he was smart and brave when he was a boy, remember? What reason would turn a bright boy into a drunkard? I won't say he is the worst ruler Byzantium has had . . . and then these illnesses. His wife died young, his heir is sickly. All of a piece.

"At first I believed Aunt Theodora when she said that Byzantium was being punished for sins. Then"—she grimaced and, for a moment, looked like the urchin Bryennius remembered—"after Theophano left, I became bored again. I'd read most of what she and Danielis would let me read in the library. They had other books that looked like they'd come the length of the silk roads. I asked about them, and they told me I could not read them yet. But they were pleased, Bry', pleased that I asked.

"You know me, cousin. When I am bored and curious, I try to find things out. I started prowling the convent. I even found a way out. One night I came upon a door I had never seen. It was locked, but I used my penknife . . ." Alexandra shrugged. "The door opened onto a stairway that wound down and around until I thought I was beneath the crypt.

"Then I saw Father Basil here. He lay on an altar" —Alexandra's eyes went wide with remembered horror

—"set up beneath a statue that had about nine arms. There were stains all about. So I drew my knife to unbind him, and he cursed me for a witch."

Father Basil knelt by Bryennius. "God forgive me," he said, "but what else could I think her? I knew she was kinswoman to the woman who bought me and planned to use me as a sacrifice. A Basil for a Basil, she said. And just perhaps, for your Emperor Michael and his son, too."

Devil worship, Bryennius thought. No wonder the City failed, while Basil rose, with necromancy to back him. He shuddered. How had it happened? Theodora had been a scholar once. Who had given her the books that seduced her from the light?

"When I think of how close I came to being what Father Basil called me," Alexandra said, "I think I ought to spend the rest of my life on my knees praying. But there? God forgive me, but they ought to tear that convent down and sow the ground with salt!" She shook her head. "Nothing . . . I don't know if I can ever believe in anything . . . I knew we had to get out. And you were my only hope."

She flung her arms about his neck, and they hugged one another as they had when they were children.

"Do you hear that?" called the captain. They neared the City. The hollow notes of the wooden semantrons and monks chanting echoed out over the water. Bryennius could smell incense in the air.

"Oh, quickly!" Alexandra whispered as they moored. Then they were dashing for the horses. Kilting her robes high on her legs, Alexandra let Bryennius heave her into the saddle. She was careering off toward the Mese, into the center of the City toward the palace, almost before he could follow.

Exhaustion and terror tasted copper in his mouth. The stink of incense grew stronger. Then they were reining in, their horses' hooves striking sparks from the stone.

Alexandra tumbled from the saddle and headed to-

ward the palace, Bryennius following. Dimly she heard
him acknowledge a guard's salute, heard the man's
muttered praises for the prince's bringing in a holy
woman to pray for the heir. Then they ran inside, this
time to the heir's quarters. They pushed past the guards
and into a turmoil of priests and physicians.

And there the running stopped.

The Imperial heir lay thrashing in convulsions. His
lips were blue and foam-flecked. Blood ran from his
nose. The little priest slipped into the room and walked
toward the bed, chanting—however dubious his
theology—an exorcism.

"Hold him, sponge him with chilled water!" Alexandra cried to the physicians. She began a feverish search
of the bed. Finally, she dived beneath it and emerged
holding something wrapped in a fold of bedclothes.

The prince's struggles ceased so abruptly that several
physicians crossed themselves. "*Kyrie eleison, christe
eleison, kyrie eleison*" filled the room as they began the
prayers for the dead.

Basil—the favorite, not the priest—grabbed Alexandra and pulled her from the bed. Bryennius hurled
himself at the man, determined to protect his cousins.
Alexandra clawed free. She screamed wordlessly and
cast what she held at Basil's feet. It was a cup wrought of
silver in the shape of demons, their claws holding what
looked like a human skull.

"Devil!" she cried. "Get the priests! Ask this man
what demons he serves. Ask him! And then ask by what
design—and whose treason—he dares to threaten my
brother and his son!" She was crying stormily.
Bryennius held her, stroking her and crooning to her
until the guards dragged out the treacherous favorite,
and Alexandra's nurse pushed past soldiers to receive
the princess into capacious arms.

Michael the Basileus summoned Alexandra and
Bryennius to the intricate gold shimmer of the lesser

Hall of Audience, where he sat between mechanical lions.

At her brother's nod, Alexandra drew up a cushion. She leaned companionably against the left-hand lion, and prayed for courage. Once again, she felt as if she stood between the jaws of a trap.

Once again, her choices were limited. There had been a riot in the Hippodrome that morning when the Imperial family appeared in the *kathisma*, or royal box, for the protracted execution of Basil. (Theodora and Danielis were nowhere to be found.) For the first time in years, Alexandra wore purple, heavy with gold embroidery and pearls. More pearls and massive amethysts quivered on her headdress and long earrings. At her brother's gesture, she had stood on a footstool and held up the heir, swaying under the weight of child, splendor, and acclamation. When Michael, pale and sober for the first time in years, had gestured Bryennius forward too, she saw her own fear mirrored in his eyes.

"For God's sake, tell me what I can do with the two of you," said the Emperor. Alexandra supposed it was a good sign that he did not speak of himself as "we," in the form that the Basileus must use—"even in bed," Bryennius had quipped once to the delight of various spies. "My advisors tell me that if you go free . . ."

"The army?" Bryennius shrugged.

"They fear you'll turn the Tagmata regiments against me. And what of you, Alexandra? You heard the crowd today. They want you named Basilissa."

"That is a title for wife, not for sister!" Bryennius broke in, though Alexandra shook her head at him. Michael's wife had indeed been the last woman to bear that title. For Alexandra to be Basilissa put her only a step from the throne, and even closer than that to exile or a convenient accident.

"Would you marry, sister?" Michael asked, and his voice was desperately gentle.

Bryennius tried to lighten the moment. "Whom do

you need put out of the way, Majesty? That oaf whose odorous ambassadors call him the Holy Roman Emperor?"

Michael grimaced. So did Alexandra, who raised a beringed hand to strike at Bryennius as she had often done when they were children.

"You know I cannot do that to my own sister," said the Basileus. No one mentioned that there had been no problem when Theophano had been married off to the equally barbarous King of Sicily. But there was no comparing Alexandra with her sister, ever.

"What about you, cousin?" Michael's eyes had gone bright and speculative, and Bryennius' heart sank.

"The Autokrator is as wise as he is powerful. Therefore he would not command me to do such a horrible—"

All three of them laughed. "That might be too popular a match, too," Alexandra observed.

"Sister, would you return to a convent?"

"Not while my aunt lives!" Alexandra swore.

"But I would guarantee your safety." Alexandra looked blandly at him. "And you would have leisure to study."

Finally, the anger and frustration of years tumbled out, echoing in the rich hall. "Leisure! What other choice can I have? Be walled up in a noble convent, or some prison, or—the straitest confinement of all—a porphyry tomb?"

Michael's face twisted. "I, and my son after me, must learn to rule now, and learn well. We need time for that, though. Think of a way you can be disposed of. Help me!"

Then the miracle happened. Alexandra's face lit up. In that moment she was two parts princess, one part rebel—and another part, by the grace of God, pure inspiration, which bubbled from her mind and heart, and carried Bryennius and the Emperor with her on a tide of joyous enthusiasm.

"Princes join the army or they can be sent to govern one of the frontier themes. You'll probably do that for Bryennius."

"Sister, I regret that I cannot give you a province to govern, too. I grant you have a soldier's heart. But a soldier's body? Never."

"This is what I want." Alexandra reached out to touch his amethyst-encrusted glove where it rested on his knee. "We all know that the palace workrooms have been closed down. I know it's been given out that new looms must be installed, but you know—as do I—that there is no silk to weave. And we know why. Theodora cursed the silkworms. We found her token."

"If ever I find the person who taught you to buy spies, my sister, I shall surely execute him." Michael himself had taught her, Alexandra reminded him. "If you know this much, know the rest. I have sent out men to steal more silkworms."

"And had no success. Who did you send? Our first silkworms were brought to us by Nestorians."

"They were expelled from the City for heresy."

"Not all, my Emperor," said Alexandra. "I found one tied, waiting to be sacrificed by our accursed aunt."

Michael leaned forward. "Would he be willing to go back?"

"With me," Alexandra said. "Only if I went too." Alexandra looked up and saw that her brother had not yet made up his mind. "Why not let me try? I may not succeed either. But I will be away and happy.

"You remember how when we were children, we used to dream of tracing Alexander's route across Persia and into Hind, to World's End itself?" Alexandra threw herself to her knees and laid her face against the cold of the marble floor in the prostration exacted only of captives and barbarians. "Brother mine, set me free to take that path, and I promise you that only death will stop me. And I swear that if I fall, I will die with my face turned toward the east."

"And if you do return, with the silkworms? What

then, Alexandra? You will be too powerful to be allowed to go free."

Alexandra smiled. "Ah, my brother, in that case, I shall have had a long flight. If I return, then you may mew me up in whatever convent you wish, and I shall write books for you."

1

Alexandra pressed herself against the icy rock of the narrow ledge. She checked her grip and, only after she knew she was secure, dared to shiver. Her caravan was halfway between Byzantium—where in what now seemed like another life, she had been a princess—and Ch'ang-an, in which she had vowed to be a thief. They had crossed one mountain pass after another. But now, she was certain that they were lost.

Ahead of her trudged the new guide. Behind her came the rest of her caravan: her cousin Bryennius, her Varangian guardsmen, priests, and, most important of all, the grooms they had acquired in Ferghana for the horses whose hooves made flinty sounds as they picked delicately along the rocks. She knew that if she dared lean out over the cliff, she would see clouds floating below her, heavy with snow, tinged with crimsons, violets, and golds—the colors of the Imperial silk that the workshops of Byzantium no longer wove. Far, far below, hidden by the clouds, lay snow, rocks, and people who lived in the shadows of the peaks without ever attempting them.

The thought of that view made her dizzy. Guides and merchants in Samarkand had called these mountains *bam-i-dunya*, the Roof of the World. At first she scoffed at what she considered typical Sogdian exaggeration to drive up prices. She knew better now. The air was thin and cold as an assassin's blade. Fever stalked behind to claim the cold's leavings; it shrilled in the temples, clouding judgment and balance.

From the breast of her tunic, she fumbled out a greasy, much-folded map. There was still enough light to read. She traced their way across Taun Meron Pass. After that, their path was supposed to descend until they reached Kashgar.

They had left the pass days ago, and climbed ever since. Still the guide led them on a twisting upward trail toward white massifs that blocked out the sky. It was getting darker now, though this high up, the sky always seemed dark to her. A blood-colored moon was rising. She glanced ahead, praying that the guide would wave and announce shelter, an end to the day's travel. No one could cross the Roof of the World by night and survive.

She gasped at the thin air. To compose herself, she ran through a litany that resembled nothing at all she had ever learned from her tutor or from her days in an Imperial convent.

They had bargained in Samarkand and Ferghana for horses and now were bound for Kashgar. From there, they would cross the desert, heading ultimately for Ch'ang-an itself, birthplace of silk. There she must steal silkworms, or their eggs, whatever might enable Byzantium to revive the industry that won its Empire beauty, money, and prestige. If she were caught, they would torture her to death . . . slowly. But if she had not dared the venture, she faced prospects almost as bleak.

She feared the convent most. One of the priests wished on her by the court trudged beside her, and she looked away. Convents and monasteries, right enough, professed service to God and the Theotokos, Mary, Bearer of God. What might lie in secret chambers behind the pious, glimmering mosaics made her shudder with more than the cold.

Haraldr, the Varangian who led her escort, came up to her. Accompanying him was the Nestorian heretic who called himself Father Basil, a little man with a round body and a Persian cast of feature, an absurd contrast to the fair-skinned Northerner.

"Do not stand still too long, my princess," the guardsman told her. Alexandra knew how she must look: tiny, even frail, dark, and fine in comparison to the massive Haraldr, whose blue eyes appalled the natives hereabouts, and whose endurance made short work of these heights. "I saw our guide talking with Father Andronicus there, and I want a few words with them both. Words like food and shelter . . ." He grinned ferociously at her. Alexandra found Haraldr reassuring, like having one's own golden bear.

She held out a hand to restrain Father Basil. "My cousin, Bryennius?" she asked.

"He said the horses were getting tired, and dropped back. When last I saw him, he decided your ladycompanion was tired too, and needed to be cheered."

Alexandra wasted breath on a soft laugh. Bryennius had two passions: horses and women. Usually he was a good judge of both. Certainly, his choices in Ferghana —now restive as the sky darkened and they saw no stables—had reduced the Sogdian merchants to wailing prophecies of bankruptcy for themselves and starvation for their children. Well enough: In Ch'ang-an, they were mad for such horses. Bryennius could sell them, or give them as bribes while searching out a way to steal silkworms.

His taste in women, though, might get him killed. In Samarkand, one lady's brothers had almost knifed him. And if it hadn't been for Bryennius' fondness for Alexandra, he might still be playing polo on the palace grounds. Instead, his loyalty to her had got him sent out on this death sentence along the silk roads—and she thanked God for it.

Father Basil, the Nestorian, raised an eyebrow at her mention of the Theotokos. "Upset by Orthodoxy, priest? You prefer, perhaps, my aunt's altars?" He winced, and she was sorry, remembering the dark figure with the nine arms, each holding a dagger, and the altar, wrought of porphyry the color of blood.

The little man drew closer, so close that his breath warmed her face. "Do not speak so much, Highness. Look above us."

Up ahead loomed what looked like a sheet of ice. It was actually a cliff, its crags smoothed out by slabs of snow, now fissured and softening in what passed for spring in this country. Any loud noise—a shout perhaps, or a horse stumbling or, worse yet, panicking and plunging aside on the trail—might bring it down upon them.

"Pass the word to the grooms," Alexandra told the priest. "If the horses seem fearful, blindfold them." She wished she could blindfold herself too. As Haraldr said, it was not good to stand still too long. She forced herself to move up the line, careful to secure a handhold before taking each step.

Three more twists on the path brought her out suddenly onto a ledge that jutted out not more than a foot from the center of the vast rock face they had to cross. She edged out, feeling like a fly crawling across a marble wall. Ahead of her, she saw Haraldr's unmistakable bulk, and the guide, who waved one arm.

What lay up ahead turned her sick with more than altitude. Above them lay yet another peak. Sure enough, they were well and truly lost. If she lived, she would kill that guide herself, she vowed. But on that peak . . . sudden relief threatened to unlock her knees and send her toppling off the ledge through miles of empty air. On either side of that peak stood one of the preposterous

clusters of steep-pitched roofs and sloping walls built
centuries ago by monks, whose successors still managed
to survive here, even in the winters.

Alexandra crossed herself. For the first time since she
fled the convent, the gesture was more than a habit left
over from a time when faith provided her something
beyond a vocabulary for swearing. Shelter. Tears
squeezed from her narrowed eyes and froze to her lashes,
and she scrubbed at the ice. She glanced back, and saw
Bryennius waving at her. Sharp eyes: he'd seen it too.

Remembering Father Basil's warning about noise, she
slowed until he caught up to her. "I want you to
interpret," she whispered. "Beg us shelter, and find out
how long it will take us to find the right road to
Kashgar." Simple enough: assuming the monks would
house women, and they would not have to backtrack to
Taun Meron, the pass they'd crossed two weeks ago.

Thinking of Father Basil's ability with the languages
hereabouts, she almost crossed herself again. She herself
could handle Persian. She knew enough Arabic to swear
in, plus fragments of other tongues. But these oddly
pitched, long-voweled languages . . . she didn't trust
that guide. The old guide had fallen ill too conveniently
in Ferghana—and he had been tended by Andronicus,
recommended by a faction she distrusted, though on no
evidence. Could she trust any refuge to which such a
guide might lead them?

She followed Father Basil along the narrow ledge.
They were coming to the intersection of cliff and new
peak, where a tumble of rocks offered shelter from the
keen night winds that were blowing, threatening to pluck
horses and men from the ledge and hurl them down, past
clouds, into an unseen valley. The moon had risen fully.
Despite its redness, the spray of clouds drifting across it
looked as white as the mountain peaks. The sense of
being entombed in rock that had haunted Alexandra for
days left her, and she glanced out with something like
love and awe.

If I go no farther, she thought, *at least I have seen this.*

There was a purity to these titanic peaks. Here, for an instant, she could forget her brother's tottering Empire, and her suspicions that political intrigue and thaumatur- gical dabblings (the traditional hobbies of Imperial la- dies) still gnawed at its heart. The mountains and the empty spaces were indifferent to such matters, and they reduced the humans who cared so hotly about them to motes even smaller than a silkworm's egg.

The wind died. The night was so silent that she could hear the bells on the harness of the pony toiling last in line. The high-pitched ringing ceased abruptly, muffled by a groom who feared to bring the snows down around his head. Now all Alexandra heard was the pounding of the blood in her ears. She almost welcomed the cramp- ing chill in fingers and toes. Soon she would be sheltered from the night in some small, noisome room, sur- rounded by familiar faces and smells, but she would not forget this exaltation.

A chant suddenly started, it came from the monastery on her left.

Alexandra's mind went back to the chants of Byzan- tine convents: the massed voices, and the semitones, the striking of wood semantrons, and the incense, floating below the long, melancholy features of the Figures in Majesty, glittering in mosaic. That was *cosmos*—order and beauty. But . . . *that order was betrayed*, she thought with an intensity of rage she had not experienced since she stumbled into a hidden part of the convent and discovered quite a different sort of ritual. *We were all betrayed*.

Male and female voices they were, some pitched well below what a human voice ought to achieve, and accom- panied with the hollow wailing of horns carved of straight bone. Instinctively she feared it.

The song that echoed down from the left-hand peak sounded like the chants she had heard the night she had found Father Basil, bound in a corner and left to gaze at a cup that had been carved from the base of a skull. What was it he was fond of saying? "The Way has no constant name, nor the Sage a constant form. According to environment, religion is set forth, quietly offering salvation to all the living." Heresy, beyond all doubt.

Still, it offered a terrible possibility. Suppose, Alexandra thought to herself, once she crossed the ledge and lay panting against the rock, suppose the Good is always the same good, regardless of the form in which it appears. What about evil, then?

Ever since she was a child, Byzantium had been tormented by necromancy; her tutor was perhaps the only person she knew who did not wear some sort of amulet or swear by some superstition. And if that were so among the Romans, how much more so among barbarians? Haraldr made the hammer sign more often than the sign of the cross, and she knew he swore by Thor.

Aunt Theodora had always been a dabbler. And she had always been ambitious and clever enough to conceal it. But from the moment Alexandra had seen that hateful figure of a she-demon with the nine arms and avid mouth and obscenely protruding tongue, she had known that her aunt had traveled beyond the dark side of her own faith to other, more exotic sorceries—and that they were all reflections of the chaos that sought to impose destruction and reign over it.

The ritual that night in the convent would have culminated in Father Basil's death if she hadn't rescued him and fled. She shuddered, nearly retching with memory and altitude, thinking of Theodora and the woman Danielis, approaching the altar, daggers in hand, to kill the little Nestorian to add his strength to the Basil they favored as Basileus rather than the rightful Emperor Michael. Oh, God, the hideous shriek of cheated, hungry rage when they discovered Basil gone, and Alexandra missing too.

Alexandra started, then shuddered as if that shriek had rung out from this monastery, echoing out over the abyss. She glanced up at the peak in fear and guilt. Father Basil had warned her against loud noises that might bring the melting snow down upon them. The terrible, low vibrations of the chant echoing against vast rocks, pulsing through the air, seeking entrance to her mind and thoughts; how had the snow not fallen yet?

Now she could sense a second set of vibrations, a second chanting, coming from the other monastery. These voices were also pitched well below the limits of normal singing, and inhumanly sustained, but where the first chant revolted her, this made Alexandra feel warmed, comforted. She glanced up at the peak again, and rubbed her eyes. Each monastery was bathed in light: the one on the left, a spectral hue almost the color of the blood-washed moon; the one on the right, a pale, pristine blue the color of water running deep below ice.

Father Basil crouched beside her. "Get down, my princess," he hissed. "Don't let them see you!"

If all necromancy was the same, did it follow that if one necromancer knew about her, they all did? This was no time to chop logic. Alexandra sank to her knees and tried to pray. No words came. She had not been able to pray since she had met the little Nestorian and fled an Imperial convent, her faith lost and her reason failing.

Now she lifted her face from her hands. "What are they doing?" she whispered.

"They call it *mantrayana.* Sound, certain kinds of sounds, can kill—or heal. The monks fight with noise, one group to bury us under snow, the other . . ."

"To defend us?"

"To maintain balance, and hold the snow where it lies. If that saves our lives, so much the better. If not . . . well, so long as balance is upheld . . ." He shrugged, the curious, Asiatic gesture that went so strangely with his cultivated Greek.

Alexandra raised herself cautiously and glanced at the huddled bodies of her caravan. Haraldr was holding his axe and an amulet, Bryennius was creeping toward her, the officer Leo (of some noble house or other; it vaguely troubled her not to remember which) and several of the grooms and packmen had collapsed in the snow. She could hear faint sobbings. From halfway down the line came the *Kyrie*s of prayers in Greek and the more sonorous *Om mane padme hum* of a bearer. Hail to the jewel in the lotus, she translated. The man would do better to invoke divine intervention, not that it would work.

They had no defense against this! she thought with fury, except to wait, and hope, and pray that the monastery that shimmered in the blue light could keep the snow from overwhelming them. She heard a rumbling, saw a white blur slide from the cliff, and suppressed an impulse to hide her face.

About five yards ahead of her, by the guide, knelt her aunt's priest, not praying for them, not encouraging the men who might find his spiritual authority—such as it was—comforting, but watching the left-hand monastery with awe and an unholy relish. She cursed him, unnecessarily, since any priest who served *that* was damned already. So her aunt's hand and power had reached out to the court, giving her this traitor, and beyond, threatening them all.

"Look there!" hissed Father Basil.

Lights flickered in both monasteries. From the one on the left, tiny figures, dark against the luminous snow, were emerging, picking their cautious, sinuous way down the slope.

"Where are our bowmen?" demanded Alexandra. One or two good archers—and the Persians usually were good archers—ought to drive them back. She and the other nobles in the party had several vials of Greek fire carefully stored, but they had agreed to keep the deadly stuff for ultimate peril. Hurling it uphill would only bring the inextinguishable, savage fire cascading down upon them.

The word was passed down the line, and bows were hastily strung.

The figures grew closer, and Father Basil gasped. "You see the ones with the elaborate headgear?" he asked. Alexandra peered closely at the advancing magicians.

They wore dark hats and reddish robes. Bones and oddly shaped amulets dangled from hat and belt. Several held bone horns and shook metal rattles. She had never seen their like.

"Devil dancers from Tibet, the Land of Snows," he whispered. "No monks of any kind fear the mountains. They travel from Ch'ang-an to Hind, from Hind to the Land of Snows, all the way to . . ."

"Where are those archers?" Alexandra gestured furiously and saw one guard wave a bow in response. They were ready. Since she dared not shout the command to fire, Alexandra rose to gesture at them. The devil dancers were coming closer. One locked eyes with her. Her arms felt sluggish, frozen, but she raised her right arm, ready to bring it down . . .

"No!" screamed Andronicus, her aunt's priest, and hurled himself at her. She elbowed him aside, and gasped in horror as he overbalanced and fell, shrieking, into the clouds that swallowed him. She flung herself against the safe, icy rock, her arm sweeping down in a desperate command to fire. One arrow struck home, and a devil dancer toppled, tripping one of his fellows. Dead and live magicians toppled, rolling down the slope, stirring up snow and rock.

From the right-hand monastery, the chant intensified. Alexandra bit the back of her hand. Monks emerged and stood by the base of the monastery's retaining walls. The chant grew louder, as if the monks fought against tremendous power. Alexandra felt herself straining to help without knowing how.

Then the very face of the mountain appeared to writhe. Huge gouts of snow erupted from it, and blasted down toward the ledges and boulders where they sheltered, tiny frail humans who would be picked off the mountainside like flies and hurled far below.

"Snowslide!" bellowed Haraldr.

The Varangians had seen this before, Alexandra thought wildly, clutching at the nearest rocks for what good that might do her. The rumbling of the snow intensified, entering her body wherever it touched rock or ground. Over it came the scream of horses maddened with fear, the shouts and wails of her people, and, throughout, the terrible, persistent chanting of monastery warring against monastery.

She found herself drawing long, desperate breaths against the time when there would be no air at all. Ice chips stung her face, and she looked away from the monasteries just in time to see whiteness engulf half the mountain. Horses and tiny figures went spinning from the ledge, some still clutching at rocks or weapons or reins. A thin shriek was the last Alexandra knew she would ever hear of her lady-companion, but—
"Bryennius!" she screamed and tried to run toward where he had been just seconds earlier.

"Save yourself!" A huge body pressed her and Father Basil down against the rock. Giant hands forced her into a tiny crevice between the stones. "Lie still until the rumbling stops, Princess. Then you can dig out." Then Haraldr too was torn from her by heavy whiteness that poured down and kept on pouring.

There was nothing but the whiteness and the cold and the terrible noise. Alexandra felt her mouth stretched in the rictus of a scream that never came. She could hear nothing, see nothing, but the snow which finally drowned out even the chant of the magics that had forced her this far from home to die.

Alexandra's eyes were still squeezed shut. Before she remembered she was supposed to be dead, she brought her fists up to scrub the snow and ice from them. She only saw a blur resolve itself into whiteness. Blind, then? The thought carried an irrational weight of terror with it. *As if it matters*, she thought, *that I see the place where I will freeze to death*.

A rock lay under her shoulder, and she eased away from it, instinctively seeking comfort. She lay beneath snow, she realized, and she was still breathing. Snow slabs must have settled above her, trapping in air and

warmth, saving her life—for now. She looked from side
to side, hoping to see a dark tangle that might mean that
one of her companions had been spared, but there was
only whiteness.

She screamed, but no sound came from her throat,
which felt seared by the screaming she had already done.
And flailing in panic only started a small rumbling that
made her freeze against the snow, remembering the
larger rumbling that had stolen her people from her.

Wait until the rumbling stops, then try to dig out,
Haraldr had said. He was gone, swept away by the snow.
Alexandra hoped he had had time to draw his axe and
shout a prayer to the Thunderer, whom she knew he
truly worshiped. Bryennius was gone. Father Basil was
gone, and without him she could not even speak to the
people in these lands. And the horses, the weapons, the
food, even the few pathetic vials of Greek fire.

What was the point of digging out? The snow rumbled
again, settling until the next fall. She went rigid, then
gradually eased into a more comfortable position, com-
posing herself as if to lie in state. Tears froze on her face.
They said that freezing to death was easy, like lying in
feathers, and drifting into dreams of warmth and light.

She tried one of the meditative exercises she had
learned, but could not concentrate for grief and exhaustion. Then she slept, and, after a while, dreamed of
sunlight on the Golden Horn, blessed warmth, and the
softness of silk.

Alexandra stirred and trembled. She was chilled all
over. Did this mean she was dying? Then she must turn
her face east, as she had pledged. Which way was east?
She woke, and recoiled in terror from the snow that pent
her in: had she died already and been laid in a tomb?
Her head spun, and she almost panicked. The lid overhead was white, not porphyry; snow and ice, not stone.
With a little whimper, she raised one hand to the snow
above her. A chunk broke off in her hand, and she sucked
at it. The cold burned her tongue, but revived her. The

rumbling was gone. She began, with agonizing care, to chip away at the snow.

Dig out, Haraldr had told her. *Sweet Mother of God, I'm tired!* If the snow were old and dense-packed as she feared, she would collapse before she saw the light of day. Keep on digging. She stamped her boots clear of loose snow and reached up. More snow fell to either side of her.

For hours she worked. She found a little dried meat in her belt-pouch, and put that in her mouth, with more snow. It heartened her. Then she was tired, she wanted to lie and rest, but she had been sweating, and knew that to sleep now, with the protective snow above her thinning out, exposing her to the cold, would be death. She wept a little and dug on.

For what? Why was she pressing on? Her friends were gone. Her kin was gone. She was alone, bereft on the Roof of the World.

"I promised the Basileus. I promised my brother." She encountered ice, and drew her dagger to knock it free. Finally, a flurry of ice fell before she could duck. Sputtering, she found herself head and shoulders above the level of the snow. She kicked and scrambled her way out.

The sky was very pale. She could not recognize the land below her, transformed as it was by crumbled slabs of snow and ice. She could not even see any bodies, a cruel mercy that spared her the task of trying to clamber down to them and provide some sort of burial. Above her on the peak, the two monasteries looked as if nothing had touched them for centuries—no chanting, no devil dancers. They could be empty. Carefully, Alexandra rose to her knees. She sobbed for air, and looked around. She was very dizzy. Weaving, she pushed herself to her feet, and started toward . . . it was the right-hand monastery that had tried to stop the snow from burying her caravan. She reeled, no . . . not into the gorge . . . and started off.

Above her, the stars faded and dawn tinged the snow

with blood. Surely she had not dreamed away an entire day and night? There was no time, just snow, and pain. She craned her head to keep the monastery that was her goal in sight, and forced herself onward, higher than she had ever climbed.

Blood made her sight dark. Blood . . . the merchants had told her that sight played tricks with one, this high up. "This way," whispered a new voice, the voice of a wise child.

She turned and looked at him. Despite the cold, he wore very little—a saffron-colored cloak, almost like an antique toga, and chains of jeweled flowers.

"Who are you?" she asked, astonished that he understood her language.

"I am your friend. You can call me Rudra. Rudra Cakrin. And if you permit, I will teach you . . .

"I could take you to my home," he wheedled. "Come!" he held out both hands to her, and she pushed them away. Something bright fell from one of them and rolled on the snow. It was a brilliant red, shocking against the whiteness of the snow. Blood? A rose? Some damned sorcery. Alexandra shook her head and trudged onward, climbing now on all fours. Sunlight struck the snow, which glinted like diamonds along her path.

"Do you wish to see your home again? Then you must take the Diamond Path . . ."

Alexandra moaned. "No! No more magic . . ."

"Come, my sister . . ." The hand reached out. In a moment, it would grasp hers, and she would consent to sorcery, though she had never consented before . . .

She pushed at the child, and her hand seemed to pass straight through him. Then, amazingly, she was running toward the monastery, her heart almost bursting with the effort.

She heard a whistle and a clamor of horns, and froze in her tracks. A gate, intricately carved, painted blue and white, groaned open. People started down the slope toward her, and she wept from relief and terror.

Several wore monks' robes. But as fast as they moved,

others moved faster: men with the golden braids and beard of her guardsmen, and a small, round man with a Persian face.

"Father Basil!" she gasped, and sank to her knees. "Make him go away."

"Who?"

"Rudra. He said his name was Rudra Cakrin, and he would teach me. But I don't want to go there, I don't! I have to get to Ch'ang-an, I promised my brother, I promised . . ."

Alexandra felt herself being picked up, carried tenderly within the monastery, where the corridors were narrow and painted with ferocious red and blue deities she was afraid to look at. "Don't make me . . ." she begged.

"My princess," whispered the Nestorian. "I saw only yourself on the slopes. And the monks found no footprints beside your own—and those of the men they rescued last night."

He beckoned, and one of the oldest, most wizened of the monks came up beside her. Awe shone in his narrow, slanted eyes.

"We found this in the snow." The monk held out his hand. In it gleamed an opened flower. A lotus, Alexandra saw, like the ones that were brought from Alexandria to float on pools in the palace gardens.

She moaned and finally let herself faint.

2

Sometime later, Alexandra became aware that her body was no longer bitterly cold, that scrapes and bruises no longer stung, and that—astonishingly—she felt indifferent to the fact that she was still alive and even relatively comfortable. Body warmth did not matter; she was floating in a vast, pale sea. She remembered afternoons of sailing in the Basileus' ornately carved barge on the Golden Horn, then put them out of mind. This was no earthly water. She felt like a sky creature, able to bathe and rejoice in the thin, pure air between mountain peaks. *So this is how angels must feel*, she thought. Somehow the idea didn't seem as blasphemous as she knew it was.

She could see immense distances. She spared a glance down at the tumble of snow, rock, and black specks that she assumed might be bodies at the base of the mountain. Some lay to the right or left, away from the abyss itself, diverted by unpredictable cascades of snow. These might live, she noted idly. But what was that to her, a creature of the upper air?

Beyond the mountains lay Kashgar. Her spirit strained toward the city she had tried to reach. Beyond that she felt waves of great heat and greater desolation, luring her to gaze on it, but her eye swept beyond, farther and farther until it came to a cliff hung with banners, then a canal, a walled city. She knew that her visions showed her Ch'ang-an, and she pressed in closer. It seemed larger and more splendid than Byzantium, the home she would never live to regain.

That thought tore her attention back to the west. Violent light, an insubstantial mob clamoring for her to notice it: Bryennius' dark, clever face and lazy voice; Haraldr. Many faces were new—a tiny, exquisite girl; a slender man, no longer young, with refined features and wise, lazy, slanted eyes. Last of all came a woman's face the color of old ivory, lined and imperious and bitter, but otherwise an older version of her own . . .

In her dream, she met the woman's eyes and knew terror. *There you are!* it seemed to say to something else, and she felt herself drawn by a black, sticky thread. She was being ripped from the ancient monastery and battered body that provided but unstable housing. She struggled in the dream, trying to raise a shadowy hand. She didn't want to return to Byzantium, if Theodora were alive and seeking her. Death was clean in comparison with what her aunt had planned for Father Basil.

She forced her glance away, but this war of wills in the upper air was alien to her. She was being drawn back to look . . . and then, she saw the child who had first appeared to her on the slope. He did not nod or shout for her attention, but stood with his attention fixed upon a glowing flower cupped in his hands. As she watched him, his face turned wizened and scarred. Finally, he looked up and their glances met. She felt a sealing there. She wasn't sure she wanted it, but it was better than the darkness. The child—Rudra, he had called himself —smiled, and his eyes expanded to dominate her consciousness. She was still floating, awash in that strange sea, but she felt herself drifting lower and lower now.

Soon she could see herself, lying on a narrow pallet in a room painted with a blue and white figure. The sight of her own body, still dressed in battered leathers, Persian trousers, and torn boots, intrigued her. She was very thin, and her hair, tumbled free of the cap she wore, was long and black, almost blue in comparison to the pallor of her skin. Her face resembled the mosaics she had grown up with: haughty, narrow features, arched brows, and a look of melancholy, even in sleep. Not beautiful, no, but familiar, that woman on the pallet. She sought to rejoin her body, but felt herself caught in an undertow, being washed out to that tranquil sea again.

Soft lights gleamed before her—white, blue, red, green, yellow, and a kind of smoke color. She drifted toward them, drowsily hoping for company.

Then she heard a whirring, as if a spinning wheel wound silk in her presence, a clangor of horns and cymbals, and strangely pitched, prolonged syllables she could almost understand. She felt herself being shaken by the shoulders, and cried out in protest as old bruises were jarred and new wounds opened. Abruptly the shaking stopped, and she was eased back on the pallet.

Alive again? Tears ran from the corners of her eyes and she could not stop them. *When I was born, I wept, and now I weep again, for truly, I think I died on the mountain*, she tried to say, but no sound came. Tenderly, someone wiped her face. Her eyes cleared. She looked up into the face of Father Basil, and saw that he wept, too.

"Praise God you live, my princess."

Alexandra turned her head from side to side. The chanting continued. They were practically dinning it in her ears.

"Make . . . make them go away," she husked. He raised a hand. The hooting and braying subsided. It was very quiet in the tiny room. Sunlight poured in from one small window. In its dazzle, the figures painted on the walls seemed to dance and wave their many arms.

Two monks slipped from the room, edging past the —that was one of her Guard who stood at the door! How many lived, then? She would have to deal with the loss of the others later. Tears poured down her chapped face, but she ignored them. For now, she would simply try to sit up. The priest, little taller than she, supported her.

"Easy. That was a hard battle you just fought."

"Battle?" she asked.

"Drink this first, then sleep. When you're rested, I'll explain."

Alexandra glanced at the cup suspiciously.

"This drink, will it make me sleep?" The idea of more sleep frightened her. If she slept, she might slip away from her body again to set out upon that sea, and this time, she might not be drawn back.

"There are no drugs in it," he said. "Is it that you fear sleep? You drifted very far, but the monks sang you back."

"Is that what that howling was?" she asked.

"That 'howling' was one of their sacred chants. If you hadn't been found babbling of a child with a gout of blood in his hand, I doubt they would have sung it for an outsider."

They knew of the child who had saved her. Perhaps he was an angel, if the pagans, devil-worshipers, and fire cults hereabouts had angels. She knew he meant her well.

"Now will you drink?" Basil still held the steaming cup.

Stubbornly, she held his eyes. "While I drink, you can explain to me which battle you meant."

Father Basil gestured, and an old man came forward. He had the fined-down look of the mountain dweller about him. Though it must be cold in the monastery, he wore only a single yellow robe, and his arms were bare. They were thin, but looked very strong.

"He knows Persian," the priest said in that language. "Also some Greek, and the sacred languages of Hind and the Land of Snows. Even one of the languages spoken in Ch'ang-an."

"Have you thanked him for saving our lives?" Alexandra asked, and saw Father Basil look guilty.

Bless the little Nestorian! Alexandra thought and fought against hysterical laughter. Once he made certain that he would survive a magical attack and an avalanche that wiped out most of his companions, he found himself another savant and—no doubt—had been discussing philosophy while waiting for her to waken. Knowledge was a passion with him. It had lured him to Byzantium, almost to his death. On the long trip out, she had been his student in languages. At least this aged monk spoke Persian; she would not have to struggle with the complex tones of Tibet, or the endless syllables of Sanskrit.

The old man smiled at her, his narrow eyes almost slanting shut in his wrinkled, cheerful face. There was something of the look of *that child* about him: a good enough place to begin.

"No thanks are necessary, daughter," said the monk. "It is our duty to prevent any interference with your path."

"The child . . . the wise child. When I dug myself free and came to you, I saw a child who said his name was Rudra."

The monk bowed his head. Clearly, he had schooled himself to silence before outsiders on the topic of this child.

"Why is it so remarkable that *I* should see him?" She had been warned that at these great heights, travelers encountered hallucinations and madness. Had any two people ever seen the same hallucination?

"Because, daughter, he is the King of Shambhala. And just as your faith has its mysteries, Shambhala is not a part of our Way that we reveal to outsiders."

The kingdom's name resonated like the gong that an ambassador to the Basileus had brought from the Land of Gold. It was simultaneously strange and familiar, like encountering a passerby and realizing that she was a long-lost twin. Shambhala.

The monk gestured at a wall hanging. Depicted in brilliant crimsons, golds, and blues was a city surrounded by rings upon rings of snow mountains in a pattern of eight petals . . . "Like a lotus," Father Basil murmured at her side. At the center of the city was one of the intricate patterns she knew were called mandalas, and at the heart of it sat some sort of figure, enthroned. She squinted against the blinding sunlight and peered at its face. If it looked like the child she had seen, she would know that she had stumbled past hope into some strange faith's stranger rituals.

"That is Shambhala, the enlightened city hidden between snow mountains. As the Wheel of Time spins, there will come an age when wealth and piety will decrease, day by day, until the world will be wholly depraved. Property alone will confer rank; wealth will be the only source of honor; passion will be the sole bond of union between men and women. Earth will be venerated but for its gold and silver."

The monk's voice deepened as he shifted from Persian to Sanskrit. It sounded like the apocalypse, Alexandra thought, and was not surprised to hear that at that time, a god would become human and raise a great army. He would ride forth on his blue horse, and with his blazing sword, destroy the barbarians—*us? the Persians? my aunt?*—and "reestablish righteousness upon earth. The minds of those who live at the end of the age of strife shall be awakened, and shall be as pellucid as crystal. The men who are thus changed by virtue of that peculiar time shall be as seeds of human beings, and shall give birth to a race who shall follow the laws of the golden age of purity."

"The apocalypse," she whispered. "We have a . . . sacred story of the end of times, of a great walled city." The words stuck in her throat, and she was glad to drink from the cup Father Basil handed her. It seemed a profanation to speak of the New Jerusalem here in this pagan shrine, and yet, and yet . . . how much alike the story of Shambhala seemed. *But it was a place on earth,*

not in heaven or at the end of days, the last remnants of
Orthodoxy argued at the back of her skull. What about
Augustine? What if there were more than one city of
earth, and more than one City of God, all examples of
order, set against chaos, and at the end of time . . . she
shook her head. Orthodoxy decreed otherwise. And yet
the ruler of this Shambhala had no reason to appear to
her, let alone save her life, and yet he had.

"Why me? What does he want of me?" she was
appalled to hear herself ask. She was less than nothing
now: a fugitive princess whose friends and wealth were
gone, and lacking even the grace to be thankful for a
visitation that had saved her wretched life.

The monk smiled and raised his hand to point again at
the wall hanging, when the room shook about them.

Cries rang out in the hall. Her guardsmen called on
Thor and Christos with equal fervor. Alexandra levered
herself up from her pallet onto her feet as the floor
heaved beneath them. The dazzling sun had been replaced by a ghostly violet glow. Thunder rumbled in the
clouds that were piling up above the highest peaks. At
this height, they were fatally exposed to such storms.

A man too young to be a monk—an acolyte perhaps?
—ran into the room and knelt before the old man.
"*Vajra*, the thunderbolt, comes!" he cried.

"There is no need for fear," the older monk reproved
him. "My daughter, we should see this. Can you walk?"

Where was there to walk? There could be no flight
from this storm. Lightning scored the dark sky. Alexandra nodded.

The floor still had that alarming tendency to shake as
if she balanced in a chariot, but Father Basil and a
Varangian let her lean on them. Moving with amazing
speed for a man his age, the monk brought them through
a maze of halls until they stood on a kind of narrow
balcony that overlooked the chasm that was now filled
with darkening clouds. *My friends . . . lost down there.*
Lightning danced from those clouds to the ones looming
above the barren white peaks, shutting out all the

mountain range except the crag on which that other, darker monastery stood.

"Power was invoked and used," Father Basil said quietly. "It was meant to strike us, but we live. Therefore it must go *somewhere*. Usually, such power recoils three-fold upon the user." His voice had a questioning note in it, and the monks nodded.

Again came that blinding dance of lightning. Fires blossomed upon the snow and rock, encircling the dark monastery, then dying away. Tiny figures ran from it, but could not cross that ring where the fires had been.

"What will happen?" Alexandra asked in a voice she didn't recognize as her own.

"They struck, knowing what they did. Now they will pay."

The wind died down, leaving the air even colder than before. Monks, soldiers, and princess huddled together, watching. Above the doomed monastery, the clouds thickened. Though the air was still, Alexandra's hair prickled on her scalp. The clouds seemed to draw strength from everything about them, to serve as a channel for some force . . . white and purple fires danced in their immense bellies. Then an immense bolt slashed down, searing through cloud, snow, and rock.

They cried out. Alexandra found herself on her knees, clutching and being clutched by the others for support. "Blind!" someone wailed.

"It will pass," came the old monk's serene voice.

Now they could hear a thin screaming. Alexandra wanted nothing more than to cower where she had fallen (assuming she could not creep into hiding indoors), but forced herself to stand and seek out the source of those cries. Across the chasm, the dark monastery was dark no longer. Flames burst out of its windows, danced on the backs of running, screaming figures, and poured down the monastery's slanted walls. Then slowly, almost as if it were a dream in which one encountered terror past bearing and yet could not flee, the walls crumbled as the rock beneath them cracked and slid down the side of the

mountain into the abyss. Any hope of begging the abbot
to order the hillsides searched for survivors of her party
died in that moment.

"*Kyrie eleison*," she whispered. God have mercy on all
of them. Whether these forces were arrayed for them or
against them, passionately she prayed for them to keep
far from her.

The clouds were dissipating. Sunlight tore through
them and blazed in a column of fire, its base upon the
living rock where once sorcerers had lived.

"What was that?" muttered one of the Varangians.

The monk met Alexandra's eyes. His own were compassionate, but quite inexorable. "That," he answered
her, "was the path of the thunderbolt. Some call it
Vajrayana, the Diamond Path. And, daughter, it is the
road you must walk if you want to survive."

In the days that followed, Alexandra felt herself under
the discipline of tutors more severe than any she had
encountered. The man she had thought of as the "old
monk" was, in fact, the monastery's abbot, who paid her
the great honor of speaking to her himself, rather than
through one of his *chelas*.

The monks here were a composite of races and people.
Some were even from the Land of Gold, which had been
sending people into the West and Hind for centuries. She
had seen accounts of such journeys by men with names
like Fa Hsien and H'suan Tsang. Others were from the
Land of Snows, where the religion had taken strange
ways, she thought. The abbot was one such; his followers
called him *tulku*, or holy one, and *rimpoche*, a title
Father Basil told her was reserved for a few very holy
men who were believed to be reincarnations of earlier
monks.

After that first visit to her quarters, he had taken to
summoning her and Father Basil to his own rooms,
presided over by a female icon with eyes on palms, bare
feet, and brow whom the monks called the White Tara,
Lady of Compassion. Alexandra usually winced and

looked away. The monks also knew of the Christ. The scriptures explaining the legend of Shambhala called him Isha.

The abbot had explained the Kalachakra, or Wheel of Time, to her, had decreed that she was somehow borne upon it, but that he himself stood apart from it. She still smarted from the way in which she had learned this.

Terrified after the manifestation of power which casually obliterated a side of the mountain, she had begged refuge in the monastery. "If I can do no good," she said, "at least I will do no evil."

But she had been refused. She should have expected it. Vajrayana—the Path of Diamonds. From what she could understand, it seemed to have as much relationship to other forms of Buddhism as the Christianity of a desert anchorite had with, say, that of a silk merchant. Less, perhaps: for while the ascetic and the merchant shared a certain orthodoxy (or, in the case of heretics like Father Basil, a few common assumptions) Buddhists appeared to be divided by region and theology into many groups, with Vajrayana, or the Diamond Path, being considered the most demanding.

According to the abbot, all paths led to enlightenment. The Hinayana was the humblest, a lesser way in which people purified their minds, tried to kill their desires, and concentrated on their own . . . Alexandra supposed she had to use the term salvation. Then there was the Mahayana, the Way that took lifetime upon lifetime to achieve. And finally, there was the Diamond Path, which seemed to turn everything Alexandra had ever believed about religion on its head.

"It is like poisons," said the old tulku. "For indeed lust, hatred, and delusion are poisons." (She would have called them sins, but never mind that.) "The follower of the Hinayana shuns all poisons. The follower of the Mahayana path knows that small doses of poisons may cure one of disease . . . in this case, illusions. But the Vajrayana adept knows that the idea of poison itself is an illusion. Lust, fear, anger, illusion . . . they are all facets of enlightenment. Such a person drains them and, in so doing, transforms passions that would make an ordinary person mad into a vehicle for enlightenment."

"It sounds perilous," had been Alexandra's comment. In its use of passions—especially sex—it also sounded like magic, in which a sorcerer might begin by studying proscribed texts, meaning no harm, but being drawn, step by step, into congress with demonic forces. But it was the energy that passion evoked, not the passion itself, that was important, she learned. Was that how her aunt had fallen—mistaking passion for philosophy? The tulku had agreed. So much for there being one true faith, then. As Father Basil was fond of preaching, "The Way has no constant name, nor the Sage a constant form." The Kalachakra scriptures might mention Jesus, but they also mentioned Mohammed and Mani, plus, of course, the host of Buddhas and Bodhisattvas that flourished in these mountains.

Each land seemed to have its own special deities, all horrifically portrayed. Alexandra did not know if she would ever learn them all, or if she even wanted to.

She had seen enough of the wrong sort of power to feel her hackles rise in the presence of any power. She had sensed it on the mountainside, when her aunt's priest began to chant. She had sensed it in the chilling of the air when the thunderbolt blotted out the monastery that had allied with him. And now she saw it in the accounts of feats by adepts, who could stop their hearts and restart them, wear wet robes into a blinding snowstorm and dry them by the heat of their own bodies, even fly. She had read of saints who could do such things; she herself, following her tutor's instructions, had slowed her heart long enough for her to escape from the snow-drifts on the mountainside.

The scholar in her—and the catlike curiosity of the Greek—awoke and kept her at these new studies, alarming as they were. At least, she told herself, the languages would be useful in her travels. She had seen how quickly these mountains could turn against travelers; from what she had heard of the desert that lay beyond Kashgar, it was less treacherous because its menace was apparent even in its name: Takla Makan . . . a warning that those who entered never came out. If bandits or a storm, earthquake, or fever took Father Basil, she would be lost unless she could live without an interpreter.

Though she balked at the meditations and visualizations that the abbot suggested, gradually she reached a compromise with her new studies that she hoped she could live with. The Diamond Path bore not even the faintest resemblance to the Orthodoxy in which she had been raised. Strangely enough, that did not bother her. Her aunt had turned to its magical side, and she herself had almost been the victim of power turned evil. Why should other faiths not have both bright and dark, open and secret aspects?

If all faiths were the same—which she wasn't prepared to admit, but would assume, shrinkingly, for the sake of argument—then all faiths had another thing in common: a hidden, or esoteric, side that could be perverted. A Byzantine's amulet or icon seemed the same as a Buddhist's statue or prayer flag; a Buddhist monk's sanctity could be as great as a dweller on Mount Athos—and the magic which perverted Orthodoxy could damn one as quickly as the Diamond Path.

It might be damnation, but it was certainly logical. And the logic was so seductive she found herself being drawn in. Clearly, the Vajrayana was dangerous even to think about.

"That it is," agreed the tulku. "Err on the other paths, and your Way is only prolonged. Err on the Diamond Path, and it is like taking the shortest way up a cliff. One false step, and you topple into the pit. You need perfect understanding, perfect self-command—and a guide."

Futile to protest that she had no place upon this Way. If all magics of all faiths were joined, as they appeared to be, then she was as likely to be attacked by a follower of the Diamond Path who had gone wrong as she was a black magician of her own kind. It was even futile to protest that the tulku had taught her up to this point; he denied doing more than setting her feet on the Way. Her teacher, he claimed, was no less than the child she had seen on the ice—the legendary, and as-yet-unborn, King of Shambhala, in whatever incarnation he might be at the time, and wherever he might be. What was worse, if she valued her sanity—*and salvation*, she thought—she would have to seek him.

"Could *you* not be my guide?" she pleaded. A desperate hope . . . to stay where she would be taught, where she could do no mischief while she struggled with the power that had been foisted upon her. Far better to stay with this man, whom she trusted, than wander the Roof of the World like one of the Magi run mad in search of some mystical child.

"I follow the Mahayana, daughter. If I followed the lesser Way, I would not have interfered; no, not if it meant your dying on the mountain. Because I do indeed see which Way you must walk, I will set your feet upon it. But you yourself must make the journey."

Alexandra had argued further, but the abbot had been as obdurate as . . . well, adamant. Finally, she remembered that victorious Byzantine generals were awarded a belt studded with diamonds. Coincidence? She was coming to doubt it. Strangely enough, the thought settled her. She had fled from a convent, forsaken what she had thought would be a life wholly of the mind and the spirit for a life of adventure. If she thought of this new life as a battle, in which she served order, wherever she found it, against chaos, wherever it erupted, she might be able to face it.

But now, risking a slow, torturous death by stealing the silkworms of Ch'ang-an seemed an easier and more comforting proposition. And how was she to do either? She had lost her friends, her horses, and her funds.

She wished she could think of those losses as illusions, but her grief was very real. Haraldr's loyalty, his laugh, his awe at new places; Bryennius' ready courage and wry humor; the grace of those ruddy horses; these tore at her until she wished she had the skill of a yogi to transmute them into some sort of escape. Those times she was not studying the texts she learned to call sutras and the strange oblong scriptures that the abbot lent her—she spent praying for her friends. She no longer asked what god might hear those prayers.

For the third time that sunny afternoon, Father Basil and a monk from Hind were correcting her translation of a passage of an epic battle in which a god appeared to a king, showed him the futility of a battle, but ordered him to fare forward anyhow. "It seems I have something in common with this Arjuna," Alexandra commented to Father Basil. "Trying to learn this seems futile."

He smiled, and tapped the page. "Fare forward, my princess—once again, from the beginning!" he ordered. She half expected to feel a teacher's corrective slap upon her hand.

She was making headway when long strides and heavy footsteps announced one of the Varangians. Slower, more decorous steps behind him indicated that he came accompanied by one of the monks.

Though he wore local clothing and had agreed not to carry his axe in the monastery, the guardsman saluted with as much precision as if he had just emerged from the military garrison in the old Mangana fortress.

"Pilgrims, my princess!" he said.

Alexandra raised an eyebrow. When the snows and winds permitted, pilgrims always found their way to the monastery, some bringing sons to enter as novices, others seeking enlightenment or bearing gifts. One such group had brought the abbot the robes of the priest whose chanting had brought down the mountain. The ground on which they were found was scorched black, in the shape of a body, crumpled by a long fall. No bones were ever discovered.

She recognized the monk who entered as the personal disciple of the abbot. "The pilgrims have come to see the tulku, have they not? How can I best serve him?" There were legends of Rome and Byzantium in these parts: As little like him as it seemed, perhaps the abbot wanted to display the foreign princess to the pilgrims. She laid down the book with some relief, and rose.

The monk was trying to keep the smile from his face, to mask his features with the serenity that his master habitually wore. But it escaped him; he practically glowed with joy.

"What is it?" Alexandra caught him and, since he was little taller than she, spun him around. "Tell me, monk, tell me! Do these pilgrims concern me?"

The young monk smiled. Not waiting for him, Alexandra ran down the shadowy corridors she knew well by now. The god figures in their eternal, titanic dances on the walls seemed to wonder at her speed; monks whom she encountered pressed against the walls to avoid being knocked down.

Panting and almost reeling in the thin air—*it was folly to run so fast and so long in these mountains*—Alexandra arrived in the monastery's walled yard. The lesser gate was swinging open, and the caravan of pilgrims winding in. Before her stood the abbot. He too seemed to smile.

Illusion, she thought, *or hallucination. I have run too fast, or my readings have made me mad. This is impossible!*

Several of the pilgrims wore the dress and mannerisms of merchants—they were the same on the Mese, or main road of Byzantium, as they had been in Sogdiana, and as they would doubtless be in Ch'ang-an. Others were villagers, bent from the backbreaking labor these mountains exacted from people who merely wished to survive. They glanced around, awestruck, at the monastery, at the abbot in splendid robes, at the images, and the banners.

But there seemed more fear than awe in their manner. And the reason for their fear became apparent when the final group of pilgrims crowded in before the huge gates swung shut. A group of villagers and merchants' grooms held . . . "My horses!" Alexandra cried, and ran forward to take the bridle of the first one. Not all of them. That would have been too much to expect. But enough, even if they lost some on the arduous road to Ch'ang-an, to make a good appearance.

Six villagers who looked as if they would rather be anyplace but where they were followed the horses. They were carrying a long, crude stretcher.

Alexandra steadied herself against the horse, its reins falling from her hand. Her eyes flooded with tears, which turned cold against her lashes. A sudden sweat drenched her, then dried quickly in the cold, leaving her trembling. "Illusion?" she whispered at the tulku, who shook his head.

That length of arm and leg, the braids of hair and golden beard—unmistakably, it was Haraldr. And when she ran to him, and shook him by the shoulders, calling his name, blue eyes opened to regard her.

He looked at her with a vague sort of attention—but no recognition, no awareness at all.

Around her, the pilgrims were murmuring of a fantastic battle, of the courage of the fearsome stranger with his horrible blue eyes, and the axe that had to be the attribute of a war god.

"What have you done, Haraldr?" Alexandra cried. "And how can I cure you?"

The guardsman's only answer was a low, terrified moan. Alexandra had never heard such fear from him. He moved, but only to crouch in on himself. Alexandra tried to pry his hands free, and felt warmth on her own. Haraldr's hand bled profusely; the blood had soaked through whatever filthy cloth they had used to wrap it. She wondered that he was not bled white by now.

Carefully, she unwrapped the hand. Though the flesh of the wrist looked macerated—*chewed*, she thought, swallowing bile—no bones seemed broken, and the gnawed flesh looked clean. Yet the bleeding would not stop. She bandaged Haraldr's hand again, and turned to call for help.

Suddenly his free hand grabbed her by the wrist and pulled her until she sprawled across him.

"What's wrong?" she asked, her voice shrill with fear and surprise.

"*En freki renna*," he moaned. "The wolf, the Fenris wolf, runs forth. My hand . . ."

No live wolf would terrify Haraldr, who had brought wolfskins to Byzantium before joining the Guard. And no wolf bite would stay untended this long without festering.

Haraldr had to wake up. He had thrust her into safety before the snow tore him away from her. He was one of her last links with her home; she had never realized how much Imperials relied on the Varangians, not just for strength and courage, but for their loyalty and humor. That the magic had reached out to harm him pained her: It was wrong for the blond giant to face anything that could not be mastered by his great axe.

Bracing herself against his shoulder, she forced herself free of his grip and turned toward the abbot.

"This is my guardsman. I think he must have fought a demon," she told him. "Help us!"

3

Without appearing to hurry, the abbot knelt at Haraldr's other side. "He's too strong, I can't hold him," she gasped.

The abbot nodded and touched a point at the Varangian's throat. Haraldr collapsed and lay alarmingly still.

"Now," the abbot said, and a clangor of horns, bells, and chanting started. The chant had recalled Alexandra to life; she prayed earnestly it would do the same for Haraldr. The old, intricately wrought bells rang with a peculiarly shrill and piercing sound that washed over the hearers in wave upon wave, and never ceased. It seemed to separate Alexandra from all the world except the man whose hand she still clutched. She could see Father Basil's lips moving, but could hear nothing but the eternal clamor of the bells. The abbot held up a horn for her to see. Instead she leaned over Haraldr, trying to wake him, shake him back into reason and courage.

An underpriest knelt at Haraldr's other side, washing

his bitten wrist with warm water. There were no wolves in what passed for lowlands here at the Roof of the World. There were, however, snow leopards, but they were notorious for avoiding human dwellings. And the bite of any big cat would have rotted by now. She ought to be praying that Haraldr would not lose his arm, much less his life. But what good would either be if the mind were gone?

"Tell me what happened!" she begged, though the bells and horns, *ghanta* and *k'alin*, drowned out her words. Haraldr's eyes opened, the blue that the people hereabouts found so uncanny, and he started, glancing about wildly until her pressure on his fingers made him look at her. He was floating in illusion, Alexandra remembered her own wanderings in spirit—and then his glance and his grasp pulled her into the nightmare which held him trapped.

As the snow pried him away from the princess, Haraldr bellowed his rage. At least he had given her a chance to survive; the Shieldmaids would know that and save him from Hela; he could cross Bifrost, knowing he had been true to his oaths to the rulers of Miklagard.

The snow bore him down the mountainside until he seized a rock outcropping and swung himself into the safety it offered. Snow and ice thundered over his head, and he grasped his amulet.

The rumbling and the mad snowslide subsided. After a time, it looked like he might live. When the snow stopped trembling as more tumbled down, he dug himself free, and looked uphill, his eyes wild. He could not even see the place from which he had been swept: clouds covered it, or perhaps that whiteness was tumbled ice and snow.

"My princess," he whispered, "Alexandra!" His voice rose to a scream, and he flung himself at the slope until he threatened to pull more snow down upon him. The footing was too treacherous; he could not climb back up to save her, if still she clung to the rock with those little hands of hers. More likely, the snowslide had buried her. He sank to his knees, dizzy. She held his oath, and he had failed her. Best to die right here, he thought.

Would that have been her way? If she held his oath, her brother held hers; and she had sworn to travel east as far as she could. Poor brave princess: if she could go no farther, Haraldr could, as long as breath was in him. He slapped his arms and legs to bring warmth back to them, then cast about for a plan. He had been taught by his grandfather how to walk out of such slides. He would descend into the valley, find a village where he could rest, then determine what might be best for a masterless man to do. Scrubby treetops showed above the snow; he could weave them into shoes and walk the more easily.

The air grew easier to breathe as he descended. He paused once to glance up at the mountain peak where he had lost friends, and the princess he had sworn to protect, and shook his fist at it. Though he knew that the Imperial lady withstood hardships like a woman of the North, she was still in his charge. Like all the house of Miklagard, she was delicate, because she lived too much inside her thoughts. That was why they had Varangians to guard them. The Rhomaioi were moody but not fools: They valued the Northerners' courage as it deserved, favoring them with special trading privileges, and honoring the Guard with its own wing in the Imperial palace.

He would probably die here, he realized. But he could not have allowed his princess to travel to the edge of the world unguarded. Though rocks and snow shifted treacherously underfoot, Haraldr reached the valley. Tumbled where they had been flung, he found the bodies of several men and and their horses, but not his princess. He plundered the dead men's packs for food and weapons.

Nearby lay a tumble of priest's robes. There was no body in them, though the ground where such a body might have lain seemed etched into the shape of a man, his limbs twisted at impossible angles. The ground scrub beneath that shape was withered. He stirred the robes cautiously with a stick. From them tumbled a medallion on a chain, insignia such as a priest might wear, though it bore no likeness to anything he had ever seen or wished to see. The image on it grinned like Grendel itself, had daggers in each of its many arms, and wore round things that looked like skulls. He might have known. Princess Alexandra had known Andronicus was no proper priest. Certainly he had always made Haraldr's hackles rise.

He touched the Thor's hammer that, for a wonder, still lay about his neck. Now what? He was lordless now. His duty had been to guard the princess and her cousin on their way to Ch'ang-an, and to cover their retreat. That need not change. Haraldr had no illusions about his abilities. He could hire on as a caravan guard and make the desert crossing. But he had not the cunning and speed to trick Ch'ang-an out of its silk. Still . . . he glanced around the valley, hoping to see smoke or flocks or fields—some sign of people who might take him in.

Something rolled across his foot, and he stooped to pick it up. A hunting horn, but curiously shaped, not like the ones he used in the home he would never see again. A circular design had been carved into it. Grumbling at the pain bending down had caused him, he tried to blow the horn until twinges warned him that his tumble down the mountain had probably broken a few ribs. He hung the soundless horn about his neck and went on. He might not know what direction to walk in, but his course was clear. "I will not flee the space of a foot, but shall fare on farther," he muttered in his matted beard. To Kashgar, when he could. And thereafter, if his fate permitted, across the Land of Fire into Ch'in.

A shrill cry brought Haraldr around, hand to his dagger. Nearby huddled a child, who tugged at a sheep that had gotten its foot caught between two stones. If he were lucky, the child would understand the mangled Sogdian he had learned from the grooms, he thought and started toward him. Naturally, the child fled, but Haraldr bent to free the sheep's foot. Let the child see he meant no harm, he thought, and let the animal leap free. The boy rose slowly from where he had flung himself, his bright black eyes as wide as folded lids would permit.

Moving slowly, not to terrify the boy further, Haraldr held out his hands, tried out the word for "friend," then thought of what else might attract him. When he was a boy, the sight of blade or axe would have drawn him like a lodestone; doubtless, this child would run shrieking from them. There was his amulet, and he was reaching for it when his hand fell on the cord of the horn he had found.

Dangling it in front of the boy lured him closer. Haraldr grinned at the little scrap; what few children he had seen in these parts were all tiny, pretty, though in a strange, amber-skinned, slant-eyed way, and more solemn than the Emperor on high feast days. This one was no exception. The child took the horn and examined it, then looked up.

"Shambhala," he breathed.

Was that the name of their village? "Shambhala," Haraldr agreed, and took the offered grubby hand. Even the foul-tasting tea of the mountain folk would be welcome now, and perhaps they would have wine.

What they had wasn't much, he learned once he approached a miserably small huddle of five huts, with a sixth one crumbled in on itself, smoke still rising from it. The remnants of the village were guarded by flags, charms, and a priest who waved bones and rattles in his face and who chanted like a Finnish *völva* when the fit was on him. The people looked hungry and frightened. Only the boy's presence kept them from fleeing. He bent down, so that they would be able to look eye to eye (even though his blue eyes were regarded as freakish in these parts). "Friend," he said in Sogdian he knew was thickly accented, and "Shambhala."

His two words bought him entry into a smoky dwelling about the size of a barrow (and he touched his amulet against the ill luck in that thought), where he was served a bowl of tea with butter in it, and a few chunks of

dried meat that he tried hard not to wolf down. Halfway
through the too-small meal, the local priest entered.

Father Andronicus, whose outline had been etched on
the rock, had always made Haraldr feel as if he were
caught alone and fireless in a black forest full of wolves.
This man only made Haraldr feel wary, though power
crackled about him. He laid down his empty bowl and
waited.

The priest handed him the horn. "Friend?" he asked,
and Haraldr nodded. At the priest's gesture, he bent
himself double to get through the door, and followed
him to the ruined hut. The priest pointed at the charred
beams and toppled rock. Haraldr could see claw and
tooth marks. He almost laughed aloud. All his life he had
enjoyed the sagas. Now, within one day, he had lost his
ring-giver, and he was expected to slay this village's pet
thyrse. It was well that the sagas had taught him irony
too, he thought, and set himself to wait until dark.

He drew out his axe and leaned on it, hoping to stay
awake. He had not slept for a full day. The air in this
valley was heavier than in the peaks, luring him toward
rest. Gradually the snapping of flags in the wind, a few
bells ringing, and gabbling voices grew distant.

When he woke, the peaks at the horizon were barely
crimson, and clouds hid the moon. He tensed and
waited, trying to recall how, in the stories, heroes slew
monsters. In the story of Grettir the strong, the undead
Glamr had ridden the rooftops, until Grettir wrestled
him to death. Something coughed. He almost jumped,
then started to laugh until he reminded himself that
snow leopards prowled the hills.

Even snow leopards could have their heads chopped
off by his axe. He drew off his boots to move with more
stealth, picked up the axe, and rose. Rocks crashed in on
the burned-out hut, and something rooted about in the
rubble, then was still. Haraldr padded forward. He heard
bones crunch, and decided that his safest course was to
attack quickly. Clouds shifted, and the bloodstained
moon came out. Now he could see clearly. He took a few

steps forward, climbing up on the tumbled walls, stalking the hunter in his turn—and then his prey turned its head.

It was bigger than any leopard that ramped in the pens at Miklagard, and its eyes glowed a hellish green. As he raised his axe to close them forever, the beast coughed. His axe dropped from his hand, and the beast leaped for his throat. With a coughing growl, it pounced down upon him. Haraldr yelled a prayer to Thor and Christ in Majesty, and got his hands up around the it's throat in time to protect his eyes.

The beast was quick and twisty, he thought, and took a tighter grip on its fur. As he reached for the hold that would enable him to snap its neck, fur became scales, and steaming drops burned his face. He bellowed his pain, and held what was now a serpent away from him, glad the demon had chosen a guise without hindclaws that could slash and disembowel. The thing squirmed like Loki itself, but he would bind and kill it! Though its jaws gaped wide, and the poison from them burned and dazed him, he twisted the serpent's neck farther, and felt the bones grind.

Scales became coarse fur again, and he heard a yelp of anguish. Now he dared to open his eyes, and immediately wished he had not. He was a Varangian and the grandson of a jarl. He could fight, he could hunt, he could read verse and make it. Because of the verse he read, he feared the thing that he grappled with in its new guise—a huge wolf, froth dripping from its jaws, the light of malice and reason in its eyes. Fenris, hound of Hel, freed of its chain! His grasp faltered for an instant, long enough for the beast to snap at his throat. Its teeth closed instead on the horn he bore, tearing through the cord and sending the horn down to join his axe.

With one hand Haraldr drew his dagger, and with the other tightened his hold on the great wolf's neck where the fur had ruffled up so that he had no chance of breaking its neck. Since there was nothing else to do, he held fast, hoped that his mail and armlets would protect him just a little, and thrust hand and dagger into the it's. Jaws clamped about leather and metal. He heard himself screaming, mad from pain, while his dagger slashed at the beast's vitals until the jaws released. He fell back, the wolf on top of him.

Haraldr rolled away from it, rising into a crouch, ready to fight until he or his enemy were torn in shreds, but the beast whined in agony. Haraldr staggered forward to give it its deathblow. His hand and wrist were covered with blood; dimly he wondered that he had not left them in the wolf's mouth like a second Heimdall. He bent and retched with pain. The beast lay unmoving, but that could be a trick. He started forward again. Its shape shifted again, from fur to scales, to feathers, and back . . . and then faded suddenly, leaving only a burn mark on the ground. The wind of its passing was sudden and foul-breathed. Haraldr heard a rattle, as of skulls bumping together, and then the whistle that one might use to call a hound.

He glanced up and saw the shadowy figure of an immensely tall woman with a fierce glare. She beckoned to him. *Hela?* he thought. *But I'm not dead!* Then the figure changed until it resembled the capering she-monster Haraldr had seen on Father Andronicus' medallion. He fell to the ground, terrified more by the creature's passing than he had been by its presence. It was the Fenris wolf. It had broken free. And though he had beaten it off, it would return, heralding the endless twilight and the last battle. And Hela had seen him, marked him for her own. Monster-slayer though he was, he cowered in dread and horror.

Then there was nightmare for a long, long time . . .

Something or someone was slapping him, cursing him in bad Norse and the language of the practice yards. Another demon, perhaps, this one in human form? He reached up and caught the wrist of the person slapping him, twisted it, and heard loud protests. In Greek. Would the demons of the hills know Greek? He didn't

think so. He opened his eyes and saw, twisting in his
grasp, the princess whom he thought he had lost in the
snowslide. His princess. He grinned helplessly at her.
Beside her stood the little Persian priest who advised
her, several other men wearing shabby robes, and two
people he recognized as villagers. They stared at him as
he might have looked at the Thunderer himself.

"Let me go, you great bear," Her Highness commanded again, and he complied. He fell back onto the
pallet, dizzy after even so little time awake. "Whatever
demon was sent to kill us, you slew it. Rest now. It
almost bled you white."

"My axe," he mumbled. His chapped lips hurt from
grinning.

"We have it safe." She turned to the priest. "Wouldn't
you know that he'd ask for it first."

Tears rolled down her face, and she brushed them
away fiercely, then wiped his face with her sleeve too. He
barely stopped himself from catching her hand when it
brushed his mouth. He could not meet her eyes anymore. She had been with him, traveled into nightmare
with him, and had not feared his pain.

"The horn . . . horn of Shambhala . . ."

"We have that too," Princess Alexandra told him.
"And when you're rested, you can tell us what you know
of Shambhala."

The Imperial family was wise, that went without
saying, though all Miklagard was supposed to say so.
And the princess was truly wise. Thus, it did not really
surprise Haraldr that Alexandra or this thin little abbot
knew of Shambhala. It seemed natural that if the same
seithr—evil magic—afflicted all of them, whatever
might be good would affect them all too. If Hela could be
a she-demon in these mountains, then why could Valhalla not be named Shambhala?

He remembered the day he had had that revelation.
He had waked from a doze—since the princess had

brought him out of his nightmares, he seemed to spend his time either eating or sleeping—to hear her protest, "But I'm *Christian!* Why do I need this Rudra Cakrin? And I'm not going through these sacraments with bell, crown, sword, scepter, and all the rest of that baggage . . . I can't even pronounce most of it."

"The initiations of Vajrayogini, goddess of the Diamond Path," said the abbot. His tone indicated that he had said it over and over. "I understand that you are unwilling to set foot on the Way. But it has claimed you. From Shambhala itself, your teacher has reached out to mark you for himself, and will, in his own time, initiate you. Otherwise you have no defense against the darker powers your aunt unleashed against you and your City. Though no flowers grow in these mountains, I can at least give you one of the objects you will require."

He had said other things that Haraldr only understood dimly: that this Way he insisted the princess must follow did not mean the abolition of all passions, but mastery over them. Rage, she had experienced, and terror as the snow buried her. (That much Haraldr understood.) But when the abbot said that she would have to endure all such emotions before she could use their strength . . . The princess shook her head, rejecting the priest's words.

With the air of a man laying aside an argument in order to take it up more profitably later on, he beckoned forward one of the younger priests, who knelt, sword and sheath laid across his upraised palms. Though the sword was sharp, both it and its sheath looked very old. The abbot clicked a long fingernail against the blade, and it rang keenly, piercingly in that thin air. Haraldr snapped into battle alertness. Old swords were things of power. "This is a treasure of this house. Would you truly refuse it?"

The princess laughed. "You have me trapped, don't you? Seeing as how you saved my life, I can refuse you nothing. And besides that, my own weapon lies buried in the snow." She accepted the blade, half saluted the abbot with it, then sheathed it, and sat studying the patterns on the scabbard.

To Haraldr's astonishment, the abbot turned to him. Father Basil moved to his side, ready to interpret. "You," the priest said. "This is yours." He held out the horn of Shambhala, strung on a fresh cord. Only a few scratches showed where the demon's teeth had closed upon it.

The abbot's thin, dark fingers, hardly more than bones themselves, traced out the pattern on the horn. "A city between two rings of snow mountains . . . Shambhala, where the king and his warriors wait for the world's need . . ."

Haraldr jerked upright. "My people too have that tale," he said hoarsely. "I blew the horn, and no one answered." No one answered because the need was not great enough, he realized the instant after he spoke, and flushed with shame. In that moment, he felt himself the barbarian that some Greeks were unwise enough to call him to his face.

The abbot nodded. "If you have need . . ." Silently the Varangian vowed never to become that needy. Against all hope, he had slain a demon. He had found help. He would have the use of both hands. He had been reunited with the Imperial princess he was sworn to serve. The abbot would help them outfit themselves and reach Kashgar. It was more than enough.

4

Bryennius choked on snow, spat out a mouthful of reddish water and ice, and flailed about until he had made a small cave in which he could rest, at least for the moment. That was good: Both arms worked. Groaning, he tested his legs and thanked God and His gentle Mother that they were not broken. Once, during a game of polo, he had fallen from his horse and been dragged halfway around the Imperial grounds before he could cut himself free of his stirrup. That time, he had felt as if an executioner had taken a hammer to each bone and sinew, yet it was nothing to the aches he felt now.

So cold . . . his thoughts were muzzy, the way they were after he had drunk too much. A priest had been chanting, that much he recalled. They had been lost, Alexandra had been even more upset than usual—and, as usual, she was right. Bryennius remembered now. The altitude and the chant made the horses uneasy and terrified Alexandra's companion, Thea. Bry' had divided his time between them until . . . his head rolled back and forth in the snow. Oh, God, the chant had sunk into his body, and then he had heard the rumbling of half a mountainside's snow pouring down upon them . . .

"Alexandra!" he called, though it came out a whimper. "Thea?" No, there was no Thea, not anymore. Practically his last sight before snow had blinded him was of his cousin's waiting-woman cartwheeling through the air, down into the clouds. Leo, his friend, the Varangians, that mad priest Alexandra prized so—they must all be dead. And Alexandra herself. He lived, though how much longer he could live without fire or supplies was not certain. Still, he had to look for her. He muttered a brief prayer, for whatever good it might do anyone, then flailed about upslope. He could feel strength draining out of him into the thin, cold air. Then the sky whirled before his eyes, and darkness closed in. He was falling backward, and his last thought was that this time he would never wake.

When awareness returned, it brought sanity with it. It was twilight. Instead of lashing out until he exhausted himself, he looked at the place where he had fallen, then moved arms and legs to make sure that he could. His hand touched something warm. He crawled toward the warmth and found the body of one of the pack animals. He raided its saddlebags for food and wine, and huddled against it, panting. Gradually the pounding of his heart and the keening in his temples subsided. He could hear a low moan, and the snorting, grunting sounds that a fallen horse might make.

He was afraid to shout, lest it bring down more snow, but anything was better than dying alone and frozen. "Who's there?"

"Here . . . I'm falling . . ." The voice trailed up into a terrified scream, and Bryennius tensed, waiting for the snowslide.

When nothing happened, he crawled in the direction

of the voice. Now he could hear muffled sobs. "Oh, God, buried alive."

"Leo?" he called. "Is that you?"

"Prince! Bry'—you're alive!"

Bryennius forced his aching limbs to dig through the last few feet of snow. His hand struck an arm splaying out from hunched shoulders. He grabbed it, heaved the man to the surface, turned him over, and sank back onto his knees, panting. *Leo. It was this or back to his regiment in Alexandria, and he came with me because we were friends. Did I bring him all this way to die?*

His friend's helmet lay several feet away, badly dented, beside a feebly struggling horse. Beyond it, another horse was struggling, first to its knees, then all the way onto unsteady legs. One of the horses, God help them all, onto which they had loaded the packs containing Greek fire. Bryennius tried to whistle at it. It nickered at him, and stood with its head down.

"Leo?" Gently, Bryennius brushed ice and grit from his friend's eyebrows. Leo's eyes opened, then drifted shut again.

"Don't leave me!" Panic threatened to overwhelm him as it had when he waked and supposed himself alone, and dying on the mountain. If Leo could walk, they had horses, supplies . . . by the Blessed Theotokos, they had hope! "Wake up, brother!" He slapped Leo's face, until the young officer's hand came up to clasp his.

"Think . . . you're not my general . . . he wouldn't hit . . ." Leo turned over and tried to vomit.

"Here. Try some of this wine," Bryennius urged him. Finally, he got him settled, his back propped up against one of the dead horses' packs, a blanket wrapped warmly about him. He staggered over to lead those horses able to walk over to where Leo lay, and picket them roundabout for warmth. One lay with a snapped foreleg, too exhausted to scream or to thrash, and he cut its throat with his dagger. He thought that the blood that splashed his hands was the warmest thing he had ever imagined. If worse came to worst . . . Father Basil had told him of barbarians who drank blood. Or, he supposed, they could use the Greek fire to burn the dead horses and warm themselves at the pyre, if they weren't consumed too. Bryennius felt his gorge rising, and turned away quickly.

He made a rough camp, and was glad to sink into the blankets and furs, gladder yet to wolf down the sparse provisions he had gathered. It was getting very dark.

Moonlight glinted on the snow. He could see his friend's face: scraped raw in some places, very dirty, his sandy hair matted. He supposed that he himself looked like a brigand in the leather and sheepskins of the hillmen. Now he wished that he had let his beard grow as most Byzantines did. It would have been warmer.

"Bry', did you find—" Leo turned and spat out a fragment of tooth with an oath of disgust and frustration.

"Any of the others? No. When it's light, we probably should dig around here in case anyone else . . . the least we can do is give him proper burial."

Or her. Alexandra. Of all the rabble of spare princes and princesses in the palace, she—three years or several centuries older, depending on how you looked at it—had been the one closest to him. He felt his throat squeeze shut against a sob. She had always provided the schemes, he the manpower to execute them (and frequently the backside that was punished whenever they were found out), when they were children. As they grew older, her wit had extricated him from numerous traps set by women, politicians, or both wrapped into one silk-clad package.

Poor little princess. If he was a spare prince, for whom no politically safe place existed in Byzantium, his life had been enjoyable. Polo, the games in the Hippodrome, beautiful and willing women—it was only when he spoke with Alexandra, sitting in her rooms among a clutter of codices and scattered paper, that he realized that his life was blurring past in wasted motion.

At least he was alive. Alexandra . . . he couldn't imagine that quick mind and quicker tongue stilled beneath the snow. But what would have become of her if she had stayed in Byzantium? There had been no place in the Empire for her either.

Leo laid a hand on his shoulder. "You and Her Highness were close," he rasped. "I'm sorry."

"So am I," Bryennius told him, welcoming comfort. "But it might have been worse. Now, do you want to try to sleep? Tomorrow we'll have to strip supplies from the dead horses before we try to find our way back."

"Back to what?" Leo echoed his own question.

Think, Bryennius, he ordered himself. *Think!* It was hard. He had been denied the discipline of a professional soldier, and Alexandra had always supplied the logic. What would she do? "I say we head back down the slope and try to retrace our path. This is a trade road. We may encounter another caravan bound for Kashgar—"

Or they might meet bandits. In either case, they had the horses, and they had their swords. It was better than dying on the mountainside. He said as much to Leo, and waited for the other man—who had been a soldier—to supply a better plan. To his surprise, Leo only nodded assent.

Bryennius had time for mild astonishment, another yawn, and then he was asleep. Sleep was shallow in these heights, and dream-filled, especially when one was tired, battered, and hungry. Bryennius found himself dreaming of Byzantium. Once again the crowd in the Hippodrome where he had often raced was screaming. This time the shouts were for Alexandra. All Byzantium acclaimed her as Basilissa. Her brother waved him forward too, and the crowd cheered him as a hero. But Alexandra's face was white, and her fear struck terror into him too, terror which fed on itself until he jerked himself upright, his cry echoing from the icy rocks.

"You were the one who wanted to sleep," Leo told him. "Really bad dreams this time?"

"She knew." Bryennius leaned forward and let his hands dangle between his knees. What he could see of the sky despite heavy clouds paled toward dawn. "She knew when they acclaimed her that she was . . . we were . . . in danger."

"Too much power. Didn't you realize?" asked Leo. "She was popular enough that even the lady Theodora couldn't sneak out of hiding to plot against her—and that made her a focus for anyone who wanted to overthrow her brother."

"Trust Alexandra to see it." Bryennius shook his head. Alexandra had understood so much, and now she was dead. Another thing she had seen was the shortage of silk, not just the first-quality silk and purples reserved for the Imperial palace, but all silk, and the goods it purchased from the merchants whose carefully regulated numbers crowded Byzantium. "She showed me the empty workshops, the women with idle hands," he murmured. "I wouldn't have thought to link it to a blight on the mulberry trees . . . but when we had them dig, we found those same devil-cult talismans buried in the orchards. No wonder all our silkworms died."

"So you came with her—and I with you," mused Leo.

Bryennius looked up. From here, he thought he could see the two monasteries toward which they had climbed only a night ago. Then the clouds obscured them again. *By God, Bryennius, you're not safe either!* Alexandra had raged. *Just you watch. Soon there will be rumors of a marriage between us, and you know that's often the first step to the throne for an ambitious man.*

But I told *the Basileus!* he had protested. *And I don't want to rule.* Both of them tactfully did not mention their horror at the idea of marrying one another.

"I wasn't afraid," Bryennius said, with a sort of dulled wonder. "But none of our ambassadors—or our spies —could get more silkworms. And when Alexandra decided to try it herself, well, for once in my life, I wanted to do something useful." He laughed a little hollowly. "Besides, this might be the only chance I would have to travel."

He fell silent, not wanting to share what had truly decided him: the compassion in his cousin's eyes as she called him a fool. As a spare prince, he had never been permitted achievements of his own. *Don't think I'm being noble*, she had said. *I need a man I can trust along, one of my own blood . . . a prince who can go places where a princess may not. You . . . please?*

He had never been able to refuse her, and so he had come. There had been plenty of adventures. If this were the last adventure of all, well, he had had a fine time.

Lightning crackled through the dense clouds. The horses screamed with terror, while Bryennius and Leo leaped to their heads to comfort them. For what seemed like hours, men and horses clung to one another while the mountain trembled and fire danced overhead. When the sky cleared, both men looked up. The crags where the dark monastery had stood, where sorcerers had chanted and brought down the snows, had been sheared away; the naked rock looked slick and blackened as if by terrible heat.

Bryennius shrugged. "No one could have survived that," he said. So much for any hope that Alexandra might possibly have survived the snowslide. Then he helped load the animals—fine horses and pack beasts alike—with the supplies they plundered from the dead. Leo tied two sticks into a rough cross, which he planted in the snow.

Carefully, they loaded the surviving horses and helped them turn.

"We head for Kashgar." Leo looked to Bryennius for confirmation.

He nodded.

"Then I suppose we head back to Byzantium by way of Samarkand? You were lucky to get out of there with a whole skin."

"We're not going home," Bryennius said. "Not now, maybe not ever."

Leo stopped so suddenly that Bryennius almost

bumped into him on the narrow path. "Where are we headed?" he demanded.

"We finish what Alexandra started, or at least try to."

Brave words, he told himself wryly. Well, what else did he have now? Without looking back at the deadly peak, the tumbled snow, and the pathetic, rickety cross, they headed down the twisting, narrow path to Kashgar.

5

Four days later, a peculiarly shaped rock spur convinced Bryennius and Leo that they had finally retraced the road to the point where the traitorous guide had led them astray. They traveled downward, always downward now. Though what passed for a road in these hills was never easy, it grew steadily less perilous. But it was still no road that starving men and beasts could take safely. That morning, he and Leo had given the last of their grain to the pack animals. They had food for perhaps two days more. Kashgar lay at least five days beyond that.

Leo, who had scouted ahead, appeared around a bend. He shouted and waved excitedly at Bryennius, who hurried to catch up. Here, where the pass had opened up into what was practically a plain, two pathways joined. He pointed, and Bryennius could see hoofprints. The marks were old, but of sufficient number that Bryennius felt new hope.

"Thank God," he muttered.

"This trail is old," Leo warned. "Just look at the dung. Besides, even if we could catch up, they might well think we are bandits. And we haven't the strength to fight them off."

"Now what?" asked Bryennius.

"I put my ear to the ground. Someone is coming. And then I remembered you used to like to gamble for high stakes," Leo commented. Then, to Bryennius' astonishment, he began to unsaddle the horses. It was far too early to make camp, Bryennius started to protest. Then he realized. They could not catch up to the travelers whose tracks they studied, not as worn as they were. They could not make it to Kashgar on the supplies they had. With good fortune, the caravan Leo claimed he heard might actually show up before starvation forced them to move on again.

Bryennius laughed mirthlessly. "Not for stakes this high, brother," he said, and helped make camp. At least Leo's gamble would give them and the horses a badly needed rest.

Leo had begun to apologize for wasting the time when one of the high-bred Ferghana horses nickered. Both men fell silent, listening. The horse nickered again, and Bryennius went to its head, stroking its aristocratic nose until it was calm. Leo loosened knife and sword in their sheaths and crept into the rocks bordering the trail.

Bryennius fumbled in a saddlebag for additional weapons. His hand fell on the slick hardness of ceramic, and he pulled out a heavily sealed jar containing Greek fire. He was appalled at the path his thoughts had taken: would he really use the fire and turn bandit? He hoped he wouldn't have to find out. At least Greek fire wasn't magic, he thought. He had had a bellyful of magic. Please God his exposure to it had died with Alexandra. He had never seen her afraid before it touched her.

A clatter of stones brought him around, sword out.

"You've gotten more alert," Leo approved. "A train of

men and animals is approaching. Somehow we'll have to stop them without scaring them enough that they'll fight."

"Persian or Muslim?" Bryennius asked.

"Neither," Leo said.

Bryennius was simultaneously puzzled and relieved. The Sogdians were by far the most numerous travelers hereabouts, closely followed by the Muslims with whom they had intermarried. While the Sogdians dealt with anyone who met their price, the Muslims could be dangerous, as Bryennius had found out in Samarkand. It wasn't as if he had meant to seduce the lady Rabia, sister to some of the Abbasid trader-nobles. He had glimpsed her once—purely by chance—voiced his admiration, and damned near been knifed in the market.

"What are they, then?" he asked.

"I don't know," Leo admitted. "Not pilgrims; they looked heavily armed. Some sort of barbarians. But they look strange for these parts. They're taller than the average Persian and, under all that dirt, they're light-skinned, almost as light as the Varangians. Where do you think they come from?"

"Does it matter as long as they let us travel with them?"

"It might," Leo said. "In any case, do we wait for them now?"

They settled themselves along the road where they could see the caravan coming, but where arrows could not reach them. The morning passed. Bryennius shook himself out of an uneasy nap, and laid a hand on Leo's shoulder.

"Shouldn't they be here by now?" he asked.

Leo groaned, stretched, and headed for a rock spur. He climbed rapidly, then shouted down to Bryennius, "They've cut across the plain about half a mile back. They're going to pass us by!"

Bryennius swore in several languages. "We have to make them see us!" he yelled back. He grabbed up a saddlebag, reassured himself that the horses were firmly picketed, and began to climb, wincing each time his shoulder even came close to brushing the rock.

"There!" Leo pointed. Bryennius fought against the panting that threatened to turn into hacking coughs. He cupped his hands over his eyes, thankful for the clear air at these heights that made nothing out of distances. These barbarians were indeed as tall and blond as Leo had reported. They were wrapped in black goatskins, were heavily armed, and looked formidable. Doubtless, if he and Leo expended their horses' strength to ride toward them, they would attack.

Bryennius reached into his pack and pulled out a sling and one of the vials holding the Greek fire. Before Leo could stop him, he whirled the sling over his head. The vial smashed against rock and scrub, creating a most satisfactory explosion that would burn fiercely until the last scrap of wood or plant life was consumed.

"That ought to give us time to reach them," he said with satisfaction. "And give them something to think about. Down!"

They scrambled down the rocks and back to their horses.

"Prince," Leo said formally, "do you want me to go first?"

"Remind me," Bryennius said, "when we get to Kashgar that I'm going to knock you down for saying that. We ride together!" Leo's question hurt. He had lost Alexandra, closer than a sister. Leo was his closest friend, his only companion now. He didn't need a courtier; he needed the brother and friend his rank had always denied him.

Leo laid a hand on his shoulder. "Remind me," he told Bryennius apologetically, "to let you try."

By the time they reached the fire, the barbarians had made a half-circle about it, standing between it and the bundled-up figures who huddled by the few straggly packhorses and an amazing number of goats, tended by the women and children. Though they seemed to move about freely, Bryennius reminded himself not to stare at them. A man older and taller than the rest and wearing, if possible, more noisome goatskins, came forward bearing what looked like a blackened piece of wood, hacked roughly into the form of a man, a flat plate of silver gleaming where the face ought to be. Two younger men carried a more elaborate statue of two men, hands on one another's shoulders, legs overlapping. Some attempt had been made, though probably with the blade of a spear or blunt knife, to carve features on the two faces, which looked like younger men. The three men's progress with their—icons? idols?—looked too ceremonial to be anything but a religious rite. And when they started to chant, both Byzantines tensed. They had known chants kill before. But it might be equally deadly to interrupt this one. Bryennius strained to listen to the chief, priest, or whatever he was.

"Can you make sense of anything of that?" he hissed at Leo.

"The only thing I can make out is 'Imra.' Their chief devil, I imagine," Leo said. Then he too stiffened. "Wait! That's Greek!"

Bryennius nodded. "You're close," he said. "I think some of those words are Macedonian." He had gained something from all those years of listening while Alexandra talked. When Alexander's armies had traveled through Persia and into Hind, some men had deserted, while others, who married local women, decided to remain behind. Legend had it that their descendants still lived in hidden valleys, waiting for Iskandar, as they called him, to return. In an undertone, he passed the story on to Leo. "They're far out of their range," he added. "Maybe they're going to Kashgar to trade." It was better to hope for that than to assume automatically that they were brigands.

"We're Greek," Leo said. "But Alexander's been dead over a thousand years. That's a long time to wait."

"It's a long time, too, to preserve the language," Bryennius told him. "Besides, what other chance have we got?"

"What chance, indeed?" Leo said, and kneed his horse forward. "They've sighted us," he muttered. "Try to look royal."

"For that, I'll knock you down twice when we get to Kashgar!" Bryennius hissed, then let his eyes go remote, his face become still and severe.

Six of the men mounted and rode toward them. Bryennius heard a snick and shook his head at Leo. "We ride in unarmed," he said in an undertone. "We are not afraid of them."

"Like I said, you gamble for high stakes," his friend muttered. "Here they come, and they've got their priest with them."

The barbarians rode straight up to Bryennius and Leo, and then dismounted. If they were going to attack, Bryennius thought, they wouldn't have given up the advantage of their horses. After an eternity, the priest walked up to them, stared, and finally prostrated himself, muttering incantations and greetings in everything from Persian to a hideously corrupt Greek.

Leo tugged at Bryennius' shoulder. "What are they saying? And why are they bowing to us?"

Bryennius nodded almost ceremonially to the priest and the men who ringed about them, awe on grimy faces that resembled the northern Greeks he had seen.

"It's not Alexander. At least, they haven't made that connection yet. As you heard, they have a god named 'Imra.' Apparently, he has twin sons, or associates, called Kassir and Bekassir. Think of them as resembling Castor and Pollux. Now they think . . ."

"They think we're these twins?" Leo cut in.

"Precisely," Bryennius said. "And that means we are in desperate trouble."

"Why?" Leo asked. If they were gods to these people, then they would be delighted to feed them and protect them all the way to Kashgar. Blasphemous as the idea was, it had a lot to recommend it.

"Why? Just look at us. Bryennius and Leo Epiphanes. Don't you think we're feeble substitutes for gods-made-manifest, trailing in hungry, bruised, and bleeding? Let's say they swallow that. What happens the first time they want their resident gods to perform a miracle or two? God, I wish Alexandra were here to talk us out of this situation."

"Iskandar?" The priest raised his head, daring to interrupt the two.

Alexandra's name had won their attention. They knew that name. Bryennius began to stitch together some sort of explanation, then shut his mouth on it as the tribesmen bowed to the earth, as if to a Great King. Then two men took their bridles to escort them ceremoniously back to camp. Now he and Leo couldn't escape even if they wished to. Surreptitiously, Bryennius crossed himself.

Bryennius and Leo huddled shoulder to shoulder, wedged in between a number of the tribesmen. As Bryennius suspected, these people were far out of their own lands, which lay far to the south, separated from Kashgar by the Pamirs. Restlessness, akin to the fabled "longing" of Alexander, had driven them north, Gumara the chief told Bryennius; after hours of debate, the chief had accepted Byrennius as a member of Alexander's royal house. Equally important had been the words of the priest who spoke for Imra, as portrayed by the crudely carved black figure Bryennius had seen worshiping: Imra had commanded them to seek the Twins, his sons, with whom these people's fortunes lay.

At least, Bryennius thought with some satisfaction, *I made them realize that Leo and I are not their gods*. But the instant they had shucked the cloak of divinity, they had been forced to assume a sort of overchieftainship, the governance of a people whose laws, as far as Bryennius could see, resembled complete anarchy. He had said as much and been told that when he returned home with them, he could teach them the Greek laws they had forgotten during the long centuries that they had been deprived of their rightful king.

Since they obviously knew little better, Bryennius couldn't quite call them savages. They had courage, honor, even art of a kind. Certainly, their silver, though harshly wrought, had a massive, sculptural beauty, and their weapons, crafted of the Indian steel they called *wootz*, were so sharp that he and Leo had accepted new blades with genuine gratitude.

But the rest of it . . . *barbarians*, Bryennius thought for the thousandth time. Their relationship with the Persian and Muslim traders, for example. It was half commerce, and half warfare. The merchant princes called them Simposh, the black-clad ones, and Kafirs, or unbelievers, and despised them. In return, the Southerners regarded the merchants as legitimate prey. Even the people of Ch'in knew of them and called them the Moonfolk, doubtless because of their pale skin. Only the empire of which they claimed to be a tiny part had forgotten them.

Within the markets, trading for horses, garments, and weapons went on, though both parties kept hands to daggers as well as clapped to purses. Outside the cities, it was war. As the "descendant" of their King Alexander, Bryennius could not refuse to accompany the chief and what seemed like at least ten of his sons on a raiding party. For now, he thought, he would cooperate. Later he intended to teach them the difference between war and robbery. He brought himself up short. Was he really thinking of remaining with these men as their king? Temptation caught at his heart: he could make a place here for himself, build something that might last beyond his lifetime. Something that might one day reach out to Byzantium and tell his City that he was more than just a pleasure-loving fool!

He stared into the distance. Though the mountains were many days' journey from here, the clear air made them seem but an hour's leisurely ride away. Below them, winding toward Kashgar, was the dust serpent that marked a caravan, not one of the huge ones that were practically armies or tribal migrations, nor one of the desperately poor, small ones, but one, as the warriors told Bryennius happily, the right size for raiding and riches. It was small enough that they could take it without being annihilated by archers; large enough to give them an enjoyable battle and fine booty—horses, jewels, spices, and more wootz. Perhaps one day, Gumara hoped, they would take a smith who was willing to teach them to forge the wootz as well as they forged silver. So far, all such captives had proved stubborn and silent, and had all died very bravely.

His companions might regard this caravan as a stroke of luck, Bryennius thought, wishing for the thousandth time that he was almost anywhere else. Those Muslim merchants were all related to one another. He needed their goodwill once he reached Kashgar in order to find supplies and another caravan to accompany across the desert to Ch'ang-an. Leo, more experienced than he in warfare, pointed to the small number of hired guards, each with his pointed helm and iron and leather armor, the smaller number of men who bore the deadly curved bows of archers in this land, and remarked that the tribe had a good chance of stealing the horses and swords it wanted. "At any rate, these sheepskins"—he fingered the coat he wore and grimaced—"will probably make it impossible for survivors to identify us. If there are any survivors," he said in a voice that meant that he doubted it. Then he lapsed into silence, waiting, like a veteran, for the signal to attack.

Bryennius, beside him, fought an urge to squirm with nervousness. He had always been nervous before a polo match, too.

"Ahhh," muttered the warrior next to him. Below them, the caravan swayed along, sending up a spoor of dust like an immensely long brownish serpent. Now they could hear the jingling of harness, the calls of horsemen and grooms, the complaints of beasts.

"A rich harvest indeed," hissed the chief and nudged Bryennius in the ribs. "We take, eh?"

Bryennius set his jaw and hoped that would pass for a nod of agreement.

As if waiting for Bryennius' consent, the chief mounted and screamed for a charge. They rode toward the caravan as fast as they could, hoping to close with it before any archers could draw and shoot. Before Bryennius could rein in, his horse had followed, and Leo followed him. Byrennius had his sword out to defend himself. A man thrust at him with a spear, and he cut through the wood, astonished and appalled when the blade sheared away half the man's arm and shoulder on the follow-through. All around him, he could hear the bellows of frightened beasts and the screams of men and women. Many of the men from the caravan wore armor of leather and iron scales. One rode against him on his unarmed side, trying to knock him off his horse. Bryennius shoved his shoulder into the man's chest, and he toppled, to be dragged by his stirrup until a casual spear thrust finished him off. Bryennius fought his way clear, then turned to view the battle.

Several of the merchants' silk banners were tattered; even as he watched, another fell half on the ground, half on a fallen horse. Bryennius looked about for Leo. Disdaining his new wootz blade for his cavalry sword, Leo seemed to give a good account of himself until . . . "Watch out!" Bryennius screamed as a man with a long spear seemed to materialize on top of a cart. Bryennius kicked his mount's sides and galloped for the man, but even as he hurled himself from his horse onto the cart, the spear flew and impaled Leo in the center of his chest.

Blood and a ghastly shriek bubbled from Leo's mouth, and he toppled from his horse. "Brother!" screamed Bryennius, and flung himself onto the man who had killed Leo. Slitting his throat was the matter of a moment, and then he could leap down and drag Leo's body free of the dust and the frightened horses that had already trampled it once. Tears ran in clean channels down his dusty face, and he dragged Leo from the field.

Leaving him in the lee of an overturned cart where his body would be safe, Bryennius looked for a horse. A man in the garb of a merchant was riding the nearest one. It seemed ridiculously easy to grab for his stirrup, pull the man down, kill him, then take his horse and go looking for more enemies to kill.

The sword seemed too slow and too clean a method of death. If he could have killed all the guards in the caravan with a word, he would have uttered it. He feared magic, but only the kind of power that had swept away half a mountainside could sate his desire for revenge. It raved in him like Greek fire. He cut down a spearman, then looked for another, and then the next— In the end, the Kafirs had to leap on him and physically restrain him. Except for a few prisoners, there was nothing else to kill. They led him to the rough camp they had made, patting his shoulder and murmuring approvingly. Bryennius remembered that Alexander, too, had been subject to fits of rage.

He sighed deeply, and shook himself. The stink of blood and excrement and sweat hovered at the edges of his consciousness, but he postponed his sickness and walked to the wagon which sheltered Leo. Someone had pulled the spear from his chest; Bryennius reminded himself to find out who had done it and thank the man.

He spat dust and bile, then knelt and tried to wipe his friend's face clean of the muck and agonized surprise that marred it. He held his hands over the eyelids until they closed, then smoothed back the matted hair. He drew a gold chain from around Leo's neck. Though the metal was dark with blood, he slipped it over his own head. Last of all, he bent and unfastened the regimental emblem Leo had clung to. "If I do make it to Ch'ang-an, I'll bury it there for you," he whispered. "I promise you." Behind him, a fire was burning, those damned savages were laughing and shouting, and someone was screaming like a woman in difficult travail. A thick, almost intoxicating smell twined itself through the stinks; someone had fed the campfires with the dried leaves they used as a mild intoxicant. His tears made him see double; it all seemed unreal.

When Bryennius rose, he found two tribesmen watching him. "We'll send him home," he told them, "on such a pyre as Iskandar himself built." At his gestured commands, the men heaped those who had died in the battle at the center of the field. Gently, he lifted his friend and laid him at the center of the pyre. Then he rummaged in his pack and extracted a jar of Greek fire. It was harsh, but clean; he didn't want to leave Leo to the ravages of this land, which had showed him no mercy. Waving the men back, he opened the jar and hurled it at the pyre. It burst into flame in midair and drifted down; silvery threads and ragged gouts of pale fire clung to the bodies.

Even the priest gasped in awe and pointed at him. Would they try to thrust godhood upon him again? Castor and Pollux, he remembered Alexandra's lecturing him, had been twins: one mortal, the other immortal. When the one had died, the other petitioned the gods to permit him to share his eternal life. Each lived and died, he thought despondently, but they were never together again. If he were a god, he'd have arranged this battle differently.

Don't add hubris to blasphemy, he ordered himself. *You're just a man, Bryennius. Because men called you "prince," do you expect to be spared pain? Then you are both man and fool.*

It occurred to him that men were usually sick after their first battle. He went apart and dutifully tried to retch, but nothing came up. After a time, he returned to the camp and accepted their deferential nods with an ease that disgusted him.

They had found several of the most richly dressed of the merchants, and had apparently been trying to make the youngest tell how to forge wootz. He had refused to tell them. When he could do anything beside scream, he was still refusing when Bryennius walked into the center of the ring. He looked down at the man, whom they had stripped of his armor, good leather and lamellar scales, which they laid at Bryennius' feet. The captive was young, with the fine-boned, aristocratic features of the trader princes, disfigured now with blood and burns.

Suddenly, he began to sob rackingly, babbling of the proper crucible and charcoal, of watching the wootz turn the color of cherries or of blood before the smith forged it. He fainted before he could say more and proved impossible to revive whether by shouts, slaps, or precautionary cuts and burns.

"Kill him before he wakes," whispered Bryennius to the chief. Gumara raised a hand, obviously reluctant to lose both entertainment and knowledge.

"I said, '*Kill him!*'" Bryennius screamed in what he hoped was a fair imitation of one of Alexander the Great's rages. If he saw one more man broken by wounds and pain, he thought he would go mad. When no one else moved, he drew his knife and gave the youth his death-blow.

As a dangerous muttering rose, Bryennius stammered out the only explanation that these barbarians might accept. "Leo needed another sacrifice."

The muttering subsided. Gumara gestured for someone to bring forward another prisoner, and Bryennius steeled himself for a second outburst. Then he leaned forward. Something about the man's face and bearing, arrogant even after seeing his kinsmen's deaths. He remembered now. In Samarkand, this man, his brother, and two of his cousins had tried to kill him for his too-evident admiration of his sister. He even knew this man's name from his time in Samarkand: Suleiman Mis'ar ibn Mulhalhil. And the man he had just killed was Abu Dulaf. The family was famous, with trading stations at each stage from Samarkand across the desert.

"Now you tell us," the chief was taunting ibn Mulhalhil, "of the proper method of hardening the wootz. I know some of it already." His voice took on a singsong intonation. "It must be heated until it does not shine, just like the sun rising in the desert, after which it must be cooled down to the color of king's purple—"

"Then dropped into the body of a muscular slave," snapped ibn Mulhalhil. "Why not kill me and have done with it? You there, the savage who killed my cousin, you kill me with that knife you probably plundered from another of our men!"

The Kafirs growled and pressed in closer. Bryennius stepped in and waved them off. For all the man's anger at him for all the fact that he was of a nation with which Byzantium was at war, ibn Mulhalhil was a civilized man, and should not be tormented this way.

And besides, so many were dead, so many like Alexandra and Leo, young and fine and brave; this merchant prince had courage and intelligence which should not be snuffed out. Bryennius smeared his hand across his face in a rough attempt to clean it, then knelt at ibn Mulhalhil's side, unbinding him.

"You are free now. You have my word that they won't harm you. Do you remember me?" he asked in Greek. "It's a long way from Samarkand where you tried to knife me. How is the lady, your sister?"

The man spat at him but missed. Abruptly, Bryennius was filled with rage. He had just saved the man's life, and his damnable arrogance along with it. The man was tall, with the dark skin and strongly marked features of the Muslim princes, made even more distinguished by black brows and a sharp beard. They had not yet stripped him of his own long scalecoat, or the tattered brocade he wore over it.

"The Simposh are strange companions for you of the Rumi," the merchant observed. "Or perhaps not so; you're all Kafirs—infidels." Damn him, he could see that Alexandra was not with him, that none of his party remained, except for a few wretched Ferghana horses, but he made no comment.

"These people vowed themselves to our service . . . Leo's and mine. My cousin . . ." He turned his face away, ashamed to weep in front of the tribesmen or their prisoner.

"How crude of you to mention the lady your cousin in an outsider's presence," said ibn Mulhalhil. Was *that* why he had tried to kill him? Because he had mentioned his sister? Bryennius knew how startled he must look. It was true that the Muslims secluded their women, unlike the ladies of Byzantium who came and went as they pleased. Bryennius would have hated to die because of a chance and courteously meant remark.

Abruptly, he decided that it was wrong for this man to die at the hands of savages. Besides, he told himself, the man came from a rich and very powerful family who maintained a thriving business along most of the outposts on the way to Ch'ang-an.

Ibn Mulhalhil studied his face, nodded with satisfaction as he read Bryennius' decision in it. "What makes you think," he asked in an undertone, "that these people will really let you release me?"

Alexandra, Bryennius thought with satisfaction, must be looking down at him from heaven and teaching him guile. "The gods have decreed that my brother be rent from me," he cried. "But they have provided in his place this man, who will serve me as did my brother."

One of the underpriests nodded approval; it was not fitting for their ruler to be without a companion.

"And may Allah have mercy upon you for blasphemy," remarked the merchant.

On both of us, Bryennius thought. The chief and the shaman were still muttering suspicion. "This man's family is known to me," he spoke quickly. "It is rich and powerful in Kashgar, and will doubtless pay well for the return of one of its sons."

"Cleverly done," said Suleiman Mis'ar ibn Mulhalhil. "I assume you and the Kafirs are bound for Kashgar, where they hope to equip their new Alexander"—this was said with a disdainful lift of dark eyebrows—"for his journey to his new kingdom? Was that why you intervened?"

"One reason," said Bryennius. "For another . . ."

"Your trip across the Takla Makan desert? You seem in an . . . embarrassed condition," said the merchant. "Horses and companions lost. Naturally, my ransom might well include my family's help in making the trip."

"Naturally," said Bryennius. He jerked the man to his feet. "Give me your word not to escape, and I'll free you. I'll even help you bury your cousin," he said. One thing he knew about the Muslims: ferocious they might be, but they held to their word.

Grief flooded the man's face, and Bryennius was sorry for his harsh tone. But it was necessary. Ibn Mulhalhil jerked his chin up in assent, and Bryennius rested a hand on his shoulder, steering him first toward the body of his kinsmen, then toward the quiet night beyond the circle of Kafirs.

Ibn Mulhalhil glanced at Leo's pyre, which still roared and smoked. "Of your kindness, poor Abu Dulaf has had enough of fire," he said. "I would rather bury him." The earth was hard, but they hacked out a shallow grave for the youth and heaped it over with rocks.

For a long moment, they stood on opposite sides of the wretched grave, facing one another. Bryennius nodded.

"I swore to have your life," said the merchant. "Under the circumstances, I give back my oath." He laughed bitterly, then cut it off when the laughter threatened to become hysterical.

The man was keeping himself on too tight a rein, Bryennius thought. He remembered him as arrogant, princely in the way that the finest of the Persian merchants were: proud of their wealth, their power, and their familiarity with the world. This must be his first experience with loss and defeat—close companions of Bryennius ever since the avalanche. Compassion for his former enemy made his eyes fill, and he shook his head.

"I meant what I said. We are the last two civilized men among them. We should stand together, or by whatever god you worship, merchant, we will both fall separately."

"You would trust me?"

"I accepted your word. Was I wrong?"

The merchant sighed deeply and rubbed his arms. "We both may have underestimated one another," he said. "And we have both lost close, close kin. I too am willing to start afresh."

He held out his hand, and Bryennius took it, both with such ceremony that each backed up, then laughed harshly. Though they would have to guard one another's backs, their losses were too fresh for either to be easy with the idea. But they had several days until they reached Kashgar, and Bryennius would have to explain why he would not return to the tribesmen's ancient territory and rule them. He thought he could think up something. Perhaps Suleiman, his newly acquired ally, might help. Unaccountably, he smiled at the thought.

6

Alexandra reined in her horse and leaned forward. Though mountains melded uneasily into cloud ranges at the horizon, the path ahead widened almost into a veritable road, and it sloped downward into Kashgar. "I never realized how wonderful a word 'down' was," she remarked.

Already she was imagining the shouts and ringings of the bazaar, the chants of alien faiths and suspicious bargains, the braying of the sturdy donkeys and the neighing of high-bred horses offered for sale; there would be a world of color and fabrics; hot food in the inns perhaps, and, even more blessedly, hot water for washing. Tears of thankfulness blurred her vision, and she was careful not to move until her eyes cleared.

Beside her, Father Basil murmured a few words. "My brethren have a congregation in Kashgar. The first thing I must do is seek it out and offer thanks to God that any of us were spared."

82

An estimable sentiment, Alexandra thought, but she suspected that the little priest, whose plump frame appeared not to have suffered at all from the avalanche, would ask among the Nestorians in Kashgar whether any remnants of their earlier silk manufactures had survived. If they could somehow buy silkworms here, they had best do so, and spare themselves the terrible journey across the fringes of the Takla Makan desert.

Though Ch'ang-an still lured her, losing Bryennius and the others in the heights had taught her respect for these lands. Alexandra had to admit that she too never expected to survive. She sighed and forced herself to look away from the town that tempted her to gallop down the slope, screaming in triumph like a barbarian, then glanced back at the men and horses halting behind her. Some six of the Ferghana horses had been saved; all, fortunately, were of the vivid bay color esteemed in Ch'in. Some of the grooms and all of the guides and porters were new, found for her by the abbot whose hospitality had saved her life. Her eyes skipped over what she could not help but regard as the emptinesses that should have held her maid, her cousin, and some of the other officers, until she came to Haraldr and Father Basil, who rode closest to her.

As always, Haraldr sat a horse with his axe slung on his back and a horn hung about his neck. His size made him awkward on horseback. He dismounted and led his horse toward Alexandra's stirrup. The fingers of his right hand twined around the reins, moving constantly as he exercised the hand weakened by the bite of a creature that most definitely had not been a wolf. The grooms with whom the monastery had supplied them moved out of his way, regarding him with fear, reverence, and a little loathing. (Alexandra reminded herself to release the men in Kashgar and hire new grooms; she had no desire to cross the desert with the head of her guard an object of superstitious dread by a pack of mountain men.) Haraldr knew her mind. He met her eyes and grinned.

He was another one lucky to be alive, luckier still not
to have run mad. There was little comparison between
the warrior at her side and the bled-out, cowering man
who lay in the monastery's courtyard as she tried to stop
the bleeding from his wrist, and who moaned in terror of
the coming of the Fenris wolf and the final darkness. His
bearers had muttered of demons.

Alexandra inspected the big Varangian, who promptly
involved himself with a minute adjustment to her stirrup.

"At least we're out of the hills. The hillfolk will be
terrified of you for generations," she remarked. "You
saved that village; God knows, you probably saved all
the villages for miles about, not to mention the rest of us,
by killing that demon my aunt wished on us, but they
won't speak to you, even to give you thanks."

Haraldr grunted. After a time, he dared glance up.
Now his princess had turned her attention to the inviting
city before them. The abbot had talked to her of trust,
even of surrender to this Rudra fellow who was fated to
teach her. It sounded like holy vows. Once she had taken
those, and almost lost life and soul to them. No wonder
if she were afraid.

"The horn, Haraldr, may I see it?" she asked. He
handed it up to her.

"He"—Haraldr knew that she meant the abbot
—"said that this is a map, had we only skill to read it."
She paused for a long time. "You of the North are said to
be without fear, and yet . . ."

"In our stories, heroes swear not to retreat even a
footstep, but to go on farther, my princess," Haraldr
said. "When I was alone, and thought that you and all
the others were dead, I swore that too."

She nodded, and handed the horn back to him. "Then
I will not insult you by asking if you still wish to cross
the desert."

A dark mood was on her; not for the first time,
Haraldr wondered if her regard for Prince Bryennius

had gone beyond the fondness of cousins for one another.

Abruptly she shook off her mood. "Well," she declared, "against all hopes of aunt, demon, or bad weather, we have reached Kashgar. Father Basil wants to pray, I want to bathe, and we all need to eat before we can even think of desert crossings or stealing silkworms." She waved her hand for the company to start again. "Haraldr, at my back. You, Father Basil, if you will, ride at my side. And pass the word that every man and horse in my service should walk and look as proud as he can. Let's enter Kashgar as princes, not as castaways!"

From somewhere, a groom unfurled a banner and handed it by its pole to Haraldr. Purple silk—the color and pride of Byzantium—fluttered in the wind as Alexandra and her train entered Kashgar. A majesty was on her, Haraldr thought, and enjoyed the sight of it, which reminded him of ceremonies in Miklagard in which the leader of the Varangians, who had the privilege of following the Emperor into battle, rode behind His Majesty on a white horse, and the entire Guard marched, clad in crimson, axes burnished, behind them.

Perhaps now they would all come back into their own again. In that case, Thor would have the white stallion he had already pledged, and a mare beside. There were guards at the outskirts of the city, more of them, and more suspicious, than the Northerner would have expected. Many peoples passed through Kashgar; surely it was to the advantage of all to keep it safe and prosperous. When the guards hailed them, Alexandra stared them down, then silenced them with the purse she threw with superb arrogance to their captain.

So small, and yet so very strong, Haraldr thought, like the chain that bound the *real* Fenris wolf. Her head was held high, her hair streamed down her slender back, and she wore the distant, haughty look that all the Imperials could summon. Heads up, Miklagard's pride rode through a bazaar that shone with burnished copper, fine embroideries, and glistening fruit, while people of all the races that thronged the city fell silent to watch.

Alexandra stretched out, and let the serving women finish drying her long hair. Fruit glowed on silver dishes, and sherbet in the Persian fashion frosted a fine glass pitcher. Equally Persian were the inn's blue tiles and its standard of luxury for guests, fresh either from the mountains or the Takla Makan desert, and eager to pay for it. She might have deduced from the armor and weapons of the guards that Persians and Abbasids dominated the trade city; the number of mosques, and the bazaar clamor at her arrival, a woman leading her own train, told her even more.

She had anticipated that particular problem, had hoped that Bryennius would serve as a second self for those dealings where a prince would be more welcome than a princess. But now she would have to be both. She rose and pointed. With obvious reluctance, the serving women helped her into the coat, boots, and trousers she had insisted upon, instead of the women's garments they had offered her. They were dark silk, so finely cut that she suspected they had been made for a prince—or a catamite. She shivered at the feel of the fabric against her skin; she had missed it since leaving Byzantium.

Father Basil was waiting for her in the outer rooms.

"I hope you said a prayer for me too," she greeted him.

He nodded as if that had not needed to be said. Waving away an offer of wine pressed from the mares'-teat grapes grown in the Turpan oasis—the inn kept a fine stock for nonbelievers—both were silent while more sherbet was brought. Once the room was empty, Father Basil moved his cushions closer to her.

"You saw the guard," he began in Greek. "Kashgar is Muslim now, but it's had several masters in the last few years, ever since the people of Ch'in were forced from their westernmost prefectures. We saw it in Samarkand, which they used to rule. Warriors from the Land of

Snows, Uighurs, the Hsiung-nu. It's frightening. And with the city under Muslim control—"

"Your people here," Alexandra broke in.

"Safe enough, for now. Heretics or not"—he grinned at her—"they're people with a Holy Book, and therefore under protection. As are the Jews, the worshipers of Mani, and the servants of the Buddha. That's much the same as it is in Ch'ang-an. But if the rulers here are threatened, they may look about for a scapegoat."

"So they can't provide us with silkworms."

"Alas no, my princess. After the last wave of trouble, the silk was put under even stricter guard. My brethren will help us pay our way across the Takla Makan, and for that—"

For that, Alexandra realized, they should all be on their knees giving thanks.

She listened to the Nestorian's report with half an ear, thinking that he made as good a spy as she had ever encountered in a lifetime of dealing with them. Byzantium appreciated fine spies and rewarded them well.

She was less enthusiastic about the number of priests and holy men in the City. While some might possess the genuine sanctity of the abbot who had saved her life, she remembered how "Father Andronicus" had turned out to be a demon. This close to the desert, other demons might creep in off the sand. The serving women's jests, half-malicious, half-fearful, had reminded her that Takla Makan meant "If you enter, you don't come out." Apparently, it was desolation itself. Travelers clustered together for protection, not just against the solitude but the whispers and giggles of demons. Occasionally, a caravan would disappear from along the desert's edge, victim of a *kuraburan*, the "black storm" such demons could summon. Along the trade routes lay the bones of man and beast, bleached and dried by the desert, alongside the remnants of their trade goods. No one wanted to touch them.

Occasionally bolder travelers came across beams or broken walls, the ruins of a half-buried town. But if they dug, seeking treasure, sand poured into the hole almost more quickly than they could remove it, and threatened to bury them too. No one dared venture into the deep desert, though there were legends of a hidden spring at its center.

Shambhala? Alexandra had suspected briefly, then dismissed the idea. Shambhala was said to lie between snow mountains, not giant, serpentine dunes.

"Thank your friends for me," she told the priest, who had fallen silent, respecting her thoughts.

He glanced at her men's clothing, then tactfully glanced away. "How else might I negotiate with these traders for passage, unless as a prince, not a woman they can cajole and cheat?" she asked.

"I heard another story, my princess. They say that a prince of the Imperial T'ang dynasty arrived some time ago from Samarkand and now prepares to cross the desert."

"Why is he so far from his home?" Alexandra asked, then laughed at herself.

"Apparently the prince is also a poet. Much of the land we crossed once belonged to Ch'in, but is now in the hands of Muslims or the warlords from the Land of Snows. He wished to see what his Empire has lost. Since one of the things his Empire lost were the stud farms to the west, if we were to show him our horses . . ."

"How would you suggest we do that?"

The Persian's round face crinkled into a wide smile. "It's my understanding that trouble hunts the entire length of the silk roads, from Byzantium all the way to Ch'ang-an. Ch'in has been plagued by revolts and civil wars for the past century. Nevertheless, life must go on. Beleaguered, Kashgar may be, but it is still full of horsemen. There will be a game of polo soon. This Imperial prince is said to enjoy the game. If we bring our horses, he'll note them."

Alexandra laughed again. Priest Basil might be, but he was also Persian, and no Persian alive could resist polo. They had brought it to Byzantium and everyplace else where nobility or warriors might be able to afford horses for it, and were willing to take the risks it occasionally entailed. Though women in Byzantium did not regularly play, as she had heard that some did in Ch'in. It hurt to remember that Bryennius had taught her.

"Shall I ride, then?" she asked. If she coiled up her hair under a hat, she might pass for a boy. Certainly the mountain crossing had left her thin enough to do so, she thought, and ate another sweetmeat.

Father Basil shook his head. "This is polo such as the tribesmen play on the banks of the Oxus, my lady. It resembles battle more than sport. Frequently, men are killed. And the ball they use is a dead goat."

Alexandra grimaced, the last time she would permit herself to do so at the thought of the game. She must make herself think of it as the sport of brave men, not of barbarians—or as a way of meeting the prince and merchants on whom safe passage across the desert might depend.

"When is this game?" she asked.

"Later today."

"We shall be there."

Once her grooms were paid and equipped for their journey back into the mountains, Alexandra and Father Basil led the remnants of their party—Haraldr and the two other Varangians who survived, several Greeks, and one or two mountain men who had taken a fancy to cross the desert—across the bazaars and outside the city. Nothing in the well-ordered stores of Byzantium had prepared her for the bazaars she had visited during her trip east. Aleppo had been fascinating, Samarkand a wonder. But Samarkand had been Persian.

In Kashgar for the first time, Alexandra saw the mingling of all the many peoples and races, from Hind to Hsiung-nu: lamas from the Land of Snows, Persian traders, even people from Ch'in, the land she had yet to reach. She and some of her officers were the only Westerners she saw, and their paler skins and round

eyes—as she learned from whispers and pointing fingers
—were esteemed an oddity. The Varangians . . . well, if
Haraldr had tried to comfort the one child who saw him
and burst into wails, he might have started a riot. She
rested her hand upon the hilt of the sword that had been
her gift from the abbot, glad to have belted it on. Any
onlookers would see only the swagger of a beardless,
probably unblooded, youth.

The markets were rich with their treasures. There was
enough in one bazaar alone to sate several armies of
mercenaries. The metal threads in fine cloth winked at
the hammered trays and pots; brilliant feathers waved
over fine lapis, a rainbow of jade, and rubies. Weapons
caught the sunlight in their own deadly display. And
over all came a constant babel of voices, trading, swearing, wooing, telling stories, or just passing the time of
day.

The incessant talk made Alexandra feel quite at home;
apparently Asians were as fond of it as Greeks. Father
Basil nosed about in—to Alexandra's mind—a highly
useful but unclerical fashion, bringing her tidbits of
news the way a cat brings home a bird or a mouse. That
man in the goatskin—whom the guards were
shadowing?—he was a Kafir, who had come north to
buy horses and, probably, to steal. What's more, he had
come in the company of a great trader and his adopted
brother, rumored to be the King of the Kafirs. Staring at
the dirty, suspicious-looking man, Alexandra thought
that claims of such people's descent from Alexander
were worse than lies.

"I have heard, my princess," whispered Father Basil,
"that today's game was the idea of the King of the Kafirs,
as a parting gift to his people whom he must now leave
for a time to travel to World's End."

Very clever, thought Alexandra. The Kafirs retained
legends of Alexander, so this "king," who was probably
no more a king than Alexandra, used them. Alexander
had longed to travel east and never stop: Very well, this
man would too—a perfect opportunity to abandon the

barbarians for the more civilized and far more profitable traders.

Beyond the Kafir were clerks, cool in their blue robes from the entourage of the T'ang prince, whose caravan was all but assembled. Seated against a wall, in a yellow robe, a man with a shaven head and eyes squeezed shut from a lifetime of facing the sun spun a prayer wheel. His lips moved soundlessly. *Om mane padme hum*.

On a whim, Alexandra stopped. "Do you know of Shambhala?" she asked. The priest looked intently at her, nodded, and smiled with cracked lips. "Shambhala!" he said in a discordant voice, then went back to his chant. The prayer wheel never ceased turning. She realized that the priest was deaf, and in the silence, his thoughts had turned inward. He had recognized only the shape her lips had made.

She quickened her pace. Soon they were outside the city walls. At the far horizon, mountains loomed up, and the sky was the color of Persian turquoise. The ground was dry with sand and a kind of coarse yellowish grit Father Basil told her was called *gobi*. Squinting against the violent sunlight, Alexandra tried to see where the desert began. But if she could not see it, she could smell something—other than camel, horse, and humanity—a kind of wildness that crept into her awareness and would grow stronger as she neared the time when she would venture out across the Takla Makan. They were coming to a wide field. She skirted the huge, cross Bactrian dromedaries and stared narrowly at the horses. There were a few here of the true blood-red breed from Ferghana, and that pleased her.

Beyond the rows of picketed animals, men argued over rules, playing space, and who should give the command to start. Alexandra's Varangians found her a good vantage point; to see better, she mounted. Across the field under a canopy was a richness of fabrics, a bevy of men and women alike who could only be the T'ang prince's court. Several Muslims rode by in full armor. Perhaps she could use Father Basil, accompanied by one of her Greek officers and one Varangian, to approach them.

The wrangle ceased. Accompanied by men from each group, an old man wearing worn black hides and huge quantities of silver jewelry galloped to the center of the field. A grayish-brown horned goat lay bleating across his saddle. Players and spectators watched intently as he shouted something, slashed at the beast's neck, and hurled it, still kicking, into the air. Blood fountained into the dust, and the mob cheered.

What followed was less a game, Alexandra thought, than a free-for-all. The teams were huge, but not necessarily equal in size. No one seemed to object. The object of this type of polo seemed as much to mutilate your opponent as to seize the now-dead goat and race back to one or two areas roughly marked off as goals, where, as often as not, your own friends tossed you back into the fray. At least twice men were unhorsed, to lie unmoving until kinsmen or servants dragged them out of danger from being trampled. Horses stumbled to their knees, screaming, then staggered back up again. Several men, bleeding from scrapes and blows, and spitting broken teeth, retreated from the game, as the crowd jeered at them.

"Not at all like the games at the palace," was the wry verdict of her officers. Alexandra agreed. Nor did it resemble the game she had seen in Persia, which was as much a highly mannered parade of finely turned-out men and animals as it was a sport. From the pointing and cheering across the field in the Ch'in prince's pavilion, she thought that this form of the game was a novelty to them too.

Gradually the game took on some form of organization. There seemed to be no set times for rest. You rode until you or your horse dropped. Then, if you could, you grabbed a fresh horse from the sidelines and plunged back into battle. The prevailing style (if she could call it that) of play was all-out ferocity in the style of the tribes who wandered back and forth across the Oxus river

. . . Tajiks, Kafirs, Turkomans, men of Ch'in, Kirghiz, and a host of others. Some men rode in the Persian fashion, two were richly dressed and armed like Abbasid merchants. Both rode fine Ferghana stallions, almost the equal of her own.

They had verve and courage, she observed. Surely that would translate into a well-planned and guarded caravan. Perhaps she should have Father Basil approach them. She herself would stay in the background, lest the sight of a woman who behaved as prince, not cloistered chattel, offend them past the hope of doing business. She beckoned to the priest.

"The tall man in the scaled armor. Find out his name for me," she whispered.

Father Basil returned almost instantly. "Suleiman Mis'ar ibn Mulhalhil," he told her. "His family hosts the Ch'in prince. We met Suleiman in Samarkand, remember?"

Alexandra suppressed a groan, then yelled with the crowd as ibn Mulhalhil and the man who rode with him dashed toward the goat, shouldering several screaming highlanders aside, then bending to scoop it up, only to lose it in the next instant, to a Sogdian who all but ripped the head from the dusty carcass. They were thieves, those Sogdians, every one of them.

Ibn Mulhalhil . . . the family had a post at Samarkand too. Bryennius had admired a woman of the house . . . She supposed there were other merchants here whom she could deal with. "Who's the man with him?" she asked.

"Strange story, that, as I told my princess earlier." So he had, Alexandra thought, but it sounded now as if he had learned more. "Several weeks ago, ibn Mulhalhil rode in with a band of Kafirs—and none of the people, or goods, he had left Persia with. The story goes that the Kafirs found him robbed and bereft on the mountainside, and that their king ordered him to be taken into the tribe. I think it's far likelier that the Kafirs attacked his train, then decided to improve the deal—and their chances of surviving it—by ransoming him back to his family."

"So that's the man who has sponsored this game, just as if he knew Roman customs. An amusing coincidence. He rides well," Alexandra observed. Then she bent forward, impressed by just how well he did ride. His trappings were indeed Persian, but something about his style, something about the rider himself—in the name of God, she *knew* that trick of leaning out to the side, almost overbalancing, at a full gallop. She had applauded it a hundred times in the Hippodrome.

"Impossible," she muttered. It was the dust, she told herself. She had to see the rider's face. She pressed her knees against her horse and moved in closer. The dust and the sunlight, damn them both, made it difficult to make out features. And it was hot; she wasn't used to this heat. It made her dizzy.

She put a disgracefully shaking hand up to her mouth and rode forward again. She was almost on the outskirts of the game, jostling for position with urchins, grooms, and lads too young to be permitted to ride with their fathers or elder brothers. There were even a few physicians and priests, some of whom stared narrowly at her: foreign, outlandish, probably an enemy.

The "King of the Kafirs" reined in his horse. It curvetted in a quick, tidy ring, sending up a cloud of dust and gobi, and he grinned at the watchers.

Alexandra screamed. Ignoring the shouts and mutters of the crowd as they realized that the foreigner in their midst was not the boy they supposed "him," she galloped forward into the center of the field.

"Bryennius!" she shrieked. "Cousin!"

The game thundered on both sides of her, and she swerved to avoid a Tajik and an Uzbek who fought a Kafir for possession of the goat. She waved one hand frantically, crying her cousin's name.

Again he reined in his horse, this time so fiercely that it reared and screamed as she approached. She swerved again, and the game roared past. To a howl of disappointment from his side, the Tajik dropped the goat.

Bryennius stood in his stirrups and stared at Alexandra. He smeared a hand across his eyes, then sat back down. "Alexandra?" he whispered. "I saw the snow bury you—oh, God, Alexandra, you're alive!" He shouted his astonishment and joy, then grabbed her into a rough bear hug. She could feel him sobbing and knew that she wept too. Against all hope . . . she had mourned Bryennius as dead. This sudden discovery—that he was the fraudulent King of the Kafirs—there had to be some reason for it. The dust swirled about them, and the riders pounded by. Bryennius slipped sideways in his saddle, or perhaps he caught her as she reeled. The heat and stench would make anyone dizzy.

One hand against his chest, she pushed herself away and shook her head at his exultant babble of questions.

"I can explain everything," he assured her quickly. "But I dare not leave the game, not now. Get back, cousin mine!" He gave her horse a hard slap, sending it back toward the spectators.

Alexandra saw a man in a dark robe point at her, then reach inside his garment. She reeled in the saddle. Halfway across the field, her guard saw and began to fight toward her. She forced herself upright.

Though the sky was clear, she felt as if a storm were brewing: hot, cold, and uneasy all at once. The ground and the air quivered as she rode toward her men. Behind her, even the players fell silent. Then one man screamed in mortal terror.

"Alexandra! Behind you!" shouted Bryennius.

Alexandra twisted her horse's head about, but she lacked Bryennius' strength with the reins. The horse stumbled, throwing her onto the bloodstained ground. She thrust against the ground, rising unsteadily to her knees, then to her feet. The field seemed to rock.

Now she could see the man who had screamed—a Kafir, the very man who had held the goat. He lay on the ground, blood streaming from his throat, gashed by the

same goat they had used as a trophy. Somehow its head
had been rejoined to its body. Now it gnashed red-
smeared teeth, and its eyes glowed.

And on stiff, but very steady legs, it headed for
Alexandra.

Bryennius rode at the goat, and slashed at it, but his
blade recoiled, and he was practically hurled from the
saddle. Other men tried to stop its rush, and were forced
back, including Haraldr, who charged it, swinging his
axe as if it were a traditional polo mallet. Helpless to
stop it, the men formed a circle about her.

Alexandra shook her head to clear it, and her hair fell
free of the cap into which she had crammed it. She heard
the riders murmur in dismay. Then the goat seemed to
scent her, or sight her with those green-flaming eyes, and
its stalk turned into a rushing attack. With a rasp of fine
steel, she drew the sword that the abbot had given her
and hacked at the thing. She hit a leg, nearly cutting it
from the obscenely animated body, but even as she
watched, the wound healed.

The sun beat down upon her head, and she was
conscious not so much of fear as of a furious irritation.
Here she was, a princess of Byzantium, trapped in an
arena and forced to fight some sort of demon or undead
thing while a veritable army of warriors was unable to
defend her. It was a vulgar display. And it came at the
worst possible time too, with Bryennius restored to her,
a Ch'in prince to impress . . . she screamed with fury
and struck again. This time her blade scraped across the
beast's spine and almost was wedged past her ability to
pull it free.

The goat wheeled and stared at her. It looked remarkably like her aunt, she thought, studying it, waiting for its
next lunge. Though the sky was very blue, she heard
thunder and sensed heat lightning building up in a sky
that had probably not known clouds for years. The
crowd was very quiet, watching.

Up and down the center of the hot, noisome field, she
battled her enemy. Snatches of prayer and incongruous

remembrances chased themselves through her mind; *Kyrie eleison* jangled against "I will not flee a foot's breadth, but will farther go," from one of Haraldr's interminable poems. There was nowhere to retreat.

The thought that she might die here seemed incongruous. She had never felt so alive, so aware of her own health and strength, of the will that kept her on her feet, learning more about the strength of the blade she held with every stroke. She was holding her own! The discovery of her own courage thrilled her. Again she heard thunder. Perhaps it would storm. Perhaps the rain would dissolve whatever spell knit this demon to the goat's unnaturally animated flesh.

Again the beast charged her, and she brought down her sword. The goat danced aside. Again, and then again. She almost stumbled, and the beast opened its jaws and rushed her. Fumes from its opened mouth made her giddy. She was near the end of her strength—if not her courage—and it infuriated her. This was no proper way to die. The abbot had assured her she faced danger on the journey east—and this, most assuredly, counted as danger. But he had also promised her aid. Where was it?

She groaned and swerved out of the goat's path, and struck desperately at its neck. Lightning pealed, leaping from sky to mountain, from mountain to the blade of her sword. As her blade severed the goat's head from its body and both parts of the beast fell to the ground, the blade trembled and rang in her hand. Light flashed along it. When she glanced down at it, the sword was clean of the goat's blood, which fell, smoking, into the dust.

Alexandra staggered. Her blade stuck in the dirt, and only that held her upright. All around her, the circle of men held where they were, staring at her in awe. Then Bryennius shook himself and started forward. He held out an arm to her, prepared to carry her off the field, but she waved him back. Hadn't she wanted the chance to make these men deal with her as a prince? She had just shown herself to be even more than that; she dare not dwindle into a mere woman to swoon and be carried back into the inner rooms.

"My horse," she told him. "Bring him."

Haraldr led the horse forward, and she leaned against its side, running the knuckles of her left hand against its smooth, warm neck. The horse rested its head on her shoulder, and she felt better for the contact. Solemnly, Haraldr knelt and made his hands into a cup. She mounted as smoothly as she could, and adjusted her fingers on the reins, waiting for the strength to ride back to her inn.

The crowd broke from its wary circle and re-formed with her at its cheering heart. She heard shouts, even the beginnings of a theological argument. Then the man she had seen praying in the bazaar was nearby. His eyes met hers, and she permitted herself a regal nod. A sudden glint of light made him bend down and pick something up. Then he offered it to her.

It was what the abbot told her was called a *dorje*, the scepterlike rod that priests used in the rituals of the Diamond Path. "Shambhala," the man's toothless mouth formed. "Shambhala." As she took it from him, she felt a thrill run from it up her arm and down her spine, banishing her fatigue and giddiness. Bryennius watched her in some puzzlement.

"For luck," she said, and tucked it into her belt.

"Cousin, can you make it back to your inn?" he asked.

"What is this, brother?" shouted Suleiman Mis'ar ibn Mulhalhil. "You send the lady, your kinswoman" —politely, he did not look at her—"back to some mangy inn when my uncle's wives would vie to take care of her?"

I wouldn't wager on that, Alexandra thought. A Greek, a woman, and a Christian. She'd be fortunate if the merchant's harem didn't poison her.

She thanked the merchant. "Before I move—or think of dinner even—I want a bath and fresh clothes," she said. "May we discuss this later?" She also wanted wine, perhaps several flasks, and a chance to rest. And above all, she wanted off a nervous, sidling horse and out of the center of a sweaty crowd that refought her battle and battled to view the thing she had slain.

"Burn it!" she ordered anyone who would listen, and pressed knees against her horse's flanks. The horse eased through the crowd. Suleiman Mi'sar ibn Mulhalhil bowed and rode off.

Bryennius was at her side again. "If you are well, then I must see to my son's funeral," he said. She blinked at him until she realized he meant the Kafir. The man whose throat the demon spirit had slashed was one of Bryennius' warriors.

"*You're* King of the Kafirs?" she asked.

"They're called Simposh, and the answer is yes; and I must go to them now."

"My guards will see me safely to my inn," Alexandra assured him.

"Leo's dead," Bryennius said. His face twisted, and the strangeness that she had sensed between them fell away. "Oh, God, and I thought you were too!" His eyes filled, and he fought for control as they headed toward the gates.

Hoofbeats sounded, and many riders rode between them and the gates. Alexandra's hand dropped to her swordhilt. But it was the men of Ch'in. At the prince's gesture, one man dismounted and walked over to her. She sat her horse, keeping her face immobile, almost the Caesar-mask she had used in Byzantium. The man knelt at her feet and touched his brow to the dust in the full prostration she had seen accorded only to her brother, the Basileus.

"This humble person has the honor to serve His Imperial Highness, Li Shou. The prince has commanded this unworthy one to bid the princess of Fu-lin, her kinsmen, and her ministers to dine with him."

Alexandra gazed about somewhat glassily. She looked over at the silken bevy of riders that was the T'ang prince's entourage. The prince rode at its heart. He was a slender man and, she thought, of middle height. His black hair and long mustaches were silvered, and he looked more like a scholar than an adventurer. She met his eyes and felt almost a physical shock. They were dark and clever, and irony seemed to dance beneath their heavy lids. He nodded faintly at her, then turned to the Muslim merchant who rode several deferential steps behind him.

So that was how the invitation came! News traveled fast in Kashgar. As if she needed further proof of that, Father Basil pushed through to her side and spoke rapidly with the kneeling man. "He's named you the princess of the Eastern Empire, of Rome, and of Antioch," he explained. "And he's used the word for princess, not merely for lady."

This was the opportunity she sought, Alexandra thought. She touched the dorje tucked into her belt. It had indeed brought her luck. "Tell His Imperial Highness I accept," she ordered the priest. "And word it as beautifully as you can." He spoke at length to the minister, who rose. A flurry of bows, and they were both off to prostrate themselves before the prince. He nodded to them, glanced over at Alexandra, and smiled. Then, quite deliberately, he waved his followers to one side and waited while she rode in triumph a second time into Kashgar.

7

Alexandra climbed into the bullock cart sent around for her by the ibn Mulhalhil household. Behind her rose what sounded like the sacking of a minor city; servants had also been sent to pack and move her belongings and her party's. Rising over the high-pitched voices of the women and the rapid-fire gabble of at least three languages came the voices of Father Basil and one of her officers, insisting that no one was to touch the pack with the tiny bottles in it, not if they valued a whole skin.

Having lost an argument about wearing his axe, Haraldr stalked to the side of Alexandra's cart, weapon in hand. "Give it to me," she ordered. He handed it in, and she set it on the floor of the cart where her sword lay. She had found herself reluctant to leave it for others to touch, let alone pack and carry away. The lightning bolt she had won only that afternoon was tucked into the sash of her new robes. An outrider drew the curtains of the cart decorously closed, and the bullocks began a pains-taking, lumbering trip down the dusty avenue.

Alexandra parted the curtains. Sand and dust seemed to cover the street, the camels, and the passersby with mauve silk veils even finer than the silk gauzes she now wore. They were a gift of Prince Li Shou. She ran a finger admiringly over the pale violet silk with its meticulously exquisite embroidery of lilacs and kingfishers. Her sash was sewn with jewels and lined with yellow—a mark of Imperial honor, Father Basil had told her, that augured well for their meeting tonight with the prince. Scent bags dangled from it; the same scent wafted from her hair, which the maid who was sent along with the garments had brushed and dressed high on her head and fastened with jade pins shaped like butterflies. She wore soft red leather boots that would not have been out of place on a Basileus riding in triumph—or on a horseman from the hills.

If this was the dress of a Ch'in lady, she could understand why silk, not gold, was the medium of exchange in the land she became more and more eager to see. Byzantine silk was darker and heavier, with elabo-rate, often Persian, patterns interwoven; this fabric was incredibly fine and luxurious against her skin after months in wools and sheepskins.

She peered out farther at the dusty lines of poplar trees and mud-brick houses as the bullock cart turned into a covered alleyway, to the vast inconvenience of the people who squatted beneath awnings, selling the ever-present plums and melons of Kashgar. The air was full of noises: voices, the clatter and ringing of the bullocks' harness, and, over all, the echoing, nasal chant that Alexandra knew was a call to prayer.

She anticipated a feast tonight, but no wine. A pity: After her battle on the polo field, she might have relished a flask. Or perhaps two flasks, she thought. So quickly had Bryennius' unlikely new "brother" and his guest, the prince, moved to provide her with gifts and servants that she had had no time to compose herself, to place the fight with the undead in some sort of perspective.

She pulled the curtain closed again and settled back. Where faith fails, she thought cynically, try logic. Question: why had the magic about which the abbot warned her chosen to attack right then? Answer: she was about to be reunited with her cousin, who had made allies . . . allies who could help her in her mission. Second question: why had she received aid? Answer: another question—why had she met that beggar-priest, first in the market, then near the field? She felt as if she stood at the nexus of events. Last time that had happened, she had faced magic. She could expect additional attacks, she thought grimly.

But the dorje-scepter . . . that was part of the initiation into the Diamond Path the abbot had prophesied she would accept, and which she had refused. *Do I have any choice at all?* Orthodoxy endowed her with free will, but the lands she had entered were dominated by karma, foreordained necessity that made her favorite tragedies seem whimsical by comparison. She sighed, then shook herself. Through the curtains she could see the flames of a sunset made more spectacular by the dust and sand. She pulled aside the curtains wholly, promptly scandalizing the people who awaited her outside the house of Suleiman Mus'ar ibn Mulhalhil.

If it hadn't been for the giant Haraldr and the rustle of shocked whispers that usually accompanied Alexandra, Bryennius realized with a pang that he might not have recognized her. Until she met his eyes and took his hands in greeting (she had started to embrace him, then realized her error), she looked much like the ladies in paintings he had seen, or the concubines who accompanied the T'ang prince. She bent and, with some effort, drew weapons from the cart in which she had arrived.

"Make certain these are stored in honor," she asked of him, and relinquished them into Suleiman's hands.

Bryennius got a look at them: Haraldr's axe, and a strangely scabbarded sword, the blade she had used that very afternoon. He felt better once Suleiman carried it out of sight; some doom seemed to hang about it. "Did you save any of the fire?" she asked him in a quick whisper.

"All but two vials. I used one for Leo . . ." His voice went husky, and she pressed his hand in sympathy, retaining it as he escorted her into the house. It was very cool and dark, thanks to its thick walls. Rugs glowed on the floors, piled layer upon seemingly artless layer, or stacked in corners. Rich cushions and low inlaid tables made pleasant-looking islands in the rooms they passed through.

Outside a carved door, they waited for Father Basil and Alexandra's officers to arrive. Within sat Prince Shou, enthroned in one of the few chairs in Bryennius' brother's home. It had been specially made and adorned with Imperial dragons. They entered. While Basil knelt and touched head to ground, and the officers saluted, Bryennius bowed as he might to an elder prince. Alexandra, being born to the purple, bowed only slightly. The prince didn't seem to miss the distinctions, and gestured them graciously to cushions.

"Our humble gifts suit the Royal Lady well," he commented in Ch'in.

Alexandra bowed again. "Tell His Imperial Highness that this one is honored by his gifts," she instructed Father Basil, who went off into a spate of oddly pitched tones. Her own command of the language was inadequate for such an important beginning.

For some time, everyone was busy with chilled melons and plums. If this were late spring, Bryennius thought, God help them on the desert that lay ahead. When he had lain in the snow of the Roof of the World, he had never thought that he might one day curse the heat.

"Most refreshing," said the prince.

"How much hotter can we expect it to become?"

Alexandra asked the diners at large, echoing Bryennius' thoughts.

"This one crossed the desert in winter, lady," the prince replied in Sogdian. "Then the Takla Makan was so cold that the ink froze in its dish when anyone tried to write."

"We have relatives in the oasis at Turpan," said ibn Mulhalhil, though, Bryennius observed, he avoided meeting Alexandra's eyes. Think of her as my cousin, not as a woman, he had urged the merchant prince. This was an honorable attempt. "They call the land hereabouts the Land of Fire. One of my uncles, who made the Hajj, says that it is hotter and drier than Arabia."

"And equally under attack by enemies," muttered a younger man in Muslim garb before he was glared to silence.

"I urged His Highness to delay crossing the desert until the autumn, but he will not wait."

"Turpan is in jeopardy," murmured Li Shou. "As Samarkand was before. That prefecture is lost to us, and soon, perhaps, these others too. So I must return home while still I can." Bryennius saw how his eyes flashed to his cousin, who nodded.

"I understand that demons stalk the desert and send terrible storms," she said.

"Travelers band together as best they can. Anyone who strays may be lost to demon voices. And then, the kuraburan, the black hurricanes . . . I survived one, thanks only to the moment's warning my camel gave. They know when the storms will come."

Alexandra's eyes flashed. She was eager, Bryennius sensed, to get on with the journey. *I must return home while still I can.* The prince's words had meaning for them too. With the lady Theodora still in hiding, with no supplies of living silkworms, and an Emperor and heir very much at risk, every day away from Byzantium was time lost for them too. Just as Suleiman shifted on his cushions, clearly uneasy that someone might commit the solecism of discussing business over food, the prince changed the subject.

"I have heard," he said, "that you have had many adventures. I would like to hear of them—and to hear of your City. Is it true that in your Emperor's palace the door leaves are of ivory, the floors of gold, the beams and columns of sweet-smelling wood and crystal, while the pillars are of lapis?"

Bryennius smothered a laugh at what sounded like the description of Hagia Sophia. Alexandra nodded graciously. "In my brother's Hall of Audience," she said somewhat grandly, "he sits on a throne mounted on the backs of lions which carry it high into the air."

"And is it true that you are all so obedient to law that there is no dissension anywhere in your land? So our stories tell us."

"Our stories," Alexandra said, with a touch of mischief, "tell us how honest your people are. I should hesitate to contradict them."

Prince Shou chuckled.

"The prince is unconventional," whispered Father Basil in rapid Greek. "Notice that he asks direct questions." Thank God for that, Bryennius thought. Otherwise they might exchange oblique half-comments for the rest of the spring.

Prince Shou smiled happily. "And this warrior of yours?" he pointed to Haraldr.

Alexandra smiled at Haraldr, then at the prince. She was obviously very much at home, Bryennius noted. "Haraldr is from our far north. His people are our allies and friends as the Uighurs are yours: far better than fighting them, don't you agree?"

Haraldr watched Alexandra as if she were fresh water in a desert. That was nothing new, Bryennius thought.

"Never in all my travels among the *hu* have I seen a man like him," said the prince. "Perhaps he might tell me of his adventures. I am very fond of the stories of the *hu*."

"That's twice he's used that word," Bryennius said to Father Basil. "What does 'hu' mean?"

"*Barbaros*," said the priest.

Alexandra started to bristle in outrage. Who dares call the Rhomaioi barbarians? Bryennius could practically hear her sputter that out. Then she remembered herself, choked, and started to laugh.

"This one would be honored if the princess would explain her laughter," the prince asked.

She dabbed at her eyes with a fine silk scarf, tried to explain, then waved to the priest, who spoke rapidly.

Alexandra looked intent, as if trying to follow. When had she learned the language of Ch'in? So much had happened while they had been separated.

The prince looked shocked at the idea that anyone might call *him* a barbarian, then laughed too. Two of a kind, Bryennius thought.

"It seems like empires are much the same—yours of the West, ours of the Middle Kingdom. And we miss our homes, both of us, and dream of what our homes have lost."

Bryennius studied him over his glass goblet, then cocked an eye at his cousin. Prince Shou was perhaps forty, but his manner, that of a man saddened by life, made him seem older. It was not that he was somber. As a Roman, Bryennius could understand sobriety, even if he had little of it himself.

"He thinks in elegies," quipped Alexandra in fast Greek, then turned her attention back to him.

"Lost?" she asked. "I am told that Ch'ang-an is the largest city in all the world. What has it lost?"

"Aside from lands? Splendor, and poetry," sighed the prince. "We have started to turn in upon ourselves and contemplate past grandeur, turning away from the rest of the world."

"Since Rokshan revolted," Father Basil interposed quickly. "An-Lushan," he translated for the prince. "He was Turkic, and rebelled against the Emperor Ming

Huang. For eighteen months, he was in exile from Ch'ang-an. Some say that the revolt almost succeeded because of the extravagance of a royal favorite . . ."

"Yang Kuei-Fei," murmured the prince. "She was wife to one of my ancestors. Imperial concubine, Kuei-Fei means. Her name was Yu-huan, Bracelet of Jade. And they sacrificed her to save the Son of Heaven."

Court favorites again. Bryennius felt his stomach chill.

"Ever since then, the Middle Kingdom has been less forbearing with outsiders. And ever since, we have lost lands. Samarkand is gone to us. Who knows? Soon Turpan may follow."

"That's true," whispered Suleiman to Bryennius. "Be on your guard. We've had reports that Turpan may soon be under attack."

"So I decided that, like the saintly H'suan Tsang, I would see what lay beyond the Purple Barrier of the Walls. I too am bringing back holy books of my faith —and many others."

If Ch'ang-an were turning xenophobic, it would be even harder to steal silkworms, Bryennius thought. And the sooner they went, the better. Suleiman had convinced him that their best hope lay in convincing the prince to let them join his caravan, and to travel not as horse-copers but as ambassadors. Thanks to the "brotherhood" they had sworn in desperation, Bryennius could present the court with an entire herd of horses—not just the Ferghana stallions that sweat blood, but fine Arabs, and the curious horses from the south.

It would be a hard trip across the desert, harder still because Suleiman could not accompany them. He would be lonely without him, Bryennius realized in mild astonishment. But he could not desert Alexandra to take up an offer of a place in Suleiman's fortunes, even if a prince might turn merchant. The best he could do was carry dispatches to their trading stations along the way. So many opportunities: he might have been a merchant; he might have ruled the Simposh—and done it well

—but he would risk his life for a city he could never rule . . . he had sworn to do so.

When his attention returned to the conversation, he realized that it had turned again to silk. "The knowledge of silk is old," said the prince. "Perhaps three thousand years ago, a princess dropped a cocoon into hot tea and saw that the thread spins off in one long strand."

My God, Bryennius thought, *before Christ, before Rome, before Homer even; at least he calls* that *old.*

"The Emperor Ch'in Shih Huang-di, who gave his name to the Middle Kingdom, had a concubine who knew how to weave and embroider with silk thread," said the prince. "Even today, the First Empress tends silkworms . . . have you that custom?"

"In Byzantium, our silk is woven by women in the Imperial palace itself," Alexandra said.

When there is silk to be had, Bryennius thought, remembering the rotting cocoons, the blighted mulberry trees that had started them on this quest.

"They say, in fact," the prince went on, "that a princess who married the King of Khotan smuggled silkworms in her headdress to her new home so she would be certain of silk garments there. Raising silk is indeed a woman's art. And how not? They love it well, and it loves them. At one time it was forbidden to all but the First Empress, but the Son of Heaven was moved by the pleas of his ladies, and the poverty of the weavers and dyers to rescind his edict. And ever since, our court has blossomed," the prince said, with another smile at Alexandra.

She looked aside. Anyone else would have thought it was modesty. Alexandra had to be considering what had just struck Bryennius: They would accept this man's companionship and protection, would accept the friendship he seemed to offer. And then they would betray him.

Bryennius looked guilty, Alexandra thought, and she knew why. *For my brother, my City, I would do anything,* she told herself. *I am vowed to do it. That story of Yang Kuei-Fei—this prince with his fondness for myths and adventures . . . if he faced a choice between his Middle Kingdom and someone's life—he would not hesitate to discard us.* Her eyes fell on the dorje that shone gem-bright amid the gems of her sash. With just such a sash, Kuei-Fei had hanged herself. She shuddered and touched the twisted wand. If she had to, she could betray this prince. But what price would there be to pay? She knew this thought was part of the obsession with order and karma that crept like the sand into her every thought.

Dinner had been served and eaten with a combination of fingers, knives, and the ivory eating-sticks that Prince Shou insisted on teaching her how to use. She had managed without ruining her garments. Then musicians and dancers had entertained, and she had drifted off into a world of deserts, caravanserais, and fascinating strangers.

A well-kept hand touched her sleeve, and she almost shuddered. It was the prince.

"Surely that is a religious symbol of Tibet," he said, carefully avoiding a question.

"Your Highness is most learned," she parried.

"In my youth"—she raised eyebrows—"I studied the magics of the Tao, and . . . other paths."

"Then I can only tell you that I found this today, after I slew the goat for a second time. I think I was meant to find it."

"I think it might be auspicious," said the prince.

Alexandra held her breath. "Auspicious" was a word of power to these people. If a thing were "auspicious," for example, the invitation by a prince to a rabble of barbarians to join a caravan, then it would be done. But if a thing were "inauspicious," then it might be a long time until another caravan was ready to brave the Takla Makan.

"So I was told," she said, "by an abbot I met in my travels."

"I would like to hear that story. It is my hope that we might trade such tales in the long nights—and days—of our trip across the desert."

Suleiman Mis'ar ibn Mulhalhil looked appalled until he remembered that female or not, Alexandra was the ranking member of her party. Now that the prince had offered the invitation, accepting it or not was her decision to make.

And it had been made, she suspected, long, long ago.

"I would gladly hear those tales," she agreed. "When might we start?"

"When the horses are assembled, and you are rested," said the prince. He raised gray-flecked eyebrows at ibn Mulhalhil. "Can you see to that, my lord?"

The trader bowed, and the thing was done.

Bryennius paused before a dune that looked like a dragon frozen in place by the moonlight. The one rearing up ahead for hundreds of feet twisted like a serpent. Ahead and behind lay an ocean of grit. Except that each day the sun burned a little hotter, their supplies became fewer, and they themselves a little thinner, they appeared not to have traveled a mile from the time when the giant dunes hid Kashgar from their sight. The only variety came in the shape of the dunes, with the giant king dunes occasionally looming over all the rest.

They had been traveling for thirty days. In all that time, the only other caravan they had sighted was dried skin stretched over bones, and cargo scattered in the sand. "Do not touch, *bahadur*," one of the Pathans they had hired to tend the horses warned him. It was the worst of ill fortune to claim what the desert had taken. One shift of the wind, or a fall of sand would hide it forever.

"*Christe eleison*," he muttered, useless as the prayer seemed.

"Amen," said Father Basil, passing by on a donkey. That one! He would survive the trip to Ch'ang-an on the strength of his curiosity alone.

Bryennius glanced down the line of march. Men,
women, camels, and horses clustered tightly together.
Above them towered the dunes. When they had first
entered the great desolation, he had watched the dunes,
sure that they would crest and tumble down like white
waves, drowning the tiny humans and beasts. He had
never been so far from the sea, from any sort of water.
The weight of all that land bore down upon him, and
then, almost miraculously, it subsided, and he was able
to survive.

Beneath the cloth that covered his mouth, Bryennius
grinned. No one had ever expected discipline or strength
from him, yet he could endure the desert better than
most. The inexorable sunlight had burned him dark,
fined him down, until he could march all night and well
on into the next day without hardship. Alexandra too
was holding up: very thin, but vigorous. The Varangians
rode "like immense Bedouin," Suleiman had chuckled
the first time he saw them, muffled to the eyes to protect
their pale Northern skin. Several had been vilely ill from
the swaying of their dromedaries; one had had to be
restrained from beating a camel senseless because it bit
him.

The Ch'in themselves? Before the caravan had left
Kashgar, Bryennius had witnessed a comedy in which
Suleiman had attempted to dissuade many of the party
from continuing onward. Alexandra and Bryennius himself could not be denied; they were the ambassadors,
and, Bryennius thought, the master thieves. Besides,
they were Romans, Suleiman a Muslim. No one knew
whether they could continue to meet Suleiman on terms
of friendship. The Varangians rejected any suggestion of
remaining behind. As for the women of Prince Shou's
entourage, "Our ladies have married into the tribes, and
lived well among them. They will survive, as they
survived the trip out."

So much for his "brother's" misplaced concern. Suleiman had warned him again of the storms, and of the
repeated tests of Turpan's ability to protect itself. They

might never see one another again. Bryennius missed him. He rode past Alexandra, who sat one of the Ferghana horses at the prince's side. She was slight enough that the horse would not be injured: so far they had not lost many of them.

"We have a legend of a mountain called Meru," he heard Prince Shou say. "It is said that the gods live there. Is that like your Shambhala?"

That name again. It clamored in the stillness like the gongs in the temples Li Shou spoke of. Bryennius shivered every time he heard Alexandra mention the kingdom she had dreamed of when she wandered alone in the snow.

This prince, whose accomplishments apparently included a little sorcery, would have to let himself in on her story. He understood, in a way Bryennius could not. Up and down the length of the column Bryennius patrolled, waving at that guard here, this groom there, bowing decorously in response to a flutter of silk from one of the Ch'in concubines. Even Alexandra had told him he looked like an Imperial eagle. She had never commented on his appearance before. But then, to his knowledge, she had never ridden and laughed with men before either.

He looked up at the sky. It seemed paler at the horizon, indistinguishable from the sand. In a little while, the sun would rise with a ferocity greater than ten volcanoes. They would ride until it grew unbearable, then rest during the heat of the day. Bryennius would sleep, guarded by the soldiers, who had accepted him as their commander after he had told them how Leo had died. He had his men, his friends, his kin, and his mission. It was more than he had ever dreamed of having. Despite the terrible asceticism imposed by the Takla Makan, he was happy.

He heard hoofbeats, smothered by the sand, behind him as two traders rode up, accompanied by several grooms.

"Don't ride alone, Highness," they warned.

"I wasn't drifting," Bryennius protested.

"It isn't sleep we fear. It's the demons. Listen!" They rode on without speaking. Bryennius could hear the groans of the camels, an occasional voice, the faint ringing of harness. He strained his ears. At the edge of his perceptions came a hissing. He stiffened.

"Ah, so you hear. Now, listen more closely. I will lead your horse. Shut your eyes."

As he forced himself to hear, the hissing separated into whistles and giggles, rising and falling in pitch as if unseen creatures all about him made rude and perhaps threatening observations. He opened his eyes and shook his head.

The man beside him nodded. "Demons," he said.

Gold appeared at the horizon, then turned copper. The wind rose as it usually did before dawn.

Then the camels' usual complaints grew into a chorus of moans. Their pace slowed. At first their riders, especially the Varangians, tried to beat them into more speed. The camels clustered together, then stopped. They dropped their heads to the sand and moaned again.

"What is it?" Bryennius asked.

"The *buran!* Cover your face, and help us pitch camp. The camels always know first when the demons bring storms."

Now the horses started to stamp and neigh. The king stallion shrieked defiance against the rising wind, the sand that started to swirl, then darkened until it blotted out the rising sun. The grooms began to wrap the beasts and themselves in heavy felt, despite the great heat.

As quickly as the kuraburan rose, it reached howling frenzy. Bryennius, helping people dismount and struggle into the protection of a circle of kneeling camels, looked wildly about for Alexandra. There she was, riding with the prince toward the hastily thrown-up camp.

Beside Bryennius men and women whispered prayers and curses. The storm swirled about them. Bryennius threw off his felt wrappings and winced as dust stung him, and stones, hurled by the wind, pounded his legs.

Securing a line about his waist, Bryennius started out toward his cousin.

"Don't go!" screamed the man who had crouched at his side. Then he started chanting. "*Om mane padme hum.*"

Giggling rose over the hiss of the sand and wind. There they were! Just a few steps more, and surely Alexandra would see him. Just a few steps . . . the giggling rose to a gabble and a shriek. The prince turned to shout something; Bryennius saw his lips move. Something howled and drowned him out. A gush of wind and grit battered against the carts, overturning three. With a scream of terror, Prince Shou's horse bolted.

"Alexandra!" Bryennius screamed in equal terror. She had to have heard, would have to ride toward him and the dubious safety of heavy felt wrappings.

"You're not getting him either!" she shouted at the storm. In a fury, she kicked her horse's flanks and rode after the prince.

Bryennius lunged forward. He hoped he would have had the courage to go after her. He tried, but two men of ibn Mulhalhil's household threw themselves at him and forced him to the ground.

The two riders disappeared into the storm. Howling and hissing, it forced them deeper into the desert.

8

The torment of sand and flailing gravel ripped away Alexandra's sense of direction. She screamed for the prince as he vanished deeper into the desert, but the only things she heard over the kuraburan were the hoots and giggles of the demons that had hurled it upon them. But she could still see a dim figure, and she turned her struggling horse in its direction.

Why had she chosen to throw her life away? She knew enough of evil sorcery to know that this storm was no part of the magical feud that had pursued her from Byzantium. The demons of the Takla Makan were more malicious and less powerful; they struck at random, and now they had struck her. The desert would engulf her. Perhaps a hundred years from now, it would cast up her bones as a warning to travelers she herself had not followed. And Li Shou with her.

"Oh, no, it won't!" she muttered to herself. There had been no reason to follow the prince except a sudden knowledge, a necessity as stark as anything she'd ever seen enacted on stage, that she had to save him. That it was inevitable that she try and that, if all went right, she would succeed. Was that what was meant by karma?

The figure up ahead grew larger and more solid. She kneed her horse for whatever speed it could summon, then leaned forward to catch the bridle of the other horse. Li Shou grasped her arm until it ached clear to the bone.

"We have to stay together!" she shrieked. He shook his head, and, putting her face where his half-slit eyes could see it, she tried again. He nodded, understanding the motion of her lips. Well enough. She pulled her arm free and signaled that they should dismount, use the meager shelter that their poor horses' bodies would provide. It was a double bind. If they were to have the slightest chance of riding out, they had to preserve the horses. But first, they had to survive the storm.

They crouched down, huddling together. Li Shou flung an arm about her shoulder as if he could keep the sand from striking her. She turned to face him again.

Twice she tried to speak, but her mouth was too dry. Finally, she spat and managed to twist her lips around words that astonished her even as they came out. "Did you really hear a child?"

He shrugged, then winced as a particularly sharp piece of rock struck his shoulder. "Probably a demon. It is no matter now. Your effort to save me was honorable, but I regret it, Princess."

A child. That must have been what drove her away from safety. When she wandered on the mountainside, there had been a child who had helped her reach safety, had promised her . . . she strained her ears to hear over the storm, closing her eyes, focusing inward.

When the sound she sought for came, she started up quickly. The prince tried to pull her back down. "I heard him too!" she said.

He shook his head and pulled harder. The kuraburan could madden, but this, she knew, wasn't madness unless it was the controlled insanity of the power working through her. And she had felt that enough times to know it. The sound came again, mingled now with a terrible screaming, as if whatever child wandered this desert were pursued by demons.

She stiffened, jerking free of the prince. ".There!" she cried and flung out an arm. "What do you see?"

"Madness," the prince said, a mere shape of the lips. Then he leaned forward. Breath hissed beneath his lips as he stared at the figure.

This was not the young child who had guided Alexandra on the mountainside, Rudra Cakrin, fated to be the King of Shambhala. If he had had an older brother, or if he had aged years since he had saved her, this might be the same boy, almost a youth, wearing clothes that at times appeared to be riding garments, and at other times the robes worn by novices in the monastery that had taken Alexandra in. He stood very still, untouched by the kuraburan, not even squinting against the fiercely blown sand, and a light seemed to gleam about him. With one hand, he held something red and shining. With the other, he pointed.

Prince Li Shou whispered something. "Of course it couldn't have been a child. We're both mad. You do go mad before you die of thirst," he said almost calmly.

"Not madness." Alexandra started after the boy. "A manifestation. A power. And he wants us to follow him. Are you coming, or would you rather die here?"

For an instant, the prince hung back. Then the curiosity that had driven him from Ch'ang-an years ago to collect mysteries and wonders of all types made him catch up his horse's reins and follow where the shining figure led.

The horses protested and staggered. They were near the end of their strength, she thought. Would their companion know it, or care? She heard laughter rise on either side of her, felt new fears and rages. Perhaps she was mad. Perhaps this was not Rudra Cakrin at all, but a particularly subtle form of demon. She could choose to turn away and accept certain death in the storm, or she could trust him.

She drew the sword she had used to kill the goat. It gleamed, blue against the ochre and black of the blowing grit. Was it her imagination that the demon laughter grew fainter, as if intimidated either by the blade or by the glowing figure she and the prince followed? Though they stumbled, at times buried to the ankles or the knees in sand, the figure seemed to move unimpeded above it.

"King Rudra." She tried the name out, and the figure, though it could not have possibly heard, turned and pointed again. The sand swirled about them, then disappeared for an instant. Alexandra stopped short, then tripped over—it was a beam of wood. They had stumbled, or been led, into one of the thousand ruined cities buried in the Takla Makan. Ahead she made out two walls, and the fragments of a roof from which time-blackened beams still projected.

The blowing sand threatened to bury her. She picked herself up, then tugged on her horse's reins. If the ruin had not crumbled in all the centuries of storms it must have weathered, it might serve to shelter two people and two horses. Once again, Rudra Cakrin had saved her life, or at least won her time enough to plan what to do to save it for herself. "My thanks," she whispered, turning to face him.

But the boy was gone.

Alexandra and Prince Li Shou staggered into the shelter they had found. Their horses knelt the way that camels did when their loads were removed, a sign of how exhausted they were. No sand stung them, and the howling of the storm was so muffled by the walls that the sudden quiet struck them like a blow.

Except for the light that clung to Alexandra's sword, almost as if left over from their encounter with the boy, the ruin was dark.

"Do we have a flint?" she asked, and her voice sounded hollow. She rummaged in her saddlebags. Water, but not much of it. Food. Various other impediments that she should probably abandon to lighten the horse's load tomorrow. Her fingers closed about a small cylinder, then jerked back. A vial of Greek fire, possibly another.

Behind her she heard cloth ripping. Then Li Shou struck a light. The spark touched the cloth and flared up.

The prince knelt, nursing the tiny flames. The elegant, languid man and silken robes of that long-ago dinner in Kashgar were gone; a humble, battered figure stared up at her. Alexandra pulled off her hat and ran her fingers through her matted, sweaty hair. She shivered. Despite the heat, this shelter was cold.

"Perhaps we can find something to burn here," she said. "We can't sacrifice our clothing, not if we hope to ride out of here."

As both began to look about, the horses nickered, then whinnied in dismay. Around the ruin rose howls and laughter.

"They have us penned like fowl at a market!" cried Li Shou.

"Not while I have this," Alexandra said, holding out her sword. She would have to stand at the ragged doorway and hold the creatures at bay, she supposed. The imbecilic bravado of that idea made her want to laugh too. If she started laughing now, she didn't know if she could stop. Carefully, she drew a deep, ragged breath, and then another and another, as she had seen monks do—had done herself—in meditation.

Li Shou drew his own sword. "Not alone."

There had to be a way, Alexandra thought. As the demons drew closer, and rocks pelted the walls, she paced the tiny shelter to relieve her tension. The T'ang prince retreated into a corner to sit and assume a posture of meditation.

"What's this?" he whispered, bending down. Then he followed his question by something in reverent tones that Alexandra could not understand.

"What did you find?" she asked, going to him.

"Sutras," he whispered. "Texts, very old. This one

bears the name of H'suan Tsang, a monk who crossed the desert two centuries ago to bring uncorrupted Buddhist texts back to the Middle Kingdom."

We have no time for rare books! Alexandra wanted to shout, but forced herself to kneel. Anything in this ruin might be a weapon, left for her to find. Prince Shou lifted the fragile paper tenderly. Something gleamed, and Alexandra seized what looked like a handle of dark wood.

A high-pitched tone filled the wretched room. Outside, the howling turned into yelps of fear, but only for a moment. Then they resumed with fearful intensity as if the demons had been infuriated by their momentary lapse. The bell had frightened them! Alexandra ran her fingers over the smooth metal, over the handle that was not wood, she saw now, but bone.

"A ghanta," she whispered. She had seen them in the monastery.

"You know Vajra rituals?" Li Shou looked astonished. "But I forget. At Kashgar, you won the lightning bolt. Think you, then, that all this is fated?"

The demons drew closer. The roof beams shivered, and several mud bricks fell from the walls.

Alexandra handed him the bell. "First we fight. Then, Highness, if we live, we shall discuss theology."

Together they stepped to the door of the shelter. Beyond the opacity of the driving sand and dust they could see figures dancing about and waving black daggers in their many arms. Alexandra showed the demons her sword. They took it as a challenge and advanced.

"Now ring the bell!" she cried, and the prince did. The ghanta's voice was pure and piercing. The horses snorted once or twice, and were silent. One demon, braver or madder than its fellows, ran forward. Alexandra gasped, then spitted it upon her blade. The demon shrieked, burst into smoke, and vanished. Alexandra retreated into the cascades of sound evoked by the ghanta. It was like standing under a waterfall. She willed the sound to cover them, to protect them, and felt a thrill dart from her brow to the base of her spine, and then another. The protection was there! The demons howled, and she tensed her will again and again, feeling some energy leap from her to strengthen that wall of sound. She was aware of thirst, and then that too was gone, washed from her by the high-pitched ringing that protected them as the demons clustered around and the storm grew fiercer.

Li Shou lowered his hand, and the ringing ceased so abruptly that they both gasped. "The walls aren't shaking as hard," he said. "I think the storm is dying."

Alexandra raised her sword and looked outside. "It's near dawn," she said. "And the sky *is* lightening."

She sighed, then yawned. She felt drained. It would be wonderful to sleep, but if they rested now, they might as well rest forever. They shared out food and water, giving the larger portion to the horses.

"I have this," said Li Shou, holding up a dark metal arrow that dangled from a chain. "A direction-finder. It points north. It may be our only hope."

"Haraldr will search for me," Alexandra said.

"No one turns back to search for what the desert has taken," the prince said. "What makes you think that your tall . . ."

"Hu-barbarian?" Incongruously, she almost laughed. "Haraldr is no barbarian as his people reckon things. He is the son of a . . . you might call his father a border lord. He can fight and make poetry. Above all, he is a Varangian, pledged to the Emperor—and, through my brother, to me. No Varangian would break such an oath. Haraldr will find me, or die here."

"A noble thought, lady." Prince Shou turned from discussion of oaths to contemplating the book he had found. "Does this mean anything to you?"

He knew she couldn't read the thousand pictures in which his language was written, Alexandra thought, but bent to look. Mountains, arrayed as if in the petals of a lotus, at its heart a city, and at the heart of the city . . . there was no mistaking it. There sat a king, and his face, though older, was the face of the boy who had guided them.

"Shambhala!" she said. "I saw this picture once before, in a monastery. That is the king, Rudra Cakrin. Twice now, when I have been in peril of my life, I have seen a child or boy with his face. And each time, I have been spared."

"I have heard that name. We too have such legends. The story is told that Lao Tzu, one of our greatest—you would call him a prophet, perhaps—left the Middle Kingdom on account of its great wickedness. Now he lives on Jade Mountain. And there is Mount Meru, in the south. Lady, do you truly seek such a place and such a king?"

Alexandra nodded, then found herself nodding off. Now that the bell had stopped ringing, she wanted only to collapse into darkness.

"Then I give *my* oath to you that I will aid you. And if it is so fated, I vow that I will go with you myself. If the master of Shambhala appeared to you, I owe you both my life. When you arrive in Ch'ang-an, I promise that you and yours shall be honored guests in my home."

"Will that be allowed?"

"Ordinarily not," he agreed. "The Uighurs have been so arrogant that private dealings with many foreigners have been forbidden. But I am a prince, I will have returned so recently that they may still be glad to see me. And when I left, I had friends enough that I need not expect the silken cord to be sent me and given until dawn to hang myself for housing not barbarians, but honored guests and friends."

She had not counted on his gratitude. In an instant, she saw how easily she might move about Ch'ang-an if she were not subject to the restrictions that the capital, like Byzantium, placed on foreigners. She could steal the silkworms . . . at the cost of betraying not just a man who trusted her, but her host. Well, if she survived, she would try to resolve that dilemma.

Her head drooped, and she forced herself to sit upright. Again, and again—until she found herself falling sideways to rest against something warm. She shook herself awake, then rose to her knees about a yard away from Li Shou, whose shoulder had supported her. The sky was paling toward dawn. She rose and turned her back to the prince, to hide her flushed cheeks.

"Shall we start?" she said. It would be well to travel as far as possible before the sun came up. If worst came to worst, they could tie themselves to their mounts and sleep in shifts, one leading the other, and holding fast to the prince's direction finder.

He nodded. They saddled their horses and led them outside. Alexandra turned back to look at the ruin, already more than half-covered by the sand once again. "I have to believe we have been guided," she mused.

Suddenly she cried out and staggered. Instantly the prince was at her side, half-supporting her, listening to her stammered tale of how Haraldr had won the horn that was linked with Shambhala. "I heard—oh, inside my head!—like the cry of a hunting horn. Something has inspired Haraldr to blow that horn, and it calls to me."

Again came that soundless blast, and she reeled.

"We have to let him know that I've heard him," she gasped. "The bell—ring it!" And when the prince hesitated, she seized it and rang it herself. In the still, open air, the sound would carry a long way. And if the bell rang as the horn did in both ears and mind, Haraldr must surely hear it.

"We can't ride yet," she whispered. "He'll never find us if we don't stay in one place."

"Madness," judged the prince, but settled himself to wait. "When my horse bolted, I counted my life as gone. If it is fated that I die, then as well here as anywhere else."

As the sun rose higher in the sky where never a bird dared fly, Alexandra alternately rang the bell, then listened for the horn call that assaulted her spirit. She could feel strength flowing from her as from a mortal wound. She sank down on the sand, and Li Shou sat down beside her, drawing her across his lap to rest.

:"It's closer," she whispered, then winced. Her dirty, scratched hands caught at the prince's sleeves, and a spasm shook her. He took the bell from her and rang it, then waited. Moments later, both winced at the call that came.

"He'll never see us!" she cried and dragged herself to her horse and its saddlebags. "Swear never to tell!" she commanded, then hurled what she had drawn from the bags against the walls where they had sheltered.

Flame sprang up. The heat from the Greek fire melded with the heat of the sun and the coarse sand. Sand, sky, and burning ruins shimmered as if in a furnace. Alexandra lowered herself to the hot sand before she fainted, but forced herself to sit, rather than lie down.

"What's that?" Li Shou's voice snapped her from uneasy sleep.

"Mirage?" she moaned, and he moistened her lips with water, restoring her to some measure of alertness. "Where?"

He gestured toward a tiny speck that danced and flickered between them and the horizon.

"Illusion," she whispered. "It must be."

"You told me that your guard would never abandon you, and I did not believe it. Now it is I who believe, and you who doubt. When we are safe, perhaps you will beg his pardon."

He drew her down to lie on the sand. Then he leaped to his feet, waving his arms, even jumping in a mad effort to draw the attention of the black speck that rapidly gained in size and speed.

It *was* Haraldr, the other Varangians with him. All were heavily muffled in robes from head to fingertips against the sun that was doubly punishing to their Northern-bred pallor. Within moments, they had reached the burning ruin, where the prince and princess they never truly expected to see again awaited them.

"You blew the horn," Alexandra said. "I heard you."

Haraldr reached inside his robes to touch the hammer
he wore. "I shall thank Freya too," he whispered.
"Come, let us get you back."

Worn by the storm, the battle with demons, and the
struggle of mind and heart to guide Haraldr to them,
Alexandra barely felt him lift her onto his camel and give
the order to start back. The camel's fast, even stride over
the sand and Haraldr's heartbeat lulled her.

Only shouts of astonishment which rapidly turned to
cheers woke her from a waking dream in which horses
and jade mountains played their part. Someone was
trickling water into her parched mouth, and tenderly
wiping her face with a silken cloth.

"Alexandra!" She opened bleary eyes to see
Bryennius. In the now-ragged dress of a Muslim merchant prince, he looked like a brigand, and she told him
so.

"Thank the Mother of God and Her Son!" he wept. "I
never hoped to see you, let alone hear you tease me
again."

She could hear Father Basil arguing with a hoarse
voice that she identified with difficulty as Li Shou's.
"Yes, I know I too need rest, but not until she is tended. I
tell you, I saw her fight the creatures while I watched,
unable to help."

"You rang the bell," Alexandra said, but both men
ignored her.

"In Ch'ang-an, you are to be my guests. And for now,
she is to be tended by my concubines. No, I will hear no
protests. The thing is done." He clapped his hands, and
Alexandra resigned herself to the ministrations of those
birdlike creatures with their delicate hands and fine
skins. Since they had survived the storm, apparently
they were not that delicate. It might be pleasant, she
thought fuzzily. Once, after a period of intense study and
meditation, she had had a fever, and the dream-filled
rest had come as a pleasure and a relief.

Bryennius was patting her hand, holding it to his

rough cheek. "Cousin, did you hear? The prince has ordered that his concubines attend you. You're not afraid they will regard you as a threat to his regard for them?"

Alexandra knew the women's quarters of the Imperial palace. At best, they were hotbeds of gossip, at worst, quiet and subtly murderous battlefields that no man could understand. But when the women dabbled in sorcery, assassination could be the least one had to fear.

She forced herself to pat her cousin's cheek. "I'll be safe," she whispered. "For one thing, they know they have me to thank for getting their prince back to them at all. For another—do you have any idea how ugly they think barbarian females are?"

9

Bryennius rode back toward the head of the caravan, content for the moment. His own inspection had reassured him that the Ferghana horses' legs were sound. He had not dared to rely on the words of guards or grooms for anything as precious as those horses. But they endured the desert well. Bryennius suspected some admixture of Arabian in their bloodline.

Ever since the Varangians had brought Alexandra and the T'ang prince out of the kuraburan, leadership had fallen upon him. He was delighted at how well he took to it. In the weeks the prince and his cousin shivered in fever, tied to their camels, Bryennius had become first man to wake, last to rest. He agonized over the horses, and settled disputes. At Kucha, Father Basil and the prince's physicians agreed that Li Shou could walk or ride as needed throughout a day's march. At Karashahr, Alexandra had finally demanded a horse, intimidated the prince's concubines into giving her the riding clothes that they had hidden, and taken up her former routines. But the merchants, grooms, and soldiers still took their orders from Bryennius.

His cousin rode at his side now, silent, the way she had been since the kuraburan. They had weathered more storms, but none, thank the Blessed Mother of God, like the one she had been lost in. She had come out of the desert half-dead and, it seemed, three-quarters mad. Now her lips moved as if she were praying or arguing with herself. The one time he had ventured to ask what her thoughts were, she had told him a tale of a thing called the Diamond Path that made him think her wits had gone astray in the sand. That storm, she told him, could have been an illusion.

"Some illusion," Bryennius retorted. "It nearly killed you. And you're still far from well."

"If I had accepted the Diamond Path as the abbot told me I must, I might simply have walked through the storm the way Rudra Cakrin did, when he brought Li Shou and me to shelter."

"You still insist you saw someone?" Bryennius had asked. He was terrified that the sun, the sand, and the arduous, monotonous trek had stolen his cousin's sanity.

"Now you think I'm mad," she told him. "Did you ever think that madness too might be an illusion?"

She stirred, glancing up at the peaks of the T'ien Shan, called the Celestial Mountains. Snow glittered at their summits. Bryennius licked his lips. If he drank now, the entire caravan might, and they must hoard their water until they reached Turpan.

"We're climbing into the foothills." He offered as a safe, sane topic of conversation the magnificence on the horizon and the line of march. Alexandra turned to look at him, she was only a tired, thin-faced woman with bright dark eyes that for now, were mercifully free of the intense, speculative glitter that had so frightened him. "It might be cooler there."

"My Bryennius." She smiled at him. "I shouldn't trouble you with my own fears. Do you know, I think you are dearer to me than my own brother?"

If he wept, the caravan might doubt his fitness to lead them. (What was that bellow? Ghazala, oldest of the camels, winning her daily war with the men who tended her, he deduced.) And without a leader, they were all lost.

Her tiny hand reached out to lie on his above the reins. "I swear to you, I do not think I'm mad. I might well be, though. The Diamond Path that the abbot said I must walk? It's like the mountain ledges we crossed—snow above, the pit below, and madness all around. And now the desert. Deserts give birth to religions, you know. I can understand why."

Bryennius suppressed an urge to cross himself. Father Basil, heretic or not, would have to deal with that astonishing comment.

"No, Bry', I'm not preaching a new revelation." Abruptly, Alexandra's voice was sharp, angry. "Damn you, man, this is hard enough without your going silent and tolerant and panicky on me! I'm telling you, I saw things, I felt things during that storm, and I can't think them through."

That much sounded like the old Alexandra, when she was frustrated by her Aristotle. Bryennius could respond to that frustration.

"Then give it a rest, cousin, please. In fact, if you could turn your lofty mind"—her nails bit into his hand—"to ordinary matters, I need to think a few things through myself. Would you help me?"

"At Karashahr, when you delivered the letters from Kucha, and picked up the dispatches for Turpan, what did they tell you that worries you?" Alexandra grinned at him. "Yes, I know I was supposed to be resting. But you're not very subtle, cousin."

Bryennius sighed with relief. Prince Shou might be their comrade and profess himself their friend, but

Alexandra was family, her complex logic familiar and reassuring.

"At Kashgar, at dinner that night, you heard that Turpan is in some jeopardy."

Alexandra nodded. "From what I've learned, it's always been a battleground. Every time some king or other wants to expand, his eyes fall on Turpan. Not to mention his armies. It's a strategic site, and the water supply is good. Not to mention its wine."

The last thing Bryennius needed now was to think of Turpan and its *karez*, the subterranean channels that brought water down from the T'ien Shan foothills, as impressive a thing in its way as the Roman aqueducts. There were almost a thousand of them, he had been told. A thousand cool tunnels, each rippling with water in the cool, quiet dark. He licked his lips again. This time he actually reached for his waterskin before he stopped himself.

"Turpan's under attack, then," Alexandra came to a conclusion.

"The Karashahr traders think that by now the Turpans have either waited them out or succumbed." Wars in the desert were not a matter of protracted campaigns or prolonged sieges: the resources simply were not there. Lightning raids, treachery, the hope of carelessness . . . these were the weapons that might win a trading outpost for any one of a band of ambitious tribes. Of all the oases along the silk road, Turpan had the best chance of outwaiting an especially well-equipped force . . . unless someone—or some power—damaged the karez.

"Do we know what we may ride into?" The question was asked lightly enough. Bryennius shook his head. That had been the hardest decision of all the ones he had had to make. Should he wait at Karashahr until word, or invaders, came from Turpan, or proceed—in summer —across the anvil of sand, grit, and stone so appropriately called the Land of Fire? Risk his caravan's welfare, or further endanger his cousin's health and reason?

"And I was too ill to advise you. Ah, Bryennius, forgive me?" He almost hugged her then and there.

"Have you told the prince?"

"When he was ill, I . . . drafted his men. It's doubled our fighting strength." It was hard to suppress the pride he felt.

"My God, what a general the Empire missed in you!" she exclaimed. "If you're doing so well on your own, what do you need me for?"

Well-content, Bryennius turned his horse. He had heard both hoofbeats and the long tread of a camel, and wanted his men's reports.

"Why, cousin? To hear what you just said."

Another possible future, Bryennius thought. But it did seem hard and damnably unfair that even as his life expanded into a range of possibilities, Alexandra's shrank and twisted. She was driven now by two quests: for the silkworms she'd pledged her life (and his) to bring back to Byzantium, and now this inexplicable fascination with the Kingdom of Shambhala. Discreet questions had told him that it lay to the south. Well, if they survived that long, they could always return from Ch'in by the southerly trade routes. From what he'd heard, they were almost worse than the ones he'd already crossed.

When they stopped to rest, he would tell her everything that Suleiman and the other traders had told him. Once she had all the facts, she could occupy that complex, fertile mind on something considerably more profitable than pagan superstitions.

Days later, they climbed down from the foothills, reached the ordinary level of the sand, and kept on descending. Here the air was thick and hot, though so dry it scorched the throat and nose. Sunlight pressed upon their backs until they were surprised that the long, black shadows that they cast were not hunched over from the weight of it. The coarse sand cast the heat back up at them. The camels protested at each step, and three horses had to be killed when they collapsed, unable to walk a step farther.

"I could almost believe," Father Basil said, "that some demon had pressed his thumb into the earth and gouged out this place. The Land of Fire indeed!"

"Please, don't joke about it!" Alexandra begged.

"This one rejoices that when he came here the first time, it was winter," said Li Shou.

Bryennius slitted his eyes. The air was a shimmer of heat. Was the shadow up ahead just another illusion or was that smoke? He pointed it out to Alexandra.

She stared too. "Smoke," she pronounced finally. "And not just smoke, either. Look at the way the light moves. After Haraldr found me, I don't think I can ever forget how riders look, coming toward one in a desert. There are riders coming this way."

She adjusted her swordbelt and signaled for her guardsmen. Haraldr rode in, his axe at hand. Prince Shou closed in on her other side. Bryennius spared time for a sly smile.

"Tell the men to arm," Bryennius ordered one of the men from Kashgar.

Brigands would not touch them if they showed too great a force. An army, however . . . "Tell them also to remember that we are traders, not a war band. We don't attack unless fired upon."

As the sun beat down on them, they waited, straining their eyes until the shimmer blurred and re-formed into a band of riders. "Horse archers," muttered Father Basil.

"Kazaks, probably," said the Ch'in prince. "They ride magnificently."

For an instant, both Alexandra and Bryennius glared at him. This was no time for artistic judgments.

"Friends?" Bryennius asked one of the traders from Kashgar.

The man shrugged. The riders drew closer, and their own archers nocked arrows, waiting.

They could stand like this until someone's judgment

snapped, or they all collapsed from the sun, Alexandra thought. She knew that as princess, it was her part to remain in such safety as there was, until her fate—and the fate of all the other noncombatants—was decided. She also knew that it was her fate to resent such arrangements. In her lost and unlamented convent, she had seen two cats stalking one another. They had crouched motionless, neither taking its eyes from the other, neither moving, until she dropped a pebble. Then the spell was broken, and each strolled off in a different direction. The distraction enabled her to break up what might have been quite a fight, though nothing compared with the bloodshed (her own included) that might come from a misstep here.

Like everything else since her escape from the kuraburan, this did not seem real to her. It was all illusion, the abbot's voice whispered in her head. But she didn't want it to be illusion. She didn't want to be some esoteric being. She was human, and she wanted her hopes and fears back, needed them if she were not to throw herself away through caprice, indifference, or despair.

She remembered Kashgar, and how she had ridden into it like a princess, her hair flowing down her back. Well, there was no wind here to make it fly behind her (and it was probably too matted to do anything of the kind), but she could try. Moving her hands slowly toward her head, she pulled off her hat and let her hair tumble. Homer might write all he cared to about Amazons: no war party she had ever heard of included women.

A man who looked much like her hosts in Kashgar detached himself from the troop and rode forward. "I am Ibrahim ibn Mulhalhil."

"Now that," rumbled Haraldr, "is what I call a brave man!"

Alexandra touched heels delicately to her horse's flanks and moved slowly forward. Behind her, she heard appalled hisses.

"Bryennius," she whispered through her teeth, "you have the dispatches. Come . . . but slowly."

"Suleiman Mis'ar ibn Mulhalhil calls me brother," Bryennius said.

The man looked skeptical. He stiffened, and the warriors behind him tensed too.

"I have letters," Bryennius added, his voice rising a little.

"Will you let me bring them to you?" Alexandra called. Her higher, clear voice carried, unmistakably that of a woman. She took the letters from her cousin's hand and walked her horse toward the Turpan merchant, holding them out to him as she might hold meat out to a growling watchdog. From what she had seen of them, they were in Arabic. They might say anything, including, "Put to death the bearer of these instructions."

Deliberately, the man opened the letters and read them, then stared at Bryennius and, a little more abashedly, at herself. She forced herself to look around as if he could not possibly decide to harm them. Today it was difficult to tell where the mountain peaks ended and the clouds began. Above the clouds, the sky looked almost indigo. And what she saw drifting behind the riders was most certainly smoke. Despite the dryness of the air, she felt sweat run down her sides. Her heart pounded as it had done in the high passes. Sights, smells, and sounds had never been as intense, or as precious to her.

"I ask your pardon," said ibn Mulhalhil after a time. "My house and all in it are yours."

Alexandra made her horse back up and she put her hat back on. No need to court sunstroke, or embarrass the man by reminding him of her presence. *Ask if there was a battle*, she wished at Bryennius.

He fell into low-voiced conversation with the man, at one point grimacing in disgust. Then each saluted the other in the Abbasid fashion of hand to lips and brow before returning to his own troop.

"Some of the tribes here have been raiding Turpan more than usual. Mosques have been desecrated. The tribes—they say they were here before Islam and will be here long after they have driven it into the sand and made Turpan into a waste like the ruins down the road," said Bryennius. "There was plague too—high fever, convulsions, but it quit when they found . . . he doesn't want to talk about what they found. Some sort of idol with many arms and skulls."

"Like the attempt on my nephew's life!" cried Alexandra. Risking her life had won her back her ability to feel. Once again, she could smell magic, close at hand. She touched her talismans and tried to sense what might lie up ahead. It all but made her gag.

There had indeed been war in Turpan, and the town had survived it by a hair. The *yurts* of the few tribesmen who still dared to live outside the town itself rested on battle-marked sand. Smoke stained the pale mud-brick walls of Turpan's buildings, and spiraled in patterns about the mosque with its spire that looked like an ivory toy carved by a master craftsman for a Titan. They rode past many homes with walls pitted by fire and heavy blows. The townspeople were out, restoring the leafy trellises that gave them shade, grapes, and comfort, even here in the Land of Fire.

"They defaced even the cemetery this one's ancestors built here," Li Shou mourned quietly. "It too must be set to rights."

A look went from Ibrahim to Bryennius to Alexandra herself. First things first. Now the prince rode at her side. "This one admired the princess' conduct in front of the archers," he said formally. "There are stories of a T'ang princess, the lady Ping Yang, whose army defended a pass. May this one express the observation that the princess and this one's far distant kinswoman have much in common?"

Li Shou, with his old names for places and his elegies . . . Alexandra shook herself. Li Shou might be more poet than warrior, but he had been a good man to have at her back during the storm.

"This one . . ." Oh, she would never accustom herself to speaking of herself in the third person, anymore than she could speak of herself as "we" the way Greek Imperials thought they had to. "I thank you, Highness," she managed to say. Then, a little more quickly, "I am very glad that I learned of your brave ancestress only now, Prince. I rode out to face the archers because I thought that the warriors in these parts could not imagine a woman as a threat. If I had known of that princess, I think I might have been afraid."

Li Shou smiled and shook his head at what he thought was her modesty. She colored and turned away, listening to Ibrahim as he spoke to her cousin.

"Many of our caravanserais have been destroyed," Ibrahim said. "You shall stay in my own home."

Ibrahim's home lay beyond the bazaars, in a narrow alley miraculously free of camels, donkey carts, and scurrying Uighurs, Kazaks, Ch'in, Muslims, and any of ten other tribes and races. The karez was open here to the air, and it frothed with clean, fast-moving water. Alexandra wanted to dip her hands and feet into it. Trellises covered its thick walls so heavily that the mud bricks were only a pale, intermittent gleam in the sunlight.

Ibrahim murmured a few words, then stepped aside for them to enter what felt like a paradise of coolness. Alexandra felt the skin around her eyes loosen at the pleasures of being in near-darkness and close to moisture. Outside, the leaves rustled comfortingly. Her eyes became used to the room's dimness, though spots still danced and glittered in front of the jewellike stacks of rugs and soft cushions to which Ibrahim steered his guests.

Bowls of fruit and Turpan's fabled mare's-teat grapes appeared almost magically. She washed her hands in the water a manservant offered her in a turquoise-glazed bowl. Beyond her, one of Bryennius' troopers bit into a plum beaded with moisture. Juice dribbled down his chin, and he dabbed at it, grinned guiltily, and took another eager bite.

Alexandra started to laugh with the rest. Then she shivered. The juice that stained his lips looked like blood trickling from the mouth of a dying man. She shook her head. She was only a trifle dizzy, coming in out of the sunlight like that. But, she decided, no plums for her! She took a cluster of the huge, ripe grapes. A grape burst in her mouth. Along with its heavy sweetness came the taste of ashes and blood.

As conversation swirled about her, she shut her eyes and, in the same instant, regretted it. The taste of the grape tore her loose from her anchorage in the tired body that reclined on a cushion in a desert outpost, and flung her awareness adrift high above the desert. She saw the mountains she had crossed, even the peak on which she had almost died—and still her thoughts soared higher. When the mountains seemed no more than a wrinkled piece of silk cast upon the earth, she seemed to pause where she was. Now, on all sides, voices and colors assailed her. Smoke wreathed around her, and she flinched from it, remembering how the abbot had warned her against demons.

The abbot! She reached with her thoughts for his comforting presence. He would not intervene, she recalled, but surely she might greet him? The attempt made her dizzy, and now she heard laughter, a woman's voice saying in cultivated Greek, "I may not even have to destroy her. One step aside on *that* path, and she will destroy herself." She knew the voice for her aunt Theodora's, and it terrified her. Bad enough that her aunt threatened her soul, but that she herself, through a misstep on the Diamond Path, could plunge herself to hell . . . *I will not*, she whispered. She had always had guides on the Diamond Path. Now, it seemed, she must struggle on by herself.

Her awareness plummeted, and she was back inside her body in Turpan, then, just as suddenly, wandering in her thoughts below the house, deep beneath the ground.

Water trickled nearby, and someone wept. Something was rotting, but not yet decently dead, and it crouched underground.

Abruptly Alexandra snapped back to the here and now and cut into the conversation. "What lies beneath your house?" she asked.

Ibrahim clearly thought that his honored guest had a touch of sunstroke. "We are near the *qanat*, Highness. So we have plenty of water, even now."

Even as Father Basil whispered to her that "qanat" was simply the word the Arabs used for the karez, she shook her head in revulsion. Blood and smoke and worse things lay in that water, which trickled along underground ways where that thing might lap at it and foul it. Her conviction that Turpan's war was not yet over grew.

Li Shou's tired eyes rested upon her and warned. *He knows that something is wrong, and suspects it is magic*, Alexandra thought. Bryennius looked troubled. *He thinks I am going mad, as well I might*. A strong hand suddenly touched her shoulder, and she relaxed under the unexpected gesture.

"My princess needs to rest," said Haraldr in passable Sogdian. Except for the time he had wedged her into the rocks lest the snowslide hurl her down the mountainside, he had never touched her before.

Her warmth and littleness struck him almost as fiercely as his shock when she looked up at him and smiled wearily. For an instant, he saw her as she had been in Byzantium: jeweled and remote, but with a flash in her eyes. And when the Basileus spoke of her journey that day, it had rekindled the wanderlust that had already drawn him from Norway to Hedeby and Aldeigsfjord, on the mad dash down the rapids from Kiev, and thence to Miklagard. Those bright eyes had kindled another type of lust on the road east, though it shamed him to admit it. His princess . . . her courage and endurance moved him as achingly as her dark eyes or her slender frame. Even grimy, and drawn, her silken hair bound up in that ridiculous cap, she seemed as fragile and perfect as the ivories in the palace. Fool, he called himself for the thousandth time. She might have wed a king, not an oaf like himself, but she had chosen to live a holy life until danger turned her into a shieldmaid, innocent and fierce. He had as much chance to win her as he would have if he approached a Valkyrie with talk of love. But his princess had smiled at him. His stubborn heart raced.

"Certainly," said Ibrahim, sounding relieved, and clapped his hands. Alexandra rose. She would, she supposed, be conducted to his female kin; she was getting used to that.

"I cannot believe," she heard Li Shou's voice behind her, clearly taking up a subject that had stirred up some anxiety, "that the Son of Heaven would exile the worshipers of Mani."

"Even the rumor of trouble distresses me," Father Basil replied, "for my own people in your land. How long will it be before you blame the Nestorians as well as the tribes for the raids, and the violation of your holy places? And yours, Master Ibrahim. If Ch'in turns inward, distrusting the outsiders who have helped make it wise and rich, against whom else might it turn?"

Alexandra turned and left the room. The women's quarters were cool and very quiet, if you ignored the dismay and murmurings of their inmates at her parched skin, her thinness, and her scandalous clothing. It was pleasant to be bathed and oiled (she forced herself to ignore the reek of blood in the bathwater, since none of the other women seemed troubled) and eased down into a soft nest of rugs, cushions, and a fine cotton sheet, as if she were an infant. The women left, leaving behind a pitcher of water and a finely pierced brass lamp that cast fascinating shadows on the walls. Alexandra stared at them, hoping to follow them into deep, dreamless sleep.

But again she smelled smoke, and death, and that unholiness that lurked beneath the ground here. It was the karez, she knew that now. The nomads had withdrawn, but Turpan's real enemy had laired within its very heart. After a time she rose and dressed in the clean clothing the women had left for her. Comfort here was an illusion; she preferred to rest fully clad against the moment when the illusion was shattered. For good measure, she picked up her sword, then laid the pack containing the bell and lightning-bolt emblem she had won where she could reach it. Only then did she lie down again.

Lazily she traced the pattern of light dancing over the roughly textured walls. After a time, the lamp went out and she slept.

Hasty footsteps and blazing lights invaded Alexandra's room, and she woke with a cry. In an instant, she had drawn not her sword, but the twisting dorje that symbolized the lightning.

Prince Li Shou took one step back. Father Basil was with him.

"Turpan is under attack?" she asked quickly. So this was why the plums, the grapes, and the water had tasted of blood! Outside, she heard wailing and running feet, and, over all, the sound of alarm, voices shouting orders, and the clash of weapons being lifted from stores and distributed.

None of it surprised her. What did surprise her was the presence of men and outsiders in the women's quarters. Then she heard other men's deep voices too, and she realized that the women were being evacuated to some place of safety . . . if indeed such a place existed.

"The dorje," breathed the prince. Alexandra spared it a glance as she thrust it into her belt. It glowed bluewhite.

Ibrahim awaited them in the reception room they had entered only hours before, armed guards at his back.

"The tribes?" asked Bryennius, who had his sword drawn, and looked eager for a fight.

The merchant looked distracted. "Down from the hills, under the houses . . . there is a guard on the tunnels: How could they have entered?"

There was no time to tell him, Alexandra thought in pity. He would only think that his troubles had been increased by the presence of a madwoman.

"The rest of your caravan has been guided to the ruins of the Han town outside Turpan. You'll see it. Take these letters"—he thrust dispatches into Bryennius' hands —"for my cousins in Dunhuang. Tell them to guard the Jade Gate well, and to pray for us!"

"I can't leave you like this, man!" Bryennius cried. "Suleiman Mi'sar ibn Mulhalhil called me brother. Would he abandon you?"

Haraldr stalked in through the main door, causing half the men in the room to reach for their weapons. "My prince," he saluted Bryennius, "I sent the others on ahead, then came back here. Do we stay with the rear guard?"

"Yes!" Bryennius cried, even as Ibrahim shook his head.

"Your first loyalty, Prince . . . it must be to your kinswoman, and to His Highness, with whose safety my kinsmen in Kashgar entrusted you. Though I would welcome your sword, this is not their battle."

Ibrahim doesn't expect to win, Alexandra thought. Voices screamed in the narrow streets, and outside, flames danced up, casting crazy shadows on the minaret which seemed to sway back and forth with them.

Bryennius' swarthy face flushed with shame. How easy it would be to agree that they should stay here. For a moment Alexandra wavered. Li Shou fingered his swordhilt, his mind doubtless full of heroic songs as well as honest fear. It was brave, it was noble—and it was probably useless, suicidal.

Another man burst into the room. His sword dripped blood on the fine carpets. "That was the last of the women! Now barbarians are pouring in from the ruined caravanserais."

"Go now, while you can!" Ibrahim ordered.

"Prince, Princess, let me stay," Haraldr begged. Alexandra might have expected that. If they didn't stop arguing, they'd have no choice but to stay and fight.

"You are sworn to me, Haraldr," Alexandra snapped in Greek. "And I do not release you."

His blue eyes were on her, troubled and even hurt, and his hands clasped and unclasped on his axe.

Alexandra drew her sword. "My Lord Ibrahim, I thank you for your hospitality. If . . ." She drew a breath . . . "If your Allah wills it, I shall come back to enjoy it in peace. Now: which way must we flee?"

"I will lead you," he said, and they ran from the house. Crowds swirled about them. Riders pounded by. Alexandra flung herself out of their path. She heard a scream, and something meaty fall before she could even draw her own sword. Then they were engulfed in a snarl of quick, dirty fights. By the time they could breathe again, and bind up their wounds, Ibrahim lay dead. Sprawled beside him, half in, half out of the canal, lay the Greek soldier whom Alexandra had watched eating a plum. Blood ran from his mouth and spiraled into the rushing water.

She dashed her hand across her grimy face. "Now what?" she asked. Father Basil, one of Ibrahim's men, and Prince Li Shou were deep in rapid conversation. "Ibrahim—Christ rest his soul—said that there was an entrance to the karez near his house," said the priest. "And this man claims to know the underground ways. He could bring us out to where the caravan awaits us."

If it waits for us, Alexandra thought. The idea of entering the karez was abhorrent to her. What if they confronted whatever undead thing she had envisioned lurking in its windings? She imagined that it looked like the goat she had slain, only larger and fouler. But they had no better choice.

Li Shou stared at her. "You think that there's something in the karez?"

She nodded. Then they heard the shrieks of their enemy and ran for the karez.

"Everyone flee," gasped their guide. "Take what torches you can carry. Quick!"

The tunnels were so low that even Alexandra had to bend down as they crawled into the twisting darkness. This had to be torment for Haraldr, she thought after she heard a thump, a scrape, and an oath in Norse. "Like the very bowels of the Midgard serpent!" Haraldr muttered.

"Do you want to bring the earth down upon us?" hissed their guide. He held up a torch. If the walls of the karez were reinforced, Alexandra couldn't see it. The weight of earth pressing down upon them . . . she sniffed blood again, and knew it for the lives of the men who had built this waterway, and who maintained it. She wondered if they were not afraid to enter the tunnels, and how it felt to be trapped down here, waiting for the torches to burn out or the air to go bad.

Their feet splashed in the shallow water. Around them, the torches flickered orange and yellow. Soot streaks marked other such journeys. Alexandra tensed. Where was the trouble she had sensed down here? Bryennius stopped so quickly that she walked into him. He started to straighten, then remembered his height.

"I hear something," he whispered.

Alexandra stopped too, though the guide hissed for more speed. Now she could hear it too, low and plaintive, rippling over the water.

"Someone's weeping!" Bryennius said, and set a faster pace. He stopped at the junction of two tunnels, dank from the knee-deep water.

"Which way do we go to get out?" he demanded.

The guide pointed with his chin. That was the direction from which the weeping was coming.

"A trap?" Alexandra suggested to Bryennius. Whoever, or whatever wept lay in the path they had to walk. Haraldr's comparison of the karez with a serpent was too apt: she felt like she walked in between its fanged jaws.

Bryennius splashed on ahead. As the water level dropped, the noise of his passage lessened. So did the weeping.

Torch in hand, he disappeared in a bend of the tunnel. The guide, bent almost double, followed, with Prince Li Shou and Alexandra, Father Basil, several soldiers, and—as rear guard—Haraldr hurrying after him.

A scream from the direction Bryennius had disappeared in shocked a scream from Alexandra too. Dust and larger chunks of earth dropped from the tunnel's ceiling. Steel rasped out and light flickered off the huge blade of Haraldr's axe.

"The dorje!" whispered Li Shou. "Check it!"

When she had waked, the lightning-bolt emblem had gleamed balefully. Now it merely reflected the torch-light. Footsteps neared them, and they tensed.

It was Bryennius. His sword was sheathed, he had thrown away his torch—and in his arms he carried a woman in wet, tattered robes that had once been very fine.

Their guide walked over to him and looked down at the woman he bore. "What do you think you're doing?" Bryennius asked indignantly.

"That necklace," said the guide. "A double strand of moonstones. Princesses of the Uighur royal house wear such things. We had heard that during the last battle, the youngest princess disappeared. We've been expecting the tribes to demand ransom for her."

The necklace dangled from his hands, like pearls, only more filled with light.

"Excellent, Your Highness," said a soldier, the comrade of the man who lay dead outside Ibrahim's house. "You have found a princess—or what looks like a princess. How do we know that that too isn't . . ."

The woman in Bryennius' arms suddenly struggled, glanced around at the people glaring at her, and wailed again. Bryennius murmured to her and kept on walking. "She's no demon," he insisted. "Let's keep walking."

"Look at her!" whispered Li Shou. "Her mother may

have been a kinswoman, or an Imperial concubine sent here as a gift."

But what if she were a demon?

Alexandra scurried up behind Bryennius. "That was a good question, cousin. There are simple tests for demons. Doubtless Father Basil has holy relics or water, and I have this!" She showed him the dorje.

"Holy relics from a heretic, and a heathen symbol!" Bryennius snorted.

"Bry', you sound as if she's bespelled you already. In the name of God, man, do you want me to have to think of you as an enemy?"

"Alexandra!" Real hurt quivered in his voice.

"I won't hurt her. If she's been lost down here, she deserves all the help we can give her. But let me test her."

Bryennius turned and knelt. Again he murmured wordlessly, coaxing the woman he bore, her face burrowed frantically against his shoulder, to turn around. Alexandra looked at her and stifled a gasp. Despite the tears and the terror that blotched her face, the woman was very beautiful, with the broad Uighur cheekbones, but the delicate brows and upswept eyes of the Ch'in. Her mouth was tiny and perfect.

"Give me her necklace," Alexandra ordered the guide.

"Highness, we must hurry!" he said urgently. "I must rejoin my brothers, and you and your people must flee here!"

Alexandra held out her hand for the moonstones and dangled them in the woman's face. "A few moments' test is safer than bearing an enemy in our midst." The woman reached out for the gems.

"Yes, yours," Alexandra agreed. "And who are you?" She tried in Sogdian, then in careful Ch'in that brought a gasp of relief and wonder from the other woman. Li Shou bent close, and modestly the woman turned her head, almost hiding again in the refuge of Bryennius' arms. But she answered his questions in a soft voice still heavy with tears.

"She is Siddiqa," said Li Shou. "And she was not lost

here. The nomads brought her here—and left her. She does not know why. She tried to walk out, but got lost."

Alexandra held up the dorje as she might display a dagger to a boychild. Siddiqa gasped in wonder and touched it. Father Basil's mutters of exorcism ended in an "amen."

"Do you still think she is a demon?" Bryennius demanded. He was angry, Alexandra could tell.

"Apparently not," she said. "Do you still think I am mad?"

"Hush!" commanded the guide, and they went on. From time to time, Alexandra could hear Bryennius whispering to the woman he bore.

Their torches smoked, then died to reddish glows. They lit fresh ones, which seemed to burn only half as long. Underfoot, the tunnels grew dry.

"A lesser-used portion of the karez," explained the guide. "These tunnels fill during the spring, when the thaw sends icemelt down to us."

He didn't sound wholly convinced, Alexandra thought. Here the air was heavy, thick with old dust and dryness. Tentatively, Alexandra sniffed. Old fears, and underlying them, the scent of blood. There *was* something beneath Turpan, some old chaos that the tribes knew, and feared, and sacrificed Siddiqa's ransom in order to propitiate.

Abruptly the Uighur girl wailed. They all stopped. Their torches, lit so little time ago, were already flickering to darkness.

Footsteps again, in a rhythm utterly unlike that of any man, woman, or beast Alexandra had ever seen or heard. They seemed to pad softly toward them. Alexandra felt the same dread she had known in the upper air, smelled fear in the thickening air and in their very sweat. Whatever approached was a predator and an angry one.

They quickened their pace, their breathing harsh in the silence of the bad air, Siddiqa's sobs the only other sound. Father Basil suddenly went to his knees, laid his ear to the ground.

"It's shaking," he said, and in the dying light, his face was very bleak. "An earth tremor, and here we are."

Now Alexandra too could hear the rumbling. It reminded her of the avalanche. She had escaped that. There would be no chance to escape this. Trembling, she sank to her knees. Her pack felt heavy on her back. If it came quickly, rest might be a blessing.

Then she remembered the bell she carried. It had warded off the demons, shielded herself and Prince Shou from the driving sand that had tried to smother them. She pulled the ghanta from her back, and as the rumbling shuddered underneath them and fissures opened up in the walls and ceiling of the tunnel, she rang it.

During the storm, it had seemed as if the bell cast a shell of protective light about her. Now, in the near-darkness, she saw that light, saw broken bricks, huge chunks of masonry, crash down against it, and rebound. A crack wide enough to engulf Haraldr opened beneath his feet. For a moment he stood only on light; then the crack snapped closed again, and the light held.

Gradually the quake died down into tremors, then into silence. Alexandra set down the bell. The resonances of its tone still lingered in the air.

The dust all about them set them to coughing frantically. When the spasms subsided, Alexandra struck a light and kindled her last torch.

"Lord have mercy," she whispered.

The others turned frightened faces to her. She straightened as much as she could, and held her torch aloft to show them what she had seen.

All around them, the tunnels had collapsed. They were sealed in.

Alexandra took a step forward, then recoiled. Her foot had almost fallen on the body of a man, mummified by years of exposure to the dust. He still wore fragments of armor.

"He'll have company now," Haraldr muttered. His breath came fast and shallow.

Alexandra knelt beside the body. The air would rapidly turn bad here, and then they would all go to sleep.

Was that how it was with you too? she asked the silent face. *Did you ever hope to free yourself*? She could not see whether the man had used sword or hands to try to dig himself free, or whether he had simply composed himself, hopelessly, for sleep.

"The child you saw," whispered Li Shou. "And in the desert, the youth. Princess, look at that man!"

Alexandra raised the torch, nerved herself to gaze again at the dead man. Even after all these years, his face still bore an expression of resignation. And his features . . . it took all her resolution not to crouch down and sob in despair (as the guide was doing). The withered features were those of Rudra Cakrin. On his breast lay a necklace, its chain snapped, a central medallion bearing the familiar sigil of Shambhala.

Here even he had no power, and here, apparently, he had died.

And here they were. Their eyes gleamed white and terrified in grimy faces.

Their torches burned sullenly. One hissed, then went out.

10

"No!" Haraldr growled and began to scrape at the earth with the blade of his axe.

"You'll only use up the air that much faster," Bryennius said. He had his arm about the princess they had found. Haraldr merely shrugged and went on digging. Alexandra understood. As long as he could hold an axe, he would not despair. But if even the King of Shambhala himself had despaired here, what more could she do? You can die without howling over it, she ordered herself.

Prince Shou dragged himself over to kneel beside her. He raised his smoking torch the better to view the dead man's face.

"But look!" he said softly. Siddiqa took one look, sobbed, and buried her face in Bryennius' shoulder.

"If we hadn't found her, she might have wandered out in time," Alexandra muttered. "Or gone mad. I suppose this is an easier death than despair and madness."

"What makes you think this man despaired, Princess?" asked Li Shou. "I tell you, look at his face! And now, ask yourself if, since we found him, we have heard that creature hunting on our trail again."

Alexandra stared at him, wondering what he meant. Another torch smoked and went out, leaving a reek of oily smoke.

"We have a story," Li Shou went on, "of the Purple Wall. It was said that when Ch'in Shih Huang-di began his Great Wall, in order for it to stand, ten thousand men must be buried within it. A man named Wan—which means 'ten thousand'—was found, and told of our need. Willingly, he entered the Wall—"

"That's hideous!" spat Bryennius.

"Perhaps so," said the prince, "but the Wall endures."

It was like the prince to while away the time between now and death with a sad story, Alexandra thought, and yet . . . and yet . . . the dry earth had lain but lightly on the face of the dead man. He did not look as if he had died in despair.

Haraldr scraped away at the earth, his breathing hoarse in the silence. She stopped him with a touch on his shoulder.

"A sacrificial death," she mused. She took up the medallion the dead man wore, wiped it clean of the crusted earth, then laid it back down on his breast.

The air was very thick by now. Alexandra felt drowsy. She leaned against Haraldr's back, let her senses drift. Except for the heat and smells, it was like being entombed in the snow again. Only she was not alone. It was very still. Only one torch burned now, and it too was beginning to smolder.

Father Basil crouched beside the corpse. Very gently he traced the sign of the cross on its brow. "We may as well prepare ourselves," he said.

Suddenly the last torch kindled and flared first orange, then yellow, then a clear, pure white.

"Air!" she cried and tensed, sniffing for the source of the tiny breeze that had fed the torch. There it was, cool, and damp. On her hands and knees she tracked it, scratching at the dried, tumbled earth until Haraldr shouldered her aside and begin to dig. A lump of rock-hard earth the size of a man's head fell forward and splashed.

"Allah the Merciful and Lovingkind! There's another tunnel beyond there!" cried their guide, who joined Haraldr at the digging. They panted in the still-foul air, but rapidly, the hole widened until Haraldr forced his massive shoulders through. Alexandra could hear him swear as he disappeared into that other tunnel. His face, sweaty and soot-dark, showed at the opening, and he grinned at them.

"It looks clear," he announced. "I'll help you through. First you, my princess." Though Alexandra gestured to Bryennius to hand Siddiqa through first, the tiny girl resisted.

"Perhaps if I do go first, it will reassure her," she said. As she clambered through, Haraldr's rough grasp on her wrists kept her from panicking. "Bryennius, push her through to me. No? Then you come through, and she'll join you."

One by one, they struggled through the opening. Even though air in the new tunnel was dank and stale, it went to their heads like Turpan's strongest wine. Even Li Shou laughed a little wildly with relief.

The guide rose to his knees, and studied the tunnel. After a long pause, he announced, "Now I can get us out."

"Wait, oh, wait!" Alexandra cried. In Kashgar, she had won the lightning bolt, and in the desert, the bell that had shielded them when the earth trembled. If the King of Shambhala indeed protected her, he would not begrudge her his sigil, and she dared not leave it behind. Before anyone could stop her, she scrambled back into the cave they had left.

The body of Rudra Cakrin was gone, the medallion with it. In its place lay a moonstone the size of a bird's egg. Sword, scepter, bell, gem, flowers, and crown, the abbot had told her, were given to those who walked the Diamond Path. Here beyond all hope was the gem.

Earth spattered down on her brow from the karez' ruined ceiling. Thrusting the gem into her clothing, she flung herself toward the new tunnel, ignoring painful scrapes as her companions pulled her free just as chunks of rock-hard earth began to fall upon her legs. "Idiot!" spat Bryennius, as they fled down the tunnel, half dragging her in their eagerness to be far from a new cave-in.

Finally, when they crouched panting against the rough wall, Alexandra brought out the moonstone. It caught the torchlight, transmuting it to blue and white fire.

"He was gone," she told the prince and the priest. "But I will swear to you by all that is holy—in any of our faiths—that he left this gem for me."

Father Basil smiled gently, though the sweat and dirt on his face made it a grimace. "Since you like the tales of the West, Highness, remind me to tell you one day of the parable of a man who gave all he possessed for a pearl of great price."

"There!" whispered their guide. "We're almost outside."

He waved his arms frantically for quiet in case enemies, and not their own caravan, awaited them. They tried to walk slowly, lest the splashing of their boots in the shallow water alert guards up ahead. Now Alexandra could see starlight reflected in the tiny stream that fed into the karez.

They dragged themselves up out of the karez and sprawled on the earth, drawing great breaths of the fresh air, which was sweet, with the wild cleanliness of the sand, into their lungs. The night seemed full of music. Alexandra forced herself to rise, accompanying the guard to a tiny rise from which she could see Turpan, from here only a tiny cluster of buildings from which reddish smoke rose in the dry air.

Then the guide turned and pointed. "There!" he whispered. If Alexandra squinted, she could just barely see ruins. Moving along the ghostly, crumbling ways of the old town was a file of men, horses, and camels. "You must go now!" he ordered.

"Come with us," she said, catching at his arm and drawing him back down toward the others. She motioned them in the direction of the waiting caravan.

He pulled away, and she remembered he was Muslim and would not suffer her to touch him. But he smiled at her almost tenderly. "I must return to defend my home," he said.

The man stared at all of them as if trying to remember them for always. Finally, he bowed deeply to the Princess Siddiqa.

"Great lady," he said. "If it is the will of Allah, we shall drive our enemies back once more. But go quickly now, before they see you. If you travel till the sun is high, they cannot catch you."

Then he was gone, a tiny figure running down from the hills, back into the burning oasis. A shower of sparks exploded up from a house as its wood-beamed roof collapsed.

Bryennius was swearing without pause or originality. When the words "Greek fire" mingled with the oaths, Alexandra interrupted. "That would only have helped them destroy their town. And in the end, we might have been taken or killed. Come on. You heard what . . . do you know, Bryennius, he never gave us his name?"

In the end, they were nearly spitted by their own guards, who had spent hours in the ruins watching the fight for Turpan, never knowing when they too might be attacked, or if they would ever see the people for whom they waited. Alexandra hated to think how close the caravan must have come to abandoning them.

"North to Hami?" asked one of the headmen. The northern route might be longer, but it spared them the necessity of crossing the White Dragon Dunes. They were said to be as bad as the Takla Makan, filled not with demons but with ghosts.

"No!" commanded Li Shou. "Prince Bryennius, Princess, this one humbly begs your pardon, but we must go to Dunhuang as quickly as we can and warn the people there."

The headman glanced at Bryennius, who shrugged and looked at Alexandra. "Dunhuang, then." A groom led her horse up, then knelt to help her into the saddle.

"I'll ride double with the Princess Siddiqa," Bryennius said. He mounted, then gestured for Haraldr to lift her to his saddle. Quiet had fallen over Turpan. The beasts made no sound. Even the jangling of their harnesses seemed muffled.

For hours they rode out of the Land of Fire. The sky paled, then kindled as the sun rose, forcing them first to a walk, then to a rest stop they had wished to delay for hours longer. It was harsher than raiding nomads and infinitely more powerful. And unlike the power trapped in the karez, the sun would follow them. Bryennius nearly fell out of his saddle, then helped the Uighur girl slide down into his arms.

Alexandra, clinging to her own horse until her knees steadied beneath her, watched the two of them. "She is too weak for the journey," Haraldr muttered for only her to hear. "If she cannot ride alone, she could slow us all."

But the desert air carried his words to Bryennius and the girl. Even as she drank from the skin he held for her, she turned and looked up. Worship shone in her bruised face.

"Don't worry," Bryennius promised them. "She will ride, and she'll ride alone. She won't fail you—because she won't fail me."

Father Basil reached for his cross and remembered once again that he had given it to the Princess Alexandra. She rode ahead of him, near Prince Li Shou, as she so often did these days. Typically, he was talking and she was listening, hunched forward in the saddle, her head down. Bryennius rode by, inspecting the caravan yet again. He tossed an off-hand salute to his cousin, then went to speak to his Uighur princess. Her Highness professed to find their devotion nauseating, though she conceded that falling in love had helped him learn Ch'in, in order to speak to Siddiqa.

At least it could coax a smile from her, the Nestorian thought. What was happening to his Greeks? Her cousin had transformed himself from a boy, entranced with helping his elder cousin (much the master spirit of the two, Basil would have said) escape from her convent in order to rescue an exotic priest—himself—and embark upon adventures, into a formidable man. But if travel and hardship had toughened him, Alexandra seemed to have lost the confidence he had gained. She never rode alone, as if she feared that the singing sands might whisper to her of despair and madness.

A hot wind fluttered a veil of pallid sand from the sharp spine of the nearest dune. It whispered by, almost singing of the many merchants, princes, monks, and warriors who had passed by.

"What will it tell me I must learn now—or lose?" Her Highness had asked. Her eyes were wide, like those of a terrified colt. "I travel laden with heathen amulets that for my soul's sake, I should not keep, though, for my soul's sake, I dare not discard them. Each time I look at them, they remind me that I am being put through tests for some purpose that isn't mine. I am a princess. I am trying to find . . . very well, then . . . to steal silkworms for my City. Isn't that enough?"

What was Father Basil to tell her? That stealing silkworms might be the least of her ordeals was probably his fault. If she had never seen him, never seen the chapel devoted to necromancy in her convent, she would never have come this far, and certainly never brought herself to the ageless and vengeful attention of the dark powers. So he had given her the cross he had treasured since leaving Nisibis, where he had studied.

He had traveled up and down Persia, Pasargadai, Persepolis, Susa, Samarkand, and the places in between. It had never been enough. Inexorably he was drawn to the West, to the citadel of so-called Orthodoxy that had exiled his church, Byzantium with its harbors, its domed Church to Hagia Sophia, or Holy Wisdom, its armies that continued the thousand-year-long war with Persia that Hellenes and Macedonians had begun. He had thought to rest after seeing Byzantium, yet here he was, companion to scions of the Greek Imperial House that was his land and faith's great enemy.

At least, she had accepted his cross. Granted, she had stared at it a long moment. That had hurt; almost, he wished he were one of the black-robed Orthodox priests in their tall caps who stalked Byzantium and drew its wealth into their eager hands. Would she have listened to one of them? He doubted it. Finding, and saving him had cost her her faith, her family, and her City. The cross was but small recompense.

Or, Basil thought, as he watched her turn her horse away from the Ch'in prince and catch up with her cousin, the cross was precisely her problem. When had it reached a crisis? Basil's sharp wits, trained in theology at Nisibis and in ancient Persian culture, could pinpoint the moment when she realized that the King of Shambhala's sacrificial death in the karez, the man Wan's willingness to be immured in the Ch'in Great Wall, and Christ's death on the Cross were all types of the same thing. All Ways were indeed the same. Failure in any one of the forces of order—call them faiths —would damn her as surely as failure in the Way to which she had been bred.

They had argued about that halfway across Asia, and now she had the demonstration of it thrust into her face. If she was being tested by some power (as indeed it looked), it appeared to be done treating her gently.

Father Basil shuddered to think of what ruthless mystery might regard an avalanche, battles, sandstorms, and adventitious demons as "gentle testing."

Alexandra had been too well schooled in Aristotle to deny the logic of her situation, but it terrified her. Like the man who had gazed into a chasm and stood paralyzed, she had confronted damnation too closely, and too often to look away. Her terror could not have distressed the Persian priest more had he been her actual father rather than a spiritual father whom she had to reject. She needed a retreat, Basil thought. Or rest in a cool, shady place, not the endless monotony of the White Dragon Dunes and their hot-breathed, ghostly songs.

Li Shou gestured him up to ride beside him. Father Basil bowed low in the saddle. "This one would be honored," he said, though "curious" was, as always, the better word.

As he guessed, the prince from Ch'ang-an wished to discuss Bryennius and Alexandra, to speculate on why they came to Ch'in, and what they might do once they arrived.

Father Basil glanced sidelong at the prince, a plump little man with the shrewd dark Persian eyes evaluating a taller, thinner man whose eyes were weary but equally canny. This was not conversation, but a combat between heirs to ancient traditions in which cynicism, evasion, and erudition were the weapons each used and appreciated. Compared to them (and regardless of their protests of master philosophers in Athens, Rome, Byzantium, and Alexandria) his Greeks were children who careered through cultures deeper than they dared permit themselves to comprehend.

"You are aware," murmured the prince, "that foreigners with Ch'in wives or concubines may not remove them from the Middle Kingdom."

What would Prince Bryennius do? Father Basil wondered. He doubted that the Greek would leave the girl behind, assuming they escaped with the silkworms. In that case, he would probably steal her too. But that was not a possibility to discuss with a member of the ruling Ch'in dynasty.

"Has His Highness thought what might be done?" Father Basil asked, almost rudely direct.

"The prince might well take up arms for the Son of Heaven. He would not be the first prince of the Hu-barbarians to seek shelter in Ch'ang-an."

A fine response, and one that punished Father Basil for his rudeness. Not long ago, perhaps just a century, an exiled son of the deposed King Yazgerd had claimed asylum in Ch'in as a client prince. Such men were given handsome uniforms, titles, and places at court: such things as Bryennius might have had if his own Empire had not feared him.

Father Basil turned to look the prince in the eye. He had suspected that the prince too regarded the cousins as "his Greeks," Bryennius to be given a future at court, Alexandra a place as his favored wife or concubine. The attraction had been clear from their meeting in Kashgar. The prince had a passion for the exotic. If Alexandra and Bryennius could be enticed to remain in Ch'ang-an, he would have not only them but their guards and servants to protect him from weariness for the rest of his life. It was a possible future, if it were not for Alexandra's vow to steal silkworms and return to Byzantium.

"This one," he began mendaciously, "dares to inform His Imperial Highness that the princess has been a nun and is still under vows."

"Yang Kuei-Fei was a nun, a Buddhist nun. Yet she put off her robes and became the treasure of the Son of Heaven."

Father Basil raised an eyebrow. Actually to remind the prince that the Imperial concubine had died in a revolution would have been too blatant.

"I am not the Son of Heaven. Yet, when we arrive in Dunhuang, I shall commission a cave in honor of my safe return from my travels, and in the hope . . ." Amazingly, the prince leaned forward on his saddle just

as Alexandra had. Once again, Father Basil braced
himself to hear a confession. "Why should she not stay?
What is there for her in her home, which sent her away?
She . . . both of them . . . deserve better than life among
the barbarians."

"Is that not up to your lords of karma?" asked the
priest mildly.

"She too is as bound by the Wheel as if she had been
born Buddhist rather than . . ." He gestured at the
impossibility, as he saw it, of comprehending barbarian
cults. "I will *make* them stay. I will make them want to."
For an instant, desire blazed up in those knowledgeable,
tired dark eyes.

Then, as if that instant of revelation had not occurred,
Imperial Prince Li Shou waved his hand gracefully at a
blur on the horizon. It looked close, but the desert air
was so clear that distance itself became an illusion.

"Dunhuang," he said. "If there are no storms, we will
reach it in three days. I have been telling Her Highness
about the caves. She has told me that in Fu-lin—you
would call it Hrum?"

"Rome."

"Your own faith used to meet in such caves. Is that
true?"

The discussion of catacombs lasted until Alexandra
rode by again, this time with a group of men-at-arms.
The prince's eyes followed her. And, Father Basil noted,
the big man who led the Varangian Guard observed it.

From desert, they rode into the green of an oasis, from
solitude into the paths of caravans starting the journey
out across the singing sand. At least, now, they were
warned; they might survive. Even Father Basil felt himself intimidated by the crowds of Ch'in, Uighurs, Persians, Tibetans, and Kashmiri, and their pack trains.
During the drastic strike direct to Dunhuang, he had
forgotten that people other than those in his own caravan existed. Then he was caught up in the exchange of
news, of congratulations or prayers for a safe journey, or

laments for caravans that had disappeared through the Jade Gate, never to be heard from again.

"All travelers enter Ch'in by the Jade Gate," he overheard the prince explaining to Alexandra. She listened intently. A trap, the Nestorian knew she was thinking.

"One would have to pass through the Jade Gate to go south too?" she asked. Shambhala, so they had been told, lay in the mountains to the south and west.

"I promise, if you wish to search out Shambhala, I shall come with you," the prince said, boldly dropping the respectful address of "this person." He leaned forward, and would have taken Alexandra's hand even out in the crowded, dusty road, had Bryennius and the guides not interrupted with shouts that an inn had been found.

Much later Father Basil was summoned to Alexandra's rooms, where he found her resting, bathed and fed, but very tired.

"I should return this," she said and held out his cross. He took it up, kissed it, then returned it.

"If it gives you comfort, keep it," he said. He sat before being invited, feeling more discouraged than he had since that time when his curiosity outran his luck in Byzantium and he found himself a prisoner awaiting sacrifice by a woman who had turned to the Dark.

"What troubles you?" she asked. "I know that you have heard all the gossip in the town by now."

"The followers of Mani have been expelled from Ch'ang-an," he told her.

"But your monastery there—you told me it was an Imperial foundation."

"Not as Byzantium knows such. One Emperor was its patron; another may turn his face away. There have been signs . . ." Father Basil bowed his head. Signs indeed: Messages came and went from Dunhuang, and he had listened well. All over Ch'in were riots. Christians, Jews, and Muslims were set upon and their property destroyed. The rumors were even worse than the messages.

He should not have come here, though he had dreamed all his life of the trip east, of seeing with his own eyes the stele that declared that all faiths were aspects of the same truth.

"This may make our task more difficult," Alexandra mused. "Your people will be afraid."

"Lady, as in Kashgar, they will help when they can."

He knew it might not be enough. They sat silently, and then, summoning good humor, Alexandra shook herself. "Prince Shou tells me that the ladies of the Imperial palace tend the silk. That might be another possibility —if I could enter the palace . . ."

"As ambassador, or as concubine?" snapped the priest.

"As God wills," Alexandra said.

"Do you believe that?"

"You have no idea how hard I try." She sighed, and might have said more had not one of Prince Shou's servants begged entrance, and their company at dinner.

"I vowed to give a cave to the Buddha," the prince had said. "Will you ride with me to the caves? They are thirty-six *li*—about twelve of your miles—" he explained to Alexandra, "to the southwest."

The prince had spared no effort to woo her, Father Basil thought. He himself had planned to gather what news he might of Nestorian congregations. But the lure of the caves of Dunhuang was too strong. Hundreds of years of carving and painting had transformed a mile-long ridge into a collection of shrines. He had dreamed about it for years, longed to see it as he had longed to see Samarkand, Persepolis, Byzantium, and Ch'ang-an himself. Gossip and fear would have to wait.

They rode out long before dawn. Finally crimson glory warmed their backs, and cast long shadows before them. Though they rode into a green valley, the singing sand lay piled up outside it in huge dunes. The air was very pure, moist to their throats after the months of desert.

Now they could see the mass of rock that held the fabulous caves. Father Basil suppressed an urge to clap heels to the sides of his horse, and glanced over to see Bryennius reining in too. Then the sun rose farther, and abruptly, splendor cascaded down the cliff face.

The cliffs were hung with immense banners of orange and gold and crimson silk so fine that they quivered from their own weight despite the stillness of the air. Father Basil gasped in wonder and a little fear. Alexandra laughed a little mischievously. "Why do you cry out, Father? Surely, you're not afraid?"

"Like the legions of Rome the first time they met the Parthians and recoiled from their silken flags?" he asked, equally mischievous. She threw up a hand, conceding the point.

Then the banners blew aside, and they could see the rock face. It was broken up into hundreds of caves, the entry to each adorned with carving, some intricate, some monumental. Niches held stone Buddhas seated in eternal meditation; there was even one enormous pagoda of seven stories. All the caves appeared to be linked by wooden platforms and ladders. A procession of monks, their arms laden with scrolls and banners, filed into one ground-level cave and came out, empty-handed.

They dismounted and led their horses toward the great ledge as if it were irreverent to ride farther. "Put off thy shoes from thy feet," thought Father Basil, "for the place whereon thou standest is holy ground." About him, grooms and princes alike muttered prayers. Tension drained from him as the sanctity and peace that quivered in the air here embraced him. He sighed, content to see that his Greeks were smiling at one another again, and that Alexandra seemed relaxed. Surely the chaos that pursued her could not penetrate Dunhuang.

They entered the nearest cave, a splendor of crimson and ochre and gold. Leaving chanting, kneeling attendants behind, they walked into the next cave, a wondrous forest of cool greens and indigos. Lifesize statues of

Bodhisattvas and warriors attended a figure seated in a posture of meditation. Its face was broad, and a gem shone in the center of its divinely serene brow.

"Can we see them all?" Alexandra asked Li Shou, leaning forward, her hand almost touching his sleeve.

"We shall try," he said and smiled at her.

Their footsteps echoed as they entered the next cave, painted in red and gold in patterns that ran from floor to ceiling. The cave was immense, dominated by a sleeping Buddha fully thirty feet long.

Alexandra gasped, then turned toward Bryennius. "Can you imagine the reaction of the old iconoclasts?"

He began to chuckle, then remembered that in a manner of speaking, he stood in a great church, and stopped himself guiltily. "They would have died of overwork," he said and moved aside to join his Uighur princess, who studied the wall paintings, her face rapt.

"Alexandra," her cousin called softly. She and Li Shou went over to join them.

"The figure is Avalokitesvara, the comforter, seated in a mandala. Below it are painted the figures of the donors," explained the prince. "Soon I will have my own portrait on such a wall."

"Surely though, this is not the style of Ch'in?" Father Basil ventured. He had seen such figures brought out of Hind, with their graceful, swaying bodies, and many arms.

"No. Here we call the Comforter Kuan-yin instead. And we see her as female. My cave will be consecrated to Kuan-yin," said the prince.

A priest came to his side, and drew him away into low-voiced conversation. An attendant also joined them. Several times, strings of cash chinked persuasively. Father Basil suppressed a chuckle. In every country, shrines—or their keepers—were much alike.

Gradually they separated, to drift from cave to cave. Father Basil found Haraldr staring at an immense wall painting broken into several registers. He followed the Varangian's gaze away from the many-headed gods and their consorts locked in ferocious and intricate embrace to the great central motif. Two circles of snow mountains, arrayed in the form of a lotus, and, at its heart, a glistening city and a great king. Warrior and priest nodded to one another.

"I hope she misses this one," Haraldr told Father Basil in a voice that sounded as though he doubted she would. Behind them was a scurry and a susurrus of whispers.

"Where is she?" Haraldr hissed at him.

"She wandered off," the priest admitted.

"Then we look for her!" The Varangian glared, then evidently decided not to waste time pounding him into the rock before he searched for his princess—a decision for which Father Basil was devoutly grateful.

They found her, finally, in a cave where the dominant color was the rich blue of pacific manifestations. Tired of wandering, she had dropped to her knees before a statue of a woman with a gentle face, carved and painted to look like a lady of Ch'in.

"Kuan-yin," Father Basil told the Varangian. "A sort of representation of peace and comfort."

"Like Freya!" Haraldr nodded in understanding.

Basil grimaced. Then he realized that while Haraldr might see the statue as a goddess, and he only a representation of a fascinatingly alien faith, the princess must be seeing it as an icon of the Blessed Virgin who guarded her City. For the first time in weeks her face was calm, her breathing slow and regular.

He heard footsteps outside the cavern and would have barred entry, if the newcomers hadn't been Li Shou and an old man carrying a handful of brushes. So the prince had found his artist, had he? Seeing Alexandra, the prince stopped short and gestured to the artist, who crouched behind a statue and began to sketch with rapid brush strokes.

Basil drifted over to watch him work. More quickly than he would have imagined, drawn in thin, nervous brush strokes, the figure of Kuan-yin began to appear on the paper. Then the artist paused. He looked from the statue he copied to the woman who knelt before it. Muttering under his breath, he picked up a brush and started work on the figure's face.

The mouth was small, the lips narrower than those on the statue. At the same time, the nose in the sketch was more determined. Arched brows, then eyes that were round rather than slanted. Still, Basil could recognize Princess Alexandra. The entire composition took on the cast of the paintings of the Blessed Virgin that Father Basil had seen in Byzantium, and yet, unmistakably, it was a Buddhist holy picture. In centuries to come, pilgrims to Dunhuang would make their prayers to an icon of the Virgin in her incarnation as Kuan-yin. Though this was probably blasphemy, Basil felt no urge to protest. Kuan-yin, or the Blessed Virgin whom the Greeks called Theotokos, Bearer of God—if, in this far-off place, she had the face of a woman whom a prince delighted to honor, why should that offend anyone?

The light had begun to fade in the cave when the artist finally rose. Still, Alexandra sat motionless. The man stared at her one last time, then bowed almost reverently. The movement broke her concentration. Sighing, she stirred from her trance of contemplation. Still kneeling, she reached into her belt pouch and drew out two things: Basil's cross and the moonstone she had taken from the karez at Turpan. She looked at the statue of Kuan-yin once again, then at the artist's drawing, startled. "She *is* the Mother of God. I don't suppose the form matters."

Then she handed him back his cross. "It appears that from now on, I shall be just as heretical as you, my friend." But she smiled as she said it, and her eyes were kind.

11

A crumbling rampart rose out of the grit, wound along their path for a time, then sank back into the earth. Finally Li Shou stopped beside one ruin, taller than most. It looked like a watchtower, but for what fort?

"'I brought order to the mass of beings and put to the test deeds and realities: each thing has the name that fits it,'" Prince Li Shou quoted.

Alexandra shuddered, as she did each time he repeated that saying of Ch'in Shih Huang-di, the ancient Emperor who had forced his name on all Ch'in. His hand lay even on the desert between Dunhuang and Jiayuguan. It was called the Land of Ghosts. After the safety and sanctity of Dunhuang, she found its starkness doubly unsettling.

The ruins they passed now were part of the Purple Wall, the immense bulwark begun by the ruthless old First Emperor. Each subsequent dynasty had added to it.

167

Now Ch'in was crossed by fortifications, some of rammed earth, some of bricks or dressed stone, many crumbling. Surely, if one made the journey, as unorthodox philosphers said one might, to the sphere of the moon, one could see those dusty walls snaking across the land.

Li Shou pointed to the ruined tower. "I like to imagine," he said, "that the signal braziers still remain up there. Smoke by day; fire by night. One column of smoke if a force of one hundred approaches by day. Two columns of flame by night for an invading army of five hundred."

What was the warning against silk thieves? Only Father Basil's misappropriation of Exodus about pillars of cloud and pillars of fire protected Alexandra from blurting out the question.

The farther they traveled into Ch'in, the more anxious she became. She had always heard that fugitives fought an insane desire to give themselves up. She could believe it now. Those walls, and the Emperor who had ordered them built, and given names to all things, awed her. Such total control and dedication over thousands of years, combined with the immensity of the lands she crossed —it was an act of hubris to even try to steal Ch'in silkworms. She would be caught, tortured till she begged to die in this land barriered by mountains and deserts, with never a glimpse of sea. Until she left the Golden Horn and the Middle Sea, she did not know how much she would miss them. The land and her conscience weighed her down, and she longed for water.

From desert, Li Shou led them into a land of blowing yellowish soil, where the farmland was carved into terraces centuries old, and the green crops grew in dark stripes by the rim of each level. Alexandra studied the people: bronzed, muscled, dressed in shabby blue. They did not dare to study her in return.

Her longing for the sea was satisfied then, in some part, by the immense Huang He river, yellow in color, half mud in texture. Along with innumerable pigs, countless peasants, and a plethora of officials (all of whom treated Li Shou with exaggerated deference), they had boarded a boat for the journey past dikes and fields and around sandbars to Ch'ang-an. Not even Haraldr had seen such a river on the deadly passage south from Kiev to Byzantium. By the time they disembarked, she no longer missed the sea. She had had enough of water, and far too much of the prostrations called kowtows, sidelong glances, and references to the Hu princess.

At each stop, there had been a flurry of runners, rumors, and dispatches. A new Son of Heaven held the Dragon Throne, a devout follower of the Way, or Tao. While the prince knew very little of Wu Tsung, *ten thousand years to the Son of Heaven!* he had cried repeatedly. But he had been more melancholy than usual. He had spent years collecting texts of all faiths to bring them back to Ch'in. Alexandra assumed he had expected that the Emperor would reward him. Now it seemed as if all his labor might be for naught. He rode silently, downcast until he remembered the many Taoist charms and alchemical texts in his baggage. Perhaps they even included the secret of the elixir of life. Alexandra found it strange to be reminded of courts and religious quarrels, so much like home, but so far away.

Still, Li Shou took pride in the First Emperor, who had once punished a mountain by hacking it away. There was a ruthlessness an excess in this land—both in itself and what its people made—that reduced Byzantium's plots to the contrivances of a moment. If the idea weren't disloyal, Alexandra might have thought that Ch'in made the Empire of the Romans seem new and petty.

"Mount Li, the First Emperor's tomb, lies east of Ch'ang-an," the prince said. "It was built to house him and his troops and his court forever. They say that he watches, and if danger comes to Ch'in, he will waken and send his armies . . ."

Li Shou was watching her too closely for her to dare shiver. "What land is this?" she asked quickly. The old man was dead; it would take a miracle to make him rise; and there were no miracles in this land.

"We are passing the graves of the T'ang emperors," he said.

"A necropolis?" Bryennius asked. He had known soldiers from the regiments stationed in Egypt, who had told how that country enshrined its dead.

"No." Surprisingly, Haraldr broke into the conversation. Li Shou raised a silvered eyebrow. "Those are barrows." Touching his amulet, the guard gestured at the mounds which rose on either side of their path, gently sloping hills with trees upon them. It was easy to think of them as man-made.

From time to time, they rode past rows of statues, only slightly less animated than the stolid workers who bent and planted, bent and pulled, in field after field. The escort wished on them by officials in Lanzhou started up a marching song that sounded, Alexandra's people complained, like the wailing of cats. And still Li Shou spoke on and on, explaining as if he spoke to her alone. At times he described his home, at times the texts he carried. They taught ways of power that one adept might study, but that required two adepts for mastery. His eyes burned, and his voice was resonant.

Alexandra thought she understood. The prince had planned a more triumphant homecoming. A student of the exotic and the strange in a culture that valued both, he had gone out to collect wonders, and returned—to a city and a Son of Heaven that might not want them. Still, he had to share with someone, and she was there.

Are we liabilities to him now? she wondered. *Strange, then, that he seeks our company. It cannot be simple gratitude for his life.*

"You must pardon me," she broke into his flow of explanations, and turned hastily. She heard him chuckle, and she greeted Father Basil's approach with relief. Typically, he had strayed from their road.

"My princess!" cried the Nestorian. "Up ahead!"

It looked like a riot, Alexandra thought. Around the

next mound or two, mounted soldiers and peasants armed with heavy mattocks belabored what seemed to be other peasants. Why? They looked no different from their assailants.

"They're Christians, Nestorians like me," cried the Persian priest. "Oh, I heard the rumors along our route, I was afraid . . ." A mounted man with a pike sent an old man sprawling; he did not move after he had fallen.

"For the love of God, can't we stop this?" he begged, eyes going from her and Bryennius to Li Shou and his newly acquired guards. Some of them were bound to be spies; God knows, she'd arrange it that way.

The prince's face went grim. He turned in his saddle, gestured for baggage and noncombatants—concubines, clerks, and the precious Ferghana horses needed to woo the court—to be led out of the way.

One of the Varangians laid a hand on Alexandra's horse's bridle. She shook her head. "Use the flat of your sword only, my princess." She hated to think what would happen if the first thing the Greeks did in Ch'in was kill someone.

Now they could hear screams of pain and triumph and, over them, what sounded like desperate prayers. Several Nestorian women had fallen to their knees. One huddled over the infant in her arms till she was pushed over.

"Hai!" Alexandra cried and spurred after the men. She grinned as she toppled the man who had struck the cowering mother with a shrewd blow to his hindquarters. A lucky blow, she realized in the next instant as mattocks and pikes were raised against her. This was cavalry drill; she had no experience at it. She had not even been able to stay on her horse for long at Kashgar. She hung on desperately and swung her sword, wincing with each blow lest she break the ancient blade.

A shriek whirled her in the saddle. Siddiqa? What was Bryennius' sweetheart doing out here? she thought. Where was she? Turning to check on the Uighur girl's welfare saved her life. A soldier on horseback rode at her, his pike whistling from the speed with which he brought it down. It would have cracked her skull like a Turpan melon if she had not veered to the side. Even as it was, Alexandra heard a roar of fury and some Norse oaths, a rush of wind that struck red fire into her brain, a roaring and dizziness, and then nothing at all.

The wheat smelled fresh and sweet. Twilight was drifting down, and the heavy heads of grain were damp. She brought a hand up to her aching head, then looked at the blood that had oozed onto her fingers. She leaned over and retched. Near her a man sprawled face down, crushing the grain. If he could be waked, perhaps he could help her. She tried to rise to her feet, made it to her knees, and gave up. But when she crawled over to the sleeping man and pushed at him to turn him over, the wound that had destroyed his face made her gag. If there had been anything left in her belly, she would have brought it up. The flies were clustering. She brushed them from the cuts on her own head and crawled away.

She . . . who was she? This was not her home: She knew that much. Slowly, she sat up and gazed around. The field was trampled, and other people lay nearby. Probably dead, she concluded, and praised herself for her cleverness. There were not that many women with head wounds who could think so clearly. Now, she must think of what to do next.

She was alone. This did not seem reasonable. She must have come here with other people, but where were they? She couldn't bring herself to investigate those who lay in the field. Perhaps there were others. But the grain rose higher than her head as she sat. Painstakingly, she began to crawl again. She saw horse dung, and dragged herself toward the swath that the horse had stamped in the field. It was easier to crawl when the grain was smoothed down. Dark feet rose on either side of her. Statues, she remembered now. They had ridden through an army of statues that appeared to guard these small hills. She laid bloody hands on the base, then the feet, then the robed knees, of one statue. It seemed to sway as if alive and protesting at this treatment. She murmured an apology, then levered herself up to stare into the face of some long-dead minister.

"I am lost, sir," she whispered. "I do not remember my name. Can you help me?" There was no answer. No wonder: She was speaking in Greek. No one but she spoke Greek—except the people she had lost.

The wind stirred the wheat. It sounded like a voice. She turned in its direction, in the direction of the next statue, and the one after that, like wise courtiers ushering her toward their ruler. Up ahead lay a gentle, breast-shaped hill. The grass upon it looked soft. If she climbed up there, she would see other people. Her people . . . they would see her, and find her. Perhaps they would give her back her name.

The empty scabbard at her worn belt almost tripped her. She must have had a sword too. So much; and now she had lost it all—sword, and horse, and name. She wept a little for the unfairness of it, and staggered from statue to statue, embracing each drunkenly in its turn, until she reached the mound, swayed, and sank down grateful for the rest. The grass was as soft as she had hoped, and she rested her aching head upon it. The night wind seemed to croon to her. Suddenly the fact that she was lost seemed less terrible than her thirsts for water and for sleep. She lashed her head from side to side, feverish, seeking comfort. It made her dizzy.

Curious; she had not seen that freshet rippling through the fragrant grass before. She lowered her face into it with joy. First, a good, long drink. Then, she would bathe her head. That might clear it. Only she was so very sleepy . . .

Bryennius pounded his fist against the nearest statue, then swore at the pain. Near him, two wounded men groaned with slightly more justification.

"Who saw her last?" he demanded. Alexandra's horse galloping back toward the herd it knew, its jaws dripping

froth, its eyes rolling, had been the first indication that
she had come to grief. Damn her! What made her think
she could pretend to be a cavalry officer?

"Why didn't you stop her?" he shouted at the sunset.
Father Basil rose from his knees and made one last sign
over the Nestorians slain in the sudden attack. The
others crouched down, heads knocking the earth, before
Li Shou. The prince gestured to Father Basil. Bryennius
could not understand his rapid, urgent words, but the
people spread out over the field, searching. One cried out
and came running up, awkwardly holding a sword.

Bryennius recognized it instantly. Alexandra had used
that blade in Kashgar.

"She is so little," Haraldr muttered. Small and slender, she would leave little mark in the grain.

"It's getting dark. We can't leave her alone, hurt . . ."
Byrennius' voice caught. Siddiqa's gentle hands touched
his arm, reached for his hand, scratched from where a
mattock had grazed it. She began to bind it with a
fragrant silk scarf, and he smiled down at her.

"That way," she whispered, pointing and speaking
slowly.

"*You* saw Alexandra?" He grasped her fragile shoulders and almost shook her. Siddiqa met his eyes
staunchly.

"A man . . . a soldier with a . . . a pike," she explained slowly, so that he would understand, "he wanted
to strike her . . . I scream, a . . . ar . . . your cousin, she
turn, fall. Hit, but not hit hard. I think . . . that she live.
We find her."

Heedless of the men about them, Bryennius gave the
Uighur a smacking kiss. "You go . . . be safe," he said,
and pushed her back toward the baggage train.

"Siddiqa says she saw her fall over there!" Bryennius
cried to Li Shou and the Varangians. The men oriented
themselves by the rows of statues and started an orderly
search.

The sky had darkened to Imperial purple when they
reported back in without his cousin.

"Torches," Bryennius said. His voice was a ragged ghost of itself. "I'll search all night."

"I'm with you, Prince," said Haraldr.

Li Shou shook his head, but did not otherwise protest. It was probably sacrilege to camp in this field of tombs, but Bryennius was beyond caring.

They began to unload supplies. "Not there," the T'ang prince ordered, and pointed toward one mound flanked with lions, winged horses, officials, and foreign envoys. "Liang Shan, where Wu Tse-Tien is buried. It's an inauspicious place."

Unlucky? The sooner they made camp, the sooner they could continue the search. Bryennius was in no mood for superstition.

"Wu Tse-Tien . . . Empress." Siddiqa was at his side again. "Very bad."

"Listen to the princess," said Li Shou. "The woman buried in that tomb deposed an Empress, then the Son of Heaven himself. Do you understand? She *made* herself the Son of Heaven, wore his robes, occupied the Dragon Throne for forty-five years. In that time, she exiled, slew . . . at least three royal heirs were sent the silken cord."

That was, Bryennius knew, the order to commit suicide and spare oneself disgrace of public execution. A female Nero, then. Byzantium had known a few women like that. Half a century ago, Irene had blinded her own son; and now, the Basileus' own aunt would kill him and his heir—and Bry', and Alexandra—if she got the chance again; she had nearly succeeded at least once with all of them. Bryennius made no further objection to their shifting camp.

But he could not take his eyes from Liang Shan either. Something about the tumulus drew him. The torches were kindled and cast long shadows. He mounted and gestured for one to be handed up to him. To his astonishment, Siddiqa bore it to him. "You . . . bring her back," she said, and her eyes were full of tears. He had not realized that the girl cared about his cousin.

Hoofs thundered past him, and he shouted for
Haraldr to wait, then cursed again, and rode toward the
hill more slowly. He reined in and stood in the stirrups,
trying to listen. Surely, he had heard a cry. Yes, there it
came again, along with the big guardsman's bellow of
joy. Very slowly, the Northerner rode back, Alexandra
draped across his saddle, her head drooping against his
massive shoulder. In just that way he had carried her out
of the Takla Makan. That time his face had been muffled
by robes. The relief and devotion Bryennius read on it
made him look tactfully away.

Bryennius leaped forward in time to ease his cousin
down from the Varangian's horse and into the firelit
circle where Father Basil waited with soft cloths and
warm water. He caught his breath at the sticky, bleeding
mess that smeared her hair and face, and found himself
sobbing.

"Put her down, Prince," said the priest. He touched
her face, peeled back her eyelids, then shook his head.
"One pupil is far larger than the other. That is not good.
But don't mourn yet, Prince. With God's help, people
struck on the head often live, even when their eyes look
thus. She needs warmth, and quiet, and time to sleep."
He gestured all of them back. "She also needs air," he
added sternly.

Bryennius crouched as close to his cousin as the priest
would allow. From time to time, food and drink was
handed to him, and the empty containers taken away
later. He did not remember eating or drinking. The
moon rose in the sky, gibbous and silver. It cast a ghastly
light on her face. Still she slept. Her breathing was deep
and regular.

Then, she began to whimper. Her breath came more
rapidly, and her hands jerked back and forth. The priest
leaned forward with a strip of leather, ready to force it
between her teeth, should she suffer a fit. He jerked his
chin, and Li Shou himself cast more fuel on the fire.

For a long time, Alexandra moaned and struggled
within herself. Then with a soft wail, she fell back.

Bryennius heard Siddiqa's sweet voice go taut and urgent in a Buddhist prayer that Li Shou echoed. *"Kyrie eleison, christe eleison, kyrie eleison,"* Bryennius gabbled. There had been no time to pray when Leo died. There never was time to pray along the line of march, and before that, in Byzantium, he had seen little need. He wished now that he were more in the habit of prayer, more adept, perhaps, in making God hear. Alexandra had survived so much. *Kyrie, spare her, and I shall . . . what will you do, Bryennius?* Promises were useless. He turned his pleas to the Theotokos. Surely God's gentle Mother would take pity on another woman, one so far from home. Had she not wandered afraid in Egypt with her family? Behind him came the mutter of prayers from the people Alexandra had helped to rescue. That these prayers were Christian comforted him not at all.

The moon was sinking down toward the horizon when Alexandra stirred again. She raised her hand to her bandaged scalp and hissed.

"Alexandra?" Bryennius whispered.

She sat up and opened her eyes. They glowed green, inhumanly green and intense. She raised her hands, adorned, as it seemed, with long, elegantly tapered nails, to her bandages and pulled them away from hair that now fell sleekly over her shoulders.

"That is not our name," she said in formal, accentless Ch'in. Her voice was very cold. "We are Wu Tse-Tien. Bow before the Son of Heaven!"

Even as Li Shou complied, Alexandra's back arched in a terrible spasm.

"This flesh is mine!" A second voice tore from her mouth, the cry of a hawk swooping on prey. It spoke in Greek, and its accents were those of the woman whose magics had pursued them across half the world.

Bryennius backed away. He had seen asps once, and their deadly stare filled him with the same horror as this nearness to a woman who was possessed. The familiarity of her face and figure made it even worse. He would hate himself for abandoning his cousin, he knew, but he had to get away.

"Invader and thief!" Again it was the voice that called itself Wu Tse-Tien. "Leave the Middle Kingdom. You have no place here."

"The body is bone of my bone, blood of my blood, and you are a ghost. You cannot stop me, or bar me from this flesh that I claim."

As each voice spoke, Alexandra's body jerked as if she had been lashed. How long could her body withstand this—let alone the spirit which two spirits assailed simultaneously? Li Shou backed away from the ghastly scene in the firelit circle. Spells, charms . . . Bryennius fixed his hopes on Father Basil, chanting the words of an exorcism. Christ had hurled demons from a man into the Gadarene swine. Would a heretic dare so much? The voice of Theodora shrieked in rage as he chanted. Laughter rose over the shrieking, as the Empress Wu's voice anticipated her victory. She would walk again, rule again. The voice turned soft, seductive, promising crowns and kingdoms to Li Shou, who ground his fists against his eyes, his languid control shattered.

The Theodora voice wailed again, and Alexandra's body spasmed, then went limp. Bryennius forced himself to move closer, as if he could atone for his earlier terror. He knelt by his cousin's side, taking her hand. "Is she breathing?" he asked the priest.

"Bry'?" Her voice was only a raspy whisper.

"Alexandra!" His tears splashed onto her face.

"Theodora's gone now, but the other one, the new one . . . I fell, Bry', and there was a hill . . . I thought if I could get to it, I could rest. Then there were voices in my head, fighting over me . . ."

"You sleep now," he told her, patting her hand.

"I can't!" she panted. "She's still there, the Empress. She thinks I'm her enemy . . . and she's right, Bry'. You know, it's not fair. She lived eighty years, but it wasn't enough. Now she wants my life too. If I let go for one moment, she'll have . . . have it all, body . . ." she gasped for breath, ". . . and soul, all my thoughts."

"You're a fighter, cousin, you can drive her out," he mumbled, feeling worse than useless.

She gave the faintest of laughs. Tears squeezed out from the corners of her eyes. "The way of Shambhala is the way of a warrior. I'm not very . . . good at it."

Her face twisted, and she shook, then lay still. "She . . . that's her. She wants out, Bry'. I'm trying . . . try to hold her off." Alexandra drew a long, deliberately steady breath. "Is Haraldr there?"

The guardsman knelt beside her. One huge hand went out to touch her hair, but fell onto his knee instead. "My princess, we won't leave you. Here we are; here we'll remain for as long as you need."

"No, that won't work. Both of you, listen. One of the things I learned once—I was curious—was how to make Greek fire. If she takes me, she'll learn it too." Alexandra forced herself to sit up.

"I can't allow her to learn that. Neither can you. If she doesn't have a body to live in, she'll have to return to her tomb.

"My final order to you, Guardsman. If she conquers, use your axe . . ." She fell back, her eyes closing.

Haraldr cried out wordlessly.

"Don't argue," Bryennius ordered Haraldr. "She needs her strength to fight."

Li Shou came up behind them. His hand on Bryennius' shoulder was stronger than he had expected. "My knowledge of your tongue is imperfect. What did she say?"

"Did you find anything, in all your books?" Father Basil demanded.

"Nothing," said the prince. "Surely your ritual—"

"The lady Theodora was brought up in Christianity. My exorcism drove *her* out. But it can do nothing against a creature of another faith."

Haraldr rose to his feet, his face gaunt with sorrow. "I will get my axe," he muttered.

"What is this barbarity?" Li Shou cried.

"You've seen the fire we carry," Bryennius replied, not moving away from Alexandra. She was trembling now, and little broken sounds came from her throat as she fought the battle within for control of body and soul. "Alexandra—you know she has a taste for odd knowledge. She knows how to make it. We have a law in Byzantium. If we disclose this secret to an outsider, the penalty is death—even for an Emperor."

The Ch'in prince started to protest. Bryennius broke in. "For the love of God, you idiot, do you want Greek fire let loose in your country? You told me that Wu Tse-Tien was one of the most ruthless Emperors you've ever had. She'll use it!"

If she wins, then Alexandra is dead anyhow, and better so, he thought. His cousin moaned, and her trembling intensified. It was only a matter of moments before it turned into convulsions again. Her eyes flew open, and green light came and went in their depths. She looked very frail. If she surrendered, this Empress would find out why Alexandra had come into her realm. Evil she might be, but she was loyal Ch'in down to the moldering bones she now sought to escape. She wouldn't let them escape, let alone take silkworms back with them.

The other Varangians joined Haraldr. His hands opened and closed on the haft of his axe. One of them spoke in guttural Norse. Haraldr nodded.

"What did he say?" demanded Li Shou.

Bryennius dashed a hand across his face. If only he could sweep away demons, foreign princes, and his grief as easily as he brushed away tears.

"'Don't weep,' Arinbjorn said. 'It will ruin your aim.'" Bryennius bent and kissed Alexandra's hand, then laid it on her breast.

He stood up and backed away. Siddiqa ran to his side, and he reached for her, embracing her, one hand turning her sleek black head against his shoulder so she might not witness what Haraldr must do. The Empress' fierce voice erupted from his cousin's lips, then was choked off. "For God's sake!" her own voice begged.

Haraldr drew a deep breath.

Bryennius was starting to nod when Siddiqa struggled in his arms. "No!" she cried, pushing with small fists against his shoulder. "Let me go!" He held tight, and she kicked him, trying to get free.

"Little one, little love, you don't understand," he said.

She thrust him away with strength he had never expected to find in her. She had always seemed so frail, so complaisant. The mouth he had kissed and learned to compare to a peony bud twisted and swore by the excrement of turtles. Her fragility had been strictly in his own imagination. She might have been in need of rescue, but she was no weakling.

"Idiots!" she hissed, followed by a spate of Ch'in that Bryennius could not follow. Then she ran toward Alexandra's horse.

"She's beside herself," Bryennius muttered and started after her. "What was that about?"

"In the karez," Li Shou said. "Remember what we found in the karez?"

They had found Siddiqa, yes, and the body of a man Alexandra had called the King of Shambhala. It was all part of that madness she insisted on talking about.

"The sword," Li Shou said. "She dropped it. The dorje she won at Kashgar, the bell, the gem—all in her saddlebags, when she fell. She was unprotected."

This was folly. Father Basil had tried to exorcise both spirits, and failed. What did Siddiqa hope to do?

Siddiqa ran back to them, Alexandra's bags clutched to her breast. She dropped them beside her and began to rummage inside them, talking all the while.

"Listen to her, Prince Bryennius. She says that the Empress Wu was a devout Buddhist. These symbols are Buddhist symbols; they may have power when the signs of your faith fail you," Li Shou advised.

Bryennius glanced frantically over at Alexandra,

whose back arched in spasms that got stronger and stronger as the Empress gained control.

Crying out in triumph, Siddiqa held up the moonstone Alexandra had taken from the breast of the warrior who had died in the karez. She ran over to Alexandra and tried to thrust it into her clenched fists. An arm flailed out and knocked her onto her side. Stubbornly, she picked herself up and tried again. Alexandra's other hand came up, and Siddiqa smacked Alexandra's face firmly, then pried at her fingers. This time, she forced the huge white gem into Alexandra's hand.

The moonstone kindled. White light rose from it until it haloed the woman holding it as if she were a figure in a mosaic. Alexandra drew a long, rattling breath. Her eyes opened. Again, the greenish light of possession ebbed and surged in them. She looked down at the gem, focusing all her energy upon it.

The light was reflected from Haraldr's raised axe. "Wait!" Bryennius cried. "At least, we can try."

The gem glowed more and more strongly. The circle of light in which Alexandra lay seemed to coalesce, then to form into eight separate parts, like a lotus. It had a faintly bluish tinge.

Disastrous as it might be if the Empress won, they closed in around her and saw the flower shape reflected in the moonstone. Moment by moment, it solidified. Around her rose the chant of prayers from Li Shou, Siddiqa, and the Ch'in guards. Alexandra's lips moved too. Her own voice, blending uncannily with that of the Empress, rose in prayer and loathing.

"Thief!" she shrieked in the Empress' voice. "Thief —but adept on the Path. How can this be? How can I fight?"

Now even the Empress was one with the watchers, seduced by her faith to fight her desire to steal Alexandra's flesh and life. The light from the gem intensified. For a moment, the face of a man in the prime of life seemed to blaze from it, and Alexandra's body bowed itself, as if in homage.

"The Diamond Path," whispered Father Basil. "Give her the lightning bolt."

But Siddiqa was too entranced in her prayers to hear. So it was Father Basil who found it and held it before Alexandra's eyes. He unclasped one hand from the moonstone that she clutched, and lowered the dorje toward it. Her body cringed away, but her will held. In the instant before it touched her palm, she reached up and grasped it firmly.

Her whole body arched again in one of those hideous, bone-breaking spasms. Bryennius gagged as he smelled burning flesh. The chanting stopped.

For a long moment, he heard only the chirp of crickets and the susurrus of wind, blowing through the wheat fields. Then it seemed that the wind rose, carrying a wail of mourning back to the tomb that should never have opened.

Alexandra fell back, gem and dorje rolling from her hands. To Bryennius' amazement, the hand that the lightning bolt had seared bore only a reddish mark resembling a lotus. Even that quickly faded.

Siddiqa tugged a blanket out from one of the packs and, glaring at what, clearly, she considered inefficient males, covered Alexandra warmly.

But Alexandra's breathing was deep and regular, and her face bore a peace that passed their understanding.

"Is she dead?" Bryennius whispered.

His lover went to him and smoothed back his hair. "Not for many years."

"I shall build another altar to Kuan-yin," said Li Shou.

Haraldr laid down his axe. Since he no longer needed to fear the ruin of his aim, he wept, and Bryennius wept with him.

12

Dawn shone through Alexandra's tent. One of Li Shou's innumerable servants or concubines (Alexandra never could quite tell which was which) brought her tea in a delicate porcelain bowl and laid out riding clothes. Outside her quarters came the usual babel of breaking camp, and Bryennius' voice rising in anger.

"Three men rode off, just like that, and you didn't stop them?" he berated someone. "I know that they know the land and could sneak off, but still—"

"Undoubtedly, they were sent to examine us and report back." Li Shou's calmer tones cut through Bryennius' anger.

"Spies!" he spat.

"Would your own Empire act any differently?"

Alexandra chuckled into her tea. Originally, she had thought it was a kind of wine. Its steaming fragrance soothed burning eyes and eased into her mind, which felt bruised. *And why wouldn't it, with two dreadful women*

184

battling inside it for possession of my soul! She was too battered to be outraged at the thought of possession, or relieved that her desperate order to Haraldr to kill her before she betrayed her land's secrets had proved unnecessary.

She finished her tea, waved away the usual bevy of attendants, then dressed in the clothes they left out, even to the cloak and hat that would give her some protection against curious stares when they entered Ch'ang-an. Last night, she had waked from fitful sleep to an argument: Should they allow her a day's rest here, or should they ride on immediately? Alexandra had dragged herself outside, stumbling over Haraldr, who had stretched himself to sleep outside her quarters.

"I can ride if I must. The less time we spend here, the better," she had insisted. She would have begged if she had had to. The firelight outlined the mounds of the Imperial dead. If Bryennius had asked her, she would have said to ride away from them immediately, as the three spies had done. If Ch'ang-an had its equivalent of Byzantium's Bureau of Barbarians, no doubt the spies were reporting to it right now. How would they describe her inner battle with the Empress? Would they say that a long-lost T'ang prince had returned home, accompanied by exotics, including a most aristocratic madwoman? She would have believed it herself; the traces of Wu and Theodora's struggle in her mind were foul, soothed only by her remembrance of the white light from the moonstone that Siddiqa had forced into her hands.

A deep voice and a light one exchanged halting courtesies. She heard Haraldr move aside. Siddiqa slipped within, dressed in the Uighur fashion.

"I owe you my life," Alexandra said, embracing her. The younger princess cast her eyes down.

"I owed you mine. You and—" She flushed at the thought of Bryennius. "Are you ready to ride, elder sister?"

Alexandra raised an eyebrow. *Why not? Bryennius is my brother, and she is beloved by him.* She smiled at the younger girl. *If she were the pretty, docile creature that she looks, I'd be dead.*

Ahead of them rose the walls of Ch'ang-an, thick and square.

"Home," Li Shou murmured. Riding at his side, Alexandra glanced away to allow him privacy. The city was huge; twice the size of Byzantium, and not confined to an area like the Horn. Canals ran through it; but the massive eastern wall was broken only by two gates. It would be a hard city to escape from. The prince had told her how the city was laid out—an orderly grid of fourteen wide, tree-lined avenues running from north to south, eleven from east to west. Except for the two huge markets, the quarters marked off by these avenues were walled.

"Not like home," Bryennius had commented to her. He missed the tangle of streets, rich and poor houses jostling on the same block as one of the great churches, with the Mese cutting through the center of the city, shop-lined, winding up to the perfume merchants near the palace, and the silk vendors' special House of Lights, dark now for lack of goods. Surely the trees Alexandra saw here were mulberry trees. And where there were mulberry trees, there were silkworms. Somewhere in those markets or the palace compounds themselves was the treasure Alexandra sought.

The walls of the Ch'un Ming Gate were at least as thick as Byzantium's northernmost defenses. Soldiers in leather and scales guarded them. They recognized Li Shou and were quick to salute him. The spies had accomplished that much, at least. As they entered, the noises of Ch'ang-an rose about them. Then they heard a rumble. The ground trembled beneath them, and several of their horses shied.

"The First Emperor stirs in his sleep," Prince Li Shou commented almost whimsically.

Alexandra forced herself to smile.

The caravan leader who had ridden with them since Kashgar came up and bowed. "We must report to the Office of the Sarthavak," he said.

Li Shou nodded at Bryennius. "That office deals specifically with the hu, I mean, merchants of Persia. But I think that they will stop off in the taverns here, or the tea shops." He gestured elegantly. "No doubt you too will be interested in the taverns down the road. Or the P'ing K'ang section. They can make a man's homecoming very sweet . . . or welcome a traveler from the West."

A number of soldiers and officials rode toward them, flanking a small, thin man in a scholar's robe and elaborate headgear. "Your pardon," said the prince. "I must speak to these people."

Father Basil nodded. "That's where they house . . . musicians, entertainers . . ." He looked embarrassed.

"*Hetairai*?" Alexandra surmised, and the Nestorian priest nodded. Siddiqa caught Bryennius' eye with a "just you dare!" look on her face.

"My own people and our churches are nearer the western part of the city. I'm told that the market is livelier there," Father Basil said.

Several of the soldiers looked wistful. "Do you think it's too late to tell the prince that we want to be merchants, not envoys of Byzantium? It sounds easier," Bryennius commented.

Alexandra sighed. She watched the officials bow low to Li Shou. From here, she could hear nothing of their conversation, but their postures and gestures were so courteous, so mannered, that she suspected some sort of danger. She touched her heels delicately to her horse, edging as far into the avenue as she could without being stopped. Other women rode by, some brash and bareheaded. The wide avenues teemed with people riding, walking, or being carried in elaborately decorated, closed carts. Over the walls of the quarter she could see the upcurved roofs of what looked like palaces.

With the air of a man making a generous and unde-

served concession, Li Shou inclined his head to the
official and retraced his steps. A flush along his high
cheekbones betrayed his annoyance.

"Ch'ang-an has changed if an official can challenge the
word of a cousin of the Son of Heaven," he hissed, and
mounted so quickly that his horse sidled. He leaned
forward and ran a hand along its arched neck. Then he
signaled for them to move forward.

"Ordinarily," he told the Greeks, "visiting envoys
who come to make submission in their prince's name to
the Son of Heaven—"

Alexandra laid a hand on Bryennius' reins, hushing
the indignant outburst he was about to make about the
Basileus' demotion.

"How else could it be?" the prince asked. "When
envoys come, they become the responsibility of that
man's office, which regulates the funerals of members of
the Imperial family."

"Cheerful," Alexandra commented.

"It also maintains hostels for foreign guests like yourself. Lu Tsung there"—he flicked his fingers at the
retreating official's stiff back—"heads up that office.
When I told him that you were *my* guests, not his
responsibility, he was outraged."

"Do they suspect that we are spies?" Alexandra asked
with all the innocence she could summon.

"Idiots!" Li Shou snorted. "Because Lu Tsung did
well on the examinations, he climbed rapidly in the
Emperor's service. I have had reports on him and his
family. In Canton, his elder brother locked away all
foreigners; Lu Tsung seems to think that if he follows his
brother's advice, he will gain great face. He has already
doubled the guard to 'protect' Ch'ang-an against barbarians."

"Isn't he succeeding?" cut in Father Basil. "The Manichees have already been outlawed. Is there not some
movement . . ."

Li Shou flung up a hand. Never had Alexandra seen
him so angry. "A movement, indeed. Ch'ang-an has

always been fascinated by the West. I have looked forward to reading you poetry like that of Tu Fu, of showing you the great paintings of the Yen brothers, who claim to have painted scenes of your home. Now men like Lu Tsung want us to turn our backs on all we have learned from outside the Walls of the Middle Kingdom."

"Xenophobes," murmured Alexandra, then translated for the prince's benefit. It sounded very familiar, very unwelcome. In such times, foreign guests were in some danger, foreign faiths at more. It was chaos again, seeking to undermine what order and cooperation it found, wherever it found them.

"You know that I have spent years collecting holy texts," Li Shou said. "Buddhist, Taoist, a few Christian scriptures . . . last year, a scholar named Li Ao died. He knew a great deal about Buddhism, had studied it for years just in order to refute it."

Alexandra and Father Basil looked at one another. Heresies. Religious conflict. And they were in the thick of it. Li Shou, they knew, was heterodox, a true descendant of those Emperors who had endowed the Nestorian churches in Ch'ang-an. But this new Son of Heaven . . ."Your Emperor follows the Way?" Alexandra prompted, using the term Tao. The little she had heard of this Way spoke of a retreat from the world, a unity with the cosmos, order, and a simplicity that was almost pastoral.

Li Shou's eyes burned. "Later," he said.

Pastorals could also include a wolf in the fold, a wolf, in this case, who might also be the shepherd. It was not an idea she wanted to dwell on.

He was silent as they rode past a lavish Buddhist temple, its curved roofs painted red and gold. Outside crouched huge statues that resembled dogs or lions, or both. Incense floated over the walls and tantalized them. Chanting and the sound of gongs rose. For an instant, Alexandra fancied herself back in her long-gone, and unlamented, convent. This temple was so rich! she thought. It seemed larger and more elaborate than the

Church of Hagia Sophia, that soaring sculpture of light, mosaic, and marble, with its domes from which, some people claimed, angels descended to help the priests serve worshipers.

Father Basil studied the temple avidly. "There must be hundreds like it. And Buddhism is not native to Ch'in . . ."

"Think you Buddhism too could suffer?"

"As your Patriarchs did my own church." He nodded. "Surely you have heard complaints that in Byzantium the monks own too much land, too many armies, and slaves, and control too much of the City's gold."

It had been wealth that had enabled Alexandra's aunt to purchase forbidden books, to bribe the people she must have bribed: wealth that made her feel all-powerful, and bred first her ambition, then her damnation.

They rode slowly through the eastern market. Each trade had its own bazaar. Except for the faces and the languages, the clamor and the familiar goods made Alexandra feel much at home. Bryennius tossed cash to a flower vendor and gave the chrysanthemums that he bought to Siddiqa, who laughed with delight.

Alexandra gazed in wonder at the number and kinds of people in the market: Sogdians, Persians, Arabs, men of the steppes, Turks, even strange-looking men in high black hats from a land she heard was called Korea; men with the dark skins, aquiline features, and long eyes of Hind, and from farther south, from the Land of Lions. Priests of ten separate faiths jostled merchants of all races. Nobles in carts or litters, or riding accompanied by servants thronged the bazaars. Many were women, exquisitely dressed and painted, jade and gold ornaments trembling in their hair. Seeing them, she felt unkempt and too large.

She felt as if they stared at her and all her people, dismissing them as barbarians—which they were not, appraising them as enemies—which they had no wish to be. But which, in one important sense, they had to be. Another enemy rode at her side: the prince who had been friend and ally, and would now be their host. It was a terrible crime to betray one's host.

Once past the market, they turned north and rode toward what looked like official buildings near the walls over which they could see trees and palace buildings.

"Administrative offices," Prince Shou observed.

"This Lu Tsung works in them?" she asked. "Perhaps we should . . ."

"What are you suggesting?"

"If it causes you difficulty to accept us as guests," Alexandra began slowly, "perhaps we should let ourselves be received by his people." Constant official scrutiny would make stealing silkworms harder, perhaps impossible, but she would not be betraying a man who deserved better.

"I will not give you up!" he interrupted, angrier than she had ever seen him. "We will discuss this after we are settled."

Already, artisans stitched gowns and jackets for her. Her rooms were bright with jewels and flowers, hair ornaments, and embroideries. Alexandra had been bathed, and exclamations for her foreignness had been suppressed. She had eaten, slept briefly, and had just begun to wonder whether or not it would do to ask for books when Li Shou's chief steward, an ancient eunuch, entered, prostrated himself, and requested the Most Excellent Lady's presence.

Alexandra followed the man across a garden, in through a moon-shaped door on either side of which were characters for life, health, and fortune, and into a room clearly reserved for her host. Here were the books she had hoped for, here were musical instruments, exquisite screens and intricately carved statues, and misty landscapes painted on silk. The room had the look of years of loving preservation; the prince's steward had

served him since he was a child. Prince Li Shou sat on a
bare platform, paper, a brush, and a cake of ink at hand.
He gazed at an ornament that seemed to be no more
than lapis lazuli sculpted into the form of a hollow rock.
Near him, and flanked by a number of younger officials,
sat Lu Tsung.

Bryennius, Father Basil translating and gesturing at
his elbow, stood beside another elderly man and someone who looked like a former soldier. A clerk crouched
at their feet, drawing.

"The Department of Arms," explained Li Shou, rising
to greet her. "It immediately meets with all foreign
envoys to learn of their lands, to draw maps . . ."

Then it *was* like Byzantium's Bureau of Barbarians,
and she would be subject to official investigation. She
expected no less. Since the officials had not been presented to her, she ignored them with the hauteur she had
learned in the Imperial palace. Li Shou appeared appre-
ciative. *Do you realize that you are making enemies*? she
thought at him. Or was it simply that he refused to
retreat from the position he had taken?

When the silence between Alexandra and the glaring
officials had grown too thick to ignore, Li Shou presented them. Lu Tsung glared at her, clearly expecting
her to bow. "In this one's land," Alexandra spoke
formally, "it is not the custom for ladies of the Imperial
House to bow to anyone but the Emperor—who is this
unworthy woman's brother."

She could practically hear the old man's bones creak
as he bowed to her. She seated herself, assumed court
manners, and agreed to accept tea while wishing she
could join the conversation around Bryennius. At a clap
of hands, servants scurried out, returning almost immediately with her Varangians. The Ch'in soldiers instinctively stiffened into a posture of defense, then realized
that any men so tall and with such conspicuously golden
coloring could not hide themselves. Garments of red silk
had been given them, and bright sashes banded their

waists: military garments, but unlike anything they had ever worn. On a bronze silk cord around Haraldr's neck hung the horn etched with the sigils of Shambhala.

Alexandra held her tea before her face, sniffed delicately at the steam, and prepared to deal with an interrogation.

The questions continued for hours. Abruptly, they turned to Princess Siddiqa.

"He tries," murmured Li Shou in Sogdian, "to apply recent ordinances which forbid Uighurs to associate with Ch'in to her. But she is half Ch'in herself; her mother was a princess."

"You!" Lu Tsung called Bryennius, who turned, brows haughtily raised. "Do you realize that you may not take a Ch'in wife or concubine away from the Middle Kingdom?"

"I thought she was Uighur," Bryennius said. He turned back, grimacing at Alexandra. "Can't he make up his mind?"

Alexandra stared at the prince and the official. This was more than a conflict over privileges; it seemed an old animosity.

"And the barbarian prince?" Lu Tsung kept to his subject.

"His Highness is my guest, to stay or go as he wills. For as long as he wills. In the meantime, I am of course requesting proper recognition for my guests," Li Shou said. "I applied immediately for official robes and for copies of the classics, which Her Highness wishes to read. I trust you will arrange their presentation to the Son of Heaven."

"What gestures of submission will they make?"

"You saw the Ferghana horses they brought. Proper ones, of the true breed that sweats blood."

"These unworthy beasts are this one's trifling gift to the Son of Heaven," Alexandra said quietly.

"And this . . . this lady?" Lu Tsung gestured at her with thinly concealed contempt.

"Her Highness is a scholar and a great traveler; she will aid me in my studies of the White and the Yellow. Surely you, as a follower of the Way, can understand the value of such a lady's services in alchemy."

Father Basil stiffened. Alexandra disliked Lu Tsung's crack of dry laughter even more than the insolence with which he inspected her. "As you know, the Son of Heaven leads us all along the Way. If the . . . lady is adept, she might best assist him."

There was silk in the palace, Alexandra thought. A move into the palace might be one way of getting to it.

"If the most honored minister will forgive this wretched priest," Father Basil interrupted, with determined humility, "Her Imperial Highness has been a cloistered nun."

Again that dry, cruel laughter. "So was Yang Kuei-Fei, and Wu Tse-Tien herself. Yet they went willingly to the Son of Heaven. And this one has already let her hair grow. If you study tantra, I tell you, *Highness*, look to yourself and yours lest you be punished! And if she also assists you in your studies of the Tao—which I doubt —assuredly she is no nun."

"Enough!" snapped the prince, though he barely raised his voice. "You will send my guests their credentials, and all else that is theirs. I myself will act as their advisor. This audience is finished!" He stared fixedly at the little lapis lazuli sculpture, as if trying to calm himself.

The night was cool, and the garden fragrant. Any storms that threatened were a result of the day's disastrous meeting with Lu Tsung. "He dared threaten me!" the prince muttered repeatedly. "And he insulted my guests."

It had taken hours to make him willing to say more than that.

"I never liked him," Prince Li Shou conceded now as they sat in the quiet garden. A few lights burned, gleaming off the golden carp that swam in the twisting stream that ran through it. Over by a huge, hollowed-out limestone boulder, Alexandra's soldiers lounged about and pretended not to be on guard. "I will admit that the scholar Li Ao was a genuine servant of the Tao, though very narrow. But this man is a place-seeker! If the Son of Heaven favored Buddhism rather than the Tao, Lu Tsung would be a Buddhist. If he favored Turks, then he would build a yurt in his gardens and eat mutton. Now, to curry favor, he feigns a resentment of all things that are not Ch'in. He thought my going out of Ch'in madness. I am certain he hoped I would die on the journey."

"Instead, Your Highness returned, not just with the texts you sought, but with foreign guests," said Father Basil.

"Indeed." Li Shou nodded. "But there is an additional problem. Before Lu Tsung was Taoist, he studied the classics. In fact, his performance on the scholars' examinations won him his office. At their best, our classics teach respect and order."

And at their worst, intolerable prejudice, Alexandra surmised. "Do they teach one to despise foreigners and women?" she asked aloud.

"At their worst, yes," the prince admitted in a low voice. "But it is not the texts as much as flaws in the students themselves."

Despite the vast distances that separated her Empire from this one, things were always the same. No one was fool enough to deny the authority of Saint Paul, and yet, in his name, fools treated women as chattel. The similarity between hate-filled misinterpretations amazed her. Authority. If a man thought he had set his feet upon the right Way, what might stop him from insisting that others follow it? Some sages of the Tao had refused power, but surely others . . . both Plato and Aristotle had tried to raise philosopher-kings, and what had they gained? Plato nearly died in Syracuse of a bloodbath. Aristotle had tutored Alexander, whose battlefield had been Asia itself. It was dangerous for a ruler to be consumed by an idea, and frequently deadly to those around him.

Had they come to Ch'ang-an only to be caught in a holy war?

"This is an ugly situation," she mused. "As for living in the palace, I know—"

Li Shou rose so fast that his cup toppled and shattered as easily as his hard-won composure. "You know nothing, nothing at all if you make that suggestion. What I said to Lu Tsung was an excuse. I tell you, no more of that!"

How dare you? Alexandra started to demand.

"You, priest!" raged the prince. "You tell her what his words actually meant!" The silk of his embroidered robes hissing and whistling about him, Li Shou strode about the garden. Shards of porcelain crackled beneath his slippers.

"Before we fall into worse problems," Alexandra spoke with deceptive quietness, "I suggest you tell me what he means."

"Alchemy . . ."

"I know what alchemy is," she said, exaggerating her air of patience. "I know that Taoists practice it in the hope of gaining immortality in this world. That is not just heresy, it is blasphemy. And if your Son of Heaven dabbles in blasphemy, then I shall pray for you. You will need it. What I do *not* know"—she turned back to the Nestorian priest—"is why Li Shou became so outraged after he himself said that I assisted him in his studies."

Father Basil hunched in on himself. "If we had come by way of Hind," he began, swallowed, and began again. "In Hind, the Diamond Path is associated with . . . I have heard that fornication plays a part in their worship. There are temples devoted to it, priests and priestesses . . ."

Alexandra flushed scarlet and thanked God that the night was dark. "Though I may have taken a few steps along the Diamond Path, I know nothing about this other worship. In other words," she said in a voice that barely trembled, "what Lu Tsung suggested was that I go to this Emperor as a concubine."

Father Basil nodded wretchedly.

"Elder sister," Siddiqa spoke for the first time, "my mother told me of the palace in which she was brought up. Many ladies pass their entire lives there with never a glimpse of the Son of Heaven, much less . . . she was glad to leave. But short of death, or a convent, there is no escape from it."

Alexandra was abruptly, absurdly furious. She had entered a convent to escape marrying a Frank, left Byzantium as much to avoid being married off as to steal silkworms . . . no, that wasn't true. What had she sought in leaving Byzantium for the East? Certainly, she meant to get those silkworms. But it was the journey, the chance to see and learn, and to keep on going, free of the cages of pragmatism and ceremony that had, once again, slammed down upon her. Upon the road, she had been traveler, warrior, even—a few insane times—magician. Now, once again, "they" saw only a female body to be awarded to the highest-ranking man available. Had she really traveled to the End of the World only to find that people and customs were no different?

Siddiqa's warning enraged her further, dealing as it did with only the logistics of escaping the palace once she took the concubine's way in. But then, Siddiqa was brought up to regard multiple adulteries as normal. What made it worse was that she had trusted Li Shou, and he had embarrassed her. He had turned the magic she had learned in the Pamirs and relied upon in the desert into a barracks joke, and she didn't know if she could ever face him again. Ridiculous tears stung her eyelids, but she restrained them.

"The prince himself first called me his assistant. Let us hope that he meant it innocently. Or, instead of one enemy, he will have two."

The soft silk of her robes caressed her body as she retreated to the rooms she had been assigned. The mirrors there showed her a stranger with flushed cheeks and blazing eyes, very slim, but graceful, with subtle curves that the sheepskins and the baggy riding clothes she had worn for months had concealed. She flung the mirror down, struggled out of the whispering, offensively clinging silks, tossed them aside, and wept for shame and disappointment. She had thought better of them all, herself included.

13

As she admired the bell tower in the center of Ch'ang-an, Alexandra felt like a bumpkin who scraped the manure off his boots and lurched into Byzantium to gape. She was glad for the hat and veil that let her blend into the crowd; twice already this morning, she had seen other foreigners jeered at. A knot of loafers had actually pursued one portly Uighur until guards caught sight of the potential riot. Alexandra thought they seemed reluctant to stop it, but the loafers had fled anyway. They would be bolder next time.

So the chaos was here, too. Again the ground trembled underfoot, and she thought of Li Shou's stories of the First Emperor. *Is it I who wake you, old man, or the chaos?* Stealing silkworms—that might mean disorder in Ch'in, harm to its trade. But if she did not bring them back, then Byzantium might fall into worse chaos. She was thinking in circles again.

Circles . . . abruptly, she thought of the paired circles

199

of snow mountains in the paintings of Shambhala.
Beyond the circles of the world might lie other circles.
That was bad Plato and worse doctrine, but if she were
really that orthodox, she would not dream of entering a
Buddhist shrine.

All her spies were out, Bryennius dispatched to the
more discreet tea shops (though Siddiqa had flown into a
rage when he teased her, and had scratched his face), the
Greek soldiers and Varangians to the rowdier western
market. Father Basil had been only too happy to follow
them to the Nestorian church founded by the saintly
Alopen. Alexandra slipped into the nearby Buddhist
temple. She was not the only woman standing by herself.
Several others, both veiled, and unveiled, meditated
before immense statues like those in the caves at
Dunhuang, or attended the complex ritual.

But the temple felt wrong. Not because it was a pagan
shrine: The monastery where she first learned of
Shambhala had been steeped in holiness. That feeling of
sanctity, even more than the chants and the incense and
the tales of the abbot, had made her willing to believe
that . . . she shook her head. This temple was far richer
than the monastery at the Roof of the World. It was
lavish, even tawdry. The statues and murals were newly
painted and heavily gilded. Under the chanting and the
incense so heavy that two people had already swooned
was a feeling of . . . fever. One summer, there had been
sickness in Byzantium. Alexandra had insisted on leaving her convent's library to help in its infirmary. Even
now she remembered how the air had quivered. The
entire city had seemed feverish, as if it were one single
body, and that body feverish. Though it was autumn in
Ch'ang-an, that febrile energy quivered here.

She wandered away from the pudgy, chanting monks,
searching the walls for signs of Shambhala. Her footsteps
echoed in the corridors as she moved away from the
crowd. Gradually, the noise subsided. Now she heard
only her own footsteps, and the padding of sandaled feet
behind her. When she stopped, those other steps stopped

too. Wishing she had the abbot's sword, she reached into her flowing silk sleeve for the dagger she carried, then turned around. Her free hand swept the veil back over her head.

A man wearing a monk's robes faced her. Like herself, he was foreign. She thought he might be from the Land of Snows. He raised a hand, and she tensed, dagger ready. But he only pointed at the wall and smiled at her.

"To the south, Princess," he said. "And go soon."

Alexandra glanced at the wall. There indeed were the snow mountains and the mandala of Shambhala, within which the king sat, awaiting the signal to ride forth to rid the ordered world of its enemies. The fever in the air subsided a little. She turned to question the monk. A lotus with a bluish tinge lay on the clean stone pavement before her. She really could not say she was surprised to find herself alone. She bent to pick up the lotus, sure that she had found a sign. To the south, then. Once they stole the silkworms, they would flee along the southern roads, back to Byzantium.

Lotus held before her, she retraced her steps. The monk had warned her not to delay, a message she would heed. She wanted to travel by winter; Father Basil had learned that the men who had smuggled silkworms out of Ch'in three centuries ago had succeeded only because they had traveled in the cold. Heat quickened silkworms to a riot of hunger and breeding; winter plunged them into a stupor.

Besides, she was increasingly afraid of the men who seemed to turn Tao into chaos. Two days before, Li Shou had vanished into the palace compound after warning her that their presentation to the Son of Heaven would be delayed, "though that does not seem to be why you have come." *Merciful Bearer of God, had he heard her questioning Father Basil about the silk?* Once, while they had been discussing it, they had heard a whisper of silk robes, and immediately fallen silent, inept conspirators as they were. Had that been the prince?

Her quarrel with him had been slow to heal. Both still

changed the subject whenever it turned to magic. Li
Shou was also reticent about the Son of Heaven. How
not? She would hesitate to discuss the Emperor of the
Romans with a stranger. Emperors were all-powerful,
all-knowing. In the case of the Emperor of the Romans,
he was bound by his service to God. An Emperor who
followed the Tao, however, might believe himself the
Tao incarnate, an embodiment of heaven and earth,
rather than its vicar. Such a man might consider himself
as far above good and evil as she considered herself
above silkworms, or barbarians. Since earthquakes existed in nature, a man who believed that he embodied all
nature might decide that the earthquake's force was
right and beautiful. He could become a catastrophe in
human form.

The earth rumbled again. *The old First Emperor,
stirring in his sleep? It is not I who am the danger, old
man. Look to your successor.* She waited for the rumbling to die down. When it did not, she hurried for the
nearest door. She had a horror of being trapped beneath
one of the twisted, painted cornices.

A mob of soldiers and men in workmen's blue tunics
swarmed into the temple, dragging worshipers from the
shrines, and priests from the altars. Another group bayed
the priests up into a ragged line beside a line of sobbing,
shrinking women clad in ashen robes. One woman's
headdress tumbled off as she wailed. Her head had been
roughly shaved some time ago.

Then the soldiers forced priests and nuns to join
hands. When several refused, swords slashed down.
Then the others were marched out to a chorus of jeers, a
ribald parody of a wedding song, leaving the bodies
behind. Blood pooled on the scrubbed flagstones.

Now comes chaos, Alexandra thought. She looked
desperately about the courtyard for her cart and the
servants from Li Shou's household. That overturned
hulk, from which the silk hangings had been stripped,
the oxen stolen, and the servants driven away—that had
been her cart. Now she would have to make her way

home unescorted and on foot. And her disguise was no thicker than the silk veil that hid her face from the crowd.

Someone shouted and pointed, and five men ran toward her. Alexandra shrank against the wall. In the desert, when the demons had pursued her and the prince, she had used the magic of Shambhala to summon a sort of protection. Passionately, Alexandra wished for it now. Her hands, gripping together, crushed the lotus between them, and its fragrance drove away the stink of sweat and blood and human fear.

Abruptly, the men who spotted her turned away, sinking into the crowd that hurled rocks and less savory missiles at the statues towering overhead. The screams and crashes of the riot seemed lessened. Even the air was different: Free from the blowing soil that yellowed the sky in Ch'ang-an, it was the dazzling indigo of the sky in the high passes. For an instant Alexandra felt dizzy, intoxicated, as if once again she trod the Roof of the World. She seemed to walk in a bubble of quiet.

She edged out along the wall into the court, past two men who kicked at the body of a monk who had chosen to die rather than be forcibly wed to the woman crumpled at his side. They might indeed have been well suited. Alexandra wanted to trace a cross over them, but dared not move her hands from the lotus that was her protection.

Carefully, she picked her way across the battleground that had been a temple courtyard. She turned to the north and east, intending to return to Li Shou's compound when the power about her shimmered. Faint yet piercingly clear in her mind came the call of a horn. She had sensed its music once before, and it had saved her life. Now it called in distress to whomever might hear it. She turned toward the south and west. Kilting up her silken skirts of lavender and blue, she began to run.

A horse stood nearby, its head hanging down from sheer weariness. She touched its lathered neck. When it did not flinch, she led it to the nearest crouching statue

of a grotesque lion, which made an excellent mounting
block. Again, the horn call! She looked about. Impossible that no one else could hear it! She tucked the lotus
into her belt and drove her heels into the horse's flanks.

Haraldr was glad that Arinbjorn guarded his side as
they strode through the western market. The small,
golden-skinned natives of Ch'ang-an moved out of their
way. Ahead of them, Father Basil scuttled around a
corner and disappeared.

Arinbjorn chuckled. "The minute we settle into a new
place, he heads off to find a church. Now, my first stop
would be a—"

"The crowd back there, Arinbjorn, is it thinning out?"
Haraldr asked. He felt as if he were striding naked
through a crowd of onlookers. The market, which he
remembered from past visits as being engagingly rowdy
at this time of day, was quiet, too quiet. You couldn't
have a better battle-comrade than Arinbjorn, when he
decided to use his head for something more than sluicing
ale through the rest of his body. The other man tensed,
started to turn, then changed his mind.

"Are you expecting trouble?"

Haraldr shrugged. "I wouldn't want to take on the
whole market, would you?"

"Not after Her Highness told us to keep quiet. I like
her idea: a quiet, friendly walk through the market, as if
there's any way we can pretend we look like . . ."

"What's that!" Haraldr dug his fingers into
Arinbjorn's brawny arm until the other guardsman
grunted.

"Leave off, you ox!"

"Over there. That troop . . ." A file of soldiers, stocky
men with knotted scarves on their heads, cuirasses of
scale and leather clattering as they moved, marched into
the market, accompanying a man in the robes of an
official, a parasol denoting his office held above his
elaborate headgear. Criminals were usually punished in
the western market, Haraldr thought. A commotion

behind the official drew his attention, and he headed toward it.

"Quietly, *she* said. When did you ever disregard *her* orders before?" asked Arinbjorn.

Haraldr ignored his friend's remarks, though ordinarily he might have reminded Arinbjorn that "she" was Her Imperial Highness Alexandra, and he'd do well to remember it. He wished that Father Basil hadn't scurried off so quickly; the instant matters got beyond drink or food (mostly, you pointed and held out cash, and someone ran and got you whatever you pointed at), he wanted an interpreter. By all the Vanir and Aesir, he especially wanted one now.

She was worried, he could tell. Usually her orders were crisp and direct. This latest one, to go out and simply listen, filled him with unease. He had long suspected not just that his princess fled magic, but that some of the magic she feared lay within herself. As if anything she could do would be evil—aside from that order to strike off her head before she could blurt out their secrets. Twice in the past week, Haraldr had wakened in a cold sweat, dreaming that he had raised his axe against the woman he . . . He felt that way because she was their ring-giver, he told himself. The Basileus had given them and their oaths over to her. She was so brave, but now she was afraid. Haraldr could see it, and it made him want to take his axe to something.

"Looks like a wedding!" commented Arinbjorn. "Lines of men and women together, all dressed the same."

"They look like monks and nuns, fool!" hissed Haraldr. "Why would *they* marry?"

Arinbjorn nodded, then smiled at a small child whom he saw staring at him. Its mother snatched the baby out of his path.

"Pretty child," he said.

"They probably think we eat babies," Haraldr muttered as he tried to puzzle out the official's words. "Probably best to let them alone. You're right,

Arinbjorn. They're marrying off those people to one another, shutting down their monasteries."

"If Father Basil isn't careful, he may find himself with a bride!" Arinbjorn laughed, then lowered his voice, remembering orders.

"These aren't Christians; they're . . . Buddhists, Her Highness told me." Like the prince—though liking wasn't precisely what he felt for Li Shou, who tried to dismiss him, jarl's grandson as he was, like a hired sword or a thrall, and whose eyes followed Alexandra about with a look that his princess (wise as she was in other ways) was too innocent to understand.

"No!" burst from the throat of one woman who stood behind the official. Haraldr understood that much of the tonal, clanging language of Ch'in. The woman's voice scaled upward into a scream, then a yammer that choked off as blood gushed from her mouth and her body fell from the platform into the dust of the market. The official kept on speaking.

"I think he's looking at us," muttered Arinbjorn.

"Back up," Haraldr ordered.

Reluctantly, the crowd parted to let them through. Halfway into the next block, it held firm. They tried to shoulder through. Suddenly the press of tiny, intense people, with dark hair and bright tiny eyes, oppressed Haraldr, and he tried to shoulder through. His axe was slung across his back. If he had to, he could free up an arm and draw it . . . unless one of these folk had a knife and was willing to try using it.

Gritting his teeth and sweating, Haraldr concentrated on pushing through the crowd. A child set up a wail at the sight of him, and he kept on going. Behind them, the official finished, and musicians struck up the sick cats' wailing, broken by the clash of cymbals and drums, that they used instead of music in this land.

Abruptly a wail rose in the market and the crowd pressed forward. Someone shouted and hurled a rotten fruit which splattered the official's fine silk gown, and soldiers leaped from behind him, their swords drawn.

"Get moving!" Haraldr shouted. "We've got a riot on our hands!" Neither man drew his weapon yet. They pushed brutally through the crowd, eager to get back to Li Shou's palace and report. The market crowds degenerated into a series of brawls. Thieves pillaged the stalls, as individual fights broke off. Two men practically rolled underneath Haraldr's boots. Swearing, he stepped over them.

"Over there!" Arinbjorn pointed. Above one stall tended only by a few children was a tiled overhang; *was*, until a knot of brawlers caromed into its supports.

"No!" Arinbjorn shouted, and dashed forward. Instants later, he grunted as he took some of the burden of the roof onto his shoulders. "Get those children!" he yelled at his officer.

Moving with speed unusual in a man his size, Haraldr dashed forward, but was only in time to keep a falling tile from dashing out Arinbjorn's brains.

Then the brawlers crashed into the supports again, and the roof slipped farther. Arinbjorn cried out and fell to his knees, then onto his face. Over the snarls and shouts of the mob, Haraldr could hear the terrified shrieks of the children trapped beneath Arinbjorn, then nothing at all but panting breaths.

"Get out . . ."

That was Arinbjorn. Haraldr had to free him, yet if the rioters caught two foreigners here, they would tear them apart. His oath was to the princess; but if he abandoned Arinbjorn, she would probably make him wish that the mob had caught him. He bent to shift the rubble, then rose to size up the crowd. He cursed it, then cursed again.

Think, man! he ordered himself. He wished he had the security of orders. He twisted one hand in his beard, and felt fingers brush against the horn he had carried since he found it. In the desert, when he thought he had lost Alexandra for good, he had blown that horn, and found her. He raised the horn, then hesitated. He might be summoning her into danger. But she held his oath.

When all else failed, he had only the oath to trust to. He set lips to the bone mouthpiece and blew with all the force of his lungs. He produced no sound. He tried again until red specks danced before his eyes, and he collapsed to his knees, the horn dangling from its cord. He could sense echoes all around him, as if the horn call rang through air in some world that neighbored this one.

He bent double, hoping that the crowd would miss him. Nearby, Arinbjorn groaned. Haraldr began to tear at the masonry that covered him.

Hoofbeats pounded into the market. The crowd parted slowly, and the hoofbeats neared him, then stopped. Knife in hand, Haraldr rose into a crouch —and faced a riderless horse. Reins dropped out of empty air onto its saddle; he heard a slither of robes, and feet running toward him. Then a hand was on his shoulder, and he saw the princess.

"Where were you?" he gasped. Had she found some Tarnhelm that let her pass unseen?

"Never mind that," she hissed. "The city is running mad. It's as much as a Westerner's life is worth to be out in it."

"Arinbjorn tried to save two children. They're trapped beneath that."

Her Highness studied the rubble, looked at Haraldr, then reached for her sash. "Give me your belt too. If we tie one end to the horse, the other to the biggest piece of that roof . . ."

He ran to the sweating horse, and the princess ran after him. "Here, take this!" she ordered, and pressed a wilting lotus into his harness. Abruptly, he could see her again. "I can pretend to be Ch'in, unless they unveil me. You can't. Get him out!"

Though the horse rolled his eyes at the unlikely looking harness, he was sturdy, and the rubble shifted with more ease than Haraldr would have thought possible. Arinbjorn rolled to one side, and the children screamed.

"That's panic, not pain," Alexandra said. "You see to

Arinbjorn." The man groaned as Haraldr patted him up and down, roughly seeking injuries.

"Only shaken."

"Load him on the horse," she ordered. "I'll look to the children." She reached down and took their tiny hands, smeared with dirt and lime. Haraldr watched open-mouthed then, as she walked up to two people in the garb of merchants, pushed the children toward them, and spoke quickly, commandingly in Ch'in. Haraldr heaved Arinbjorn up across the horse's saddle, then turned back to see Alexandra, having found adults to take charge of the children whom Arinbjorn had rescued, turn back, and look puzzled.

"Haraldr?" He remembered that he held the lotus; she couldn't see him.

"Here, Highness. Here's my hand."

"Let's go home. I hope that flower lasts till we get there."

The mob swirled about them, but they passed unseen, heading out of the market toward Li Shou's compound, and whatever small safety could be found there.

14

A carp splashing in the narrow stream that twisted between pines and a great, freestanding rock startled Alexandra. This quiet garden, devised by a scholar for contemplation, and the riot outside its walls belonged to two separate worlds. Arinbjorn's bruises were proof of the existence of the other; they had been lucky to be able to retreat back to the safety of the palace. Lucky, or divinely favored, and she was coming to suspect the latter. Father Basil had still not returned from his church, nor Li Shou from the Imperial palace.

Alexandra sighed. Though she dutifully turned to the books that had been left in her rooms, her attention wandered to servants' gossip overheard while she bathed. It seemed that silk in Ch'in was the product of women—just as it had been in Byzantium. In all circles from the poor family that owned only a few mulberry trees to the women's quarters of the Imperial palace, women tended the silkworms, chopped leaves for them, tended the fires that kept them awake and feeding, and then, when they began to spin, watched over the cocoons until they were ready to drop them into boiling water, then unravel the silken thread.

Well enough. I have only to convince some family to break the law and sell silkworms to a foreigner . . . just when the whole Empire looks like it's turning against foreigners. Simple.

She opened the *Lao Tzu* again, and bent over the unfamiliar characters. What was that? "Heaven and Earth are not benevolent; they treat the ten thousand creatures ruthlessly. The sage is not benevolent; he treats the people ruthlessly." How had a gentle Way turned so fierce?

But was Byzantium any different? In just one of her City's riots, over twenty-five thousand people had been slaughtered in the Hippodrome alone. Chaos was the same the world over. She laid aside that book for one wrapped in scented silk. Idly she opened it and began to leaf through.

The book was illustrated, each picture as cunningly painted as any devotional manuscript from the West. But what these pictures were devoted to! Her cheeks flamed. On each page, a man and at least one woman twisted and twined about one another in the act of union. Unable to look away, she noted that the tiny figures were pale, the women paler than the men, except for their private parts, which the artist had tinted a rosy color.

She dropped the book as if it burned her fingers. But before she could clap her hands to order a servant to take it away and burn it, she remembered that for some sorceries union was a sacrament, a liberation of power. That was why she had quarreled with Li Shou when he had told that minister that she assisted him in his alchemy. If she had seen this book, she felt now that she might have tried to kill him.

How could a brothel transform itself into a shrine? Her fingers trembled on the fine paper. The book had been lovingly crafted, the figures finely drawn. Against both her better judgment and her will, she turned page after page. She had been a nun, then a traveler; even the thought of performing the least and most chaste (not that any of them were) of the acts pictured on these pages appalled her. Yet her mouth went dry, and her face scalded, and her curiosity, never long asleep, awoke and pulsed along her veins.

She had heard titters in the women's quarters, giggles if clouds or rain were mentioned in proximity. Now she understood why; and she didn't think she would ever again hear people speak of jade or peonies without blushing fiercely.

Li Shou had included the book among those left in her rooms, she realized. *You're not truly such a fool as to ask why, are you, Alexandra?*

Approaching footsteps made her push the book to the bottom of the pile she had had brought into the garden. Anyone coming this way would see only her contemplating the whorls and caves within the rock he had paid gold for and ordered set in his garden.

As she dreaded, it was Li Shou. Alexandra started to rise, then thought better of it. Her knees were weak and she stammered over her greeting to him. Fury at her own embarrassment helped her control her speech.

He gestured at the stream. The sky was darkening toward twilight, and vapor rose from the water.

"The mists are sluggish, confused today," he said. "We call them *chi*."

"Does that surprise you?" she asked.

"Today I tried to speak against the recent madness," he said. "But those old men who seek to return us to the days of Ch'in Shih Huang-di shouted me down, called me half-barbarian. Were you caught in the street brawls?"

"I saw monks and nuns dragged from a Buddhist temple," she said, looking down at her scratched fingers. "They were wed to one another while the rabble jeered, except for those who refused."

"Were they slain?"

Alexandra nodded.

"They were sworn to renunciation," Li Shou spoke softly. "But there are other ways along the Path that are sweeter." His hands drifted over her books (including the scandalous, silk-wrapped one), and he dropped down beside her on the carven bench.

"Why do they do this?" The cry burst from her before she could control her voice.

"And you in the West, have you not your holy wars? Did I not hear Father Basil describe how your own City cast his people out?"

Alexandra shook her head. "This is worse. This is . . . chaos."

Li Shou's hand touched hers, and she forced herself not to flinch. "I agree. Destruction, and greed. The monasteries have become fat and sleepy. The Son of Heaven—may he live ten thousand years!—follows the Tao. He *is* the Tao. But little men like Lu Tsung will make their fortunes." He sighed, and was silent, as if waiting for the garden's serenity to purge his spirit of bitterness.

"At least, I may not be forbidden my own studies," he said. "The Son of Heaven is fascinated with immortality, and so will not hinder any scholar who claims to seek it. You too, lady; you are a student."

His hand stroked hers. One finger touched the center of her palm, which was sweating, then traced the veins on her wrist. She pulled her hand away, and he laughed.

"What do you read, Princess?" he asked in a low voice that made her tremble. "No. Look at me." He tipped up her chin with one well-kept finger. "That is better. You blush. Will you not answer me?"

Her lips were trembling, and she hated it, despised the gush of tears to her eyes, her involuntary response to that gentle, knowing voice and practiced touch.

"It may be a long time before the Son of Heaven will agree to see you, and you can fulfill your brother's commands. With all that time . . . there are other ways of enlightenment than the road to Shambhala, you know, and ways more satisfying when shared."

She knew how ill-favored many people in Ch'in found Westerners, had counted on it. But Li Shou, she remembered, had always been fascinated by things and people from beyond the Middle Kingdom. His life was bound up with them.

Alexandra had faced avalanches and black storms along the way to Ch'ang-an without half the panic she felt now. He smelled of sandalwood. He was bending over her, and she felt paralyzed. In an instant, he would touch her, and she would learn whether a body—her own body—could really twist into those astonishing postures that seemed burned into her memory.

"Your Highness!"

It was Li Shou's aged steward, his wizened face looking almost anguished. The eunuch had his arms outstretched, attempting to bar two other people—*from interfering in his master's pleasures*? It was Haraldr, and with him a much-singed and bleeding Father Basil. Alexandra leaped to her feet.

"After I saw Arinbjorn settled, my princess, I went out again hoping to find the rest of your people. All but two are safe."

She bowed her head. "Last of all, I found Father Basil. He should be in bed, with a healer sent for, but . . ."

"But I had to speak to you, to both of you!" cried the little man. "They're killing us out there! Do you know what they did? Today they torched the church that an Emperor had built. Two hundred years of faith and hard work—burned to ashes in an afternoon!"

Tears rolled down the priest's grimy face. "I helped save the children in the school, praise God. But our entire community, they're making plans to flee."

Then it would be useless to appeal to them for silkworms. It was inevitable. If no one would sell them or supply them, she would have to steal them from the only source left. The palace. Perhaps Siddiqa's mother's stories would help her sneak in—or they could bribe a guard. Involuntarily, she put both hands to her temples.

Too much was happening at once. The Manichees, the Christians, the Buddhists . . . if no foreign faith was safe, it would be only a matter of time, perhaps just hours, until foreign merchants too were under attack.

"We are behaving like savages!" hissed Li Shou. "This chaos is unspeakable!" He rose. "Lady, kindly excuse me. You will want to question your people. And I, I must write a memorial to present to the Son of Heaven. Han Chu, you will see that a surgeon attends to this good priest. And, lady, remember what it was we spoke of."

The languor that had characterized the prince since his return home was gone. The man who walked toward his study was the comrade of the journey east, the ally who had not despaired in the Takla Makan, nor flinched in Turpan. Even Haraldr granted him a curt salute.

"Father," the steward began in that woodwind eunuch's voice of his, "we must salve your burns. Come and rest."

Father Basil flinched violently away from the alien features that resembled the hundreds of rage-twisted faces that burned what he had most prized. "Forgive me," he murmured the moment afterward. "Call the surgeon for me, and I'll submit."

Alexandra reinforced his request with a curt nod. Reluctantly, the eunuch retreated.

"What is it?" she asked.

"If we do not leave soon, I fear we will not be able to flee at all," whispered the priest. He began to weep again. "Lady, they're killing us!" Alexandra took a scarf from her sleeve, dipped it into the stream, and began to clean his face. The blood-scent seemed to taint the cleanliness of the pines and gingkoes.

"You are exhausted," she murmured. "Go with Han Chu, go and rest. Leave the problem to me." The priest staggered off.

"You should help him," she told Haraldr, who lingered by the pool. He had not yet changed out of the crimson he had worn in the morning. His tunic was torn at the shoulder. The weal of an old scar was pale against the heavy muscle and red-gold hair of his chest. Her mouth went dry as she looked at him.

"My princess," Haraldr began, his voice hesitant as always when he thought he intruded on her thoughts. "What did you and the prince discuss?"

Alexandra's brows flew up, and the blood rushed into her face again. But she had control of herself in an instant. "Weather," she said softly, staring out at the stream and the troubled, cloudy mists that rose from it. "Clouds . . . and rain."

He was standing over her in just the way that Li Shou had. The warmth of his body drew her; she had always felt safe among her Varangians. But now she was unable to meet the earnest, anxious gaze that willed her to be his keen-witted and confident leader. Haraldr thought of her as an officer, perhaps, or as a princess put in his care; nothing else. She rose. When he offered his hand to assist her, she evaded him, and picked up her books, clutching them to her breast.

"Can you find Bryennius for me?" she asked. "I need to talk with you all."

Even Father Basil and Arinbjorn insisted on joining the meeting in the garden. Bryennius thought that both of them would do better to rest. Ch'ang-an, exciting as it had looked, had proved to be a trap they might have to run from before it caught them in its jaws.

Siddiqa, desert-bred, shivered in the cool of the evening and Bryennius laid a cloak over her slender shoulders. She screwed up her forehead in a way that always made him want to kiss her, as she struggled to find words in the Sogdian that they all used to confuse any spies.

"Think!" Alexandra urged her. "We can't just go wandering about the palace."

"My . . . mother never told me where the silkworms were."

Alexandra sighed.

"Stop badgering her, cousin!" Bryennius snapped at Alexandra. Nothing about Alexandra's plan to smuggle herself and his Siddiqa into the Imperial palace in the closed carts often used to convey new concubines pleased him. Small, quick, and female, they might go unnoticed just long enough to cram the dormant silkworms into hollow cane staves and flee. The rest of them would be waiting outside the northwest gate. Assuming they could find the silkworms, steal them, and get out.

"What makes you think that they don't have the same level of protection for their silkworms as we do . . . did . . . for ours?" he demanded.

"Eunuchs might not stop two women who look like they are engaged in legitimate work. I've been in the Gynaecia, I know that silkworms need a lot of work," Alexandra said. "As for . . . magical protection, I can only rely on what has helped us before."

Her voice was a little too cheerful, Bryennius thought. She had to know how full of holes her plan was. But he had nothing better, and the need to escape this city was upon him, as much as on the others. If the chaos here had grown so strong, what must it be like in Byzantium? At least now he was a soldier, fit to defend his home . . . assuming he could get back there.

Bryennius gazed up at the moon and shuddered. It was a thin sickle, tinged red, as if it had reaped the harvest he had seen today in the streets and inns. Not a single tavern owned by Westerners was still standing unburned.

One of the soldiers stationed along the winding path near the stream whistled. They all fell silent, then started talking too loudly and at random.

Li Shou, elaborately dressed in court robes, stood before them.

"Bring light," he said over his shoulder. Bryennius flinched at the sudden torchlight.

The prince seated himself beside the stream, nodded at the towering rock that cast its shadow across the group, then looked them over.

"Tell me what you are planning," he ordered, then held up a long-fingered hand in a gesture that was both commanding and elegant. "And please, do me the justice of not asking 'what do you mean?' I am a man of sense. And I have long suspected that more than a desire to pay your respects to the Son of Heaven brought you to Ch'in."

Haraldr was creeping up behind him. In a moment more, he could catch him, gag him before he could cry out . . . but Alexandra too held up a hand and forbade it.

"Other than the courtesy we owe you as our host," Alexandra said, "why should we tell you?"

"Because I suspect that it is bound up with magic, with the chaos that has stalked you since you left your home . . ."

"Earlier than that," she put in.

"And if it's a matter of magic, I can possibly help. Certainly, I have earned the right to try."

Alexandra raised an eyebrow.

"This evening, after I left you, I wrote a memorial condemning the Son of Heaven's actions. It is worse than you thought. Do you know how many thousands of people have already died? Ch'in will be one vast grave-yard before he and his court of carrion-eaters are sated."

"You said that at court?" Bryennius asked.

"I did. Needless to say, I was shouted down and accused of treason. The ministers called the guard, and they hurled me—me, a prince of the Imperial House—to my knees before the Dragon Throne." He laughed grimly. "A prince, did I say? Not any longer. I was demoted to commoner and sent home to await . . . this may be it now."

Han Chu appeared on the curving path and prostrated himself at Li Shou's feet.

"Didn't you hear, old friend, that I am prince no longer?" the younger man asked. "Get up, man, get up! And bring in my guests."

The eunuch rose. With immense dignity, he ignored

the tears that ran down his face, and ushered in five armored soldiers. Their ranks parted to let Lu Tsung, a roll of dark silk in his hands, approach the prince.

"Even now I find you with your barbarians, not decently worshiping at the altars of your ancestors," the minister remarked, disgust evident in his pursed lips and flaring nostrils. "You have become a barbarian yourself."

Li Shou sat, watching his enemy. His breath came a little faster, Bryennius noted, but he neither moved nor spoke.

"I believe that this will be no surprise," the minister said. "The Son of Heaven remembers that once you and he were distant kin." He unrolled the dark cloth he carried. Shrouded in it was a long, silken cord.

Siddiqa stifled a gasp, and Han Chu sobbed aloud. Bryennius darted a look at Alexandra. "Think of Nero," she whispered in rapid Greek. "He would command men to open their veins by sending them a sword. Here, they use a silken cord."

Suddenly Bryennius could not get enough air, or take his eyes from Li Shou, who leaned forward slightly, touched a finger to the cord, then took it into his hands and tugged on it.

"It appears to be quite sturdy," he remarked. He glanced up at the night sky. "I have until dawn, I assume, to make my arrangements. You need not wait."

My God, does he really expect the man to sling that cord from the branch of the nearest tree and hang himself? Bryennius thought. It wasn't decent. He heard himself growling, and saw Haraldr start forward.

"Unnecessary," Li Shou told the Varangian. "But if you could show these men out, then come back, you would have my thanks—for whatever they are worth now."

Haraldr signaled. Abruptly, the Varangians seemed to materialize from the shadows and tower over the minister and his guard. The Ch'in soldiers looked at Lu Tsung, then at the Varangians, and went quietly.

"You see?" asked Li Shou. He let the silken cord fall into his lap. "I am considered a Westerner. So, naturally, I shall help you—provided you work no harm on the Son of Heaven."

Alexandra took a deep breath. "He has the right," she told the rest of the group. "We came for silkworms. A blight killed the silkworms in Byzantium, blight and foul magic that stretched out to menace the Emperor and his son. The silk trade is vital to our Empire. I thought that if we had could restore it . . ."

"That the balance might, in some way, be restored?" Li Shou asked patiently. Alexandra nodded.

"There are no silkworms to be had here," said the prince. "You will have to go to the palace and take them."

"So I thought too," Alexandra said, and told him their plans thus far.

He turned and stretched out a hand to his steward, who crouched weeping at his side.

"Han Chu." The man scrambled up, then made to flee.

"No, don't go. Or you, Prince Bryennius. Stay with me for as long as you can. I—we—will need your help before the end."

15

By moonrise, the servants' lamentations subsided and
were replaced by a steady stream of farewells. Each man
and woman received a final gift from the prince whom
they had served, then slipped out of the compound. A
while later, Bryennius' soldiers, Greeks and Varangians
heavily muffled to hide their alien features, were escorted to the eastern gate.

Last of all, the eunuch Han Chu prostrated himself
before his master, then took charge of a richly capari-
soned cart bound for the Imperial palace, and bearing
Alexandra and Siddiqa. They wore elaborate robes,
suitable for soon-to-be Imperial concubines, and, because the night was cool, overrobes of warm furs. But
beneath their robes were riding clothes and boots, and
hollow staffs were hidden among the cushions of the cart
in which they rode.

"What if they fail and are caught?" Bryennius stood in

the doorway, shaped like a moon for good fortune, until the cart disappeared in a bend in the road.

"Han Chu will not let them suffer." The condemned prince's voice seemed to come from very far away. Bryennius turned on his heel and reentered Li Shou's study. The lamps cast wavering shadows on the walls and gilded silk hangings, and glowed through a jade screen by the prince's writing table.

Inevitably, there would come a moment when Alexandra and his Siddiqa would have to leave the old man behind. What if they were caught then? For all the strangeness she had been through, Alexandra still preserved a Christian horror of suicide. Siddiqa might not, but the idea of that delicate throat pierced by a blade —he saw Li Shou watching him with that too-perceptive gaze of his, and shuddered.

The prince set his seal to a paper, rolled it, and handed it to Bryennius. "Yours, for the journey. Now, come look at the map." Bryennius stood over the older man, stood so close that he was aware when he shivered. Behind them, in its wrappings, coiled the silken cord that both struggled to ignore.

"I know Alexandra feels compelled to escape south, but don't expect to travel by sea. The harbors will be watched. And no city in Ch'in is safe for outsiders now." The long, elegant hand began to trace out a route. "Your only hope of safety lies on the frontier, back the way you came. To Dunhuang." Li Shou shuddered. "I wish I could say that the people now alive in Ch'in are all you may have to fear. Just remember that the First Emperor promised vengeance against *any* foe of Ch'in."

Li Shou was talking about magic again. In that case, Dunhuang, where the timeless sanctity had touched even Bryennius, and given Alexandra rest, might shield them from any magic that pursued them from Ch'ang-an, just as it had protected them from what drove them from Byzantium.

"You have kin there, of a sort," the prince continued

with a quiet intensity that made Bryennius sweat, despite the autumn chill. "Warn them to flee. But if you value them, do not travel with them."

"Why? Surely, the bigger the caravan, the safer the journey."

"And the slower! I tell you, speed is safety for you, and nothing else. When you leave Ch'ang-an, make haste. Especially—" He looked up. "You remember the tombs of the Emperors. Your road . . . there is no other way . . . takes you past Mount Li. By all the gods, do not dally near the tomb of the First Emperor. Promise me!"

Bryennius nodded. "From the Jade Gate, go south. At Khotan, you can choose again: back to Kashgar, or into Hind or Tibet. I had hoped to go too, and help your cousin find Shambhala . . . perhaps she will now. I do not think she will be at peace until she tries."

Prince Li Shou rolled up the map and gave it to Bryennius, then sat gazing at the gem carved into the form of a hollowed, water-smoothed rock, drawing its serenity into his own spirit.

"Why not come with us, man?" Bry' cried. "Come back to Byzantium, and be our guest, as we have been yours!"

But the prince was shaking his head. "I cannot leave here."

"In the name of God, why not, when all they can think to do is sentence you . . ." Bryennius gestured at the deadly, bundled silk behind them. "You're even helping us steal silkworms . . . why stop at that?"

The Ch'in prince chuckled, a sound incongruous in the still room. Outside, the night wind blew and a nightingale sang. The scent of pine prickled at Bryennius' nostrils. Briefly he cursed the trees outside. In a few hours, the prince would pick up that cord, go into the garden, and choose the sturdiest branch he could find.

The older man turned and smiled at him. "In case you had forgotten, the punishment for stealing Ch'in silkworms *is* death. Even though I am sentenced to die, I cannot leave. For all my years traveling, the Middle Kingdom is my home."

Bryennius shook his head, the beginnings of angry sorrow welling up in his chest as a growl. "Consider it like this. I am a child, forbidden by my mother to give food to strangers. Yet I like the look of the strangers, so I disobey. But, just because there is punishment in store, shall I run away with them? I shall stay here, where my ancestors have died. Let it go, younger brother."

Bryennius knew he looked startled. "Oh, yes, I call you brother. People usually come to regard you as a brother, do they not? And in our case, there might have been rather more truth to it—if matters had but worked out as I hoped. We might truly have been brothers, you and I."

Bryennius shook his head in sorrow. "Alexandra is cousin, not sister, to me."

"In all the important ways, you are her brother, even more than that Emperor you serve. You . . . I planned for you to serve the Son of Heaven as a soldier. You might even have enjoyed it. And the lady . . . she would have been my first wife, my companion, and my partner in study. I would have treasured her . . . you knew that, did you not?"

"I saw how you looked at her," he admitted.

"So did she," mourned the prince. "Such a brave lady, yet I know I frightened her. It might have been very sweet. Had we only had more time . . . We are bound together on the Wheel, all of us. Perhaps it may reunite us one day. You will tell her what I have said?"

"My oath on it!"

But the prince shook his head, amused by Bryennius' fervor. This was the last time Li Shou's poise would make him feel raw and untutored, Bryennius thought regretfully. "Your word on it is enough. I trust you. You should be long gone, but—" He looked up. Abruptly he shivered, and the sallow skin at eye and mouth ticced convulsively. For a moment, he looked ancient and dying. Then he gazed at the miniature rock and drew a deep, shaking breath. "Stay with me, for just a while . . ."

"To the end," Bryennius vowed hoarsely. "I promise you something else. My first son, Siddiqa's and mine . . . he will bear your name."

"Among those impossibly long names you Western barbarians use?" Li Shou laughed in quick delight. Then his mood turned somber again. "Promise me nothing. But, as I said, we are all bound. It may be I shall come back into flesh as a Hu-barbarian. Certainly, I spent years enough—and love enough—upon them. Perhaps, I might even return as a child you love."

Bryennius ventured to lay a hand on the seated man's shoulder. Li Shou reached up and grasped it for an instant. "Enough. Take the map. Take this ring as my gift to you. Give your cousin Alexandra this trifle." He pointed at the rock. "It is not so heavy that it will weigh her down, no matter how fast you travel. And remember me."

Sensing that Li Shou had schemed to keep them all in Ch'ang-an, Bryennius had never trusted him. Now his mistrust struck him to the heart. Once again, a brother passed beyond his reach, as Leo and Suleiman had both done. And this one he had never appreciated. He reached into his heavy travel clothes and pulled out the insignia he had carried since before Kashgar.

"This belonged to a man I honored," he began, but already the prince was shaking his head.

"I have no need for gifts now, nor for any of the treasures I stored up. Illusion, all of it. Do your holy books not say so too?"

"Vanity of vanities," Bryennius murmured.

"I give them to you, all my beautiful vanities. Use them to cover your flight. Feed them to the flames . . . when I am gone." Bryennius knew he must have looked even more dense than usual. "The fire! Your cousin would have died rather than betray how to make it. I know you have a few vials left. When I am gone, use

them to burn this place. It will look like a riot. Perhaps
they will think all of you died in the flames . . ."

Li Shou turned and looked up at the sky. Moonset had
passed hours ago. The air was freshening, the sky turning
pale. "By now, I pray, they should be through. And safe.
You must go." He bent and reached for the silken cord,
slipped it from its wrappings, and let it slide from hand
to hand. "At dawn, Lu Tsung will come to check that I
have obeyed the Son of Heaven. Let him find only ashes.
Perhaps, if we are very fortunate, the fire will catch him
too." He looked up, a kind of wry mischief glinting in his
long eyes. "You see, the rock in the garden, the one by
the stream, is one he covets. And since it is an old
companion of mine, I want to cheat him of it."

"I can't believe you're not afraid." To his disgust, the
words he had suppressed all night blurted from
Bryennius' mouth.

"Afraid of death, no. I shall be reborn. Unless, of
course, I have earned sufficient merit to win release.
Though I doubt it, my friend, I truly doubt it." The
prince smiled, then turned serious again. "But I do
fear . . . pain, a long struggle, disfigurement. One reason
I asked you to stay . . . do not let me suffer."

Bryennius bowed assent.

"Why then, we make an end. Come, younger brother.
First we will burn these papers that I no longer need, and
then I shall inform my ancestors to expect me among
them almost immediately." Swiftly Li Shou cast papers
on a burner, then went to an austere altar on which
tablets rested, and prostrated himself before it.

Banners of violet were starting to glow at the horizon.
A nightingale's piercing song made the night almost
unbearable. Then a brief tremor shook the earth, and the
bird flew away. The prince raised an eyebrow and
watched it go. "Quickly, now." He led the way into the
garden where they had often sat and talked, then gazed
about. "That tree, I think."

He had chosen the pine beside the stream, near the
huge, free-standing rock he loved. Looping the silken

cord into a noose, he tossed the other end over a branch and secured it. Then he climbed onto the bench and slipped the noose over his head.

Though Bryennius longed to break, to run and hide like an irresponsible, grieving brat, he forced himself to stand firm, as he had done at Leo's pyre.

"God watch over you . . . whichever god you choose," said the prince. Then he smiled. For a little while, he stood meditating, his eyes shut. Bryennius found himself praying, both the prayers of Church and childhood and the heathen ones he had learned in this strange, cruel land.

Then Li Shou jerked himself away from the bench. His feet kicked spasmodically, and his mouth gaped and gurgled.

Bryennius drew his dagger and stabbed the prince to the heart. His blood stained Bryennius' tunic as he stepped forward to catch him, to cut him free, and ease him down to lie beneath the tree.

He folded Li Shou's hands over the wound. They were still warm, and his blood warmed them further. Then he closed the dead man's eyes, and let his hand rest for a moment of farewell upon his forehead. Finally he placed Leo's regimental insignia between the prince's clasped hands. Hadn't he promised Leo to bury it honorably in Ch'ang-an?

"As I promised . . . brothers," he whispered.

His eyes watered as he lurched back to the now-desolate rooms where he might have been content to live out his life, and he swore at his tears. A pack lay on the floor. He almost stumbled upon it. Then he rummaged through it fiercely, finding the vial he sought more by feel than sight.

Shouldering the pack, he returned to the garden. A few long needles had drifted down upon Li Shou's body. The nightingale had returned, to open its throat in one last torrent of song before dawn. Bryennius clapped his hands to frighten the bird away. As its wings flapped, and it flew to safety over the palace walls, Bryennius hurled the vial of Greek fire down beside Li Shou. Then he ran before he could see the flames start, catch, and consume his friend. And if he pulled his hat down upon his face and wept as he mounted, then rode frantically toward the Ch'un Ming Gate, he was not the only man in Ch'ang-an that dawn to be stained with blood, to weep, and to flee.

The walls of the Imperial city were high and thick, and the gates sloped inward. Alexandra lifted the curtains of the oxcart that lumbered in through the gates, toward the silkworms and away from escape. She wished she could see Han Chu, who drove the cart. He claimed to be distraught at his prince's death sentence, but she had seen good actors before.

Half-smothered by cushions in the place beside her, Siddiqa breathed too quickly, and her eyes glinted. Fear? Excitement?. Alexandra knew that the Turpan princess had nerve and courage, but even if her nerve broke, she needed her now for her fluent Ch'in, and her features, which were not as alien as Alexandra's. She looked like she might be an Imperial concubine; after all, her mother had been.

Siddiqa shifted awkwardly, pulling at her robes. Desert-bred, she found the weight of furs and wadded silks, plus the riding clothes they concealed, distressing. Her hand went to her waist, and Alexandra knew she caressed the dagger Bryennius had given her. She would turn it on herself, an option Alexandra did not have. If they were taken, her best course would be to compel guards to kill her. Han Chu, she suspected, had orders not to let her live to face slow torture for theft, but Han Chu could not pass within the walls protecting the silkworms from the rest of the Imperial compound.

The cart rumbled over paving stones now, past rows of long-needled pines and gingkoes, past columned buildings that seemed barred against them. In the moonlight, the round entryways of some buildings looked like mouths—but to think that way was to open herself to

fear, and to court chaos. The wheels rattled over an
arched bridge, then beneath another gate, over which a
tablet hung. Guards halted the cart and Han Chu hailed
them, speaking too rapidly for Alexandra to follow. She
tensed, and Siddiqa squeezed her hand. In the darkness,
she could not see the reds and golds that the walls were
painted. From the distance came the yapping of a hound.
The cart jolted forward and she dared to breathe again.

Finally, Han Chu slowed the cart beside a narrow
building, and edged it into a pool of shadows. Alexandra
forced herself to remain seated until he came to open the
cart for her; mannerly shyness, even awe, suited her role.
She glanced sidelong at the old man whose swollen eyes
and sagging posture relieved any doubts she might have
had that he would betray her. Then she and Siddiqa
followed him across a wide space in which their footsteps rang too loudly, and the hound's yapping was
louder yet. Their shadows sprawled across the field, and
up the next wall. The bundle of canes that Han Chu
carried looked like spears. Surely a guard would see and
stop them.

The gate in this wall was very narrow. Though her
fears screamed that this was a trap, a cage, she let Han
Chu bring them to the tiny gate. Here he bowed, handed
them the hollow canes they would fill with silkworms,
then slipped back into the darkness to wait. No man, nor
once-man, could pass within these walls, for the making
of silk was women's business.

Ahead of her, mulberry trees swayed in the night
wind. Their branches were bare, sign of a recent harvest.
Silkworms, she knew, fed voraciously before they spun.
To keep them from food for even one hour was to kill
them. The branches hissed and rustled as clouds scudded across the moon, and cast dappled shadows on the
building ahead. The wind was freshening. With God's
favor, they might expect the weather to turn cold and
remain so. A good frost would ensure that the silkworms
would sleep in their cocoons, raising the chance that she
could bring them, still living, to Byzantium. Despite the

chill, she and Siddiqa dropped their fur cloaks, since the
building housing the silkworms would be kept hot to aid
them in spinning their cocoons.

The barking Alexandra had heard earlier became
louder. She hissed a quick oath. That was all they
needed, to have some imbecile come out to investigate a
barking dog or to hush it—and find them. "We'll have to
quiet it ourselves," she whispered. But beside her
Siddiqa shrank away and looked wretched. She certainly
picked a fine time to show that she was afraid of dogs.
Alexandra sighed, and waved her on ahead.

The barking ceased. A scrabble of claws on stone told
her that the dog, or dogs, drew nearer. Then she heard a
low whine and a growl. She drew her dagger and moved
forward slowly, stopping herself just before she whistled.
In an undertone she hissed out noises that she knew
calmed dogs, praying that they worked here too.

"So, boy, so . . . what do you have?" she whispered.
She made her way over to a dense tangle of bushes where
something scrabbled and whined. To her relief, the
animal was small, one of the golden hounds from
Samarkand that seemed like nothing but a collection of
tufts of fur. But a whimpering revealed that she was
alone in finding the beast harmless. A tiny fox kit cried
and tried to curl its way beneath a rock. It was alone;
clearly, at some time before, the hound had killed its
brothers and sisters.

"Oh . . ." Alexandra sighed. Though this was no time
to rescue small animals, she had to drive away the hound
in any case. Her sash, looped about its collar, made a
convenient leash. She tethered the hound to a branch,
then picked up the kit and set it on her shoulder. When
she finished inside, she would free it.

The door opened at a touch, and she slipped inside.
The place resembled Byzantine workrooms in the wom-
en's quarters before the blight had killed their silkworms: the meticulous cleanness, the faint hum of life
and growth, the stacks of trays, and, above all, the heat,
like a summer on the Golden Horn. Briefly, she was

homesick, then exultant. She wanted to dance or cry out her victory—even though she was thousands of miles and many months premature.

Seizing her canes, she almost ran to the nearest tray of cocoons and began cramming the small, thready capsules inside them. She thanked God that the worms were not in their feeding frenzy; the one time she had witnessed that, the relentless crunch of leaves had sickened her.

The humming intensified. She found it soothing. After the chill of the outdoors, the warmth of the room and the heartbeat of the fox kit against her breast lulled her. She felt faintly drowsy.

Then she saw Siddiqa, crumpled up against one rack of trays. Bile rushed to her mouth and she swallowed hard, remembering that strong odors—sweat, fear, sickness—killed silkworms.

"Younger sister?" She knelt and began to turn the Uighur girl. Desert-born, she would not have been harmed by the heat; a survivor of the karez of Turpan, she would not have fainted from terror. All this Alexandra knew without thinking. She laid Siddiqa down and went into a fighting crouch, her dagger springing into her hand as she heard slippered footsteps.

"Your sister thief tried to pretend that she was here by right," said a woman's voice. "I am glad you do not lie." There was a deepness, a richness, and yet something wild about that voice, like piled furs. Even though Alexandra knew that perfumes were never brought near silkworms, she smelled a faint musk. This must be the woman called the "silkworm mother," guardian of the cocoons. In its way, the position was as demanding as that of an abbess: no scents, no cosmetics, and chastity for months on end. The woman Alexandra faced didn't look like an ascetic. She was tall and supple. The sleek hair that sprang back from a V on her brow was thick, with a reddish glow. Strongly marked, arched brows set off huge, black eyes and a dark, passionate mouth, open now in a smile that showed sharp, perfect white teeth.

"Fox . . ." the word shuddered from Siddiqa. "Fox-woman . . ."

Alexandra had heard tales from the Varangians of "weres," creatures half-human, half-beast; she had never thought that a were-creature could be lovely, even though its long-nailed hands were extended like claws to rend her. The Varangian tales were of wolves; in Ch'in, the tales spoke of creatures that had the souls of foxes.

She had no silver, no cross upon her, none of the arsenal of countryfolks' or priests' wardings against such a creature. Her exultation of but a few moments past seemed as far distant as Byzantium itself, or the moon. It seemed unfair that she might be stopped, not by chaos, nor princes, but by the damnable, unpredictable wild magic such as she had encountered in the desert and in Turpan.

"I won't hurt you," she began, trying to reach the animal in the fox-woman.

"Thief!" the woman hissed. "I shall put the sleep on you, and drag you outside to feed my little one."

Wakened by the voice and probably, Alexandra thought, by her pounding heartbeats, the fox kit nestled in Alexandra's robes chose that moment to squirm and bark shrilly.

"My kit!" cried the woman in a voice that sounded like a fox's bark. "My son, my only one left by those accursed dogs! Give him to me!"

She advanced, and Alexandra backed away from her long, sharp nails.

"What will you have?" said the mother of silk. "These insects I guard? That foolish, sleeping thief? What are they to me beside the life of my child? Take them, take them all, but give me my son!"

She gestured with one of those quick, clawed hands, and Siddiqa stumbled to her feet, rubbed her eyes, and picked up the canes she had filled.

"Fox-spirits are treacherous," she whispered to Alexandra. "Do not trust her."

So Alexandra dared not trust any bargain she struck.

The fox-spirit's eyes grew as bright as polished onyx, then spilled over. Alexandra had not realized that a beast could weep. "Please," she begged. "Give him to me!"

In the name of God, or the Bearer of God, or whatever names anyone worshiped, did the woman really think that Alexandra would dash the poor kit's brains out, right before her eyes?

She pulled the fox kit from within her robes and stroked the small, soft body that squirmed in its eagerness to reach its dam.

"Don't torment me!" cried the fox-woman.

Alexandra gestured to Siddiqa to head for the door. Gathering up her courage, she walked toward the woman who shook her head from side to side in her grief. Her hair flew free and lashed like a fox's tail.

"I tied up the dog that would have killed . . . your son," she told her. "I meant to set the kit free after I finished here." She held the kit out to its mother with trembling hands and dared to make her own plea. "I ask you to believe that I do not steal for sport, nor take more than I need. I . . ." She thought (as she had not done for months) of her nephew, the prince whose life she had saved, of her fevered homeland, and her voice choked . . . "I have kits of my own to protect. If I cannot bring them what you guard, they may die. But I will not bargain with a child's life. Here. Take your son. Keep him safe."

She placed the kit in its mother's hands. For an instant, they closed over her own, and she felt their hot, inhuman strength. Sharp nails bit into her flesh briefly, then pulled back.

The fox-woman clutched the kit to her breast, and backed up against the wall. One tray spilled and its precious contents rolled onto the floor.

"You do not bargain?" Her eyes were bright, suspicious.

"Yesterday, I saved children in the marketplace. Today, I saved your son. I tell you, I will not hurt a child!

Now," she bluffed, "call your masters. Will you watch while they kill me?"

Alexandra had never felt such pity as she did then for the confused, wild creature who saw her usual defenses fail and was faced instead with kindness. Suspicion warred with relief in the brilliant eyes. Clearly, she trusted no one, even the people who had set her as a guard, yet loosed the hound that killed her other kits. Fox-spirits were treacherous, unpredictable. They would not keep a bargain for longer than might amuse them.

But they could be moved by gratitude and love.

Moving faster than any natural human, the fox-mother darted forward, seized Alexandra's hand and, doglike, sniffed and kissed it. "Take what you need and go. I shall remember your scent and teach it to my children. Woman"—and the word was almost a title of nobility—"know that Russet Silk is grateful to you —and that she is not the least of the vixens."

Alexandra bent and began filling her hollow staffs from the cocoons that had rolled on the floor. Beside her worked Siddiqa, though more slowly from her fears of the fox-woman who circled them.

"You will go west," said Russet Silk. "That is good. Ch'in has no place now for kind strangers, or any strangers at all. Keep going west. Do not stop, not for anything. And perhaps, if you come home to your own earth, perhaps you will tell your kits about me."

At that, Siddiqa looked up and smiled. "I shall tell them that you were very beautiful and very true," she said. Alexandra nodded.

The fox-woman smiled. For a moment, the three of them simply looked at one another, and the warmth they felt had nothing to do with the heat in the building. Then the earth shivered, and Russet Silk sniffed the air.

"You must go . . . now!" she cried softly. "I myself shall be your guide."

Swiftly, using every scrap of cover and shadow (but, in the instant it took Alexandra and Siddiqa to scoop up their cloaks, pausing to spit at the tethered hound),

Russet Silk led them through the tiny gate back to their cart. The air was damp; soon it would rain. Han Chu lay sprawled on the ground beside the cart, his shoulders shaking. Hearing them approach, he lifted his head, then forced his aged body stiffly up.

"Excellent ladies!" he cried. "But who is with you?" he asked and looked around.

At the moment that his eyes turned to Russet Silk, a large fox of unusual beauty and her kit darted away from Alexandra, back into the night.

"We have it," Alexandra whispered. "Now let us leave, if we can." They leaped into the cart, hiding themselves and the precious canes filled with cocoons beneath the heavy fur robes. As Han Chu plied the goad on the lazy oxen, they stripped off their overrobes, then forced themselves to lie silent and unmoving as the cart lumbered through a gate, over a bridge, then through another gate. It began to rain, and the oxen slowed, mourning the rain with loud bellows. That was a dreadful moment. For an even more dreadful one, Han Chu was questioned by guards. Then they were out of the Imperial city and moving toward the Ch'un Ming Gate.

Banners of light the color of an Empress' veil streaked across the sky. But more violent fires, unchecked by the rain, stained the ground and sky as they rode past Prince Li Shou's compound.

Siddiqa gasped.

"Bryennius," Alexandra whispered quickly. "He must have torched the house with Greek fire." She crossed herself and muttered a quick prayer for Li Shou, who had wanted her, and who had spent his life to aid her and her City.

"*Ai-eee!*" Han Chu began to wail. The cart stopped as he let the reins lie slack. He sat staring at the white-hot glare.

"No! Keep driving!" Alexandra cried. "We don't dare stay here. Once we're outside the gate, we'll be safe!" A lie, very probably, but outside the Ch'un Ming Gate waited Bryennius, please God, and their guardsmen, horses, and packs—all they would need if they were even to try surviving the trip home.

Wailing that he would die with the prince whom he had served his whole life, Han Chu tumbled down from the cart and ran toward the burning house with a speed that was astonishing in a man his age. Siddiqa, younger and faster, leaped out and started after him.

"Come back!" Alexandra cried, hating herself as she caught the girl by the robes. "If you ever hope to see Bryennius again, we have to get out of here!"

She hunched her shoulders and tugged her hair about her face before whipping up the oxen and heading for the gate. She wished she had even the fragments of the lotus that had let her pass unnoticed through yesterday's riots. Many carts crowded the gate, though. Since they looked like two terrified women trying to flee the fires, they were waved through.

Once outside Ch'ang-an's eastern wall, Alexandra drove swiftly along the road. The rain made it hard to see the landmark by which they had agreed to meet, a ruined shrine by an ancient, twisted tree. She kept on driving, cursing the oxen, ready to weep from worry.

"We have to turn around," she called to Siddiqa. "I am sure I've driven too far."

The possibility of driving back and forth in the rain while pursuit might be assembled (no matter what Russet Silk had promised!) ate at her nerve. Then the ground trembled again, the oxen bellowed, and Alexandra realized that she might not be able to keep them from panicking.

"Gather the canes," she ordered, "in case we have to jump. I'll try to turn now."

Even as she turned, the quake came again, stronger this time and echoed by thunder. The rain intensified. She fought to hold the oxen.

Then, like the welcome shock of cold water on a hot day, she felt the demand for her attention that always meant the horn of Shambhala.

"That way!" she cried. "Thank the Blessed Mother."
She goaded the oxen into a run and cried encouragement
to them as the thunder pealed once more. Lightning
seared across the sky, and she saw her Varangians, axes
raised, guarding their horses. Behind them, wrapped in
an oiled cloak, was Father Basil. Two grooms leaped
forward to seize the oxen's heads. Alexandra and
Siddiqa jumped down from the cart.

"Bryennius?" asked the Uighur as Alexandra ran to
one of the packhorses.

"Not here yet," came Haraldr's deep voice. Alexandra
hoped that Siddiqa wouldn't hear the concern in it. Her
hand fell on the thing she sought, cool and cylindrical,
and pulled it free.

A horse galloped toward them. The guardsmen
growled and formed a line between the rider and the
women. Alexandra readied what she held in her hand for
a throw. The horses screamed. Even in the rain, Alexandra could smell blood too.

"Friend!" cried a voice in Greek at the exact moment
when Siddiqa darted by the guardsmen.

In a moment, Bryennius was down from his horse and
had her in his arms. Alexandra started forward, then
held back. Siddiqa had the right to embrace the new-
comer, not she. She busied herself, turning the cart.
Then she slashed the reins of the cart almost through. In
a moment, she would toss the Greek fire onto it. With
luck, the burning cart and stampeding oxen would foil
pursuit for a brief time.

"That's blood!" Siddiqa gasped, terror in her voice as
she clutched at her lover.

Alexandra's heart went cold. The rain poured down
her face and plastered her clothes to her body.

"Not my blood," came Bryennius' voice, more sub-
dued than Alexandra had heard it for weeks. "Li Shou's.
I couldn't just let him strangle slowly. God have mercy
on his soul."

Feeling as though nothing would ever warm her,
Alexandra threw the vial of Greek fire, and the cart

exploded into flames. The oxen dashed away, bearing the burning cart. One good jolt would sever the reins, and the cart would careen on its way, free of the terrified beasts.

Haraldr tossed her into the saddle, and they were fleeing Ch'ang-an as the earth trembled, and lightning, not the rising sun, supplied light for the journey.

Mount Li loomed up along their path. The horses screamed in terror of the storm. Inevitably, they slowed down.

"Hurry!" Bryennius screamed. "As you love your souls, Li Shou warned me to get by Mount Li as quickly as we can. Ride!"

What good is speed if we break our necks? Alexandra bit her lips on the words, then bit them in earnest as she fought to keep her horse from bolting. Foam whipped from its jaws, to be washed away in the driving rain.

A blinding peal of lightning brought them all to a stop. Not ten feet away, a huge crack opened in the road, then snapped shut. The earth's trembling reverberated along her spine; her teeth were chattering. If they had ridden a second longer, they would have been engulfed. Again a rumble of sound from deep in the earth. Purple-white lightning crowned the smooth shape of Mount Li, but even as they watched, landslides deformed the carefully tended slopes. Then, with a crack, the mountain itself split asunder.

16

Mount Li cracked open. Rocks and clods of earth flew from the rift and struck the fugitives. Siddiqa's horse screamed and reared. Heedless of the hooves flailing near his head, Bryennius grabbed the mare's bridle.

"We can't ride till the tremors stop!" shouted one of the Greeks, whose horse plunged and curvetted while the ground under it shook. Then he and the horse were down, rolling on the ground.

Boulders and mud tumbled down Mount Li, crushing the pomegranate trees that grew there so that the mud turned the color of blood from the splattered fruit. The slide was slower than the avalanche that had nearly wiped out the caravan at the Roof of the World. Let one of those boulders hit someone, though, and it would be equally deadly.

Though Alexandra fought to control her own horse, she couldn't stop glancing at the tormented slope. Then, almost as quickly as the mudslide started, it subsided to small tremblings along the ruined hillside, as if the mountain shook off the last troublesome concealment.

Concealment . . . Alexandra gasped and crossed herself. "There's a cave in the hill," she cried. "It's huge!"

Now a ghostly violet light gleamed from the gash in the hillside that the sliding mud and rock had revealed.

"What's inside there?" asked Father Basil. "Some sort of figures?"

"Keep back!" Bryennius screamed. Behind him, the man who had been unhorsed tried frantically to catch his mount. *If he can't ride, I'll have to abandon him,* Bryennius thought. Even as he recoiled from the idea, he shouted for the man to unload one of the packhorses.

"Stay back, priest!" he cried again. With almost his last words, Li Shou had warned Bryennius to keep his people clear of Mount Li. He had to get them away!

As the light about the cave brightened, as if a spectral dawn had come, the shadowy figures that Father Basil claimed to see shuddered, as if waked from their twelve hundred years' sleep. Ch'in Shih Huang-di might be dead that long, but he had set his guards before his death, and set them well. Now, alerted by the chaos and the thieves of silkworms that some . . . some spirit perceived as a threat to Ch'in, his guards waked. Living men? Revenants? Bryennius shuddered and bile gushed into his mouth.

"Statues . . ." breathed Alexandra from beside him.

Years ago, merchants had shown him statues stolen from a tomb in Egypt. He had marveled at their precision, their completeness, and the miracle of their long survival. But those statues had been tiny. These . . . they were as tall as the men and horses that had posed for them a thousand years ago.

Chariots drawn by four terra-cotta horses, their nostrils eternally flared in rage, their manes sculpted into windblown shapes, rumbled down the ravaged slope. In each stood a charioteer, his bronze and wood weapons ready for use.

"An army of statues!" Bryennius cried. Siddiqa screamed, then bit her lip until it bled.

He turned his horse's head savagely, gesturing for everyone to flee. Single horses could outrun chariots, and if not, the twisted ground might stop them. The chariots jerked and rolled down the slope. One toppled and rolled downslope; its fellows drove by as if it had never existed. Behind the chariots emerged archers, who took up positions on either side of the gaping cave, arrows already nocked on their bowstrings. They fired as one creature. The man who had been unhorsed fell with a scream and an arrow in his eye. A slinger whirled its weapon with unnatural strength and speed, and a Varangian fell, his skull shattered.

Behind them marched a troop of warriors, their head-gear and scaled armor modeled down to the last knot or nail, their bronze swords real and deadly. Their eyes, the gelid eyes of lifeless clay, gleamed in the violet light: purpose smoldered there, and a vengeful rage. The statues would pursue them throughout Ch'in.

Bryennius galloped down the cracked road. He could feel each step of the terra-cotta army at his back shudder down upon the earth. He tried to reason his way out of his panic. If the figures were slow, they might be outrun. Since they were mindless, "knowing" only that they had been set to chase enemies the way a hound is set after its quarry, perhaps they could be outguessed. They were clay: Perhaps a catapult could pound them into shards. But, unless the earth opened to swallow them into the clay from which they were formed, they would not cease their pursuit.

Bryennius remembered the endless, agonizing miles of the journey through savage land ahead of them, then thought of the mindless, tireless enemies behind them, and despaired.

Behind him, the army of Ch'in Shih Huang-di trampled the dead soldiers into the mud.

* * *

They rode west, ate in the saddle, and begrudged every brief pause; the warriors behind them had no such need to eat or rest. Bryennius felt himself reel in the saddle. Remembering the passage east across the Takla Makan, he signaled a stop, just long enough for the riders to bind themselves to their saddles. Siddiqa's haggard face, with purplish shadows beneath each eye, tore at his heart, but he dared not strain his horse by riding double.

Mud splashed underfoot as they fled past empty fields. Gradually the rain stopped. By afternoon, people had emerged from their houses and the caves cut deep into the loess, the slopes formed centuries ago by blowing earth. Though a rope drawn across their path might have brought half of them down, the villagers did not intervene.

"Guards up ahead!" gasped Alexandra.

Bryennius heard the hiss of blades being drawn, though what good that might be against archers, he didn't know.

"They're riding away," Haraldr spoke.

Bryennius turned around in the saddle. He could not see even the chariots at the vanguard of the lifeless army. But he thought he could sense each step that the First Emperor's clay warriors took by the way the earth quivered.

"We're unclean," said Father Basil.

Despite the need for haste, Bryennius drew rein to look at the little monk.

"You know how good the messengers are in Ch'in," he explained. "Do you think that the guards don't know who we are, and what pursues us? They think we are as good as dead already."

"Or they fear to be caught between us and the statues," said Alexandra. "I think they trample anything in their path."

Unclean. Bryennius had seen a leper once, abhorred even by the guards sent to drive her off. He remembered commenting that it would have been merciful to kill her, but "Who wants to get that close?" asked a scared mercenary. He had survived to be old—but not by touching what was already condemned. *We are ghosts, undeads ourselves*, Bryennius thought. *We ride through the paths of the living, and they flee us.*

Haraldr chuckled, an incongruously bright sound. "Then supplies should be no problem. We can take what we need." Bryennius remembered that he had been a trader and that, among the Northerners, the distinction between trader and pirate was frequently blurred or forgotten altogether.

Bryennius signaled for them to slow their horses to a walk. They would rest them, then speed up again, riding west until they dropped, Bryennius foresaw, or until they were overtaken. If they outraced the statues, they faced other perils: the desolation of the land itself, solitude, bandits perhaps, who might decide that a small band racing across a frozen desert must carry treasure that outweighed the risk of taking it.

"Perhaps once we are outside the borders of Ch'in," Father Basil suggested, "the statues may not be able to move."

"First we have to get there!" snapped Bryennius.

Alexandra shook her head. "This is . . . unbalanced," she began. "Set a guard to protect Ch'in: well and good, if vindictive. One might expect that of the First Emperor. But this visitation . . . this is not ordered." She shivered and struggled with one hand into a heavier cloak. "It is too harsh. And law perverted turns to chaos, which has no law at all . . ." She stopped herself before she could finish, looking guilty and terrified.

They rode through village after village, and none would face them. The fields shone with ruddy stubble; harvest had come and gone. From time to time, they saw animals: rabbits, a stray goat that some family would regret losing. Twice, Alexandra wasted energy and breath to point out a fox to Siddiqa. Only the foxes seemed unafraid. The air was cold. Soon it would be winter. Perhaps the statues would crack and break, but Bryennius doubted it.

"Up ahead!" Siddiqa called. Bryennius had not realized she had kept enough strength to speak.

Ahead of them glinted the twisting, silted coils of the Huang He River which heavy rains had swollen until thick waves crested against the dikes, tearing at them hungrily.

"Can they cross running water?" Alexandra questioned Father Basil. There was no need to ask who "they" were.

"Can we?" asked the priest.

"We can ride onto a boat," Bryennius said, "and take it. The boatmen will have no choice, and we have money to reward them."

"If they won't?"

"Haraldr?" asked Bryennius. "How different is this Yellow River from the waters of the North?"

"Far bigger," said the guardsman. "More treacherous. We do not pass the rapids during flood season, or times like this . . . yet that is what we have to do now. The water road to Byzantium I know. I'd like to see these statues take it; we'd see the last of them! But I do not know these waters." Still, if they ran into trouble on the river, Haraldr could be set to command the boat. It might work after all, Bryennius thought. If they could cross the river, and the statues could not. They could leave them standing on the opposite bank! Bryennius grinned at the idea.

But when he spoke his thought, no one else laughed.

Their horses limped toward the river, reaching it by late afternoon. Many times all of them were thankful that they had bound themselves to their saddles, as they reeled and sagged, asleep as they rode. On the trip east, Bryennius had seen Scythians and Hsiung-nu who could sleep in their saddles without danger. Perhaps they would learn that trick . . . though they would never escape the danger.

Unless the river . . . the river like a strong, sullen god . . . hooves clattered down onto the docks where boats swayed at their moorings along the swollen waters. Men fled from them on either side.

"That one!" Alexandra pointed to one boat, larger and finer than most, on which sailors lingered as if reluctant to abandon it.

"Quick!" Somehow they flogged that last gallop out of their horses. Once they were safely aboard, they could rest, and tend the horses' slender legs.

Bryennius tugged at the scarf that bound him to his saddle, leaped onto the swaying dock. It seemed to respond not to the pulsing of the river but to the tread of oncoming, human feet. His legs buckled, but he threw out a hand against the boat and saved himself from falling. Haraldr almost toppled down, then lurched to Bryennius' side on the dock, his axe at the ready.

"We need Father Basil!" Bryennius called back. Scuffling noises and a yelp of pain behind him told him that the little priest was making heavy weather of his dismount. Dusty and exhausted, Father Basil staggered to his side. Bryennius leaped into the boat. As a torrent of protest and curses poured over them, Haraldr boosted the priest into the boat, then turned to help the others.

Father Basil spat dust into the river, then began to argue loudly, a clangor of threats and entreaty that rose but did not drown out the footsteps of that marching, inhuman army.

"At the horizon," Alexandra said, and pointed. Beneath smears of dried mud, her face was gray. In her arms, she clutched the precious bundle of hollow staves that held silkworms. Siddiqa held another such bundle.

"Cast off!" shouted Haraldr. Father Basil broke off the argument to echo that cry.

"No use," Alexandra said, running toward the big Varangian. "All the men on the dock . . . they've all run away."

Haraldr started to hoist himself over the side.

"Where are you going?" Alexandra cried, reaching out to catch his arm.

"Someone has to cast off," he said, as if explaining it to a child.

"Feel the current!" she argued. "Once this boat is free, it will be swept downriver so fast . . . you will be left behind!"

The guardsman looked at her. Then, very gently, he removed her hand from his arm and kissed it.

"No!" It was a wail of protest. Haraldr stared at her, willing her to withdraw her command. The darkness at the horizon drew closer, and he jerked his chin toward it: *Look at that.*

Bryennius shut his eyes briefly. They ached from sleeplessness and dust; tears might wash them clean. As he opened his mouth to tell Alexandra to release Haraldr, Siddiqa cried out and pointed.

"Elder sister! There . . . all along the ropes . . ."

If ever they reached Byzantium, Bryennius thought, he would teach her the terms sailors used for ships and all things pertaining to them. Then he too gaped as he followed her pointing finger.

There, gnawing on the mooring ropes, crouched the largest foxes he had ever seen. From time to time, one would look back, as if checking on the approach of the terra-cotta warriors, then give a sharp bark to which others would reply. Like a work gang and its foreman! Bryennius thought.

"Bless you, Russet Silk!" cried Alexandra. One fox . . . a vixen, Bryennius decided, with a remarkably fine, ruddy pelt, raised its elegant head and looked right at Alexandra. She barked once, as if in reply, then chewed at the rapidly fraying hemp.

The fox-guards yelped more sharply. Even as the boat swayed at anchor, it began to shake in response to those thousands of pounding feet.

"Quickly," Alexandra gasped.

"They've got it!" Bryennius muttered, and managed to restrain Haraldr from swinging ashore and helping out.

The last strand snapped.

Father Basil let loose a flood of orders which, as the boat swung away from the dock, the sailors began slowly to obey . . . just as chariot wheels and clay hooves clattered through the village.

"Beware archers!" cried Alexandra. Siddiqa clapped her hands to warn the foxes, who turned and fled soundlessly as the ancient chariots approached.

"My God, look at them!" cried Alexandra.

The first wave of chariots rolled onto the dock. The horses that drew them clattered over the docks, and then, without a pause, leaped down into the roiling, silt-laden surges of the river. The foot warriors followed, sinking without a splash.

As the boat came about, heading toward the middle of the river, the soldiers cheered. Two Varangians hurled up their axes so that the autumn sunlight flared onto the blades. They were facing west. Toward home.

Father Basil clapped his hands and began to chant. "Give thanks to the Lord for He is good. The horse and his rider He hath thrown into the sea!"

"Careful, priest," said Alexandra. "This is the Yellow River, not the Red Sea and the chariots of Pharaoh."

"Do you really think we deserve a miracle?" Bryennius asked. Abruptly, his exhaustion caught up with him, and he found himself sitting on a coil of rope. Siddiqa tugged at his boots until he pushed her hands away. She was even more tired than he. With exhaustion came depression, almost a return of his old despair. He could not believe that Ch'in Shih Huang-di's army had simply sunk into the water. Not being alive, it couldn't drown.

But it could be swept downriver, dashed against rocks or floating logs, even against other boats, he thought. The chariot wheels would stick in the mud of the river's channel. Perhaps . . . he tugged at his boots. First he would tend to the horses. Then, after a meal, a wash, a chance to change from the clothes crusted with Li Shou's heart's blood, he might permit himself to hope, even to sleep.

But after all those things, even as Father Basil started to tell their story over bowls of potent rice wine, he fell asleep. He knew enough to protest muzzily when he was carried to an improvised pallet, but to do nothing else.

When Bryennius rose and stretched, cursing and groaning at the thousand aches he had acquired during days of riding, he saw that the sun was high. The sailors and his own people had reached an uneasy truce; some of the soldiers were even allowed, now, to help with the operation of the boat. All looked better after their night's rest.

They looked better still by the time they landed. Perhaps they might escape, Bryennius thought. Perhaps that order, or cosmos, that Alexandra always lectured him on was strong enough to prevail, even this far from home.

He tossed gold to the boatmen, led his horse onto the dock, and mounted. The others followed. They climbed a hill and paused to look back at the river. Then Bryennius swore, long and foully.

"Do you see?" Alexandra whispered, pointing. "There, in the shallows . . ."

All but one chariot had been caught in the mire at the river bottom. Only three horses drew it now, and they struggled up onto the riverbank, onto dry land. It was followed, Bryennius saw, by other horses, their snapped reins dangling from metal harnesses. One terra-cotta horse limped on three feet; the fourth must have been snapped off by a rock or snag. And the horses were followed by what looked like a veritable legion of the thrice-damned warriors, water and mud pouring off their armor. All were battered, and many cracked, even broken in places. He knew what must have happened. Since there was no bridge across this mammoth river, and since no boat could take them, the statues had formed their own bridge, file after file of warriors marching over their fellows' heads, leaving behind without pity those who cracked apart, or sank too deeply into the mud at the river bottom.

A trick of the sunlight caught one "warrior's" eyes, and they appeared to glare at Bryennius with ancient, implacable hatred. But why should they have pity? Bryennius thought, in rage and despair. They were not alive, they hated any living thing, and they would harry him and his to death, and beyond.

The only alternative was simply to lie down and be trampled—and that was no alternative at all. Very well. He would go on as long as he could . . . as long as he must for the sake of the cousin who would never give up, the princess he loved, and the men who had become his to lead.

Biting his lip against shameful tears, Bryennius led the retreat west.

17

Dunhuang's peace wreathed about Alexandra, palpable as the frost in the morning air. The light turned the dust in the air to gold that shimmered like the mosaics in a chapel; the sere ground cover, now an orange hue that faded as autumn yielded to winter, crackled beneath her boots. After weeks in the saddle, with only brief pauses for relief or rest, she practically had to learn how to walk all over again. Now her feet seemed to register every scrubby brush, stub, or rise in the ground as she headed slowly for the caves.

Eased by sweet oil, her saddle galls only ached when she moved suddenly. But they were nothing to the pain that blurred the golds and ochres of Dunhuang into an inchoate splendor that *he* would have found beautiful. *He* had loved the frontier, and would not be seeing it, or anything else from now on.

Alexandra's hand closed hard on the lapis sculpture

250

that had once rested on Prince Li Shou's table by his inkstone. The pressure should have hurt. She wanted it to hurt, but her hands were too heavily callused. Bryennius had given the stone to her that morning.

"You should have had this earlier," her cousin had told her after he had unearthed it from his saddlebags. "But . . ."

In the flight from Ch'ang-an toward Dunhuang, nothing had mattered but putting as much distance as possible between themselves and the First Emperor's avenging army. No human force had pursued them or tried to stop them; it was as Father Basil had predicted. They were judged accursed, unclean. Somehow the word had spread, and all along their route, people's concerns had been to provide them with what they needed and get them gone as quickly as possible. On the other hand, there was that one village they'd found deserted —except for the people staked out along the road. Outsiders, all of them: foreigners, heretics, the mad, the simple, and the misfits. They had lost precious hours freeing and consoling them while Ch'in Shih Huang-di's army advanced. Father Basil still prayed for the souls of the villagers who had planned the murders. Bryennius still waked shouting in rage at the idea.

Here in Dunhuang the monks had accepted them, promised them rest and care while they prepared for the desert crossing. Bryennius didn't trust it. When they traded for camels in the markets, Bryennius steadfastly refused to contact his adopted Muslim family or to join any other caravan. "I know that a larger caravan is safer against bandits. But it's also slower. Why doom anyone else?" he had asked just that morning.

"Is that what you think? That we're all going to die?" Alexandra challenged him. He had denied it, but his words sounded hollow.

She turned the precious little carving over and over in her worn hands.

"Li Shou gave it to me before . . . he died. He asked

me to give it to you and say that he regretted frightening you. That you might have had something very sweet together. For as long as it lasted."

Despite Alexandra's weathering, the flush that spread from her throat to her face burned, and she looked down.

"I knew he wanted me." The words came out hoarsely, and she remembered her shock and embarrassment that day in the garden when she had become aware of the prince's desire. More shameful yet, she had waked to her own body's needs.

"You couldn't trust him," Bryennius said. "I didn't trust him either. Now I wish I had."

The prince had traveled with them, fought with them, sheltered them, and, at the last, died because of them, and thousands like them. Alexandra had muttered something she hoped Bryennius would interpret as thanks, and walked quickly away.

"Don't go far!" Bryennius had called after her. "As soon as the camels are loaded, we take the pass southwest for Miran."

From Lanzhou to Jiayaguan, from Jiayaguan to Dunhuang, and now, south along the rim of the Takla Makan with rarely a stop . . . the statues would not spare them time, and time was what she needed. The caves of Dunhuang were holy; she didn't think that the statues could penetrate the aura radiating from them.

As she reached the ladders and scaffolds that led to the caves, she blinked back her tears. A short climb, and into this cave with the wall paintings of Bodhisattvas painted the blue of compassionate manifestations, past the long, long red and gold hall with the recumbent Buddha, and—yes, here it was, the cave that Li Shou had commissioned in honor of his return to the Empire that had killed him. The paint still smelled fresh.

If she slitted her eyes to avoid the alien shapes and patterns that scrolled over walls and smooth-carved ceiling, she would see only the Kuan-yin, lady and comforter, painted on the far wall. Despite its elegantly elongated eyelids, she could pretend it was an icon of Mary, Bearer of God.

Placing the lapis lazuli before the painting, she knelt and tried to compose herself for meditation. But Li Shou's face kept intervening. She had at first been unaware of how he felt. Once she realized, she had had no idea of how to cope with his desires. He had known that. She supposed that, in a way, he had loved them all—and had died for it. Passionately she thanked God that Bryennius had intervened in what otherwise was suicide. Foolish, that thought; Li Shou's faith didn't damn the suicide, but sent him back onto the Path to try again. Even the Bodhisattvas, beings so perfected that they could escape the world, chose to remain in it to guide others. Li Shou was far from the Buddhist notion of sainthood, but he had loved the world of art and adventure he'd created for as long as he could. He would be happy to return, she thought, and she wished him a speedy, happy rebirth.

If only he might have seen how beautiful the priest artists had made the cave! He had told Bryennius that Ch'in was his mother, and he could not leave her again. Like Socrates, she thought, and was irrationally angry at her mind's attempt to escape into philosophy.

Philosophy was no consolation, despite one Latin treatise to the contrary. But its author had also died a political death. Consolation lay less in reason than in emotion. Not to extinguish it, but to face it and harness it. Love it, if one could.

Tears poured over her cheeks, and her hands, upraised to hide her face even from Kuan-yin. Had she failed in love and charity toward a man who had saved her life? She didn't know, and she shook with the force of her grief and bewilderment.

The painting's gaze drew her, even though she knew that she had served as its model. She forced herself to meet its somber, compassionate eyes which guided her into deep meditation. For the first time in weeks, she remembered where she had learned about the mastery of emotions: the monastery in the Land of Snows where the abbot had spoken to her of the land called Shambhala. Li Shou had promised to help her find it, had wanted to seek its enlightenment for himself.

He had been with her when she had found bell and gem, tokens that indicated her path toward the mystical initiation that might take her there. Bell, gem, lightning bolt, and sword were still with her, almost as precious as the canes filled with silkworms that each one of her people carried. Light as they traveled, nothing tempted her to discard those talismans.

Now that she was facing west, apprehension about her return home warred with her quest for Shambhala. She thought—admit it, she ordered herself—she prayed that the statues could not pass the borders of Ch'in to invade the cities of the West. Yet, if she escaped them and returned to Byzantium, what triumph could she expect with her aunt in hiding, free to work evil magics upon the crippled Empire? In Shambhala, she might learn a power that would enable her to cleanse Byzantium of the evil that blighted it.

And it drew her. She could feel some power pulsing in the cold, pure air, enticing her back toward the terrible serenity of the desert, and the even more terrible calm of the mountain peaks. If Shambhala lay anywhere in the physical world, it was probably beyond Khotan far to the south.

She shivered and crossed herself. "Forgive me, Lady, that I pray to a graven image and call it Thine," she whispered. "And forgive me for where I must go, if truly Thou thinkest it sin. For truly, I no longer know what sin is, or Truth." Her meditations turned bizarre again as her thoughts drifted toward unimaginable mountain peaks.

She retrieved Li Shou's carving. This was not the place to leave it. If there were altars in Shambhala, she might leave it there.

Footsteps, deliberately noisy, brought her whirling up from her knees, her hand reaching for the sword she had left in her baggage. Haraldr stood in the doorway to the cave, calm and trusting. If she had been a child, she would have run to him for comfort and buried her face against his chest. But she had seen the look in his eyes once before, in a dead man's face, and it would be wrong to exploit her most loyal follower.

"My princess? Prince Bryennius says we must leave."

"Did he send you?" Alexandra asked. Bryennius' mood had been so dark that the Varangians had muttered among themselves.

"No. His lady did."

"How does my cousin seem to you?" Alexandra looked carefully away as she asked the question, knowing that it strained Haraldr's loyalty to discuss one member of the Imperial family with another.

"If he were one of ours, I might call him *feigr*. You would say 'touched by fate.' But he has hired some fine grooms and guides. Some are from Hind and Tibet." Haraldr shook his head to forestall her next question. "They understand that we are all, in a way, pursued by fate. But they want to return home quickly, so they accept the risk."

That was good, Alexandra thought. Talented Bryennius might be when dealing with horses, but it took men born to the deserts to master the tough, quarrelsome Bactrians, and men mountain-bred to handle the beasts they would need in the dizzying passes of the Kun Lun range.

Booted feet hurried toward them, raising more noise than was proper in these caves. More of Bryennius' messengers? Alexandra had trespassed on their peace long enough. As she rose, she caught sight of the paintings on the farthest wall: a double ring of snow-capped peaks and, in their center, a great city, ruled by a king whose face haunted her dreams. Opposite, reclining at her ease, sat a goddess, eyes painted on brow, palms, and the soles of her feet. Except for the eyes, Alexandra could almost see her as the Lady of Compassion. The old abbot in the Pamirs had called her White Tara.

So Li Shou had included all their hauntings, she thought, and felt fresh tears start. She knew the exact instant when Haraldr detected the tear stains on her face by the way his own face saddened. He raised one large hand as if to wipe her eyes.

"Even though you have never gotten it to sound, you still wear the horn you found," she said, stepping back quickly and pointing at it where it hung from his neck. It too, she remembered, bore the sign of Shambhala.

He shook his head, diverted, as she had hoped. "I am neither sighted nor a scholar, Princess. But I found this horn, and I must keep it."

He walked to the door and stood aside to let her pass through first.

Dunhuang had withdrawn its protection, and it was time for them to be gone.

Blown by winds so cold that Alexandra's ink froze as she tried to do accounts, they fled south and west. Veils of dust and grit wreathed about them and caught the remote winter daylight when they met a slower caravan. At Alexandra's insistence, they screamed warnings to leave the trail, then dashed by before frightened archers could nock arrows, or priests begin a rite of exorcism. If they were not overrun by the First Emperor's army, one more legend would rise in the markets—of a caravan of ghosts clad in light, warning travelers of disaster.

Alexandra's saddle galls bled afresh, then healed and troubled her no more. Siddiqa suffered terribly from the cold, lost all her plumpness and some of her beauty. Then, like the others, she changed. Now her eyes, like Alexandra's, squinted against the ever-present dust toward a trackless horizon or looked nervously behind her, and her body was fined down for enduring the Takla Makan by winter. It was colder than the gales that swept from Scythia onto the Golden Horn, Alexandra thought, cold as the Hel by which the Varangians no longer spared the strength to curse.

There was no need, and no time, to curse it. A kuraburan struck, and they had barely time to wrap themselves in thick felt against the violence of flying rocks and gravel. When they had journeyed east, Li Shou and she had survived just such a storm, Alexandra remembered. Even if its howling—whether it came from wind or demons—made speech impossible, her lips were cracked from the cold; unnecessary talk hurt. And if she had wasted strength on tears, they would have frozen on her cheeks. Unable to rest, they waited out the storm, wondering if it had stopped their pursuers.

When the winds subsided to a faint howl, Bryennius, in the grip of the blackness that filled his heart since Ch'ang-an, took two of the scouts on a mad foray to the rear. Two men returned with news of the army of marching statues. Only one chariot still rolled along on cracked wheels, drawn by clay horses that lacked manes or limped on only three hooves. The footmen's armor was crazed and pitted by windblown gravel; several of the spearmen lacked arms. Statues blown onto their sides or backs jerked and rolled until collision with another statue or a standing rock pushed them back onto their feet or broke them beyond use.

Bryennius had lost one of their scouts, a trained slinger, after he hurled a stone that hit an ancient captain, and waited too long to see if the now-headless statue could rise. So there was a method of "killing" the statues, but there were still so many statues and so few of them that Alexandra insisted that there be no more such forays.

Outside Keriya, their water ran short. Now they could spare none for the beasts, and they thanked God for the camels. Still, each day, their humps diminished and their long-legged strides slowed.

And the distance between them and the deadly army of Ch'in Shih Huang-di, which needed no water, dwindled.

Days blurred into nights of too much watchfulness

and too little sleep. This close to any town, they had to
fear bandits as well as their pursuers. They began to
travel by night again.

One night Alexandra flogged her groaning camel to the
head of the line of march. As had become his custom,
Bryennius usually rode alone.

"Leshi, one of our Tibetans, tells me that there is a
lake at the desert's heart," she said. "If we found it, we
wouldn't have to risk entering Keriya."

"The desert *has* no heart," Bryennius said. "We have
to enter Keriya to buy more animals. Two camels have
mange, and one is near to foundering."

The Bryennius she remembered would have been afire
to quest for the mysterious lake. This silent, driven
stranger knew what their presence in a market town
might cost it, but dared not turn aside. She suspected
that his decision would give him screaming nightmares
again tonight, and all the nights that followed. She would
have taken his hand if she thought he'd have permitted
it.

Bryennius saw the gesture. Something struggled in his
gray eyes, so pale compared to the night and his weathered skin . . .

"Brother . . ." she stammered.

"In the name of God, don't call me that!" the words
tore out. "Don't look at me like that! Everyone who has
ever called me brother—Leo, Suleiman, even Li Shou
—is someone I've lost. Everyone who has ever offered
me a future is someone I've had to leave. I beg you, leave
me alone to think about the trail and the desert, and
nothing else."

"There's me," Alexandra whispered. "And Siddiqa."

"And what happens to you, Siddiqa, and me when . . .
if we return to Byzantium with the silkworms?" The face
Bryennius turned on her was drawn and desperate.
"There is still our aunt, still the magic. And don't, for
God's sake, tell me again about Shambhala."

"If you think we all will get ourselves killed, then
why—"

"Why do I go on? Because there *is* you, and there *is* Siddiqa. And maybe I'm more a Roman than I thought, enough of one to go on until I drop."

"Would it help you to talk with Father Basil?" she asked, her voice breaking.

"Why?" Bryennius shrugged and turned to look up at the stars, huge and blooming above the emptiness of sand and sky. Alexandra rode at his side that night, struggling against a grief that she prayed was premature.

Light and warmth on her back made her whirl around. Sunrise slanted toward them from the east, drenching the desert with growing splendor. The rising sun seemed shrouded in rainbows, a star inscribed in a circle that reminded her of Shambhala.

"Cousin," she ventured. This time Bryennius turned and even smiled at her.

"You love it, don't you?" he asked. "Even now. Cousin, I envy you your joy."

The sunrise hid her guilty flush.

They reached Keriya that day. To call their dealings in the market "bargaining" was an arrant lie. Merchants saw their need for camels, water, and news, and charged accordingly. They lost two grooms there, but gained a guide from Ladakh, who knew the trails that led south toward his home.

"Send scouts out, post slingers at your walls!" Bryennius told the merchants as they mounted fresh camels. Their breath steamed in the frigid dawn as the kneeling beasts grunted, then swayed to their full height. "Tell them to aim for the heads—but keep your distance!"

Then they were running toward Khotan. The new camels tired, then grew thin as their riders tested their limits. One night they stopped briefly. An impulse made Alexandra take out the moonstone she had found in Turpan and gaze into it. At its heart firelight pulsed and played tricks with it; she almost thought it formed mountains, then a lotus, in its depths.

Was that Shambhala, beckoning to anyone with the eyes and heart to see?

Bryennius, who had lain with ear to the grit and gravel of the frozen desert, rose unsteadily and came over to her. "I know I promised a rest, but we'll have to mount up again."

"Are the statues closer?" Alexandra asked. Bryennius claimed that the earth shuddered under their feet, and that he could hear it.

To her surprise, Bryennius shook his head. Father Basil had hoped that as they neared the borders of Ch'in, where the power that drove them must weaken, the statues would slow. Had he been right?

"Not statues," Bryennius said. "Statues would approach from the east. I thought I heard riders. From the west—and north."

Khotan lay to the west and slightly to the north of them.

"Bandits?" She mouthed the word soundlessly at him, and saw his face turn grim and more drawn under the ragged beard he had grown.

He nodded. "We should edge south. Perhaps we'll miss them." But his tone robbed his words of any hope. He turned away, laid an arm over Siddiqa's slumping shoulders, and urged her toward the strongest of their camels.

Hurriedly, Alexandra ordered her camel to kneel so she could mount. She hardened her heart to its moans. As the beast broke into a travesty of its usual ground-covering stride, it bellowed in an anguish she wished she could echo. Only bandits or desperate men would ride these trails at night; only bandits, their quarters near the trail, would use fast horses instead of the safer, tougher Bactrians. At least the moon was up. It would light their way, preventing a stumble into a ditch or deserted town. They might even see the bandits before they struck.

Suddenly the gem's light flared, then pulsed like a living heart. Alexandra leaned out perilously over her saddle. A little way to the left, amid a confusion of torn bales and overturned carts, lay the stiffened bodies of men and beasts. She held up the gem like a torch. The wind had not yet swept the desert clean of the limping tracks of the survivors of that attack: more men than beasts—and right in the path of their enemies.

18

Light flared behind Bryennius, a counterfeit sunrise. He turned to see Alexandra hold aloft the gem she had won in Turpan—and saw what its light revealed. Quickly he turned back before Siddiqa could see it too. Her back, pressed against him in the saddle, felt sharp and fragile. If she hadn't grown so thin in this mad flight home, he wouldn't have dared ride double, even on the best of their camels. He tightened his hold about her waist and felt her body relax in his clasp. His own spine felt like a column of fire. He hoped that, for once, a long night's ride and the need to keep alert for bandits or treacherous footing would numb him to the pain.

The night passed in a stupor of haste and pain. At dawn, he shook himself back to full awareness and found Father Basil riding beside him. The heretic priest's roundness was deceptive: Persian-born, he had tremendous endurance in the saddle. As vast cloud formations

262

scudded overhead, the wind spat sharp gusts of dust at them. Bryennius blinked hard and buried his face in the sheepskins he wore. They were rank. He could not remember when he had last been clean. Ch'ang-an, perhaps. He had been clean then of Li Shou's blood, as well.

Father Basil's cry of joy made him raise his head again. "'I shall lift mine eyes up unto the hills whence cometh my help,'" whispered the priest.

Abruptly, Bryennius hated him and his relentless hope. *We're not there yet*, he wanted to say. *We could be caught in a pincers between bandits and those statues. What if they don't slow at the border, as you hope?* He forced himself to silence for the sake of the woman who rode with him. In Ch'ang-an, she had glowed like a plump peony bud. Now she held herself upright in the saddle in order not to burden him. He must not trouble her with his despair.

Behind him came a cry of triumph from Alexandra, echoed immediately by a hoarse shout from the guardsman whose camel trailed hers, and whose eyes rarely left her. As she forced more speed from her beast in order to catch up with Bryennius, Haraldr followed.

Bryennius had seen that look on her face before, when she had ridden east in a delirium of wonder, myths of some god-forsaken paradise ringing in her head from her days and weeks in an equally heathen monastery.

"That way!" she called, gesturing ahead of them. "Leshi tells me he expects the passes south will be clear."

Bryennius grimaced. Any sensible caravan master knew that from Khotan, he should travel north and west, completing at Kashgar the great circle around the deadly Takla Makan, then head back across the Pamirs into Persia—toward home. But Alexandra still insisted on heading south, where she dreamed she might find Shambhala. She was likelier to find death for all of them. Li Shou had warned him of the passes in the southern mountains: rotting fiber bridges, dizzying plummets for thousands of feet into clouds, and through them into ferocious, unseen torrents, trails stacked with the bones of men and beasts who had fallen along the way.

If he tried to make her see reason or, failing that, turned the caravan around (and tied Alexandra to her camel, if need be), the Varangians would back her, not him, and he knew it. She, not Bryennius, was full sibling to the Basileus; the guard had sworn to follow *her*. A good general might have changed their minds, but he . . . he looked more brigand than Byzantine now in his stained garments and his beard.

Alexandra too was fined down to skin, bone, and grime. She also wore filthy sheepskins, Persian leggings, and boots, and she had dragged a fur hat over her matted hair and down to her eyebrows. Underneath it, her eyes blazed with the sort of mad faith that drew men after her . . . had drawn Li Shou even to his death, and still compelled Haraldr to follow her. Did she realize how much of the big man's loyalty sprang from love?

Alexandra might dream of Shambhala, but Bryennius dreamed too, and woke screaming. He knew that she comforted herself with her belief that they had rescued people staked out along the track of the First Emperor's army. He had never told her everything he had seen when he had doubled east, scouting along their track. Thank God, he had managed not to betray that even to Siddiqa, despite his dreams.

Alexandra had her dreams. He . . . these days, he prayed only to survive another day, when, please God, he would fight to survive one day more. It was, he thought with an odd stab of pride, the choice of Achilles between a life that was brief but noble or one that was long and inglorious. In Byzantium, Bryennius had been rich and safe, with his horses and his seductions and his fine wines. He might have lived out a long and useless life. Now, he did not expect to reach Khotan, much less ever see his home again. But he had crossed the Roof of the World, had ruled, however briefly, the Kafirs, crossed the desert, and been a confidant to princes. He had even found love.

It might be all he would have—but it was not enough. He forbade himself to escape into resignation. Quickly he reviewed his defenses. He had the soldiers whose leadership Leo had bequeathed him. If he did not argue against Alexandra's obsession, he had the Varangians. There was even some Greek fire left yet. And—who knew?—the magic she pursued might aid them.

Though the markets at Khotan were full of horror about bandits, Bryennius saw and heard no traces of them. As they left Khotan, heading south, he dared to hope that they had disappeared. At least Khotan was well protected. And the statues . . . Father Basil appeared to be right. They were slowing down. If the statues could not cross the mountains, perhaps Alexandra's obsession with Shambhala would be worthwhile.

For days they climbed steadily. Far below, in the desert basin, the worst of the winter had passed. But it clung to the foothills of the Kun Lun, mounding about the frozen bodies of dead horses and camels, the goods their bodies still bore marked with the names of merchants who would reclaim it (if they lived) during the mountains' brief spring, and briefer summer.

At Shahidulla, they traded for fresh beasts and pressed on toward Suget Pass. Ahead of them towered peaks that dwarfed any Bryennius he had seen. Though Li Shou had told him of monks who had passed this way on foot, he did not see how.

"The statues can*not* cross these," Bryennius comforted Siddiqa during the breathless nights when they clung together more for warmth than passion.

Then they mastered the pass, and were climbing again. The trails became tortuous, then, abruptly, widened onto a high plateau where wind blew across melting snow, bringing them winter and a hope of fairer weather at the same time. There was no track to follow: even the guides born in this land shook their heads, baffled.

Then Alexandra drew out the gem she bore and stared into it for a long, long time. When she raised her head, Bryennius shivered with a new horror. His cousin's eyes seemed glazed, reflecting the light of the gem. "That way," she breathed.

"That way" led toward white peaks. Beyond them lay mountains even higher, tipped with the purple-white of everlasting snow. This was only the first of such ranges. They seemed to circle this plateau like some behemoth serpent with an egg in its mouth.

As they drew closer, the peaks' huge shadows blotted out most of the sun. Now the guides checked the harnesses and adjusted loads to prevent slippage, removing bells, silencing whatever might jingle.

"Bandits?" asked Bryennius. It was one of the few words he knew in all the languages of the silk roads.

"Snowslides," said Leshi, the guide.

Thereafter, they rode in silence, except for the growls of ice and snow as it rotted and slid down the mountainsides. Bryennius could track such avalanches by the plumes of snow and cloud that shot up.

Then they spotted hoof- and footprints, stamped deeply into the mud and the remains of the snow. There did not seem enough of them to be bandits.

"Lamas," said Leshi. Bryennius did not miss how Alexandra caught her breath. She had been dreaming again, he knew. He had set one guide to watch her even more closely and to lead her mount.

The day before they reached the foot of the massif, they saw more footprints. This time, there were many of them—plus several corpses that had not yet turned black from the cold.

The peaks drew Alexandra like nothing else in her life had ever done. All the while they crossed the plateau, she had abandoned fears of the statues behind, the bandits that might be ahead, and the mountains themselves to her companions. A ring of snow mountains, she thought.

Shambhala was girded with rings of mountains like the ones that lay up ahead.

When they finally stopped, and she woke from her waking dream, the sun was still high. Why stop now? Even her own guide had dismounted, to join the grooms and soldiers who clustered about something. There seemed fewer than usual. Alexandra looked about. Probably Bryennius had dispatched many of them to scout.

Bryennius rode over to her.

"Send Father Basil there to translate," he told her.

The Nestorian hastened to join the knot of anxious guides. Alexandra followed more slowly, pausing to glance at the mountains. How did she know that up ahead, if they headed for what looked to be a mere scratch on the snowy mountainside but was actually a narrow path, they would find themselves in a sheltered area where they could pass the night, yet stand guard against their enemies? She must tell Bryennius, she decided, and signaled him.

Her cousin tore himself away from the guides and the priest who translated for him. He sawed at his reins and headed back at a pace that brought a jangle of protest from his groom.

"At your command, Alexandra," he said. This close to a fight, he shed the darkness that had been on him for months, and grinned at her, bowing in a parody of court manners.

"What are they saying?"

"Leshi says he remembers this place now. There's some kind of fortress up ahead."

Alexandra gasped. To cover it, she asked, "What don't you want Siddiqa and me to see over there? Another body?"

"Some sort of monastic. The guides call him a lama. He died from a head wound; it looks fairly recent. We're in for trouble."

"What about Leshi's fortress?"

"I'd assume that the bandits have probably taken it for their own."

Certainty struck Alexandra, and she almost reeled. "It's safe," she said in a voice she did not recognize as hers. "It is not a fortress so much as a holy place. No enemy can cross its bounds."

Bryennius looked narrowly at her. His eyes were reddened, and lines from squinting into the sun and immense distances narrowed them. He was burned almost as dark as the guides from the sun on the plateau.

"Alexandra . . . I can't order my men to ride into what might be a bandit's lair because of some intuition," he said. But a ghost of the trusting, affectionate princeling he had once been emerged from behind the wariness and begged her to be right.

"By my hope of salvation, Bryennius . . . I swear to you. And look at this!" The same faith that made her certain of the fortress' security made her pull out the gem that had served as lodestone. It caught the sunlight and sent it up in a column of blinding light.

"And the statues?"

"They too . . . I do not think they can approach. And have they not slowed? We are far from the grave of their master."

Reluctantly, Bryennius nodded.

"Then let's get the pack animals moving," she suggested. She herself rode toward Siddiqa and smacked the rump of her mount to get the lazy thing moving.

A shout from high above them made her stop short.

"Haraldr volunteered to scout that fortress," Bryennius told her when she glared at him. "You told me how he survived the avalanche!"

The glinting snow rumbled and crumpled down a stretch of the massif the width of a market. Gradually the fine dust of ice chips and snow subsided, and Alexandra saw that hidden under the snow, carved into the living rock, was an enormous statue of an idol she had seen once in the monastery in the high Pamirs. It must have towered at least two hundred feet, dwarfing utterly the colossal figures she had seen in Dunhuang.

Female and fierce, the statue leaned in a position of ease against the rock.

Vajrayogini, she had been told the statue's name was. The female patron of Vajra, the Diamond Path. Its face was supremely calm. It would watch their escape or their massacre, even their being stamped into bloody pulp on the snow by their pursuers with the same indifference. Alexandra was tempted to curse, then thought better of it. She had seen enough of the power of alien gods—and rulers—not to insult them.

Now she could see Haraldr descending the cliff from which Vajrayogini had been carved by unimaginable sculptors. He waved his arms and ran up to her, panting in the thin air.

"Quickly!" he shouted, then collapsed, his immense body racked with coughing from exertion and high altitude. He was bleeding slightly from the nose.

"We'll die if we don't have some protection. And night is coming fast. Did you see the fortress?" Bryennius demanded of Haraldr.

He shook his head, coughed again, then fought to speak. "Bandits . . ." he whispered. "Ahead of us."

"In the fortress?" Bryennius persisted.

Haraldr shook his head. Staggering somewhat from the spasms of coughing, he headed for the beast to which he had strapped his axe. Alexandra wondered at his endurance. The blinding headaches and dizziness that struck newcomers to these heights no longer troubled any of them, even Siddiqa. But she was breathing hard (how much harder it must be for the guardsman! she wondered). As she left the flat plain and wound through the narrow passage that led to the fortress, red specks danced before her eyes, tiny lights that had nothing to do with the now-setting sun—or the greasy fires that smoldered before them in the long, bloody shadows from the peaks.

They had not been the first caravan to pass this way recently, or to hope to reach the fortress for shelter. Thus

far, however, they were more fortunate than the people
sprawled at their feet, packs strewn over the rocks. Their
bodies bristled with arrows, and the snow had melted,
then frozen again, purplish-black.

Father Basil crossed himself, then reached for the bow
that he, as a Persian, preferred. Siddiqa's delicate face
went taut, but she drew her dagger and did not look
away.

An arm rose, waved feebly, then fell. Leshi and
another man, Diu from Tibet, Alexandra remembered,
cried out and rode forward. Bryennius swore earnestly.

"By the One, they're all dead or dying, damn you!" he
shouted. "Tell them what I said!" he screamed at the
Nestorian.

Basil started to translate, but the guides rode toward
whoever still survived in the carnage of the caravan.
Alexandra shook her head at the Varangians, then
glanced warily at the men hired at way stations along the
desert route. Unlike her Guard, the grooms and guides
were not sworn to her. She could not stop them, no
matter if they decided to betray them to robbers, lead
them over a cliff, or simply abandon them. All she could
do was pay them, treat them as well as she could, and
trust to their goodwill. Assuming as they must, that
bandits watched nearby, they risked their lives with this
attempt at rescue. Therefore it was important to them. If
she helped her own men to help, she might win the
grooms' goodwill.

On the other hand, if they dallied too long, they might
freeze, unsheltered, in the dark. Or the statues might
catch up to them, if the power that forced them forward
could command them this far from its grave.

Alexandra rode over to where Diu and Leshi knelt.
They gabbled at one another, their wizened faces twisting with concern as they worked over a tangle of filthy
plum robes. A lama! That explained why they had
stopped. She knew from the old abbot that plum robes
meant that this man was relatively far advanced along
his Path.

Her two guides wiped blood and dirt from his face, it was contorted with pain and the wrinkles of a rugged old age. Alexandra knelt beside them. She meant to offer her own help. But the lama's words drove the words from her mouth.

She had seen that face in childhood, in youth, even in death—and always when she had been in peril of her life.

"They're coming!" shouted one of her soldiers. Behind her came the clatter of hoofbeats and the yells she had been braced for. Swords and axes were drawn with a hiss of fine metal, and she heard the twang of men testing bowstrings.

"To the fortress!" shouted Bryennius.

"They'll never get the old lama across a saddle without killing him," Alexandra called to Haraldr. "Help him!" Slinging his axe on his back, he came running. Tenderly he lifted the old man across the nearest pack animal.

"Get inside, my princess!" he shouted, but Alexandra waited until she saw all her people moving.

Her guards formed a protective wall about her and forced her toward her mount. She overheard the guides, Tibetan and local, gabbling earnestly to one another, and she made out two words, "tulku" and "rimpoche," or precious one.

"If they can see anything precious in that poor, dying man who won't last out the night, they're welcome to it!" Father Basil grumbled, infuriated, as always, at senseless cruelty. "God forgive me!" he added.

"He will, if you ride like your wretched life depends on it!" Alexandra shouted. She was as furious as he. Many times she had come so close to meeting the man they had found, but never to speak to him. Now, he lay within easy reach—but he was dying.

The bandits were gaining on them. In moments, they would be within arrow-shot.

"Take my reins," she shouted at the nearest man. It was Bryennius. She reached into her packs, fumbled, and drew out the bell she had found on the desert.

It had held demons and storm at bay; it might serve here.

As the first flight of arrows whined toward them, she rang the bell. The sound exploded. She could feel it as an actual force, pressing against her ears, resonating behind her eyes, quivering in the air, deflecting the bandits' arrows to spatter harmlessly onto the rock and snow. She kept ringing the bell, and the sound grew, forming a dome of music about them. Haraldr rode back, snatched up Alexandra's reins, and dragged her and her mount up the track into the fortress and safety. She tumbled out of the saddle, and he steadied her, flinging a spare sheepskin about her shoulders.

"How many . . ." She glanced around.

"We lost Topgye and one of the pack animals," Haraldr reported. He gestured for archers to take up guard by the narrow slits of windows. Already the Tibetans had vanished deep within the fortress.

A moment earlier, she had been exhausted, near to fainting. It must be something within the fortress, she thought, something that restored her. No wonder the bandits had not taken it for their own. It was indeed guarded by the magics of those who had built it.

Who were they? Alexandra could see that only the outermost walls had been built by men. Inside those massive walls were immense natural caves which generations upon generations of pious travelers had vaulted and painted over with images of gods and mortals in vivid shades of rust, red, and blue. One figure had the head of an elephant, another of a maddened water buffalo. Some had many arms and legs which writhed ecstatically in the embrace of chalk-skinned female demons. It resembled Dunhuang, only the caves were much vaster. And the rock was hard: it must have taken centuries to hollow out these caves.

Alexandra turned away from the caves to look outside. Below the circle of safety cast by the fortress lay the man and beast they had lost to bandits.

"Topgye," she murmured. He had been one of the

steadiest of their guides. Alexandra had trusted him, even loading his camel and his yak with several staffs filled with carefully preserved silkworms and two phials that even her soldiers handled with care.

"I hate to see that," Bryennius growled, and pounded his fist against the wall.

The bandits were closing in, swarming over the corpses. One rummaged in a pack and emerged with two ceramic flasks.

"He carried fire," Alexandra said. She reached for flint and tinder.

"Do you want me to make him drop it?" Haraldr asked. He borrowed a bow from one of the other men, bent it experimentally, and grimaced.

As he shot, the bowstring twanged discordantly. The arrow had misfired, would fall short, was already faltering . . . and then the power of their wills, amplified by the place in which they sheltered, pushed at it. The arrow fleshed itself in the bandit's arm. He shrieked with pain, the flasks he held toppled from his hands to smash against the hard ground into a golden conflagration as exquisite as it was lethal. Five of the bandits died then and there, their bodies writhing as they shrieked and tried to beat out the fires that shriveled them. The rest fled.

"Perhaps they will think we are demons, and not return," Father Basil said. Haraldr grunted disbelief, his eyes on the broken bowstring. Then he cast the bow down.

"My princess!" he cried, and reached out to Alexandra just as her earlier exhaustion, coupled with the strain of this last battle, crushed down upon her. She stumbled to her knees and felt the warmth of a cloak tucked about her. Then sleep ambushed her and dragged her away into starless depths.

"So you think you can escape me?" The Imperial abbess towered over her, and her mouth was blood-red. Father Basil had escaped. It was Alexandra who lay bound naked to the blasphemous altar hidden deep within the convent in which she had spent so many years. She brandished a torch, was bringing it closer and closer to Alexandra's face. Alexandra woke up with a shriek.

The muffled hiss of a fire collapsing into itself as it died was what had waked her. Now she recoiled with a low cry. Despite the cold, she was sweating. Why had she dreamed of her aunt? In the sullen bloodlight of the dying fire, Alexandra stared straight up at a huge female figure with blue eyes painted on its white hands, face, and feet. It was not her aunt after all.

Beside Alexandra sat Father Basil.

"Dreams again?"

"Of home, this time. My aunt. God help us, as we get closer to home, what if she reaches out to attack us, as she did in the Pamirs?"

"Pray, daughter. Look, that's the White Tara, Lady of Compassion," he pointed out to cover any embarrassment Alexandra might feel.

"Just like me." She laughed hoarsely and saw him wince. She hated Greek fire, hated the fact that once, to atone for her knowledge of how to make it, she had been willing to order Haraldr to slay her.

Father Basil handed her a steaming cup.

"The guides made this specially for you." Since there was no way to refuse, Alexandra sipped at the strong tea, heavy with salt, grain, and butter. She forced herself not to grimace. Even in the dark and quiet, one of the guides might be watching.

"A fine warrior, fainting like that . . ." she muttered. "When even Siddiqa . . ."

"The guides have been whispering about you," murmured Father Basil. "Foreign you are, female you are, but you rescued the rimpoche, an act which will buy you freedom from the Wheel."

Over the quiet voices of men changing guard, the strangely musical tones of the men of Tibet, and the rippling speech of Hind, came Haraldr's voice, in guttural and angry Norse she couldn't quite follow.

"Which wheel?" asked Bryennius, who came in and sat on his heels beside her.

"The Wheel of Time, to which—these pagans say —all men are bound. You gained great merit when you allowed the guides to rescue the tulku."

"All you priests look out for one another," Bryennius commented. "Why is this particular priest so precious?"

Alexandra opened her mouth, then closed it. Just as well not to share her suspicions about his identity with Bryennius.

"He is a tulku," explained the Nestorian, "that is, almost a saint, reborn generation after generation to bring enlightenment to the world. There are many such. Her Highness and I met one, in fact. But this is one of the greatest."

Heavy footfalls came up behind them, and the fire blazed as Haraldr doled out fuel. It would have to be rationed strictly, Alexandra thought.

"How safe are we here?" she asked him.

Haraldr's face was somber. Alexandra braced herself to endure his report.

"There's no way to tell you this gently, my princess. A storm has blown up."

The day had been clear.

"You think it may be sorcery?"

"Lady, if we were in my home, I would swear that some völva, some witch, pursued us. As it is, I can only suggest that we wait it out. A spring flows through these caves. If we had food enough, we could last out a three-year siege. Unless the statues can overrun us."

When she looked at Bryennius, he shrugged. Clearly he had expected no better.

"What I want to know is this: What is this veritable bishop among lamas doing wandering about outside his home?" Bryennius tried desperately to change the subject.

"He is trying to *go* home," Alexandra said. "He is searching for the way back, the way back to Shambhala."

Father Basil looked down into the reviving fire. "I do not think he will find it. I examined his wounds when they brought him in. The tulku is dying."

"No!" Alexandra hissed it, and sprang to her feet. "Not this time! Not to be so close and miss him again!"

"He may linger for several days," the priest said. "Long enough, at least, to speak with you. He has asked that you attend him."

"Then let me go to him. Now!"

Father Basil patted her shoulder and handed her more of that damnable tea. Though Alexandra suspected that it was made not with the butter of yaks, but with their excrement, she drank it down for its warmth. Then she swilled out her eyes at the spring Haraldr had pointed out. It was ice-cold. She followed him to where guides and soldiers alike were quartered. Those who were not on watch slept or gamed quietly, weapons tended and near to hand. Two of the men from Tibet had kindled small lamps before the more horrific of the wall paintings. Alexandra wrinkled her nose at the smell of burning butter.

Deeper and deeper into the caves she followed Haraldr. This fortress . . . once it must have housed hundreds of industrious monks, all busily chanting and painting.

Light shone from a passage leading to the right. From it emerged Leshi. Waving Haraldr aside, he bowed deeply to Alexandra, then led her within.

The tulku was very old. His bare arms seemed no more than sinew and bronzed skin covering thin bone. His hair was thin, shorn against his skull, and his face was a mask of wrinkles that curved down to a thin mouth that seemed, despite pain, to harbor a warm smile. Though blood seeped through the bandages that wrapped his side, when Alexandra entered, he sat up and raised a hand in greeting and blessing. His other hand rested on a dented brass wheel that spun and rattled continually. But his eyes . . . his eyes were very wise, and very familiar. With his face cleaned of blood and dirt, there was no mistaking that visage.

"My daughter," said the lama.

It seemed natural for Alexandra to kneel at his feet.

"You are Rudra Cakrin," she whispered. "The King of Shambhala. I have longed to speak with you."

The old man nodded. "Once I am reborn, I will be the man you name. But before that, I had to speak with you. You have much to learn before I die."

19

Alexandra stared at the man whom she had seen before as babe, youth, and corpse. *I endured hardships, just as the abbot warned me. I have weathered every strong emotion . . . or almost. And now I have found you. Where is my power? Will you give it to me?* Behind the wounded man, two of her guides set out a narrow drum, a horn made of what looked like a thigh bone, a blunt dagger, and an array of dishes, each of which contained a red, green, or white powder.

The lama turned to dismiss them, then gasped as his movement strained his wounds. The bloodstains on the wrappings around his belly grew wider and darker. Magic forgotten, Alexandra reached out to add more bandages before she recalled that he, like some monks or the holy men of Hind, might abhor being touched by a woman. "I do have some skill," she murmured.

Rudra Cakrin shook his head at her. "This will serve long enough."

278

Their eyes met, and Alexandra tried to suppress an incongruous urge to laugh. She was a princess; this was her caravan; and she had, after a fashion, rescued him. But he looked at her as if she were a student he had summoned—and a tardy one at that. Around them rose the clash and hoot of Tibetan chants, each man sustaining three notes at once.

The stare continued. Finally, they both chuckled simultaneously, then inclined their heads in such a stately fashion that they laughed again. The lama pressed one hand to his side but waved off an offer of help.

Alexandra could well believe he was a king; he had the manner of one, and a warmth that could win hearts and minds quickly and forever. Her brother had had that manner before their aunt Theodora's curse had beset him.

Alexandra clapped her hands, and one of the guides (whose awestruck gaze told her that he had already been won over) knelt with more of the ghastly tea.

"Serve my guest first," Alexandra commanded in halting Tibetan. The lama smiled again.

They sipped the thick brew silently. Then the lama set his bowl aside.

"So, what is it you have found?" he asked, a grandsire telling a riddle to a child, an adept training his disciple.

Alexandra drank more tea. She seemed to be getting used to it. What had she found? Did he mean the silkworms, peace of mind, a safe road home—or journey's end right here and now? The enigma resolved itself in a moment, and she matched his smile.

"I have the silkworms I claimed I sought," she told him. "But what I truly sought was the journey. And if I am spared to return home, I shall cherish its memory for the rest of my life."

"Are you content?" It sounded like contradiction.

Behind the lama swelled the chant. *Om mani padme hum.* "I should be," she said. She had never desired to forsake the world. In Byzantium it had forsaken her, having in it no place for a spare princess whose skills were smuggling, arms, and some minor magics. Here she had found a world of her own, a wealth of knowledge and emotions. Gazing into the dying man's eyes, Alexandra tried to say she was content, that she had found what she sought, and what she loved most.

But she could not lie to him.

He smiled a smile that belonged either to children or the ancient and saintly. Then, deliberately, he cleared a flat place before him and reached for a saucer of gleaming white powder. As she watched, he sprinkled three white circles, then cut the outer two into eight sections each. Then he looked up, as if waiting for her to ask what he did.

"What do you know of Shambhala?" He asked her.

"It is a hidden, peaceful land," Alexandra began.

"It is more," said the lama. He began almost to sing. His voice was as clear as spring rain dripping into a garden pool, flowing over rounded rocks, natural, timeless, and simple to comprehend. Though he sang in Tibetan, Alexandra found herself able to follow every word about the gardens and the palaces that awaited.

Yet it seemed natural that Father Basil knelt at her side and murmured a translation in Greek, more natural yet when his translation changed into holy words that she shared with him. "The city was of pure gold, crystal-clear. The foundation of the city walls was ornate with precious stones of every sort . . ."

"Between the mountains, locked in by snow, lies Shambhala." Its ruler continued the song that Alexandra had first heard years ago in the Pamirs. "When this age of darkness turns so wicked that the Way is lost, and war devours the world, then shall Shambhala ride forth to battle . . ." Harsh coughing broke in on his chant. This time, blood oozed not only from his side but from his mouth. Leshi darted forward, eased him down onto a pallet, and poured more tea.

He needed rest, Alexandra thought, more than he

needed to teach a disciple as unlikely as herself. She rose to leave.

"Come back . . . later." His voice was almost a death rattle.

Escorted by Bryennius, Alexandra walked back toward the central hall where her Guard assembled.

"The bandits have returned," one of the Varangians reported.

"Even despite the storm?" she asked.

"Even so. I counted their fires. They could starve us out."

"What do you suggest?" Alexandra asked.

"We have to break out," Bryennius spoke first. "The timing is the worst risk: We must avoid the storm, yet not wait so long that our food gives out or the statues reach us . . . though that, at least, would eliminate the problem of bandits."

Bryennius was right. Soon the statues would tramp through the plateau and find the winding path to this fortress. It seemed ludicrous, however, to hope for their coming.

"Do you think we can take the bandits?" Alexandra asked.

Arinbjorn, the guardsman who had spoken earlier, laughed. She knew that he would fight like ten devils as long as she lived and then, probably, leap with a yell from the nearest cliff.

"There is another problem," Alexandra pointed out. "The . . . lama. I doubt that he'll ever be fit to travel. But our guides won't leave him until he dies."

The soldiers looked at her, and she sighed. It would be her duty to go back and reason with the King of Shambhala. She turned on her heel and started back through the painted caves, echoing to the ancient chants raised by her guides.

Rudra Cakrin had not rested. Inside the circles of white powder lay other colors. Now they truly resembled mountains that embraced a city that shone in powders crushed from malachite, cinnabar, and lapis.

Though the dying man's hand shook, he reached forward to place dry wood, saffron, and incense at the pattern's heart. "That is for the king," he whispered. "To help me on my way."

It looked like a tiny pyre.

"Tomorrow you must go. When you do, I shall make sacrifice to thank you for your teaching."

"*My* teaching?"

"Indeed, my daughter. Never, in all my lives, did I dream I would have a student who was not brought up in the Way, yet who followed it unaware. You have sought me faithfully. Your people have tended me as if I were their own father. I must bear this lesson to my people. Remember me, child of mine."

Alexandra shook her head to clear her eyes of the tears that threatened.

"Please," she whispered, her voice breaking. "I have sought you so long . . . you cannot leave me like this. Tell me, at least, not to despair."

The lama looked up, his eyes flashing.

"I tell you no such thing! You know the Diamond Path: not to abjure emotion but to wield it. All emotions, not just the ones you call good or bad. Take them, and use them. And at the moment of your greatest need, your 'despair' as you call it, think of Shambhala."

Rudra Cakrin's head slipped sideways, and Alexandra threw herself forward to catch him. But he had only fallen into the fitful sleep of the dying, which comes more and more often until they cease to wake or breathe.

What of the powers that the abbot had said she might gain from him? She needed them to protect herself and those who were hers. She had hoped for magic, and he had given her only riddles and maxims. Could they teach her anything at all? One thing was certain; she would learn no more from him tonight—and tomorrow she must flee. Before then, she must understand what it was that he had said.

Fearing to disturb the mandala he built with his last strength, she rose carefully. "I shall see him before I leave," she whispered to the guides. "I shall not ask you to abandon him. But I must have at least one guide. Choose whom you will send. You heard the holy man. We must be ready by dawn."

She left the cave, where the fires were burning down and the chant had fallen silent, and stood outside, unwilling to go back and face the hopeful faces of her people with nothing more than the riddling words she had heard. She would have to return soon. There were plans to be made, supplies to check, the precious, awkward bundles of hollow canes to be loaded on each pack animal so that if only one of them should win through, her City would get the silkworms that would restore it to health and power.

Voices rose and fell. After a long time, there were footsteps, and she tensed, her hand reaching for her sword.

"It is Arinbjorn, my princess," said the Varangian.

Alexandra looked closely at the guardsman. Now that she remembered, he had reported to her before, too.

"Where is Haraldr?" she asked.

Arinbjorn looked aside, then forced himself to meet her eyes.

"Is he ill?" Oh, God, not Haraldr, she thought. From Byzantium across the mountains and desert, he had always seemed the one stable thing, the one man she could trust above all others.

"He is not . . . ill. But I fear he is feigr."

The guardsman touched the hammer that hung about his neck against that ill luck that even speaking the word might bring. A man who was feigr was fated to die, the Rus thought. Whether or not it were true, they believed it. If Haraldr thought he was doomed, then all that magnificent will and endurance of his would turn toward what seemed his inevitable death.

"Take me to him," Alexandra ordered.

Arinbjorn led almost at a run through the drafty caves

to a tiny fire where Haraldr sat cross-legged, arms propped on his knees, his head with its matted fair braids resting on his hands. Surely after this long, he knew her footsteps. But he did not rise at her approach. He did not even move.

"Leave us," Alexandra ordered Arinbjorn. "And tell no one."

Then she sat down beside Haraldr, waiting for him to speak. For years, she had leaned on his strength, used him as shield and bodyguard until now he was as dear to her, as necessary to her, as Bryennius or her brother. Why would he not speak? Every moment was precious!

When the silence became more than her strength could bear, she laid a hand on his shoulder. A tremor ran through his body. The touch made him look up, and she almost shrank from the expression on his face. Haraldr's eyes were haunted by his conviction of impending death and shame.

"Arinbjorn should not have brought you. I wanted to spare you the sight of me like this. Forgive me, Highness. I have failed you, failed my oath. But it is Ragnarok. All things fade and wither, while outside the frost giants gather, waiting to devour us. I am ashamed, but I cannot face it."

A gout of rage warmed her as he spoke.

"Do you truly think I have come to charge you with breaking your oath?" she demanded. "I would never call you a coward, Haraldr. And until tonight, I never thought I would call you a fool."

His gaunt face looked puzzled.

"Arinbjorn came to me because he hoped that I could move you where he failed. And I came . . ." She was on her knees, trying to shake him. It was like trying to move one of the peaks that circled Shambhala, she thought. He was so solid, and so . . . so stubborn. So damned, imbecilically stubborn that he might die merely because he mistook honest fear for the notion that fate had marked him for death. *Was the power Haraldr called Wyrd any stranger than the karma they spoke of in Ch'in?*

a voice whispered inside her head. Frantically she shook off the thought. She needed all her confidence to reclaim her officer.

His hands came up and cupped her shoulders, holding her immobile.

"You, my princess. Why did you come?"

"Do you think I want to go home without you?" she demanded, her breath coming fast. "That's like asking if I want my swordhand hacked from my arm. Haraldr, I need you!"

He had always responded to that need. His hands shifted on her shoulders. Then, the nature of her need changed with such speed and intensity that she gasped aloud. Her thoughts flashed back to a garden, now ash and rubble, in Ch'ang-an, and a book that had struck her shamed and restless, unable to speak to the prince who had given it to her, or to meet Haraldr's eyes thereafter. She had flushed and lied to him, stirred by his presence in a way she refused to admit. The prince had tried to arouse her—and had done so. But not for him.

Now she swayed in Haraldr's grasp. His strength and warmth forced her to recall the passionately entwined figures in that licentious, exquisite little book. How could people touch so? she had wondered at the time. How could they resist? she asked herself as he bent closer.

"My princess, are you truly so desperate that you would give yourself to me to pretend we have a chance at life?"

"Don't *be* that way!" she wailed softly. Though his hands loosed their clasp, they still rested on her shoulders. He smelled of dirt, and sweat, and something else that left her breathless.

The Diamond Path was built on strong emotion, Rudra Cakrin had told her. Desire, her body's need for the man who held her, stunned her in the instant that she recognized it. Passion washed over her in a flood that left her clinging to him, her face pressed against his shoulder. She could have stayed that way for hours, listening to his heartbeat, but he raised her chin in long, hardened fingers.

Their faces were so close together that his breath warmed her face.

"Stay with me, Haraldr."

He traced the path of a tear down her cheek. His eyes were wide with wonder.

"At least that will leave a clean streak," she muttered, and felt a chuckle rumble through his deep chest.

"You have always been the shield at my back," she murmured. "Tomorrow, too, you will guard me. But, my friend, must it always be fighting?"

"My princess," he whispered. "My little princess." His big hands drew her firmly against him, and she flung her arms about his neck.

"You have called me Alexandra before," she told him. "Why should you fear to use my name now?"

"It's not your name I fear to use," he told her. "My . . . Alexandra, I have dreamed of you, longed for you to give me what you should not give."

"Who says I should not give myself?" she asked, trembling with amazement and delight at the passion that made her voice husky. "When I left the convent, it was forever. Even if we have only one night, Haraldr, I want it. Keep me with you."

One hand pressed against her back, while the other twined itself in her hair. "So fine and dark. It was like silk in Ch'ang-an," he said. "You were lovely, but he was always with you, always watching you."

"And you were jealous?" The possibility came as pure joy to her.

"Gods! I ached for you . . ."

"He never touched me," she told him. "I never wanted anyone until now."

Carefully, Haraldr bent his head and laid his lips against hers. They were roughened, cracked from the cold, but their touch woke a fire in her blood, and her own lips parted. As their kiss deepened, Haraldr fumbled open her clothing and fondled her with such care that she knew he had imagined touching her a thousand times.

Then he released her. As the cold air brushed her nakedness, she whimpered.

"Alexandra . . . dear heart. You're certain of this?"

She was cold now, and his body against hers would be warm. She reached for him, to draw him down beside her.

He glanced about warily. "Anyone might come here," he said. Hastily he tugged her garments closed and wrapped her in the furs of his bedroll. Lifting her, he strode deeper into the stronghold. At a sheltered corner, he set her down. Alexandra watched him, her eyes wide, her lips parted, as he undressed first herself, then himself. His hands were eager but very sure, and he waited until she pressed against him before he moved carefully above her.

In Byzantium, they would call this a sin, she thought wildly. But in these lands they made love into an art, and they were right. She wanted to say that to Haraldr, but his mouth came down on hers ruthlessly. Some miracle of desire taught her to slide her hands down his sides to his hips, to move so he might kiss her breasts, and, when his hands parted her thighs, to arch her back to receive him. Hardy from months of riding, she did not feel the pain that women always warned younger women to expect, the first time. Instinctively she tightened her legs about him, welcoming him.

"*My* princess." It was almost a growl of triumph. Then he whispered her name over and over, and she clutched his shoulders as the tremors shuddered over her like an avalanche. But this time, she was not left alone and afraid. Once again, Haraldr was with her, holding her as waves of feeling swept them over the edge of consciousness. They were floating in each other's arms, drifting in the dizzying pure air of the high passes. Power seemed to flow from the air into their bodies. Fair and tall, dark and tiny, the warrior and thinker: each complemented the other, and they were one.

Alexandra squeezed her eyes shut. Lights exploded behind them, and she seemed to see a circle of shimmering reds and greens draw nearer and nearer. The vision formed into a city with a palace at its heart. And in it sat the king she had searched for, restored to youth and health. He was aware of her, and he nodded recognition, even joy, before he turned his attention to the mandala before him, adding color and strength and richness to it. Power seemed to sweep out from it, enveloping her, moving beyond her to embrace the entire valley. With so little a thing as a gesture, he held back his enemies—and hers. She was so close to understanding now! One more moment, and she would possess more strength, more joy, than she had ever dreamed existed.

Alexandra gasped with delight. Then she was back in her body again, rubbing her face against the hair on Haraldr's chest, listening as his powerful heartbeat slowed. She laughed briefly, and felt his hands smooth her hair.

She rubbed her face against him again, then looked up. "I'm glad," she said simply, and raised her face for his kiss. There had been power here; she knew that now, but it had not been for power that she had given herself. Her last thought, before sleep claimed her as deeply as her lover, was that she had fled a Frankish royal bed, only to find herself wrapped in sheepskins and the embrace of a man from the North.

The clash of prayers brought her laughing up out of a dream full of peace and wonder. She lay alone, warmly wrapped, and her body felt very light. Haraldr sat beside her, and the shadow that had lain on him was gone. He was armed for battle, axe at his back, the horn of Shambhala dangling from its frayed silk cord.

"Did you watch over me all night?" she asked, smiling warmly.

"Not all of it," he said, and touched her cheek. "The old lama . . . the king . . . he has asked to see you."

She leaped up, exulting in the way Haraldr's eyes followed her, and tugged on her tumbled clothing.

"It is a pity to hide you," he said. For an instant, he held her against him, and her body tingled with response. Then they released one another. Alexandra headed down the passage to where the horns and rattlings were loudest, and he followed her.

The old lama sat hunched over his mandala, as if he willed himself into its center. Little showed of the splendor that she and Haraldr, united, had seen the night before. His skin was yellowed and drawn, with bluish shadows about the mouth. Death could be no more than hours away—if it did not come in the next moment.

Alexandra knelt, hoping that his death was not so near that he would no longer recognize her.

"You have your talismans, do you not?" he asked.

She nodded. "Sword, and bell, flowers and gem." She even had the rock that was her legacy from Prince Li Shou. Everything but the crown of the adept.

"I will hold your enemies at bay for you as long as I can. When I can fight no longer . . . again, I will not say, 'Do not despair.' Instead, I will tell you this: use all that lies within yourself. At the moment of your deepest anguish, think of me and Shambhala."

Alexandra bowed her head.

"Your guides . . . I have no need of them. They will go with you." Relieved of his care, they bowed before her, and she gestured them out of the cave.

The dying man shuddered. Quickly he reached into the tiny fire burning near him, and plucked out a twig, then kindled the sandalwood in the center of the mandala. The wood scattered pungent bronze sparks in the still air.

"Now go!" he whispered. "With my blessings, and my hope."

Alexandra strode to the great central hall where the rest awaited her. They were armed and ready to flee or turn and fight. It occurred to her that they must know how she spent the night, but she saw no grins, no knowing looks, only joy, as if the power that had brought her and her lover together had somehow encompassed them in its embrace of the entire valley.

Bryennius walked toward her. The darkness that had haunted him was gone, and he smiled with his old jauntiness.

"You must see this, Alexandra," he said, and drew her to the gate.

She braced herself to bear the sight of bandits blocking their escape, waiting over fires until hunger should drive their quarry out to them. But the ground before the fortress was white and smooth. Snow had fallen during the night, hiding blood, flames, and the charred bodies of the men who had died yesterday.

"I thought they would come back," she said. Her breath froze in front of her face.

"Perhaps they did. Look beyond," said Bryennius, and gestured.

Beyond the expanse of virgin snow stood a host of warriors such as the ones that had pursued them. The scales of their armor were cracked and chipped, their weapons battered and bent. Many of the terra-cotta warriors lacked a hand, an arm, or parts of a shoulder or hip. Fresh snow helmed each of them. The First Emperor's warriors stood arrayed in semicircles before them. If Alexandra's people were to escape this place, they could only do so by passing through the ranks of their most relentless enemy.

For a long moment she stared at the creatures that had pursued her. Experimentally, she started forward. They did not move.

"I knew it!" exulted Father Basil. "We've passed beyond Ch'in's frontier, and they cannot follow us!"

It might be true that beyond his realm's vast borders, the First Emperor's power dissipated and his creatures stood helpless. But the lama had said he held her enemies at bay, and Alexandra believed him.

"Well," Alexandra said, drawing a shaky breath, "let us move before the day passes."

Steadily, carefully, they led their yaks down the slope to the track they must follow. Snow churned up in powdery drifts about the huge beasts, frosting them with white. Their footsteps crackled and hissed in the dry snow; there was no jangle of harness, no shout of orders as their column narrowed to pass between the ranks of the lifeless statues.

"Don't look at their eyes," Bryennius whispered to Siddiqa, who trudged at his side.

Now they walked through the middle of the host. A faint wind began to stir, brushing at the snow helms that each statue now wore. They seemed almost to creak with a terrible eagerness to break free of whatever held them motionless. Alexandra dared look one in the face, and saw a hatred made doubly frightful by its mindlessness.

They had only five files of the clay warriors to pass through . . . four now . . . in a moment they would be beyond them and could run toward the defile that led to the south. Perhaps they should start a rockslide to block the path to any enemy who might dare it.

Abruptly a cloud passed over the sun, and turned it the color of a tarnished coin. Overhead, the sky darkened further. Out of nowhere appeared a huge black bird which flew over them, shrieking.

The timbre of that shriek chilled Alexandra's blood. She had heard it before, a cry of insatiable hunger. Only that time, it had torn from a human throat.

Her aunt Theodora had cursed her when she fled Byzantium. That laughter had pursued her halfway across Asia. And now, as they returned, and the other powers that oppressed them waned, hers grew strong once again.

That laughter . . . the night of the avalanche, Alexandra had sensed that she laughed then too.

"No . . ." she breathed. Now the wind sounded like the last feeble breath of a dying man, and she shuddered.

So did the First Emperor's deathless army.

The guides screamed, pointed, and ran ahead.

"They're freed!" shouted Bryennius. "Run for those spires up ahead!"

Grasping the harness of the nearest pack animal which bore wrapped bundles of cane, Alexandra plunged forward. She slipped in the snow, recovered herself, and tugged on the beast's reins. Behind her came Father Basil. He dropped one hand long enough to cross himself in memory of the dead lama.

She broke into a stumbling run that sent icy knives into her throat and lungs. It was perilous to run in these heights, even more perilous to lag behind. She could endure for just a moment longer. Haraldr seized her arm and half dragged her along beside him.

Leshi, who had already run between the rock spires, looked up. Then he shrieked and waved his arms to bar their way.

"We can't stop!" she screamed.

But the clatter of rocks, high overhead, silenced her. Ice splintered free of the peaks, and began to fall upon them like a rain of daggers. Boulders ground against the rocks, and earth that had imprisoned them for centuries tore loose and clattered down toward them, gouging out other rocks that followed. Though it seemed that the ice and rocks took forever to shake free, Leshi had only time for that one scream before the slide toppled a huge boulder down the slope, into the air, to smash him against the opposing rock wall.

Escape south was blocked.

"Take what you can, and climb!" Bryennius shouted. Using a bundle of canes as a lever, Alexandra forced herself up the newly fallen boulders. Rocks and ice slid beneath her feet, and threatened to hurl her sprawling. Gasps and cries beside and behind her let her know that the others too tried to cross the rockfall Theodora had caused.

It shuddered beneath them and threatened to cast them down. Finally they had to stop.

"Once the tremors subside . . ." was on everyone's

bleeding lips. They sagged down onto the frozen ground
or leaned on packs and weapons. Once the rocks settled,
they would try to walk out.

Again huge wings cast a black shadow overhead, and
the shriek Alexandra dreaded rang out. The bird circled
three times, descending lower and lower as it flew over
the silent gray statues that ringed the plain.

Once again the bird cried, as if in summons. Very
slowly the soldiers of the First Emperor stirred. They
stepped forward, halted as if reluctant to serve a new
master, then began heavily to advance. Their terrible
stone eyes glittered with hatred and renewed power.

20

The statue advancing on Alexandra was an officer. Though river, desert, and mountain had scored its face, gouged into the folds of its robe, and chipped away at its right hand, the left still clutched its bronze spear. Slowly the statue raised its weapon and brandished it.

"Get back!" Haraldr and Arinbjorn hurled themselves between her and the statues, backing her into a crack in the rock.

"Keep Her Highness safe!" Haraldr shouted at Arinbjorn.

With their bodies protecting her, she would be the last to die, trampled once they fell to the warriors who now belonged not to the First Emperor of Ch'in, but to the sorceress Theodora.

"No!" Alexandra cried.

Haraldr whirled to face her, his blue eyes anguished.

"Don't make me die alone," she asked. Even if she escaped, what chance would she have in these mountains, alone, without supplies besides the silkworms she could carry on her back?

"Use the rocks!" Bryennius screamed. He turned to the rockslide, scooped up a head-sized boulder, and hurled it.

The rock smashed against the topknot of a spearsman. The head shattered, the statue toppled, and the men-at-arms cheered hoarsely.

"We *can* stop them," Bryennius cried. "Come on!" His hands full of rocks, he ran forward.

"No!" Siddiqa's shriek of protest followed him long before anyone else started forward.

Another spearsman moved forward, a horrible, awkward deliberation in its chipped limbs. It raised its spear and hurled it. Sharp sunlight glinted on the bronze, and it flew like a violent leaf in the instant before it slashed into Bryennius' throat. Blood spurted from the wound, impossibly red, steaming in the cold, thin air, and Alexandra's cousin pitched forward onto his face. Siddiqa shrieked again, an agonized, thin sound. She ran forward and hurled herself across Bryennius. As the spearsman advanced, she raised a tiny hand that held a jeweled dagger to prevent the figure from trampling her lover's body.

Even as Alexandra cried, "Save yourself, sister!" the statue's heavy arm clubbed the Uighur girl between neck and shoulder, and she dropped like a flower with a snapped stem.

Tears froze on Alexandra's face. She clawed at the rocks, passing them to soldiers who could hurl them at the oncoming statues. Beside her, Haraldr grunted as he pried loose a huge stone, flung it into the path of two more warriors, then bent for another.

Father Basil, his lips pale, murmured prayers as he pried rocks free and passed them to the soldiers.

They had dared to hope that beyond the borders of Ch'in, the First Emperor's strength would wane, and the statues lose their power. So they had. But as the First Emperor's power withdrew, another power had reached out. Finding the clay warriors masterless, Theodora had seized them for herself. Now that she could control the lifeless, insatiable warriors, she would march them west across the mountains.

They could storm Byzantium, and all the cities of the West. A spasm of horror shook Alexandra and made her drop a stone reddened by her torn fingers. She had tried to bring life to her City. Instead, she had loosed upon it an army that no city could withstand. She swore and rolled the stone on to a man who could use it.

"Get one of the guides. You, man! Take the princess, and you, you, and you . . . get over that rockslide if you have to fly!"

So Haraldr was still trying to rescue her, whether she wanted to be rescued or not. He had his axe out now. In an instant, he would charge the statues.

It was an instant he didn't have. Clambering above his head on the unstable footing that was the best that the rockslide gave them, a guide stumbled and fell with a shrill cry. His fall set off a second slide. Boulders caromed off boulders. One bounced, and struck the Varangian on the side of the head and he fell.

Alexandra tore free of the soldier who tried to urge her up the treacherous slope, and ran to Haraldr's side. She wanted to scream and fling herself across her lover's body as Siddiqa had done, waiting for pain and blackness. But as long as her mind could hatch one more plot, come up with one more gambit that might buy them time, she refused to give up.

Now she stood over him. His axe had fallen from his hand, but she knew she could not lift it. She sought for a weapon—a rock, a knife, anything—and remembered the prince's gift to her: polished stone, apt to the hand. She fumbled in her tunic for it. What she pulled out instead was the gem she had taken off a dead man's body in Turpan. It was dull, lifeless now, but it was hard and would be easy to throw.

Haraldr's body jerked as he tried to rise. His head, with its blood-matted beard, lolled to one side. "The horn . . ." Words bubbled out with the blood. Then his eyes shut again.

Where was the horn he had carried since fighting a demon in the Pamirs, the horn carved of some bone, and marked with sacred signs of Shambhala? The cord holding it had snapped . . . there it was, a little in front of her.

But if Alexandra retrieved it, she would be right in the statues' line of march. They could trample her.

What difference did it make if she fell to them sooner or later? Haraldr had asked for the horn, and he should have it. She darted forward and bent to pick it up. The cries about her had diminished, and she realized how few of her people remained alive.

It was time for her to die, too. Her life flashed through her mind: years of learning, and then these past years full of fear and adventure and brilliance. She hated to have it end. Then despair, more powerful even than the lust she'd known last night, drowned out her anger. The statues drew closer, sure, now, of their quarry.

At least *try* to defend yourself, fool, she told herself. The gem felt smooth and cool in her hand as she flung it at the statue nearest her. Her aim was good.

When all hope fails, think of me. Think of Shambhala. As the white gemstone arced across the sky, Alexandra remembered Rudra Cakrin's parting words to her. She raised the horn of Shambhala to her lips and blew.

The horn made no sound. She blew harder, until her chest ached with the effort to force the thin mountain air from her lungs into the horn. Now she sensed the prickle of nerves and unnameable senses that had always been the horn's summoning call. But no sound. She coughed, and blood stained the horn. She shook it empty, then drew breath for the last try she would have strength to make. At least, she thought, reeling, she would faint and never feel the stone warriors stamp the life from her.

She drew more breath than she had ever done before. Blood suffused her vision, made her temples throb, and her heart beat almost to bursting.

Sound belled out across the sky. Then the gem struck the stone warrior full in the chest, and the statue shattered, bursting into flame as the power contained in the gem was released.

Still the echo of Alexandra's last horn call rang out, forming chords as it reverberated against cliff and peak, like the chanting in some ritual of Asian magic. The clamor was overwhelming. Alexandra sank to her knees. She had mastered despair enough to act. Now she waited either to live or to die.

Beneath her, rock and earth trembled as if battered by many hooves. The air quivered as the light splintered into the sort of rainbow brilliance that had dwelt at the heart of her white gem and formed into an incandescent mandala pattern. It gleamed like the mosaics in the Church of Holy Wisdom itself.

Then the hoofbeats she had sensed echoing through the rock grew louder. The mandala burst asunder. Through it rode the hosts of Shambhala.

Their steeds pawed the glistening clouds and fragmented, rainbow light, and arched magnificent heads on which manes waved like wildfire. Riding ahead of the others, on a horse whose glossy coat gleamed indigo, came a young man with long eyes and amber skin, and a face that Alexandra had seen in all stages from infant to corpse. He saluted her with a wave of his hand, a touch to lips and brow.

Then his army rode down from the sky to charge the now-burning warriors. They raised swords much like the one Alexandra herself bore against the statues and charged into their ranks. Each time a warrior touched one of the statues with his sword, the statue shattered. Its fragments coalesced into a shining figure, pure light, pure fire, that leaped out at all the other statues and ignited them. In a very little while, pillars of light blossomed where Alexandra's enemies had been. The light was so strong that she squeezed her eyes shut. Perhaps, she thought, it would be a pyre for her friends as well.

Gradually, the terrible brilliance subsided. When Alexandra dared to look up again, she saw the statues crumble into dust. Sudden winds whipped up out of the mandala, fragrant with the air of the gardens of Shambhala, and blew the ancient powder away. She heard a wail of rage and frustration, and thanked a power she had no heart to name.

Now the troop of Shambhala rode toward her, and the ground glowed beneath the hooves of their horses. Then the warriors of Rudra Cakrin reined to a stop. Alexandra forced herself to her feet. She flung out a hand blindly, and felt something warm: the flank of Rudra Cakrin's horse.

Alexandra drew her own sword and presented it to him. He touched its hilt, then pushed it back toward her. She was aware of strength at her back and knew, without having to turn, that somehow, against all hope, Haraldr not only lived, but had managed to rise to greet these new allies.

"You called us," said the king. "I hope we have served you well."

Ceremoniously, Alexandra inclined her head. Then she smiled.

"Will you ride with us?"

Warriors in armor and robes such as she had seen in the hidden caves of Dunhuang rode forward, each leading a horse. All about her, the men who had survived the last battle with the First Emperor's warriors were rising. At a gesture from Haraldr, each moved to stand beside one of the horses. The least of them was so fine that it made the horses of Ferghana, the pride of an Emperor, look like battered wrecks.

"There may be others whose spirits are strong enough to make the journey," said the king. "They are yours as well. Shall I ask them?"

Bemused, Alexandra nodded. Rudra Cakrin raised a hand, and the air quivered, grew taut, then rang like a temple gong. As the sound reverberated and combined, then died away, other figures rose from the ground.

Blood had dried on the throat of one young man with dark hair and a grin that looked wise now, instead of careless. He brushed the dark gouts away, wiped his hand, then offered it to the tiny, fine-featured woman beside him. When horses were brought them, he thanked the men who brought them in careful, aristocratic Greek, and lifted his love into the saddle before swinging up behind her.

"Bryennius!" Alexandra whispered, and crossed herself. Nothing happened—no wail, no puff of brimstone, no fiends turned upside down and flying into the air. She supposed she was not surprised.

"He wants to live. As much as you do, he wants to live, and has earned another chance. Ride with us, Princess, to Shambhala and beyond!"

Horses were brought to Alexandra and her guardsman. Haraldr knelt and cupped his hands, as if waiting to throw her up into the saddle. But Rudra Cakrin himself dismounted. Taking the reins of the horse meant for her, he backed the animal expertly until it stood before her. Then the beast bent one foreleg, and extended the other, and the great horse knelt until Alexandra could mount without assistance.

"My silkworms!" she remembered.

"They are safe," said Rudra Cakrin. Alexandra glanced behind her. A wide bundle that she knew concealed hollow staffs lay strapped behind her, and behind each one of her people. She bowed again, in acceptance.

"You have endured and mastered danger and the greater, because more hidden, dangers of your emotions . . . Finally you conquered even despair and dared to summon us, long before the Wheel turned and we were destined to ride forth."

The tears Alexandra would not shed before leaped once again to her eyes. Trembling, she made her plea for her City, for the need that had sent her out on the silk roads, for its continuing danger as long as that frustrated necromancer raged through its streets.

"I saved my brother and his heir once," she concluded. "I hope that they still live. I pray that they do." Her voice broke, and Haraldr rode closer to comfort her. His arm on her shoulders felt warm, but she forced herself to slide free of it.

"Do you dare to ask our aid for outsiders, those not of our faith, who have never set foot on the Diamond Path?" Rudra Cakrin asked.

Another test? Alexandra stiffened. Yet his words had the tone of ritual, not of challenge. "Yes," she said. "I do dare. I summoned you to ask your aid. By the challenges I have met, I demand it!"

"Ride with me," said Rudra Cakrin. " 'Seek, and you shall find. Ask, and it shall be given unto you.' "

Alexandra gasped. Behind her came delighted laughter. "I knew it!" exulted Father Basil. "I always knew it. 'The Way has no constant name, nor the Sage a constant form.' "

For once, she had no heart to defend Orthodoxy. That argument had been lost long ago.

"We ride home!" cried Rudra Cakrin to the hosts of Shambhala.

The horses started forward, gained speed, broke into a gallop, and then, effortlessly, lifted above the surface of the ground, soared past the cliffs and peaks of the mountains, and into the mists that wreathed them. A maze of light, sound, and color engulfed Alexandra's consciousness.

Gradually, she became aware that she rode at Rudra Cakrin's side. She glanced back to reassure herself that Haraldr rode in his accustomed place slightly behind her. Even though it had been midmorning in the world they had left behind, the sky was dark and the stars glittered practically underfoot. They had passed from color into a realm of night.

Those of her own people whose love and will had survived death rode mixed in among the supernal army of Shambhala. Siddiqa nestled in her cousin's arms; and both of them seemed far more intent on one another than on the wonders through which they rode. Father Basil practically trembled with joy and the gratification of his passion for knowledge. And Haraldr rode with wonder on his face. She knew them, and loved them all, so well. God—whatever god ruled here—bless them all.

Responsive to her merest thought, her horse slowed to enable them to ride knee to knee across a carpet of glistening stars.

"Are we dead?" Haraldr asked her. "I remember a rock struck me. I fell, but I have a hard head. I saw you take the horn. Now, do we ride with the Wild Hunt, or shall we cross the rainbows of Bifrost into Valhalla?"

So Haraldr, like Father Basil, recognized elements of his most deeply rooted beliefs in Shambhala.

"And I"—Alexandra smiled at him—"shall I be the battle-maid who has chosen you?" They laughed knowingly.

"You are my princess," he said. His tone transformed her title into a caress. He swept out an arm, clearly intending to draw her onto his own saddle, but the horse she rode quickened its pace and bore her away.

Stars winked about their heads as they descended through night into a region where rainbows shimmered and dawn turned the sky rose and violet. They stood in their saddles, knees tight against their horses, as if they rode down a steep slope. The angle of descent diminished and they were riding through clouds that bathed Alexandra's face and burning eyes with welcome moisture. Downward again. Now they could see diadems formed of cliffs and peaks, two great rings of snow mountains, a smaller range nestled in against a greater. Smaller ranges divided each ring into eight regions that looked like the petals of a celestial lotus.

As they rode lower, crossing the outer ring of snow mountains, gold roofs of palaces and temples winked up from rich green fields like enamels wrought for an Emperor's shrine. They approached the mountains that guarded the heart of Shambhala. Here the snow had turned to ice; the ancient peaks gleamed like adamant or diamond.

Rudra Cakrin pointed down at the city they embraced. "Kalapa, my capital," he said with love and pride.

Alexandra gasped. Like Byzantium, Kalapa was a gem set in water: two exquisite lakes, one the shape of a half moon, the other a crescent. The lakes were so clear that she could see the rocks that gleamed in their depths. As they descended still farther, she realized that the very rocks themselves were precious stones. Waterfowl swooped over the lakes. The scent of lotus floated up from the petals scattered on their water, which was the color of fine lapis.

They rode past a park in which gleamed a mandala that was twin to that built by Rudra Cakrin in the fortress only one night ago. Then they touched down before his palace. It reminded Alexandra of the center of a flower. Its roofs were built pagoda-fashion, as she had seen in Ch'in, but with tiles of beaten gold. Ornaments of pearl and diamond hung from the eaves. The walls themselves were adorned with statues of goddesses carved, like caryatids, from single blocks of fine coral. White-robed servants and officials hastened from doorways set with sapphires and emeralds, or peered from windows hewn from fine sheets of lapis, shielded by golden awnings.

This city makes Byzantium look like a slum, she thought unwillingly.

Rudra Cakrin had dismounted and was holding out his hand to her. She nodded thanks, but slipped down on her own, amazed that the pavement (fine marble, with gems gleaming between the slabs) felt like normal stone. She followed the King of Shambhala into the palace, through rooms in which carpets and brocade cushions glowed like gems themselves, into a throne room fragrant with sandalwood incense. Here Rudra Cakrin took his seat on a throne, mounted, like the Basileus', on the backs of great lions.

She and the others sank down on piles of silken carpets.

"God forgive me for thinking that heaven itself could be no finer," whispered Father Basil.

Gratefully, Alexandra accepted the warm water and thick towels that servants offered, and washed her hands from which all cuts and bruises had vanished. All the soreness had vanished from her muscles, and her garments were miraculously cleaned and mended. But she let the golden cups and dishes full of honeyed fruits lie untasted before her. Persephone had been condemned to remain in Hades for eating pomegranate seeds, and she wanted to run no such risk.

"There are no conditions on my hospitality, Princess," said Rudra Cakrin. He sounded so much like Li Shou in Kashgar that she found herself laughing at her own suspicions. She accepted a peach, and saw her friends help themselves, Haraldr to golden apples, Siddiqa to grapes. Bryennius—as she would have guessed—concentrated on the wine.

"I have given you my word that we shall ride to Byzantium and cleanse it," said the king. "But we do not need your help to do so. Why not remain here?"

The great throne room was silent as he waited for a reply.

Alexandra was silent, waiting. *Now that I have seen Shambhala*, she thought, *is there power here for me beyond the king's promise to heal my City?* She had mastered the austerities that the old abbot had foretold. *Now what?* Though no words passed her lips, she was certain that her thought was clear to everyone in the room.

"Now, we determine fates and futures," said Rudra Cakrin. "You have proved to me what a thousand incarnations failed to do: that outsiders can walk upon the Diamond Path and prove themselves worthy. And having proved yourselves worthy of Shambhala, I offer you a welcome. Will you take it?"

"If I do not stay," asked Bryennius, "what then?"

"Then I return you to where I found you."

"In short," said Bryennius, "to my death. Of course I shall remain here."

His eyes gleamed with more than the hope of renewed life. Bryennius had always been a man denied purpose, a productive future. Friendships he had treasured were ripped away. No sooner did he find some path—as King of the Kafirs, or a trader prince, even as an Imperial Ch'in officer—than it was snatched from him. In Shambhala, he would be a warrior on guard, awaiting the orders to ride for the good of the world. And until that call came, he and Siddiqa could roam parks and halls such as no other lovers had ever enjoyed.

One by one, Alexandra's people made their choice. The surviving guides chose to return to their mountains, not yet fit for the circles of Shambhala. Many of the soldiers, rapt by the beauty of the place, elected to stay.

"I am a Christian priest," said Father Basil reluctantly. "And much as I could learn here, I fear that I must not spend my life and the life hereafter awaiting a heathen apocalypse. I must beg you to return me to Nisibis, my home." He sounded so downcast that the court laughed, but their laughter was kind.

Finally all but the surviving Varangians had spoken. Then the king turned to Alexandra. "They await your word, Princess. What is it? Will you remain here, immortal, free from the Wheel? You are one whose presence we would treasure."

The offer intoxicated Alexandra like the air in the high passes. Here was the answer to her loneliness, a future surpassing any that might await her in Byzantium. She might even ask King Rudra to see that her silkworms arrived home. Shambhala was so beautiful that she could forget that she missed the sea, and would never lay eyes on it again. There would be years . . . centuries . . . to study.

But what of her guardsmen, most of whom had family somewhere, either in the City, upriver at Kiev, or in the far, far North? She realized that they were looking at her as their leader, willing to accept her choice as binding on themselves. They would be content here, she knew. None of them was more than nominally Christian; they would easily regard Shambhala as a manifestation of their own beliefs. And Haraldr, who meant the most to her, would accept any future in which they could claim one another. In Byzantium, their bond would be a scandal. Here they would have eternity together.

What would become of her City if she stayed? Beset by magic, how would her brother regard jeweled outsiders who claimed magical power and brought them gifts? Michael—please God he was still alive, still fit to rule—had suffered so much that he could not be asked to deal with what he had a perfect right to suspect was an invading army. Someone had to explain things to him, to aid him during the transition from Basileus of an Empire besieged by sorcery and full of turmoil to ruler of an Empire that she would try to make a reflection of the splendor of Shambhala.

She sighed, then reached into her tunic and pulled out the carved lapis Li Shou had bequeathed her.

"In Ch'in, there was a man who wanted very much to find this place. He promised to come with me . . . but he died. I think that Prince Li Shou was a man you might have welcomed, Majesty. Will you accept this stone? It was his last gift to me."

"I will accept it gladly," said Rudra Cakrin. "But what of your own choice, Princess?"

Alexandra sighed, and felt her eyes prickle with tears. She knew it would be hard to get the words out, and so she said them quickly, before she could betray herself. "I must return," she said.

"Think carefully," said the king. "Will you give up immortality and freedom for mortal cares and obligations? Will you forego enlightenment to help men and women who may blame, rather than thank you?"

She remembered her final interview with the Basileus. *What happens if you return, Alexandra? We will have to face the problem of what to do with you all over again.*

Unless, of course, her brother were dead. In that case, she must secure his Empire for her nephew, for whom she had an obligation to be regent.

Unless you wish to rule yourself. Fear that she might seize the throne had been the politically expedient reason for sending her east in the first place. *Not while my brother or his son lives*, she vowed. She had an obligation to serve them while they lived, and, if they died, to avenge them and rule after them.

"I must return to my home," she repeated.

"Even if they turn against you?"

Alexandra wanted to cry out for him to stop tormenting her. There would be no retreating from a third refusal, she sensed.

"Even so."

The throne room rustled with soft whispers. All about the room, white-robed people turned to look at her with sorrow and, she realized, with awe.

"Then, Princess, accept this token from me."

A gem like the one she had found in Turpan materialized in the dish from which she had chosen a golden peach. Even as she lifted it, the gem warmed and stirred in her hand, transformed in an instant into a blue lotus, its petals closed.

The whispers that wafted clouds of incense about the vast hall rose in power, then resolved themselves into a chant she remembered from her days in various shrines. *Om mane padme hum.* Over and over the white-robed figures repeated the chant. Hail to the jewel in the lotus.

The lotus bud in her hand stirred. Its petals unfurled, and at their heart, gleaming with a pure blue light, lay a diamond.

"It is yourself," the King of Shambhala told her. He rose from his throne, descended the steps to the floor, and bowed himself at her feet.

Alexandra gasped. She had been stupid again, blindly stupid. She should have considered the questions he had posed her. Would she accept the cares of the world instead of immortality and escape from the Wheel? For a person brought up in the Church, that was the only choice. But in Asia, enlightenment and escape from the Wheel were the ultimate goals.

Only one type of being chose mortality and sorrow instead of joy and freedom. That being was a Bodhisattva—a being so perfected that he, or she, would accept incarnation to aid human beings toward their own salvation.

The thought wasn't just blasphemy; it was incongruous. She was Alexandra, not some aspect of the Comforter whose many aspects had smiled at her from so many paintings and statues. One had even worn her face. That too was incongruous. Yet to respond to these people with the wild laughter that bubbled up in her would be the worst type of cruelty after they offered her the greatest homage in their power.

"Rise, Majesty. How should you kneel in your own realm?" she asked Rudra Cakrin. "Please believe me. I am no Bodhisattva. I am a human woman—or I could not have felt and mastered the emotions I needed on the Diamond Path."

"If you are not a Bodhisattva," asked the king, "what shall we call you?"

The burden of her birth, her City, her shadowed future, all of which she had managed to shed while on her quests, settled upon her shoulders like court robes made of gold and lead. There lay her answer.

"Call me a Roman," she said softly. "A Roman who may not abandon my Empire as long as it needs me."

Alexandra rose to her feet. If she stayed any longer in Shambhala, her renunciation of all it promised would break her heart.

"I beg you, let us ride soon," she said.

21

Mercifully, the King of Shambhala spared her any attempts at persuasion, and led the way out of the palace. Their horses awaited them outside, grazing in a sunny court. At the king's approach, his magnificent stallion trumpeted, and the rest looked up, then arched their necks in welcome. They did not look at all blown from their earlier journeys.

Alexandra's eyes blurred—*from the sunlight on all the gold,* she lied, when Haraldr reached out to steady her.

"Ride with me," Bryennius was urging Siddiqa. "I may never have a chance to show you Byzantium again." His eyes met Alexandra's. "At least I can bear you company that long, cousin," he told her. "You'll remember . . ."

"I will tell my brother," she promised. Then she swung up into the saddle.

Once again, she rode at Rudra Cakrin's side through the park, past a pond as blue as Prince Li Shou's lapis lazuli. The gem would remain here forever, as the prince had wanted. If she were lucky, she would control herself before she started to envy the stone. As they passed, waterbirds burst from the glistening reeds, so bright themselves that they appeared to be clad in gems, not feathers. As the birds rose, Alexandra raised her head to follow their path, and found herself looking down upon them. Unobtrusively, smoothly, the horses had risen from the raked path into the air, and now their hooves struck bright sparks from the clouds as they broke from an easy trot into a gallop.

She slitted her eyes, afraid of the glare from the snow mountains that loomed up ahead. Then they were climbing still farther, soaring over the inner barrier, rushing toward the incredible massif that protected Shambhala from the world itself; and she found herself able to bear the light. They passed through thin cloud. A fine veil of snow stung their faces, and the clear air filled them with joy. Alexandra, who had thought to weep, found herself laughing as they rode back above the Roof of the World toward Byzantium.

At a sign from the king, Haraldr sounded his horn. Soon they were joined by other riders, all spendidly dressed and mounted. This was not an escort. It was the army of Shambhala that she had seen painted on temple walls.

"Did you think to face your enemies all alone?" asked Rudra Cakrin.

Alexandra shuddered, remembering how Theodora had tried to own her, mind, body, and soul. She remembered the story of Shambhala: that when the world grew too wicked to bear, then the forces of Shambhala would ride forth to purify it. Were they at the end of days then? Perhaps this was merely the action of a wise king unwilling to let an enemy grow, unchecked.

They rode from bright afternoon into another night. Father Basil gazed about at the nearby constellations. Bryennius wound his arms about Siddiqa, though she had not complained of the cold. When Alexandra turned in her saddle, she saw her Varangians riding as if to a hunt.

The wind whipped into their faces. They were descending now, riding down the night clouds as if they were the slope of a snow-clad hill. Clouds hid the earth from them: surely they had passed the cities of Persia, had ridden over Antioch, and the ancient towns of Asia Minor, even Troy itself. Still lower, and they dropped through the last wisps of cloud.

As the shadowy bulk of Byzantium's walls loomed up, Alexandra cried out. The Golden Horn was black; a sickle moon shivered in its depths. The City was too dark and too quiet. Very few lights trembled at the docks or along the wide Mese that wound up toward the palace itself. Byzantium seemed to crouch in upon itself like a dog with a fever.

"My brother," she whispered. "My City."

"Behold," said the king, and raised a hand.

In an instant, Byzantium gleamed with light, and Alexandra would have preferred the old darkness back. *Witch-sight*, her panic shrilled inside her skull. Now the king let her see as the great mages saw. The City crawled with lights. A greenish phosphorescence rose from the docks, crept up from the island convent where she had spent so many years under Theodora's orders, and spread upward, into the City. Worse yet, patches of it appeared to glow from some of the churches, even in the palace itself.

"Like a rotten fish!" Haraldr muttered, and reached for his axe.

Alexandra drew her sword. Its blade too gleamed, but with a ruddy light she found comforting. Just such a light shone through other parts of the City: in many of the churches, about the Mangana and those parts of the palace which housed her own Varangians' kinsmen, in rich houses, or in hotels. She herself and the riders with her, descending with a spark of hooves on stone, were limned with the same light, like saints in a mosaic.

"Show me your enemy," ordered Rudra Cakrin. There

came a tugging at Alexandra's mind, as he sought the vision for himself.

The last time Alexandra had opened her mind thus, it had become a battleground for two evil women. But now she felt as if she had abandoned fear in the defile where spring snowmelts would soon pour over the fragments of her enemies. She met Rudra Cakrin's eyes with trust, and let him see what he would.

"Is that she?" he asked, and pointed.

A pool of that unholy light grew, down on a stone wharf, spilling over into the Horn itself.

"She wants to flee!" Alexandra hissed. If she had dallied in her choice, agonizing whether to go or to stay in Shambhala, Theodora might have escaped her, gone elsewhere—whether to Rome, Alexandria, even ruined Troy itself—to prey on other cities until it was safe for her to return.

Alexandra pressed her heels into her horse's sides and rode out ahead of the king.

"Help me stop this!" she demanded.

Desperation and a hot, righteous anger that Theodora continued to exist at all led her to a wellspring of strength she had not known she possessed. Now she drew on it, felt it surge through her body, rise in her spine like a tide of fire until her eyes burned, and she knew that ordinary humans, if any dared be out, would shrink from the sight of her face.

She dropped embossed reins on the horse's arched neck, and held out her hands. White fire leaped from them into the sullen glow that was the visible manifestation of her aunt's power. It roared up like oil poured upon flames, like the Greek fire she herself had used in her travels.

Now it bent toward her, seeking to curl inward and devour her. She held out a hand, denying it passage, and felt the men and women at her back pour their strength into her. She drove the white fire onward. It was like cautery, she thought, a blazing iron held to a wound to heal it. She must heal her City.

I am not worthy of this. The thought crept into her head, and she recognized even humility as a danger. She had mastered other emotions; now she turned on her own sense of unworthiness and used it to fuel her anger. *Worthy or not*, she told herself, *this must be done, and you are who is here to do it.*

Of course, it was absurd that she should fight a sorcerer with flame borrowed from a heathen king. Nevertheless, she was here to fight, in any way that she could. The fire lapped against stone buildings, seeking entrance any way that it could. Now it was driving some of her aunt's servants out of cover. Two of them, their heavy cloaks on fire, ran shrieking toward the water and leaped from the high wall. They sank with the hiss of quenched metal. Not even a bubble or speck of ash marked their fall.

"Let no one escape," Alexandra whispered. Behind her, the army of Shambhala spread out. "Some of you guard the palace. I must fight my aunt myself."

The evil phosphorescence was in retreat! Once, as a child, she had walked on the shore and seen a strange fish washed up to die. It too gleamed. Instead of normal fins, it had had tendrils that extended, then shrank back on its central core. Even as a child, she had not been surprised to learn that the creature's touch bore poison. Now the light dispelled by Theodora's dark magics reminded her of that fish. It too curled in on itself.

With Rudra Cakrin to guide her, and Haraldr's unquestioning loyalty at her back, she followed the green fire to its source. Though her mind felt curiously free of her body, she was aware that she dismounted, that she led her horse through Byzantium's tortuous streets (lit now with warring fires), across the Mese, and down into a section where she had never explored. Here were the worst stews, and, as rumor had it, the sordid shrines of cults that centuries of Orthodoxy had not been able to expunge. Here one could buy poisons, curses, or ritual murders.

And here, of course, she expected she would find

Theodora. The green fires intensified, leaped high overhead, as she led the forces of Shambhala to the cross-
roads she expected to find. Though the doors and
windows in the half-wrecked buildings looked like de-
cayed teeth, she shivered at the power that bubbled from
one of them, a shrine to some dark goddess.

"Come out!" she cried, hawk-shrill, and extended her
hands toward the door. Fire lashed out from her fingertips, blasted through it, and into the building.

"Niece." Abruptly, Theodora stood before her,
wreathed in flames, the white and the green. They licked
at her skin, but she showed no sign of the agony any
human would feel. "I welcome you."

Puzzled, Alexandra raised her hands. "Is this surrender?" It seemed much too easy. A general might have
thought to retreat, even surrender, but conquer in some
later battle; Theodora was no general, but a destroyer.

"Yes," said the sorceress. "Yours!" In an instant, the
green fire soared up between Alexandra and the forces of
Shambhala, formed into a cone, and began to descend
upon her.

She could see through it. Bryennius was shouting, and
the king himself had to hold Haraldr back. Her eyelashes
began to singe, and she raised her hands to call the fire.
Without the king to back her, it came more slowly, but it
came, intertwining about the green flame in a terrible
beauty. Her pulse beat in her temples like the great gongs
in the temples of Ch'in, and sweat ran down her sides as
she drew on her reserves for more strength, more fire.
The white fire intensified, took on shadows of blue and
purple. The effort of forming it into a weapon left her
gasping, but she hurled the fire at Theodora, and sank to
her knees.

The flames engulfed her aunt. This time, Alexandra
saw the woman's skin sear, saw the features—so like
hers!—twist with pain, then control it. Her mouth
moved, spat, and then Alexandra could hear her.

"You can destroy me, niece. But what then?" she
cried. "Return as a subject to a City I might have ruled,

that you might have shared? Do you think that the palace will welcome you back, that your brother will embrace you, trust you?"

Alexandra remembered that her brother had warned her if she returned in triumph, steps would have to be taken to control her. She would have damned the memory, except that to curse was to play into Theodora's hands. The curse would recoil upon her.

"I may die," said the sorceress. "And so I will prophesy to you. The best you can expect is isolation and mistrust, perhaps on the island I once ruled. Remember the shrine there, the one you defiled when you robbed it of its sacrifice? Can you tell me that the hour will not come that you will kneel before its altar and try for my power to add to your own? Or will you be content as a prisoner, or the victim of a 'lamentable' palace mishap?" Theodora laughed, though the air had to sear her lungs.

"Little niece," she whispered, her voice honeyed, "take my hand. Release me from this. Let me heal, and I can show you such wonders . . ."

Fire licked the face, yet still it was an older, more beautiful version of Alexandra's own. Power had marked it, glowed in it still. That power reached out to Alexandra, drew her, left a briny taste in her mouth.

They were akin. Theodora had always recognized the tie of blood, had sought to strengthen it—until, finally, she tried to make Alexandra another of her victims. Why had she listened so long? She knew what she could expect, had known it even when she refused to remain, safe and honored, in Shambhala. She shook her head, repudiating her aunt's words and her own knowledge. She had done what she had sworn, and must be content. She spat the taste of power from her mouth. The tiny, rude action broke the last hold that the dying sorceress might have had on her.

"One more duty," she muttered. "Let me make this quick."

The flames wreathed up again, pure and almost totally blue. They twisted about Theodora, twining more and more tightly, condensing into a thin spiral, and then winked out of existence, leaving only a circle of pure white on the spattered pavement. Beyond it, the shrine's roof collapsed in a shower of sparks. In the instant before it was consumed, Alexandra saw the statue that the shrine protected. Its features twisted and ran, then re-formed into the aspect of compassion that she knew and loved best.

Theodora and her dark goddess—were they glad to be cast free?

Alexandra collapsed on the stones. The barrier of flames that separated her from her allies vanished, and they ran toward her. Haraldr reached her first and embraced her possessively, then, fearful of burns, released her.

"She is unharmed," Alexandra heard the king tell him. "She breathed the air of Shambhala, ate its food. For a little longer, she cannot be harmed by the outside world."

But I might have been harmed by my own choice, she thought, and the king nodded.

She let herself sag gratefully against her lover, who ran fingers over her face and hair to reassure himself that she was unharmed. She might have drifted into sleep then and there, but Rudra Cakrin reached out to touch her cheek. Strength ran from his fingers into her body and she opened her eyes.

Rudra Cakrin rose and turned toward Asia. The horizon had already begun to pale. Alexandra smiled at Father Basil, who raised a hand in farewell, then looked over at Bryennius, who seemed unsteady as the sky paled.

Thank God there would be no time for long farewells. She bowed to the King of Shambhala as if he were the Emperor of Byzantium himself.

"Set us on our way," he said.

They mounted, and at a hand signal, his troop started away. Light and wind swirled around them once again.

* * *

The sun shone at her back, as Alexandra and six guardsmen—all who remained of the soldiers, priests, and companions who had ridden out from Byzantium years earlier—rode toward the City's eastern wall.

"The Horn, my princess!" cried one of the men.

Light gleamed off the blue water. It was good to see it again, better yet to see Byzantium. Alexandra breathed a prayer of thanks. She had survived, and she was returning with the silkworms that she had promised. Bryennius would be safe and happy in Shambhala with his love; Father Basil would no doubt entertain all Persia with tales of his travels. She wished that she might hear them. But she was home! And soon she would see her brother, the Basileus, and tell him of her own adventures.

"You there!"

Soldiers at the first gate shouted at them. Up on the walls, archers held their bows ready.

Jolted back to reality, Alexandra realized how they must appear: six huge, ragged men who bore the axes of the Guard and rode behind a thin, dark-haired creature who could be man, boy, or camp follower, all mounted on horses that made the Arab and Persian steeds of Byzantium look like nags.

Haraldr rode forward cautiously, shouting out his name and mission. Alexandra raised her head, looked at the officer who had come out to question him.

"I am Alexandra," she said. Even to her own ears, her Greek sounded accented. "I am back. Let me through to see my brother!"

By the time Alexandra and her six survivors rode up the Mese, they had acquired an escort composed, she suspected wryly, of half a regiment. This close to noon, the Mese was crowded, though the guards forced shoppers and staring passersby back to allow her to pass. Traces of the sickness Alexandra had sensed in Byzantium the night before still remained in empty buildings and rude scrawls upon church walls and monuments that should have been inviolate. But the air retained the purity of air in the mountain passes, the sun shone, and all about, people swept up rubble and marveled at the flamelike clean streaks upon some of the walls.

Closer to the palace, the silk merchants' shops were empty, but she had expected that. Though she had also expected messengers to precede her, she was not prepared for the onslaught of guards, cubiculars, logothetes, and the rest of the army of palace functionaries who waited outside, and swept her into their complex wake.

She recognized several men, knew one, in fact, to have been her spy in what seemed to be another lifetime, and summoned him to her side. "I have the silkworms," she said.

Somewhere during the uproar, she oversaw the unpacking of the canes in which the silkworms were packed. It was spring. By the time the silkworms awoke from the sleep into which the cold had cast them, the mulberry trees would be in full leaf again, and the weavers would be busy. She wondered if any of them resembled Russet Silk.

"When can I see the Basileus?" she demanded, not at all content with the torrent of reassurances and promises that her words evoked. They had separated her from her guardsmen, she realized, and she protested that too, all the way down the miles of corridors to her own suite in the palace's women's quarters.

Here serving women reacted with such horror to the sight of an Imperial princess with sun-browned face and hands, and wildly straggling hair, wearing ragged men's garments, boots, and a long, strangely marked sword, that they cut short the bows her position demanded of them in order to fall upon her with a babble of lament and propel her into a bath more luxurious than anything she had seen since Ch'ang-an. She laughed weakly as she was bathed, massaged, and perfumed—all with cries of amazement at her journey (not to mention regret for broken nails and ruined skin)—and refused an opportunity to rest for a week each time it was offered, and ate lightly.

She started to demand to see her brother, but remembrance of court ceremonies returned to her. "When can the Basileus receive me?" she asked instead.

The brief silence, followed by a flurry of activity involving jewels and robes, did not please her. Nor, she found, did the robes themselves. They were purple silk, as befitted her rank, woven with gold thread, and brocaded in an elaborate pattern that looked Persian. But even the gold embroidery was somber; and they were so heavy! The earrings they put on her hung down to her shoulders, and her headdress scratched her brow. With longing, she remembered the gauzy silks and hair ornaments of Ch'in.

Finally, a richly dressed eunuch invaded her suite to announce that the Basileus would receive her. She took up the cane filled with silkworms that she intended to present, carrying it as if it were a sword. Then, slowly —given the weight of all the trappings she wore, she could hardly rush—she followed more officials and guards toward the throne room.

So it was to be a formal audience? she thought. That didn't please her at all. Neither did the whispers that buzzed behind her back in each corridor, or her sensation of being watched and reported on to the various palace spymasters.

The doors were flung open, and Alexandra was announced.

His heir at his side, her brother Michael, Emperor of the Romans, sat on the lion throne. Behind the throne was a freestanding tree wrought of silver, ornamented with golden fruits and birds. The throne had been hoisted high over the heads of his courtiers, as if she were a barbarian who must be overawed. Alexandra bowed herself in full court prostration, suppressing both the irritation she felt and a mischievous urge to knock her head against the marble in the style of Ch'in. At her

brother's command, she rose, the cane holding silkworms resting on her outstretched palms. Despite the
rigor of ceremony, the courtiers whispered. There was
something Alexandra did not know, she realized.

The throne descended with a creaking of engines. Now
she could see the Basileus' face. Despite her training, a
gasp of dismay broke from her lips, and the cane
dropped from her hands to roll, unheeded, onto the
floor.

"There was no way to tell you, sister mine," said her
brother, and removed the bandage from his eyes. They
stared out at her, white and sightless like the eyes of
beggars.

"More magic?" she whispered as if no one but she, her
brother, and his quiet, pallid heir were in the cavernous
hall.

"I think so. After you left, my son fell ill again. I went
to Hagia Sophia, and prayed that whatever curse fell on
him be aimed at me instead. And, as you see . . ."

"Theodora is dead," Alexandra said, ignoring the
gasps as she interrupted the Basileus.

"Yet I am still blind. I wish I could see you, little sister.
I can hear you; you speak with an accent now. They tell
me that you arrived in a scandalous condition, with only
six guardsmen—and the silkworms. What of the others?"

Alexandra shook her head, then realized he couldn't
see the gesture. "They won't be returning," she said. At
another time, she would explain further.

"So. We shall miss our Cousin Bryennius." She didn't
miss her brother's use of the Imperial "we." "But We
welcome you, our most beloved sister. Once again, We
are deep in your debt."

Alexandra bowed her thanks. Then the Caesar-mask
fell from her brother's face, and he beckoned her forward with a pale hand from which he slipped a heavy
ring.

"Sister, before you left, you promised to write me tales

of wonders. Since I can no longer read them, I fear you must tell them to me."

"Any time you wish." Alexandra forced the words out and blinked against the tears which would ruin the cosmetics her waiting-women had layered onto her face.

"It must be soon," said Michael. "Now that you are back, I intend to resign the diadem and retire to a monastery. You will serve as regent for young Michael."

Unless you want the crown yourself. The words hung unspoken and ominous in the hall, and the courtiers leaned forward. Michael was aged beyond his years, wearied, despairing, but his sister seemed strong. Would both Michael and his heir be packed off today to a monastery? When Alexandra made no reply either to the spoken or unspoken words, Michael continued. "Here, take this ring . . ."

"*No!*" Heedless of eunuchs, courtiers, and about five officers who started forward, Alexandra hurled herself at her brother. His arms circled her, and he shook his head at the outraged crowd before he bent and kissed her cheek.

"I brought the silkworms . . . for you, all for you," she wept. "I fought for you. And now you would simply give it up, give it away? To me, when you know I don't want it? Don't!"

"Little one, little sister," he whispered against her face. His hands patted her back the way they had done when she was a child and had fallen, or been punished for some offense.

Her tears fell on his face and into his eyes. Then, as she felt some sort of power flow out of her, she sighed and sagged against him. Suddenly her brother gasped and stiffened, and he thrust Alexandra unceremoniously aside. She caught herself on the arm of the throne, and knelt, looking up into his face.

The Basileus raised a shaking hand. Even as Alexandra looked, the whiteness that had stolen his sight dissolved. He blinked, and drew a long, sobbing breath.

"You too, little sister," he whispered. "Are you also a sorceress?"

It was Shambhala, she wanted to protest. A little of the magical city's virtue must still remain in her, enough to heal her of all weariness, and to restore her brother's sight. A black-robed priest started forward, holding up a crucifix and chanting exorcisms.

As Alexandra grasped the golden cross and kissed it, the silver tree behind the throne burst into white flowers, and the enameled birds began to sing. People shouted from the throne room and she could hear cheers outside.

In a moment, she and her brother might have to fear deafness, not blindness, she thought. Then she tore her eyes away from her brother's face with its shining eyes.

The court watched her every move avidly. Did they really think she might turn into a demon and fly out a window, or proclaim herself Basilissa—or what? All the strength she gained in Shambhala had left her, draining into her brother. Using the throne to lever herself back onto her feet, she studied the courtiers and soldiers, trying to read their loyalties in their faces and acts. She was very tired now, cold, and afraid.

I shall have to buy myself some new spies, she realized.

22

Ink spattered Alexandra's stone table as she pushed away from it once again. Not even her battered copies of Homer would help her describe her travels in a way that her brother—and his priests—would accept. But she could not, for the life of her, describe Ch'in as a land of barbarians, or Shambhala as a shrine for devil worship: not after she had seen devil worship too.

If, by some miracle, she could capture the wonders, terrors, and splendors of her journeys on parchment and ink, they would probably charge her with heresy. Though the charge was true, admitting it would be the death of her. There'd been far too many heretics around in recent years. Besides, one Byzantine abbess (especially one born in the purple) addicted to sorcery was one too many. If Alexandra showed tendencies in that direction, she knew how quickly her brother's ministers would contrive a "lamentable accident." She had to be above suspicion.

She strode toward the garden. Her slippers caught in the folds of her stiff silk overtunic, and she swore in three languages at the glittering nuisances. A gardener and at least two servants slipped discreetly out of sight: spies, probably.

If she paced to the garden's stone wall and leaned over it, she could scan the entire City, with the Horn beyond it glinting bronze in the late afternoon. It was a view she had longed for all the time she crossed the mountains and the deserts of Asia. Ingrate that she was, now she longed for the mountains that she would never see again—and the freedom that went with them.

She laid a thin hand on her breast. A note rustled beneath her hand. Last night one of her servants had smuggled it in to her from the Varangians' barracks. Haraldr had resigned from the Guard, and he planned to leave Byzantium. Colored sails moved slowly over the water, and she studied them resentfully. Surely that small one belonged to a Rus merchant, come to sell furs and amber. Haraldr would leave her on just such a boat—maybe on that very one.

Weeks of interrogation by her brother, his suspicious ministers, priests, and generals had kept them apart. She had seen Haraldr once, the disastrous time they had allowed her to appear in the Hippodrome. The crowds had hailed her as Basilissa; she had been hustled back to her quarters, prisoner because of her popularity; and now it didn't look like they would let her go anywhere else in a hurry . . . except back to the convent she had fled. She could feel its walls closing in on her, as if her yellowed bones already lay in the crypt. She gasped for air.

She had forced herself to glance idly over Haraldr's note, then fold it as if it meant nothing to her. She had wanted to weep and to pace, then stalk through the palace and ask Haraldr what he thought he was doing. But the women's quarters did not work that way, not in Byzantium, not in Ch'ang-an, and probably not anywhere else where they had women's quarters. If she had

had Siddiqa here, the girl migh have advised Alexandra.
As it was, Alexandra relied on guile, flattery, and gold to
hire a messenger and to ensure privacy if Haraldr
answered her summons.

If he stayed away, was it because he did not dare to
come—or care to?

Her fingers worked at the throat of her gown. There
was not enough air anywhere in this palace for her! Her
weeks back in the City she had longed for had cost her
her serenity and the sure power she had gained in
Shambhala. Now they would cost her the one man whose
love and loyalty she had thought were absolute. She drew
a gasping breath, then walked slowly back inside.

If she wept in the garden, spies might report it to men
who tried to undermine her brother's trust in her. They
had heard her reject even a regency, but they did not
believe it. Well, if she hadn't been the one who swore she
had no wish for the diadem, she didn't know if she
would have believed it either.

Footsteps in her suite made Alexandra whirl around,
her hand trying to clench on the hilt of a sword she no
longer wore. The eunuch she had bribed nodded to her, a
complicit gleam in his eyes. She raised her brows until he
bowed with more respect, and oozed his painted,
scented self out of her rooms.

Then, and only then, did she dare to look at the man
whose fair hair blazed in the light of the windows. He
had changed the crimson and the axe of the Guard for
blue silk that matched his eyes, and a richly chased
dagger on a belt clasped by a gold buckle the length of
her hand. Haraldr's face was taut, the way it usually got
before a battle. She would never be able to stop looking
at him.

"My princess," he greeted her, then stood quietly.

That very quiet robbed her of speech. He acknowl-
edged that she had a right to summon him, to storm,
spit, or rage at him, as she chose—and that it would not
alter his decision in the slightest.

His mere presence made her feel more at ease. Even

now Haraldr meant warmth, loyalty she could trust. As she relaxed, he cocked his head slightly and smiled at her.

"Haraldr, why?" As the words burst from her in an anguished whisper, her hands went out to him. Swiftly he caught them in his own, kissed them, then drew her into his arms. His hands rubbed along her shoulders. She could feel the tension in his body pass into her, then dissipate as the embrace reassured them both.

Finally he held her away from him and looked down into her face. "The Guard swears loyalty to the Emperor. But *you* hold my oath now. How can I serve your brother?"

He pulled her close again, more roughly this time. "When I heard the whispers, that they feared you would try to seize control . . ."

"Haraldr, I don't want it!" It was a low-voiced protest.

"They will never believe you. Once I realized how my presence in the Guard might endanger you, I resigned. I am moving in with the merchants soon. I shall probably leave on the next ship."

His hands held her as if she were precious to him, and she felt herself warming. "How could you endanger me?" she asked.

He gave her a little shake. "You know the history of your line. Whenever a princess takes a soldier to her bed, it usually means she wants to seize the throne. You know that. You, though: I know you are trying to convince the court that you have no such plans. Isn't that why you agreed to return to your convent? Besides," he said, brushing his bearded lips against her forehead, "I didn't want to pine away for an abbess."

"I am not an abbess yet," she murmured. "Haraldr, I don't want you to leave me."

"Then come with me," he urged and bent to kiss her. "Come north. I can show you ice that floats on the sea's back, bubbling pools of mud, and boiling water that spurt into the air. I could set you to rule men and women who would trust you at your word."

In his own land, Haraldr was almost a prince, she recalled. "It won't work," she tried to say, to explain that if she fled Byzantium for the North, her brother would almost certainly expect a war. "They'll send an army," she began, but he shook his head, and his lips smothered her protests. She clung fiercely to him, then broke away.

"Not here," she whispered. Taking his hand, she led him to her bedroom. Very gently, he tugged the head-dress from her braids and removed her jewels. Then he loosed her hair so that it flowed down over his hands as they unfastened her clothing, and covered her in the moment that she stood naked under his gaze. She removed his belt, and flung it aside before he lifted her and laid her on her bed. Then, as she watched, he pulled off his own clothing.

"It's good to have a proper bed instead of sheepskins, and no enemy outside, isn't it?" he asked her as he lay beside her and brushed her hair off her shoulders. It was too hard to keep from touching him, so she didn't try. She flung her arms about his neck and pulled him down to her.

"We have time, sweet one," he told her. "Here, let me . . ."

He stroked her body, then cupped her breasts and rubbed her nipples with callused thumbs until she gasped, and his caresses slid over her belly and thighs. When she reached for him, he taught her how to please him with lips and fingers. Then he embraced her strongly, and rolled until her body lay impaled on his own, and they both cried out in pleasure.

"Come away with me," he muttered against her neck, twining his fingers in her hair so he could look at her. Then he kissed her deeply, deliberately seeking to rouse her again.

Alexandra closed her eyes, drowning in the waves of pleasure that washed over her. His hands and lips moved over her again and again.

There had been mischief in his gaze, she thought. Did he really think that he could seduce her into following him blindly? Well, he was welcome to try. She laughed and accepted his body's persuasions with joy, matching him touch for touch, until they lay spent in each other's arms.

When the haze of passion that had wreathed them both thinned out and returned them to the world, he asked again, "Will you come with me?" She hadn't imagined the humor in his blue, blue eyes. She met it with mischief of her own. "No," she said, and kissed him deeply. "And you already knew that. We have tonight, Haraldr. Let's enjoy it."

"I ought to turn viking, that's what I ought to do," he told her. "But there's only one treasure I want to steal from this City. Do you know what that treasure might be?"

"What stops you from trying?" Alexandra teased him.

"You do," he admitted. "You'd kill me if I carried you off without your consent." He laughed. Suddenly his face twisted, and he buried it against her. He no longer sounded as if he laughed. Alexandra wrapped her arms about him comfortingly as far as they could go.

Sunlight swept down the wall of her chamber into evening while they held one another thus. Finally, Alexandra stirred and ran her tongue over her bruised lips. "Do you want some wine?" she asked drowsily.

"You should not serve me," he said.

"Really?" She moved out of his arms, and left the bed. "I will remember you said that. Or, my Haraldr, we can look at it this way: I know where the wine is. You don't."

"Sweet gods, I shall miss you," he muttered.

It pleased her to brush her long hair back over her shoulders and walk toward the wine flagon which lay in a frosted silver bowl filled with half-melted snow. She swept her fingers across the bowl's damp edges, brushed them over her throat, behind her ears, and between her breasts. The coolness made her shiver with pleasure. She poured wine into a goblet, turning back with a smile toward the man who opened his arms to her. Then she stopped dead.

A wind like the air in the high passes wrapped about her, then subsided, leaving behind it the smell of lotus. And there were no lotus blossoms in Byzantium at this time of year. Light welled up behind her, and she gasped, almost dropping the wine.

She bent over a table on which jewels lay scattered. Among them was the ball of moonstone she had brought home with her. The light was shining from it. She caught it up, and the light poured over her.

Haraldr exclaimed in his own language. Pulling a blanket from the bed, he padded over to her, and wrapped the soft wool around her shoulders. The radiance from the gem limned them both as she held it between them.

She had seen visions in its depths before. But this time, Haraldr's eyes widened with amazement, and Alexandra realized that he shared them.

"That's Shambhala," he whispered. "I thought . . ."

"So did I, my love. When I chose to come home, I thought it was irrevocable. But it looks like the king may give us another chance. Will you take it?"

"Will you?" he asked.

"This is a way, the only way, we can be together—and I can be free. You have the horn, don't you? I have the gem; you have the horn. We can go back, Haraldr!"

Laughing, he whirled her around exuberantly until she begged for mercy. Then he picked up the goblet she had filled and held it out to her. Looking into his eyes solemnly, she drank and gave him the cup. He turned it, and placed his lips on the rim where hers had touched, then drained it.

They went back to her bed and lay in each other's arms, lip to lip, talking quickly, urgently. But it was a long time before they spoke again of love.

Alexandra looked cautiously about, then boldly entered the part of the City reserved for Rus merchants, where Haraldr had moved after leaving the Guard. A few inquiries brought her to the inn where he had taken a room; she ignored the smirks that accompanied the information. In Ch'ang-an, she had used a lotus to conceal herself. Here in Byzantium, where the City's faith had been her own, and where so much of it still influenced her, such minor magics didn't seem to work. She had done the best she could, she decided, and tapped on Haraldr's door.

He flung it open. As she stepped out of the shadows of the corridor into his room, and closed the door behind her, he started to hug her. Then his grin faded.

"Alexandra! Have you no sense of shame?" he asked.

She looked down at herself, at the gems and luxurious tunic purchased from the middle-ranking palace eunuch who had been her go-between, then laughed. "Very little shame, when it concerns you," she said. "This costume got me out of the palace. Eunuchs are always prowling back and forth, scheming or shopping." She shrugged. "I think some have lovers in the City . . ."

A choking noise from Haraldr set her laughing. "And you don't want other Northerners to think that you and a palace eunuch . . . oh, Haraldr!" She leaned against the wall, practically bent double, then wiped her eyes. Since deciding to flee, she had found herself quicker to laugh than she had ever been. Perhaps she was drunk on hope. Then she would also hope it lasted. Her hand came away smeared with kohl, and that made her chuckle too.

"Let me wash this paint off," she said. "Then, since you don't like these clothes, I shall take them off."

"I have our gear packed," he protested, "and the ship won't wait for us."

"And I," she said, her voice muffled by laughter and folds of cloth, "am wearing a second suit of clothes. A good thing that most eunuchs are plump; otherwise I might have had to carry them. That would have looked suspicious. There!" She flung the glistening silks into a heap on the floor. "Do I still offend your sense of propriety?"

Under the eunuch's clothing, Alexandra had hidden the garb of a young merchant, an assistant sent to the harbor to deal with one of the younger, less important Rus.

Haraldr chuckled. "No one would mistake you for a man," he said and handed her a long bundle wrapped in a cloak.

She unwrapped it. "My sword!" she said. She belted it on with relief.

"Let's go." Haraldr hoisted one bag to his shoulder and reached for the other.

Daring him to object, Alexandra picked it up and slung it over her shoulder. It was heavy, but she thought she could manage. It would cause talk if a merchant struggled under a double load while the youth at his side walked free.

They headed down to the harbor. As she walked, Alexandra gazed about the City for the last time. The churches, stores, and monuments looked cleanly scoured, beautiful, familiar—but a vision of the high passes and of Shambhala beyond them flashed across her mind. She would not miss her birthplace.

"Are you sure no one saw you?" Haraldr muttered.

"Not at all. I'm not even sure that the people I bribed will stay bought." With her free hand, she pulled out the gem that now contained a vision of Shambhala in its heart, breathed on it, and tried to concentrate. "If only we had stayed longer there! I might know what I am doing."

I am not here. You do not see me. I will pass unnoticed, she told the crystal. Her head began to ache and strength to pour out of her, a sign that something might be working, but the flow of power was so ragged that she distrusted the results of her own magic. An older Northern woman walked right into Haraldr and bounced back. She let out a cry, reached for a talisman, and fled.

"Seems to work," said Haraldr.

Ahead of them she could see the masts of the ship that would carry them away from Byzantium to a port where they could join a caravan for the trek east. She stumbled.

"This *is* heavy," she admitted.

"Not much farther," he said.

"I hear hoofbeats."

"Probably from the Mese."

Not daring to hide, or to take to their heels, they kept to the same steady pace while what sounded like a troop of cavalry trotted by.

"Haraldr, they're turning," Alexandra said without moving her lips.

"We are almost at the dock. Keep walking."

Surely her escape hadn't been discovered so fast! Alexandra lamented silently. Just let her board the ship. She'd go below, and stay below until they passed beyond the reach of Byzantium's harbor guards.

Up ahead was their ship.

But fanned out in front of it was an armed guard drawn from one of her brother's most aristocratic regiments. At the center of the crescent formed by men and horses, conspicuous on his white horse, was her brother, not the wan figure whose blindness she had cured, but a tanned, able man in the purple and armor of an Emperor.

Alexandra dropped her bundle. Now that she had been discovered, she felt outrage, not fear. "I bribed that eunuch well!" she complained.

"Sister, remember that I taught you to buy spies! I bought that one first, then passed him on to you," said the Emperor. "Together, we have made him a rich man."

Alexandra snorted. Then her brother's guards moved in. She glanced anxiously at Haraldr. Thank God: His axe was nowhere in sight.

She held her hands away from her sword and moved cautiously toward her brother. He dismounted, and she fell to her knees.

"Most Sacred Majesty," she said, and bent her head. "I beg you to believe that I mean no harm to you, that all I want is to leave here in peace."

Her brother raised her and drew her away from his soldiers, who were as curiously faceless in their armor and helmets as the figures that had pursued her out of Ch'in. "Is it Shambhala?" he asked.

Alexandra took a deep breath. If the truth were the wrong answer, then she was probably dead. She let out the breath, then decided not to speak. If her voice broke, she would die of shame before they could execute her.

"I thought so. I told you, Alexandra, that if you returned, there might be little future here for you. And I heard the longing in your voice when you spoke of Shambhala."

"Your ministers," Alexandra cried softly. "They would force . . ."

"I sometimes think that Emperors come and Emperors go, but the civil service goes on and on. Yes, some of them are insisting that I put you out of harm's way. But thanks to you, I *am* Emperor. That means they still have to obey me."

He held out his hand to her. She kissed it and pressed it to her brow. Again, Michael raised her, this time drawing her into a brotherly hug. "I can either see you off on this ship—which looks seaworthy enough, I suppose—or send you out the gates in triumph as befits a prince, or princess, who has saved the City. My own recommendation—" He smiled at her, then looked at Haraldr, and shook his head.

"Sister, I will never understand women. I remember how fiercely you refused a Frankish king. And now, I find you offering me as brother-in-law one of my own former Guard."

Haraldr bristled, took one step forward, then thought better of it.

"In his own land, he is a prince!" Alexandra protested.

"They all are," sighed her brother. "I make no protest. I merely observe. But I do suggest that you return to the palace, at least long enough to kneel with your chosen Northern 'prince' before a priest."

Alexandra held out her hand, and Haraldr joined them. "A priest?" he said. "Your Majesty honors me.

But our way lies through Persia, and there is a priest in Nisibis—"

"Father Basil!" Alexandra laughed.

"A Nestorian heretic?" Her brother raised eyebrows, then shrugged. "But then, I suppose that you have your own Orthodoxy . . . Alexandra, go with God Who created the tides, which, as I can see from the shipmaster's face, wait on no man, Emperor or not. But accept this from me."

The Emperor reached into the breast of his clothing and brought out a narrow golden circlet. "The crown of a Basilissa," he said. "You have earned it."

She knelt, and he placed it on her brow.

"Wherever you go," he whispered, "think of us."

Alexandra smiled and inclined her head. In Shambhala she would be able to watch, and to study, and to protect her City should it need it. The crown tingled. The last token of an initiate along the Diamond Path was a crown. She could feel the circlet tingle on her brow, feel power collect and rush throughout her body until she felt the same well-being she had known in Shambhala.

The shipmaster gestured wildly. At a nod from the Emperor, he sent sailors down to take Alexandra's and Haraldr's gear. Alexandra threw herself into her brother's arms, then rushed on board. Slowly, the ship moved into the Horn. Light shone down on her brother, who held up a hand in farewell. His figure grew smaller and smaller. When she could no longer see him, she turned her eyes and dreams eastward.

Epilogue

The mountains loomed up before them, wreathed with the first hints of the deadly winter storms. When the way grew too steep to ride, Alexandra, muffled in sheepskins, walked at Haraldr's side, gazing into her crystal as he steadied her with an arm about her shoulders.

They climbed higher and higher. Now the sky was a deep, rich blue, arching up toward indigo. The sun shone down on the peaks and made them cast impossibly sharp shadows. Within those shadows, it was fiercely cold; outside them, almost as warm as spring.

"We are almost there," Alexandra whispered.

Behind her, Haraldr was ordering the bearers and guides to return to the previous night's camp, to wait three days there, and only then come in search of them.

She wondered if they would bother to search at all. Hillmen accepted miracles as a part of life. The first time these men had seen her sword, they had all but abased themselves before her, muttering prayers in which she

335

caught the name of Shambhala. They had been bearers, not guides; from the moment in her bedchamber that she had seen Shambhala glow in her crystal, she had known how to find it, and where.

"Just a little farther," Alexandra told Haraldr, and took his hand.

They walked between two rock spires. Even this early in the autumn, ice glinted upon them. Beyond them stretched a flat space, large enough, perhaps, for a small band of horsemen. Beyond that lay only the abyss.

Alexandra's gem kindled in the afternoon sun. A column of fire shot up from it into the sky.

"This is the place," she whispered. She could almost see the gleaming ice of the peaks that hid Shambhala from the world, hear the cries of waterfowl in the clear pools near its heart, feel the fine silk cushions of the palace. Haraldr's hands grasped her shoulders, and he turned her to face him.

"Alexandra, if we do not find Shambhala, you must not fear," he said urgently. "We can always go to Kashgar. Prince Bryennius' friends would welcome a man with a strong back and a princess with a brave heart for their own sakes, as much as for his."

She reached up and kissed his face. He was as eager as she to regain the land they had had to renounce, but Alexandra knew that if he could spare her pain by turning his back upon it once again, he would.

"The last time we traveled these roads, I left despair behind me," she whispered. "I cannot believe that we will be disappointed."

He embraced her fiercely. Then, as if reminding himself of his usual notions of how fragile she was, he started to ease his hold. She flung her arms about him, welcoming the surge of love and desire that heated her blood. For an instant, she toyed with delaying their search to enjoy this moment, then put the thought aside without regret. There would be time, in Shambhala, time for them to delight in one another and to learn the paths on which their love might guide them.

They clung together for a moment longer. Then Alexandra laid her hands against Haraldr's chest and very gently pushed him away.

"I think we should try now," she said.

Haraldr nodded, his face somber. Slowly, he drew the horn with the sigils of Shambhala from about his neck and lifted it to his lips. The sun shone down on him until he gleamed like an immortal, and Alexandra had to glance away. Haraldr was so beautiful. She would never understand why he loved her.

Then he sounded the horn, sending a merry, musical call up into the hills.

Winds rushed down from the peaks, bringing a faint powdering of snow and a fainter scent of lotus.

"Again," said Alexandra.

With the second blast, a garden sprang up from the barren rock all about them. Birds began to sing, while white clouds massed before them.

Haraldr grinned. Raising the horn a third time, he blew it until jubilant echoes rang out from peak to peak, blending like the chorus of some awesome festival.

The winds swelled again, bringing them the fragrance of Shambhala's gardens. Eyes shut, Alexandra basked in the sunlight and the warmth, the comfort of Haraldr's arm over her shoulders as they waited.

Then they heard a sweet clamor of silver and gold horns. The clouds lit, then parted in two shining arcs.

Out rode a troop of men and women, richly dressed as if for a wedding, and mounted on splendid horses. In the lead, his right hand outstretched to welcome them, rode the King of Shambhala.